HOLLOW BAMBOO

HOLLOW BAMBOO

A NOVEL

WILLIAM PING

HarperCollins*Publishers*Ltd

Published by HarperCollins Publishers Ltd

First edition

HarperCollins books may be purchased for educational, business
or sales promotional use through our Special Markets Department.

HarperCollins Publishers Ltd
Bay Adelaide Centre, East Tower
22 Adelaide Street West, 41st Floor
Toronto, Ontario, Canada
M5H 4E3

www.harpercollins.ca

Library and Archives Canada Cataloguing in Publication

Title: Hollow bamboo : a novel / William Ping.
Names: Ping, William, author.
Identifiers: Canadiana (print) 20220442606 | Canadiana (ebook) 20220442622
ISBN 9781443466530 (softcover) | ISBN 9781443466547 (EPUB)
Classification: LCC PS8631.I5275 H65 2023 | DDC C813/.6—dc23.

Printed and bound in the United States of America
22 23 24 25 26 LBC 5 4 3 2 1

CONTENTS

To William Ping
Past, Present, and Future

hollow bamboo   noun

[**hol**-oh bam-**boo**] /ˈhälō/ /bamˈbo͞o/ /

1. the empty, compartmentalized core of the bamboo plant, used for various purposes.

2. English translation of Cantonese term jook-sing (竹升). A pejorative to describe those of Chinese descent who identify more strongly with Western culture. As the stem of the bamboo plant is both hollow and compartmentalized, water cannot flow through it. Therefore, people metaphorically referred to as jook-sing cannot connect to either culture.

This is the kind of story my dad used to make up about people
he never knew. But I met a professor once when I was young
who had heard the same story about his family.
So maybe there was some truth in it after all.

THE FIRST WILLIAM SETO PING

As loved our fathers, so we love,
Where once they stood, we stand.

SIR CAVENDISH BOYLE, "ODE TO NEWFOUNDLAND"

This is a true story.
More or less.

JANUARY 2020

I

THE OYSTER SHELL

"It's just a little white lie," she said, which struck me as an awfully charged way to describe the situation I was facing.

"All right, I won't tell them about Montreal. But am I supposed to bow or something when I meet them?"

"Will, listen. You just let the elders order first and eat first and— just let them do everything first."

"What about hugging? Do I hug? Or hand-shake? Is that allowed?"

What I want here is to make a good impression, you know, meeting her family for the first time. I already know what to wear: black Timberlands to give my height a boost, black jeans, a white V-neck undershirt, and my favourite Patagonia Synchilla pullover, a plain grey one, looks smart and professional yet casual. But I need to make sure that it seems like I know and understand—and respect—their culture. Er, *our* culture. Thank you, Poppy Ping, may you rest in peace. It's times like this when I wish my one-quarter Chinese DNA came encoded with some innate understanding of cultural practices.

Since I've been dating Alicia, my first Chinese girlfriend, I've learned a lot about Chinese customs. Like last week, when she met my family, we cracked open some Christmas crackers, you know, those hollow tubes that go *pop* when you pull on their ends and inside there's a paper hat and a shitty toy and a trivia question with an obvious answer? My mom stocks up on them during the after-Christmas sales, something to placate my niece when she comes to visit. We all crack open a cracker, offer our toys to the child, read out our trivia (*What eastern Canadian city hosts the most easterly point of North America?*), and don our ceremonial paper crowns. I like the crowns. The thin paper they're made of blots the grease from my forehead—very refreshing after a big meal.

Alicia didn't put her hat on, probably because she didn't want to mess up her hair or her makeup or something. I let it go, but my niece asked Alicia why she wasn't wearing her crown.

"In China," Alicia said, "wearing a green hat means that your partner is cheating on you."

Big yikes for me at the dinner table, but the whole Ping family was delighted by this knowledge of the cuck hat. Poppy Ping was Chinese, came all the way over here in the 1930s and built a new life for himself, but he didn't really pass the culture on to his kids, or if he tried to, his kids didn't listen. I wasn't there, so who am I to say what did or didn't happen? One thing I do know: *St. John's.*

But when it comes to meeting Alicia's family, I need to be a bit more prepared. She's fully Chinese, not mixed like me. A purebred, if you will. I've heard others say that, "purebred," but it feels wrong when I say it. Alicia was born here in Newfoundland but raised in Hong Kong. She and her mom moved back to St. John's when she was around sixteen. In a sense, she's more mixed than me, having gotten a taste of two cultures from a young age.

2

"Look, Will, if they want to hug you or shake your hand, they will," Alicia explains as she drives us to the restaurant. "Just be yourself. Don't worry so much."

"Okay," I say. "But when I give them the cakes, how should I do it? Do I make a big to-do of it or do I just give them to them without saying anything?"

"You just give them the cakes the same way you would give a cake to anybody."

"I've never given a cake to anybody. Do I need to bow?"

"Don't bow. Bowing is for funerals."

"So I just hand them the cakes, I just put the cakes in their hands—that's it?"

"Don't worry!" Alicia says, her eyes unmoving from the road in front of her. "I know you want to make a good impression, but they already like you! The only thing they've ever wanted was for me to date a nice Chinese boy."

"Okay, but they know I'm white, right?"

"You're *kind of* white. They know that William Ping was your grandfather—you're, like, local Chinese royalty."

"Yeah, but my skin is white. They know that, right?"

Alicia lets go of the steering wheel with one of her hands and makes a shrug motion, gently waving her flat palm back and forth as if to say "meh." "I told them you're pale. Just be yourself. They're just happy to know I'm not a lesbian."

Her family is under the impression that I am Chinese, and while Ancestry.ca and 23andMe might prove that genetic fact, one look at me will tell them I'm not. My skin is white. I guess I could say I'm white-passing, but really, my skin is so white, it's beyond passing, it's past. And culturally, of course, I'm entirely Western. My exposure to Chinese culture comes by way of a couple Jackie

Chan movies and some anime shows I never finished watching. I read a manga once and was underwhelmed. Don't get me wrong, I have a respect for the culture. I want to know more. I'm fine with admitting my ignorance. But in meeting Alicia's family, I need to at least make an attempt to appear knowledgeable.

Alicia told me there was only one Chinese custom I really needed to observe when meeting her family: I had to bring them a gift. "It's important to respect your elders," she said. So I bought them a couple of those jiggly Japanese cheesecakes from Montreal. Well, I should be clear: Alicia *told* me to buy a couple of those Japanese cheesecakes.

Alicia and I had been in Quebec for the past few days, which brings me to the second rule I need to follow when meeting her family: don't tell them that Alicia was with me in Montreal. Apparently it would be frowned upon to have her travelling with a boy so soon in a relationship. Whatever, so be it. It's a small lie to protect others' sense of themselves and her. It's fine. And she also told me to not drink at the meal. That wasn't a cultural thing—her mom just frowned upon drinking.

"Very judgmental," Alicia said. "Besides, you keep repeating yourself when you drink."

She also said to compliment her mom's hair, which was a very expensive wig. So four rules: pay respect/give gift, lie about trip, don't drink, and compliment wig. Okay. Got it.

The entrance to the restaurant is a quarter of a way down an alley off Duckworth Street. We're heading down the stairs now, Alicia and I, and it's time for me to go in and do my little dog-and-pony show, be the good boy that her family will love.

"Wasn't this place closed for a gas leak?" I ask Alicia.

"Was it?" She grips my arm so she doesn't fall on the unsalted concrete steps. "Are you excited to meet my mom and Uncle Gucci and Auntie Versace?"

"I just hope they like me," I say, gripping her arm just as tightly as my boots slip slightly. I hold open the door for her. We got this: pay respect, don't drink, compliment wig, lie about Montreal. Very good.

The hostess greets us in the porch. "Come in out of the cold, my son," she says. "Welcome to Black Monolith. Are you here for the DuMont Corporation's late Christmas party?"

"Uh, no. Reservation for Ping," I say, out of habit.

The hostess quickly consults her sheet. "No reservation for Penn."

"It's not under your name," Alicia says.

"Oh, right," I say, avoiding eye contact. "We're looking for Uncle Gucci."

Alicia does this thing where she gives nicknames to her friends and family so I remember who they are in relation to certain stories about them. She calls one of the girls she works with UTI Girl. I don't ask Alicia what their real names are; she seems to enjoy coming up with these private nicknames. Uncle Gucci gained his moniker because he's rich and, like a lot of rich people, or just people in general, he has a penchant for luxury goods.

Alicia says, "We're here for Dr. Kris?"

"Right this way," the hostess says.

The restaurant is dark and probably used to be someone's house, given its myriad of narrow hallways connecting to small dining rooms. Canvases depicting barren rural landscapes, saltboxes in the snow, rough waters crashing into the shore hang from the walls and I always have to watch my shoulders to make sure I don't knock into them. The hostess takes us left, then right, another left, up four stairs, down three more, deeper and deeper into the building until

5

we enter a dining room that reveals Alicia's family seated at a long table. From what Alicia's told me about him, I'm guessing that's Uncle Gucci at the head of the table. A spry eighty-nine-year-old, he springs to his feet to come greet us, as does his similarly elderly wife, Auntie Versace. They're both around four feet tall, and I can see how gravity has compressed their spines during the course of their long-drawn-out lives.

"I know William Ping," Uncle Gucci says as he shakes my hand with a stronger than expected grip. "I know your grandfather. Very nice man."

"Thank you," I say, and I turn to Auntie Versace, who smiles at me. I shake her hand, and she says something in Chinese and everyone around me says, "No, she wants a hug." I bend over to hug her a little too fast and my head collides with hers, leaving a ringing sensation in my ears. She's still smiling and nodding but her ears must be ringing too. God, I hope that doesn't kill her or something.

"Auntie Versace only speaks Chinese," Alicia says to me.

I hug Alicia's mom too. I can see it in her eyes: the disappointment that I'm white, that I have the name and the legacy but not the legitimacy. I can feel it in her hug, the way her arms form not a welcome embrace but rather a weak, reluctant greeting.

"I brought you guys cheesecakes," I say, lifting up the box.

Was "you guys" too informal? Maybe.

No. It was casual, like "this is no big deal, you guys." Four rules: pay respect, compliment wig, lie, don't drink.

"Oh, thank you," Alicia's mom says. It occurs to me that I don't know her name.

Uncle Gucci looks puzzled at the presence of the cakes and says something to Alicia's mom.

She says something in Chinese, then she says: "Cheesecake, cheesecake."

Uncle Gucci smiles and nods.

"They're from this bakery in Montreal," I add. "Uncle Tetsu's?"

"Why were you in Montreal?" asks Alicia's mom.

"I was there to see Obama."

"Who?"

"Obama? Barack Obama? He used to be the president?"

"Oh, okay," she says. Then she turns to Alicia. "What he bring back for you?"

"He got me a cake as well," Alicia says.

"Your grandfather very kind to everyone," Uncle Gucci says. "He help all the Chinese here. Very honest man."

"Thank you. He was well respected," I say.

"He own a big house."

"It was a big house." I nod. I barely remember it.

"Nice house," Uncle Gucci says.

"Yes." An awkward silence falls over the table. Auntie Versace keeps talking in Chinese to Uncle Gucci. They're both looking at me, smiling, nodding.

"What are they saying?" I whisper to Alicia.

"It's too low for me to hear," she says. "I'm sure it's fine."

A beat passes. I hear the clinks of forks and knives on plates in other dining rooms.

"I like your hair," I say to Alicia's mom.

"Thank you," she says.

Another silence, punctuated by the clinking of cutlery. Fork-knife dances.

"I meet you before," Uncle Gucci says.

"You have?" I don't recall seeing him before.

"Yes, yes. A couple years ago, when we unveil monument."

Ah, so that's what it is—a monument for Chinese immigrants of my grandfather's generation. A big rock with inscriptions and a laser-engraved picture from back in the thirties of a hundred Chinese guys in suits in front of an old movie theatre. It's only a couple blocks from here.

"Oh, yes," I say. "Yes. I remember you."

"You speak Cantonese, William?" Uncle Gucci inquires.

"Uh, no, unfortunately," I say.

"Okay, we speak in English to not be rude," he says.

Auntie Versace smiles and nods.

"You order cocktail," Uncle Gucci says to me.

"Oh no, I don't drink," I say.

"You no drink? You drive?"

"Well, no, Alicia drove. I'm just not drinking."

"What your age? How old?"

"Uh." I remind myself that I'm not twenty-one, even though I keep thinking I'm still that age. "Twenty-three."

"You man," Uncle Gucci says. "You drink. You order drink."

"Well, if you say so," I say and pick up the cocktail menu. I won't order from it, but I'll look at the menu to appease Uncle Gucci. He truly lives up to his moniker. Tonight, he's wearing a Gucci bomber jacket, with the double-G pattern embossed on the silk.

"Young man drink," he says with a laugh. "You go George Street. Young men go George Street."

The most bars per capita in North America. Terrible place. Reeks of filth and debauchery and crime and social circles.

"Heh," I say. "No."

The waitress arrives at our table. She's one of those people who blinks a lot and talks fast. Must be from around the bay, although I don't detect an accent, just that general aura of a bayman—or bayperson, I should say. You just know she used to live in one of those tourism ads where a technicolour quilt dries in the wind in front of a field of vibrating grass so vibrant that you swear the field must be alive.

"Hi, guys, welcome to Black Monolith," she says, chipper. "Before you guys order, let me just tell you about our specials that aren't listed on the menu. So, we have our famous seafood soup, it's the house specialty, featuring cod, shrimp, and other types of fish that Newfoundland is really well known for. We also have a seafood platter, featuring fried whelks, calamari, tuna tartare, and smoked mussels. All locally caught. For mains, we have halibut with a beautiful lemon-caper sauce. We only have three pieces of that left so I'll let you guys fight over it."

The waitress is primarily addressing me as she says this. I know why: I'm whitey-white guy and so I must be able to understand what she's saying even if the rest of my party doesn't. This is another thing I've been experiencing since I started dating Alicia: my whiteness. The way the waitress says "Newfoundland" and "caught locally," verbally italicizing the words, I can tell she's thinking that the Asians are tourists, maybe even that I'm a tourist. Uncle Gucci and his wife have lived here probably in the vicinity of seventy years. And yet they remain foreign.

The waitress continues droning on about the specials, "We also have every Newfoundlander's favourite dish, a real local classic, fish and chips! Which you can get with either one piece or two pieces of deep-fried cod."

It's not *this* Newfoundlander's favourite dish. It's quite possibly my least favourite dish, an absolute waste of a beautiful fish.

"I'll leave you guys to consider the options—and let you fight over the halibut," the waitress says and departs down one of the restaurant's narrow hallways.

"What you gonna order?" Uncle Gucci asks me.

I don't need to look at the menu, I've been here before. "I'll get a couple oysters and a half rack of lamb," I say.

"Oh, very good order," he says as he pats his stomach. "I used to love oyster. Now, is too hard on my stomach."

"He has to stand up for five hours to let his food digest," Alicia's mom says.

"Is that right?"

"Yes," Alicia's mom says. "So he won't be able to sleep after this until two or three in the morning. It will ruin his whole week."

"Oh, wow."

A brown-hatted man walks into our dining room with two suitcases and rests them on the floor. His eyes widen when he sees us. "Oops," he says, and he picks up his bags and walks back out.

"Why does he have suitcases?" Alicia's mom asks.

"I think there's a hotel upstairs," I say, remembering the night I spent in a room upstairs. A night spent with Alicia. The telling of that story would violate the rule requiring lying, so I don't elaborate.

"I love golf," Uncle Gucci says, beaming at me. "I used to play golf in PEI. Man in PEI tell me PEI oyster are best. What you think?"

"Oh, absolutely," I reply. Mere days beforehand, I was slurping back oysters from PEI at an oyster bar in Montreal.

"Oh yeah, you think so? Okay, back when I golf in PEI, I order twelve oyster for myself in July and man say to me, 'Oyster better in September,' and I say 'Oh, really?' So, in September I call man in PEI and I get him to send me one hundred oyster. I get big box of oyster, straight from airport. Then I open box and I realize—I not know how to open oyster! So I go to Newfoundland Hotel with three oyster in my pocket. I walk into kitchen and I say, 'Chef, show me how to open oyster.' He show me but I still not know, so then I say, 'Chef, I pay you come to my house, open oyster for me.' So he come and open all the oyster."

Damn, this guy *is* rich. "Wow, were they good?" I ask, but the waitress returns.

"Okay, guys, you ready to order? Who won the fight for the halibut?"

I let the elders speak first—that was part of the rules. Pay respect, lie, don't drink, compliment wig.

Uncle Gucci orders first: "My wife have steak. I have half rack lamb."

"I'm sorry, can you repeat that?" the waitress says, moving closer to Uncle Gucci.

"My wife have steak. I have lamb. Half rack."

"Okay, lamb, got it." The waitress makes note of it on her little pad. "And what about for the little lady herself?" She looks at Auntie Versace, who smiles and nods in return.

"No, he ordered for her," Alicia's mom says. "She wants steak."

"Oh, okay," the waitress says. "How do you want it?"

"Medium," Uncle Gucci says.

Alicia and her mom both order steak as well. I order my oysters and lamb.

"I want bottle of wine," Uncle Gucci says to the waitress. "Pinot noir."

"I'll be right back and let you taste one," she says to him.

"Me and you drink it," he says to me.

"Okay," I say with a nervous laugh. Oy vey.

"Pinot noir is my number one wine," Uncle Gucci tells me. "Merlot, my number three. Shiraz, very bad. What you think?"

"I like pinot too," I say. In truth, pinot varietals are so passé, I've been drinking pét-nats and orange wines lately.

The waitress returns and lets Uncle Gucci taste the wine. He lifts the glass to his nose. "Okay, I smell and it smell good. Is good wine. I like."

As the waitress pours his glass, she looks directly at me and says, "You guys know there's rumours that this building used to be a Chinese casino?"

I immediately feel an increase in my heart rate. Am I bearing witness to a micro-aggression?

"Yes, is true," Uncle Gucci says. "Used to be Hop Wah Laundry. In back room is mahjong." He nods as the waitress begins to pour his wife's glass. Auntie Versace smiles and politely shakes her head. The waitress continues to pour.

"They say there's a ghost here from those days," the waitress says, rushing to pour my glass. Apologies to Alicia's four rules. One failure out of four, could be worse. It seems to me that it would be more rude now if I didn't drink. I'll refuse refills, though, let the old man drink the rest of the bottle. It's fine.

"Ha!" Uncle Gucci laughs. "Must be Little Joe. He live in casino. He live upstair. Ha! Little Joe always make sandwiches for the kids."

"There's all kind of ghost stories about him," the waitress says. "One time the manager came in one morning and there was some bottles of wine and food missing. The staff said a ghost must've ate it. That must've been Little Joe." The waitress winks at me and then, gesturing towards Alicia, asks me, "Could you pass me her glass?"

"Oh, no, I'm not drinking," Alicia says.

"I'm not drinking either," Alicia's mom says, directing the words towards me.

"Is just me and him," Uncle Gucci says, pointing at me.

"Oh, okay," the waitress says. "Well, guys, the food will be out in just a minute. I'll run back there and make sure Little Joe isn't eating the halibut."

Uncle Gucci takes a sip from his glass. "Good," he says. He takes another sip and then gently pats his stomach. "Is too much wine for me. Bad on stomach. You drink."

I can feel Alicia's mom's eyes on me. I chuckle. "If you say so."

He slides his glass in front of me. "My wife not drink wine either," he says. Auntie Versace smiles and nods. He slides her glass in front of me too.

I take a sip from my own glass. I won't finish all these glasses, just let them sit there. Be polite and finish my glass. This *is* good wine, though, quality wine. I take another sip. Light, yet flavourful. A good balance of tannins that will keep my palate clean for each bite. I take another sip. Alicia's family is talking about some guy they know who died and left a business he owned to his mistress. Okay, I'll finish my glass, and possibly have some of one of the other two. But I won't touch the rest of the bottle.

I finish my glass.

It's fine, need to make a good impression: drink the wine, don't be rude, but don't drink too much.

Uncle Gucci leans back in his chair. He seems to be having trouble with his eyes, squinting and widening them. He puts on a pair of sunglasses. "Lighting in here, bad for eyes."

Auntie Versace says something to Uncle Gucci.

Then he says to me, "My wife say you look very pale."

"Ah, yes, I'm white," I say. Alicia's mom chokes. "Uh, I mean, I'm *light*, pretty light skin."

"You remember William Ping?" Uncle Gucci says to me.

"I am William Ping," I say.

"No, you grandfather," he says.

"Um, well, my grandfather is dead, to begin with." Wine talking, must self-correct. "He died when I was young. But yeah, sure, I have memories of him."

"Like what?" Alicia's mom asks.

I start on the second glass. I can feel Alicia's eyes boring a hole into my head.

I'm going to drink that fucking bottle.

No, I won't. I shouldn't.

I will.

"Well, actually, I only have one memory of him, really. Sitting in his lap, watching *Wheel of Fortune*. The game show? Spinning wheel, flashing lights? I would've only been three, so I was probably just entranced by the glow of the TV screen, all those pretty colours." There's silence around the table. This is the way I get when I'm drinking, too talkative.

"Or maybe I just liked watching Vanna touching those little screens, making those letters appear."

More silence. Forks, knives hitting off plates.

"But yeah, that's my only memory of him. Watching TV with Poppy Ping, him not even realizing that he's going to die the next morning." I've said too much. "I mean, I don't know for sure that he died the next morning, that's just how I've always remembered it for some reason. Even if he didn't die the next morning, the morning after *Wheel of Fortune*, he may as well have, because that's the only memory I have of him anyway."

I finish the third glass.

There are too many glasses around me. Where will they place the food? There's not enough room on the table. I'll nurse a fourth glass for the rest of the meal and that will be that.

Complete silence. I can't even hear the fork-knife tango now. See, I wasn't even planning on drinking, even before Alicia told me I couldn't. I just get too talky, too eager to reveal.

"This memory, of sitting on his lap and watching TV, it's one of those memories where you're not even really sure that what you're remembering is even the actual memory or just a memory of remembering that memory."

Alicia's mom is staring at me. Uncle Gucci and Auntie Versace smile and nod. I don't want to see how Alicia is reacting. Okay, no more drinking for me. Uncle Gucci gets out of his chair and grabs the wine bottle, thank God.

"Might as well," he says, hovering the bottle over his glass. Thank god. Then, with a surprising litheness, he pours the rest of the bottle into my glass.

"Oh no, I couldn't possibly . . ." It's too late, it's already poured. This is a good thing, actually, having all the wine poured. It seems like it's not as much of a waste if it's all in the glass. I'll just pace myself on this one.

The oysters arrive.

"They big? Let me see." Uncle Gucci leans in to eye my plate. They are around the size that oysters normally are, not overly big or small.

"They small. That good. More flavour in small oyster."

He sits back down.

I slurp an oyster and take a sip of wine to clean my palate.

"Your grandfather, he help everyone." Uncle Gucci slowly waves one arm over the table. "Everyone. He bring community together."

Slurp, sip. "Yes, he was well respected," I say. Slurp, sip.

"Everyone think highly of him," Uncle Gucci says.

I take another sip. "Yeah, I mean, that might be the only memory I have of him, the *Rota Fortunae*, but the memory of him, the communal memory of him, is kept alive and well by people like you." I gesture around the table. "People who knew him and tell me about him and what aspects of myself and my life would've made him proud." I take another sip. "He was a very respected man, very honourable man. But I didn't know him. Not really. So I can't speak to this respect." I pause, not wanting my message to land the wrong way. "I'm worried it might sound like I'm complaining or something. Maybe it doesn't sound like I'm complaining at all. I'm not complaining. My grandfather, he was charitable, and benevolent, and he held a critical, uh, maybe even essential role in establishing the Chinese community in Newfoundland. I know this. I know this to be true." I pick up the glass as if to sip but think better of it and place the glass back down quickly, causing some of the wine to slosh over the edge.

"See, these are things to really celebrate, and if it comes off like I'm complaining, just 'cause I don't really know anything, then I'm going to seem like a jerk. And that's not what I want. Everyone always tells me how proud of me he would be—for my grades, for being the first person in my family to graduate university, for dating a Chinese girl." I raise my glass to Alicia. She is furrowing her brows. "Maybe I feel like I missed something sometimes, regarding all the respect for him. But it's not complaining, I'm not, I have nothing but respect for my grandfather and all his . . . accomplishments." It takes me a moment to get that one out: ah-com-plush-munts.

"That being said, you can only respect a man you don't know so much, right? Like, there's a finite level of respect for the unknown and the absent, inherited second-hand respect enforced by . . . by social conventions and, and, the opinions of others." A gesture towards the audience with my glass. "Informed by people like you, telling you—er, I mean, telling me—telling me how respectable he was and how I should respect him, and of course I do respect him, of course, but still, sometimes I have to wonder how to respect a mystery. A mystery to no one but myself, that is, as everyone else knew him, and you all knew him and interacted with him and loved him and respected him. And of course, even if people didn't love him or respect him, they would probably just tell me they did anyways. Because that's what happens when people die."

Alicia is shaking her head at me. Oh god, I'm talking. I need to stop talking.

"Anyways, you didn't come here to listen to me complain, which I'm not doing, I'm just saying that I don't know the man that everyone else knows."

Blank stares all around. I need a breather.

"I'm gonna use the washroom." I get up from the table and slightly trip on the leg of Auntie Versace's chair. Fucking chair. Don't look back.

I stagger down the narrow dark hallway and push open a door and stumble into mops and off-brand cleaners. Back down the narrow hallway, taking a left instead of a right at the door of my dining room, their dining room. A light at the end of the hall glints off the edge of a toilet bowl. I walk in, shut the door, lean on it, catch my breath. I shouldn't have said that stuff. I guess I didn't say anything bad. Maybe I'm overthinking it.

This is a nice bathroom. Big rectangular chartreuse tiles covering the floor and walls. There's a paper towel dispenser, but there are also fabric cloths, real hand-drying cloths. And a big flat-screen TV behind the door, cycling through ads of drink specials and discount condoms. This place, the epitome of class.

I take off my Patagonia, just to cool down for a minute.

I walk over to the toilet to rock a piss and check my phone, but suddenly I feel a little woozy. Must be the wine hitting.

I should sit down.

Black spots cloud my vision. I'm getting cold. Also sweaty.

Oh fuck, I—

* * *

17

feel like a lightning rod, a hollow core zapped with words out of darkness, split open from shock. A voice calls to me. My own? No, that halibut in the kitchen is speaking to me, it's calling my name.

"Eat my dream," the fish says, burbling the words out from beneath his lemon-caper sauce. More butter, that's the secret ingredient. "Eat my dream." Like that Bart Simpson bon mot. But different. Eat my dream. To consume an unending longing, to summon light where I know only shadows, where I

wake up. Green tile. No, *chartreuse* tile. Close to eyes, feels nice on face. Oof. I'm awake, I think, my body covered in cold sweat. It's quiet. Must've only been passed out for a second, no one's looking for me. I feel . . . wet. I can't see through my glasses, the colour of rust obscuring my vision. My hand slips as I try to right myself.

Oh geez, I pissed on the floor. And I pissed on my pants. Damp denim.

Why is my vision rusty? I pull my glasses off. What the fuck? A puddle of blood on the floor, smeared into a print of my face. I push myself up so that I'm standing. Stagger over to the paper towel dispenser, tear one off and wipe the blood off my glasses. In the mirror I can see I'm bleeding from the top of my forehead, right on the hairline. I guess my head hit off something when I fell, the toilet maybe, although there isn't much blood around that. Maybe the sharp edge of the paper towel dispenser. There's blood on the shoulder of my shirt and there's blood down the side of my neck. I'm not in pain, but I should go to the hospital. Now I've really made a bad first impression. Got so wasted on wine that I passed out in the bathroom and gave myself a head wound.

They'll love that one. What a way to honour my grandfather's legacy, by being an idiot in public. Do I bow? Should I bow? And what about the part when I start bleeding from the head, is it better for me to just lie down and die? Just die, yeah. Yeah, that makes sense.

Maybe it's not so bad. Maybe I can clean it off. Paper towel all my bodily fluids off my pants and my shirt and my head and the floor. Go back to the dining room. Pretend nothing happened. Eat my lamb.

I dab at my forehead with the paper towels. It is an unending stream, albeit a small one. What a strange dream. A talking halibut? Oh my.

Hungry. Thirsty too.

What did the fish say?

"Eat," I mumble, "my dream."

A certain ring to that.

"Eat my dream," I say again.

I need to write that down. Opening the Notes app on my phone, I smear a little blood across the screen. "Eat. My. Dream," I say, confidently tapping each word into the cloud.

There's a dragging sound outside the door, like a heavy trunk is being hauled across the floor. Then, a knock. Oh god, I haven't stopped bleeding yet and there's still blood on the floor. Maybe I *should* just lie here and die. Or get someone to call an ambulance.

"Better off to not die." The voice emanates from the other side of the door. An unfamiliar voice, genderless. "Sober up and recall yourself. What has been will be again and what has been done will be done again."

Is that supposed to be ominous? I stare at the door, blood dripping on my lenses once again. The hauling noise gets louder and green gas seeps around the edges of the door frame and out of the TV's speakers.

"Ay, someone'ssss in here . . ." I force out, getting woozy again.

The gas stops, but the voice continues.

"You called."

2

THE NECROTIC TOUCH

I need water. I must be hallucinating. Concussion symptom? Water. I drink so much fucking water every day, you don't even understand, I'm like the prime minister of Hydration Nation. The talking halibut, and now a talking gas cloud? What's next? Is the condom dispenser going to sing me a lullaby? Dehydration, that's all it is. Guess I could drink from the sink.

The sink. Maybe that's what I hit my head off of. Or the toilet bowl or paper towel dispenser or something.

"I'm sorry to interrupt," the alien voice calls from outside the door, "but I really must come in." Pale green gas floods out of the flat-screen TV as the bathroom door flies open with a boom and a great burst of wind billows more gas into the room.

I suppose these gas works are intended to be frightening, but there's really only two options here, either I'm still dreaming or I'm dead, so it is what it is at this point. The talking gas cloud can feel free to use the restroom if it wants.

"All right, just watch where you step—er . . . float?" I say, gesturing towards the blood on the floor.

"I'm not here to use the chamber pot," the voice from the

cloud says. The voice reverberates through the gas, like the waves a pebble makes when it's dropped into a puddle, but I can't locate a single point of origin. Soft and gentle, the voice is so low and distant it seems beyond this very room.

I'll play it cool.

"Hey, man, I don't care," I say. "I'm just waiting to move on to the next phase of my life in here, so go right ahead. I won't watch. I'll close my eyes."

"You called me," the cloud intones, all solemn and grave.

"How, now? I never called you!"

"Yes, you did."

"I don't even . . . know who you are."

"Be that as it may, you still called me."

"How did I do that?"

"You asked me to eat your dream."

"*What?* No. No, I was saying 'eat my dream' to myself."

"You going to eat your own dream?"

"No, no one is going to eat any dreams. I just liked how the phrase sounded. It'd be a good Instagram caption. Or a tweet."

"So you called a dream eater and now you don't want your dream eaten."

"I . . . I don't even understand what you're saying, and besides, I have larger problems right now." I gesture towards my head wound.

The cloud hovers. Is it annoyed? I hope it doesn't think I'm rude. I was out to make good impressions tonight, anyhow.

I ask, "Who are you?"

"Ask me who I was," the cloud says.

I take a moment to think about it. If I'm dead, this guy is probably a ghost.

"Oh my god, are you Little Joe? I've heard so much about you tonight."

"I'm not Little Joe." The gas cloud begins to spin and compresses into a smaller form. "I am not anybody anymore."

"So . . . what you're saying is, you *were* Little Joe?"

"I am not Little Joe."

"Yeah, I know, you were *once* Little Joe but now you're . . . a sentient cloud of vibrating gas? How do you identify yourself? I'm sorry if that's not PC."

"I was never Little Joe. I am a spirit with powers beyond your petty mortal understanding."

"Okay, you're a spirit, that is noted. I will remember that."

"You can call me Mo," the spirit says as its cloud condenses, then bursts outward with pulsating, jagged edges.

"Okay, Mo," I say, wiping some beaded sweat from my brow.

An awful silence falls between us. It's as if the gas cloud is staring at me, even though it has no eyes. You don't realize the value and importance of eyes until they're not there. But it can see me, so it must have eyes. Otherwise it's just a cloud, growing thicker by the second.

"Can you see me?" I ask the spirit.

"Yes," Mo responds. For a moment I can see a face in the gas. A strange figure, like a child. But not really like a child, like an old person. I can make out a couple limbs, but what is bright one second is dark the next in the swirling gas: a thing with one arm, now with one leg, now with twenty legs, now a pair of legs without a head, now a head without a body. Dissolving parts, melting away, and yet the figure remains distinct and clear from moment to moment.

"Are you, like, here to take me to the afterlife?"

The gas cloud is getting hazier and denser, to the point that I can no longer see the other wall of the bathroom.

I tell it, "I don't believe in any organized religion, so I don't know if that impacts my destination or anything."

Mo's cloud begins to bubble and boil like a cauldron.

"I will admit that I have thanked God on several, um, fortuitous occasions, so maybe I believe in him? No particular sect, though. I like the pope. The pageantry and all that, not the leading-a-cabal-of-molesters angle, that's bad vibes. Um, I like his shoes, right, that sort of stuff, the bulletproof car, the big hat, the foreign tongues. The new guy, he seems all right."

What was once a translucent pale green cloud is now as dense and deep as a slab of jade.

"Okay, I'm just acting dumb, yes, I know his name, I love Pope Francis, he seems like a cool guy. 'Who am I to judge' and all that. You've seen the tweets, I'm sure."

"You don't believe in me," Mo responds, at last.

"Look, y'know, it's not personal, I just don't really believe in anything, and like, I'm kind of bleeding and . . ." I stop talking.

The spirit has become a strange shape, something indescribable, rather like a pig but much longer than any pig I've ever seen. Around seven feet long and three feet tall, its body is a twisted amalgam of things I could recognize separately but can't place when they're arranged together. A long snout, like that of an elephant, concealing two rows of short jagged teeth with ample space between them. Its skin is striped like a zebra's but textured like a pig's, with white dots dappled around the eyes. The eyes themselves are like those of a rhinoceros perhaps, emotive and small compared to the size of its head. On the end of its long back is a wiggly tail, like a cow's. And it has the paws of a tiger, soft, furry, rounded. I wonder if it has toe beans. All in all, the gas-cloud-turned-beast seems to be proud of its manifestation and stands in a confident pose.

Not how I would picture a dream eater. Not how I would picture anything, really.

"What . . . are you?" I ask.

"I was created from the spare pieces left over when the gods finished creating all the other animals," Mo says, its snout wagging back and forth with every word. The spirit's movements are ethereal, and laggy as if it were underwater. The snout doesn't wag so much as it floats. Mo's lips peel into a smile, and although I think it meant well by it, the ugly nature of its mouth shakes me.

Mo saunters towards me. "What evidence could you have of my reality, beyond your primitive senses?"

"I . . . well . . ." I shrug.

Mo's snout is so close, I feel its exhalations. My glasses steam up.

"Why do you doubt your senses?" Mo asks.

"Dude, I literally just drank a whole bottle of wine and struck my head off something. You're probably some concussion hallucination. Or maybe some other thing altering my senses. A bad oyster, perhaps, or a crumb of cheese or something. Look, I thought there was a little bowl of parmesan cheese served with the oysters. Turns out it was horseradish, because obviously. I ate a big spoonful of it and, boy, was I surprised. You could be that. You could be a big spoonful of horseradish rolling around in my tummy."

No response.

"Spirit, what do you want from me?"

"I was under the impression that you wanted me to eat your dreams. Then I show up and you have the audacity to not even believe in me," Mo says in the tone of a scorned lover. I half expect it to throw a coffee at me and storm out of the bathroom and not answer my texts or calls for a week. Alas, Mo saunters towards the mirror and looks at its body. It emits a thoughtful purr. "I was once like you too. If I had heard about me, I would've never believed it."

"Wait, what? You were human? How did you end up like this?"

The spirit walks in circles around my body, weaving figure eights between my legs, rubbing its head on my calf the way a cat does. "I myself am uncertain," Mo purrs from between my legs, "and I have no comfort to give in knowledge or belief myself. Nor would I tell you if I could." One of Mo's beady eyes winks at me. "I cannot rest, I cannot stay, I cannot taste. In life, my corporeal form disrespected the beings both corporeal and spiritual that preceded it. I did not venerate my ancestors and I lived in ignorance of their lives. As such, I no longer know myself. I do not know who I was or even when I was. I now bear witness to all things across this realm. From the births of universes to the deaths of the tiniest germs, I see it all. As punishment for my ignorance, I have been granted total knowledge."

"Well, it's not total knowledge if you don't know yourself," I say. I can see some similarities between my dilemma and the former life of the spirit. Big whoop.

"I know the incessant torture of remorse. No space of regret can make amends for one's life's opportunities misused."

How can you have a "space of regret"? I hesitate to ask.

A cold air settles into the room, and Mo opens its mouth rather wide, almost 180 degrees. Maybe I shouldn't be so flippant.

"There remains a chance and hope of your escaping my fate," Mo says, its pointy tongue flapping back and forth in its wide-open maw. "Let me eat your dream. Let me replace it with a better one."

"No," I say, "that's quite all right."

It's too late. I struggle to stay still as Mo's mouth emits a bright green light. A tremendous force of wind sucks our surroundings into Mo's mouth, stripping the walls of their decorative tiles, depriving the ceiling of its dim light fixtures. Mo even sucks my blood off the floor along with the tiles and pipes. Mo turns its beam of light towards me and I too am sucked into that wide mouth until I'm shut in tight like an oyster, my body surrounded by the green gas.

"You are small and you are brief. Do not presume you can understand what I am about to show you." The green gas swirls and darkens, turns as black as a deep abyss.

I find myself standing on pavement. In a suburb. It is a spring day, that unmistakable dewy scent of renewal in the air. I recognize the neighbourhood.

"Oh my god, you've brought me to my grandfather's house. Who lives here now?"

Mo's voice floats to me, close yet distant as always. "Go inside."

As I approach the wide front porch, there are a thousand scents in the air, each one connected to a thousand memories long, long forgotten. A thousand thoughts, hopes, joys, questions. The front door opens before me, and that soupy scent, characteristic of the homes of the elderly, overwhelms the thousand other odours.

"Hello? Is anybody home?" I call.

No response.

"Mo, are you sure I should be here?"

"They're in there." I hear the voice although I cannot see where it's coming from. "They will never be able to hear you."

"They have tinnitus, huh?"

"Go inside," says Mo.

"I'm not walking into a stranger's house. They could call the cops or—"

"Go. Inside."

"Very well," I say under my breath, and I walk in through the open door.

The house is just as I remember it. Narrow hallway, adorned with an old floral-print wallpaper. I peek around the corner into what I think was my grandfather's TV room. Sure enough, the radiant glow of a TV illuminates the edges of the orange back of an old chair, its material fuzzy like wool. It doesn't look pleasant to sit in. Itchy, probably. I can see the backs of someone's feet hanging underneath. It's a familiar chair. I remember crawling around under a chair like that when I was young and seeing a loose staple on the underside, something I would gently prod with my pointer finger, enough to feel the sharpness but not enough to puncture.

"Spirit, is . . . is that my grandfather's old chair?"

No response from the spirit. I guess I know what it would've said anyways. Go inside.

I can't go in there. The old guy is probably too deaf to hear me calling from the door. I'll probably give him a heart attack if I just walk into his living room. Imagine some random guy with blood rolling down the side of his head just walks into your house. *Oh, hi, my grandpa used to live here.* If they don't drop dead from fright, I'll be lucky if they don't kill *me*.

Via the tinny audio of the TV, a crowd of thousands yelling "Wheel . . . of . . . Fortune!"

No. It can't be.

Can it?

I step into the TV room as the jazzy theme song plays, trumpets and saxophones wailing.

"From Hollywood, it's America's game!"

I can see the spinning wheel as the camera quickly pans the audience. Looks like old footage. Must be a retro rerun on GSN or something. Does that channel even exist anymore? It's an old TV too, one of those with the really big backsides. The way they used to be.

It cannot be. How is this possible?

"A show the whole family can enjoy . . ."

I peer around the edge of the chair, not wanting to scare whoever is seated there. An elderly Chinese man, pinstriped shirt and a wool vest with little tree patterns. A toddler in his lap.

". . . filled with fun, glamour, excitement, surprises!"

My grandfather and me, sitting on his lap, watching *Wheel of Fortune*. This is it, my memory. This exact moment.

"Here they are, the stars of the show, Pat Sajak and Vanna White!"

I feel woozy. I want to sit down but I don't want to be seen. I need water. "Spirit, can we take a swing by the Health Sciences Centre before we go back to the restaurant?"

"Thank you very much for joining us here on *Wheel of Fortune*. We might have a three-day champion here in our midst. We'll find out that a little later on, but we're gonna meet some players who have some other things in mind." Pat Sajak. Say, Jack, why do I know the proper way to spell Sajak but know next to nothing about my grandfather? There he is sitting there. And yet, I remember the TV as much as I remember him.

"Do not worry, they cannot see you," Mo intones, slithering out of the TV screen like that girl from *The Ring*. "They will never see you, they will never hear you in this realm."

I look so small in my grandfather's lap, the young me. Impossibly small. Like a little dog. And happy. Big smile. He looks happy too.

"It is easy to forget the states you used to inhabit, no? Even if you think you recall correctly, you do not get a full sense of what you were."

Bouncing his knee, the light of the TV illuminating us. Him. Them. The old me.

"Have you given thought to how 'the old' you and 'the young' you are the same being?"

Ugh. I want to make fun of that, but it's kind of right. "That's more of a linguistic distinction than a temporal one," I mutter.

I kneel down on the floor. The loose staple glistens in the glow of the television.

"Your sarcasm will be of no help to you," Mo says. "I am here to replace your bad dreams with pleasant reveries."

"Sorry. I guess I caught a case of irony poisoning when I knocked my head off the fucking toilet. Public washrooms being what they are."

"Your arrogance does nothing for you. You will end up like me. You do not understand."

Why does Mo even care?

"Oh that's right, you said I would not be able to comprehend what I'm seeing here. I comprehend just fine. It's the memory I just described in the restaurant. What a wondrous ability you have, to conjure the one fucking memory you already know I have. 'You cannot comprehend.' I thought you were going to show me the birth of the universe or something like that."

"You wouldn't have the intelligence to comprehend the birth of the universe."

"Um, okay. Ouch."

"Don't you wish to know how I bring you this shadow of the past?"

"Look, y'know, I hate exposition. Let's just move on. Take me back to the restaurant, or to the hospital, or just let me die already."

"It is not your time. You must see more of that which once was. You called me."

"It is my time. You're just a vibrating cloud of gas. I'm leaving, I'm leaving."

I run towards the porch and the walls of my grandfather's house dissolve into murky green gas. I burst through Mo's mouth and find myself back in the restaurant bathroom. I dive for the door and push it open with all my might.

The restaurant is not as it was. The hallway is barren, empty. I run back to the dining room, only to discover that it's empty too.

Everyone and everything is gone.

There are confused noises in the air, incoherent sounds, wailings of lamentation, regret, sorrowful and self-accusatory. The air is filled with gas clouds, spirits, all different colours, if only by gradient. Spirits wandering, floating here and there, moaning as they go. There exists a sadness. The palpable misery of them all.

"This is the fate that awaits you if you do not heed my call," Mo says.

"I thought you said I called you," I say, my voice faltering, my hollow illusion of disaffection being exposed for what it is.

I turn to face Mo. It reaches its paws out to me, claws curled like hooks, and pierces my shoulders. Before I can cry out with the pain, Mo pushes me back into the bathroom and onto the ground, boring deep into my shoulders like a lobster pick. Another set of hands emerges from the cloud and pins my arms to my sides, and yet another set of arms holds down my legs.

"No more!" I cry. "Mo, please."

"They are mere shadows of things that have been. They are what they are, do not blame me. You must bear witness. You must remedy your ignorance. Let me eat your dreams and I will show you what you need to see."

I writhe on the floor in a struggle to escape the spirit's grasp. If it can even be called a struggle, seeing as the spirit is undisturbed by any effort I make to escape. I am trapped.

Mo raises an eyebrow as its mouth opens. For a brief moment I can see in that mouth the mutating jumble of body parts I saw in the cloud before. In the depths of its maw, there are fragments of every face I've seen in my entire life, from my grandfather, smiling as he pinches a piece of broccoli to feed me, bringing the tiny green tree ever closer to my mouth, soy sauce beaded, about to drip, to Alicia, trying on high heels and flats at the shoe store I used to work at as I idiotically mumble "You know, I'm Chinese too," to Mr. Morrison, my fourth grade teacher whose cheek had a strange discoloured patch of skin that he once explained was due to a bad case of frostbite, slamming a metre stick off a student's desk and yelling "Adrenaline rush," to Mom, walking me home from school when I was just a young child and a flock of crows had gathered outside our house, all of them perched totally still, all of them having grown wise to the plastic outdoor owl, all of them knowing exactly who the culprit was that tried to deceive them with such trickery, and Mom says, "Go inside. It's me they're after, not you." The spirit's mouth slams shut.

"Wait," I say, realizing Mo knows more than just what I shared at the dinner table. "Wait!"

"Hrm," Mo says. "On second thought, you really should go to the hospital." Mo releases its grip on me. A burst of wind blasts in my face and I see all matter of objects fly through the air. Carrots, an old brown briefcase, a toilet, and dozens upon dozens of envelopes. One of the tiny envelopes blows onto my chest and the force of the wind keeps it there. The wind dies down and all the objects I saw blowing around disappear. Except for the letter that landed on my chest.

The envelope is tattered and yellowed. It's addressed to a post office box in the Avalon Mall, but the return address is written in Chinese. Presumably. I guess the characters could be from any Asian language.

"Hold on to that," Mo says, eyeing up the envelope on my chest. "It's been lost before."

"Hold on to the envelope?" I say as I stuff it into my pocket. "But you said—"

"That head wound," Mo interrupts. "It's bad. You really need to go to the hospital."

"I thought you were, like, taking me through time or something."

"Yes," Mo says, its snout starting to crumble like sand. "But later. You need help. Then summon me again."

"How?" I cry, watching Mo decay.

"You know how. You need to be in a more private space for a longer session," Mo says with a grin as the washroom's TV absorbs it back into the screen as an ad for Screech illuminates the room.

"That sounds gross," I say under my breath.

With another bright flash of light, the gas clears out and the wailings stop and I'm staring at the ceiling and the speakers are playing a British rapper I used to hear all the time when I was in Europe last summer, rhyming about how he has the same name as his grandfather.

"Heh, a bit on the nose," I say to myself as I get off the floor and look in the mirror. Still bleeding, still woozy, blood drip-dripping down my ear.

Big oof.

I open the bathroom door. It's back to how it was, narrow hallways with inconveniently hung paintings sticking out like an underbite, the fork-knife dances clinking through the dining rooms. The hostess is just down the hall. I stagger out, leaving behind my blood on the floor. I'll clean it myself, but I should tell the hostess to, like, put a sign on the door or something.

"Hey," I call out to her, and she keeps walking down the hall. "Hey," I call out again, a little louder, walking a little faster to catch up with her. I stumble on a rug and pitch towards her, my arms outstretched like a zombie, grabbing on to the hostess's shoulders from behind.

"Why, Mr. Pynn, what are you—? Oh my god!" she screams when she sees the blood running down my head, soaking my white undershirt.

"The bathroom," I mumble, woozy. "My head. I hit it off something."

"Glenda!" she yells. "Glenda, call an ambulance! It's happening again! Mr. Pynn, let me get you a seat. Just breathe, okay?"

"Ping," I say as the hostess gently pushes me into a spare chair in the supply closet. "P-I-N-G."

"Oh my son, don't strain yourself," the hostess says, grimacing as blood drops onto her arms.

"I called 'im," a woman says as she walks into my vision. "You don't tink the gas is acting up again now, do ya?"

"Sure, b'y, I don't know," the hostess says. "He gave himself an awful smack. He can't even say his own name right."

"My name is Ping," I say. "I don't need an ambulance, really."

"Me son, your name is Pynn. And you really do need an ambulance."

"Do I?" I touch the wet spot on the side of my head.

"Coming through," another voice rings out, the sound of metal rattling through the myriad halls. "You're lucky we were only a couple blocks over when the call came in."

"We were just parked on George, waiting for somethin'," another voice says.

"'E's right 'ere," the woman I presume to be Glenda says. "'E's after smacking 'is 'ead off a sometin' in the batroom."

"He might be concussed," the hostess says. "I'm not sure that he can even say his own name properly."

The two female paramedics lift my body onto their gurney.

"I'm fine," I protest. "Really. All I need is some water. I promise."

"Son," the older paramedic says, "what's your name?"

"William Ping," I say. "P-I-N-G."

"It's Pynn," the hostess whispers.

"I t'ought you said it was Pink," Glenda says.

"How many fingers am I holding up?" one paramedic says and extends three fingers.

"Three," I say.

"Hmm," the paramedic says. "Probably he's saying his own name right."

They roll me down the narrow hall and we pass by the dining room where Alicia's family is seated. They're putting on their jackets, dessert plates left crumby in front of them. I give a gentle wave as I roll by, blood still streaming down my face.

I wait outside the emergency room for a couple hours, sandwiched between other people waiting, some moaning in pain with no visible ailments, another wiggling on edge as a bone juts through their shin. I sit holding a Kleenex to my head. *Breakfast at Tiffany's* is playing and I imagine Mo slithering out of the screen. Alicia calls but I don't answer. There goes that one, I figure.

The door swings open and a doctor surveys the room. "Mr. Pong," she calls out. "Come right in."

After clearing up some confusion regarding the name on the chart, the doctor looks at my head wound and says, "Stitches or staples?"

I look at her, waiting for her to continue.

"You choose," she says.

"Oh," I say. "I . . . I don't . . . This is your work, whatever you think is—"

"Staples," she says, and steps over to a cabinet, takes out a staple gun that looks like one they use on construction sites.

"Okay," she says. "Lie down. This'll be over before you know it."

3

DONKEY

Two weeks' rest, that's what the doctor ordered. I spend the first day after I get stapled back together lying in bed in my apartment, watching *John Wick* movies and dodging calls on my cell. I don't want to have to explain to anybody what happened. There's a part of me that would like to never get out of bed, to just be in a constant state of recovery, to never have to face the world.

I haven't been able to stop thinking of the spirit's grotesque visage, wagging snout over jagged fangs. I would've thought it was all a dream, the time-travelling spirit and all that, but the letter is still in the pocket of my pants, flung over a chair in the corner. It's all in my mind, I'm sure, but I feel a dark energy coming from that pocket. I've thought of tearing it up or throwing it away, but I hesitate to take it out or look at it too long, a loneliness emanating from its yellowed, bent corners, like a black hole in the corner of my bedroom. Every time I see it, it speaks to something portentous, something dug out of the past that I don't know but feel that I should. I could drop the letter in a mailbox, let the post office take care of it, but I fear what Mo might do if it found out. I could place it on my shelf of curios, alongside the Pope Francis bobble-head, jade Buddha, and a set of Supreme-emblazoned chopsticks. But no, the letter's radiant otherworldly energy would harsh the vibe. I must summon Mo again and give the letter back. It's the only way to resolve this anxious feeling I've had since that fateful night.

To make matters worse, I left my Patagonia sweater in the restaurant's bathroom. That's not related to the ghost stuff, but I bought that sweater at a Nordstrom in Vegas, so it has a real sentimental value, in addition to a monetary value. I should go back to the restaurant, see if they have my sweater, and while I'm there I can tuck that old letter behind the toilet tank. After all, there must be some logical reason for it to be there. Surely the ghost wasn't real, and that old letter must've been knocked into my pocket somehow when I was blacking out. The dark, portentous weight of the letter would be away from me then, locked away. Plus, I could once again be cozy in a casual yet still professional way with my favourite sweater. I mean, that's what's really important here. Getting both the letter and the sweater back to their rightful owners.

"Alexa, pause *John Wick: Chapter 3*," I say.

Keanu freezes midway though jumping onto a horse's back, his body suspended in the air. I look towards my pants pocket holding the letter, and sigh. One leg after the other, it's time to return to the world.

I skip down the alley off Duckworth. When I open the restaurant's door, the hostess looks up at me.

"Sorry," she says. "We're not taking walk-ins tonight because the DuMont Corporation has booked the restaurant for a late Christmas party." She notices the wound on my head, and a flash of recognition brightens her eyes. "Oh, Mr. Pang," she says. "Oh my god, how are you doing? I've been worried half to death about you."

"Hi," I say, nodding towards her in such a way as to show off my staples. "I think I left my sweater here."

"Did you?" she says, her eyes affixed to the wound.

"Yeah," I say. "It was a grey Patagonia Synchilla pullover."

She shakes her head. "No, my son," she says. "I haven't seen anything like that."

"Hmm," I say. I thought this might happen. Those are good sweaters. "Could I possibly take a look back there?"

"Well, I guess, if you want, but I'm sure I would've seen something like that."

"Oh, I believe you," I assure her. "I'll just take a quick look in the bathroom, just to put my mind at ease."

"Go ahead," she says. "You know the way."

"All too well," I say with a smile.

"Don't fall in," I hear her call out as I make my way through the labyrinthine arrangement of hallways.

There's a sheet of loose-leaf taped to the door with OUT OF ORDER scrawled across it. When I push open the door I see that my blood has stained some of the green tiles on the floor, and some tiles surrounding the toilet have been removed, revealing ancient piping and withered old pieces of wood. Part of the toilet bowl is missing too, presumably having been shattered by my noggin. There is, of course, no sweater, but I shut the door behind me anyways. I look in the mirror at the staple scab just under my hairline.

"Eat my dreams," I whisper.

I look around. Nothing happens. The TV is advertising a Toonie Tuesday special on Brews and Dews, and the Sonos is playing Robbie Robertson crooning about an old river. I take the letter out of my pocket, my arm leaden and unsteady, as if the small square of paper weighs a hundred pounds. The words are illegible to me, the meaning of it all illegible to me. I wish I knew more, not just about the letter but about the meaning behind these scribbled characters, about the language, the culture. I wish I knew my namesake, the man I live under the shadow of, the mystery of myself.

I could leave the letter right here on the edge of the sink, get rid of that weight of the unknown, return to my TV and the endless reveries of streaming, or . . .

"Eat my dreams," I say, with a slight waver in my voice. I can't just leave the letter here. I should give it back to Mo at least.

"Eat my dreams," I say a little louder. Give letter to Mo, then find my sweater. Easy. And if the spirit doesn't come back, then I leave the letter with the hostess. Easy.

"Eat my dreams," I repeat for the third time, grimacing, uncertain whether it was all delusion and misplaced understandings.

The lights flicker and the speakers skip a couple beats and then go silent as the lights go out.

"You rang?" Mo's voice slithers into my ears as the TV comes back on, with a picture of the Narrows advertising a brunch special. Oh god, does that mean I passed out again? The hostess is going to be pissed.

Mo twirls out of the TV with a burst of gas, having already assumed the form of the strange animal that it took on last time.

"Oh, it's you again," it says, its dry lips smirking, revealing yellow pointed teeth.

I stand there staring at it, speechless, as the lights flicker back on.

"Well?" Mo says, its words trickling out of its mouth. "Aren't you going to say anything?"

"I . . . I didn't think this was real. I didn't really think that would work. Again."

"My child," Mo says, floating closer to me. "You knew this would work. You've taken heed of my warning. Be prepared, for it shall now begin."

"No," I say. "Your letter. I only called you to give it back to you."

"You have a question that needs answering," Mo said. "I will show you the truth of who you are."

I feel a sensation of ugly anticipation, like in the moments before getting a needle; I know I have to do this regardless of how uncertain it makes me feel. Is the spirit right? Sure, I want to know my grandfather, but do I really want to subject myself to Mo's strange conjurations?

"I really must be going," I say as I reach for the doorknob. "I have places to be."

"Too late," Mo says as its mouth opens extra wide.

The door fades into splinters, the knob melting through my fingers like the T-1000. Ugh, I guess we're doing this. The room becomes darker, dirtier. The walls shrink, windows crack; fragments of plaster fall from the ceiling, and support beams become exposed.

"I'm not the litigious type," I say to the spirit, "but if that's asbestos, you're going to see me in court."

The beams fall away and we're outside again. Except we aren't outside my grandfather's house this time.

It's hot. The kind of heat that hits you in the face the second the airplane door opens on a trip to Disney World. Sweat dripping down my back already, T-shirt clinging to my body.

"Are we . . . in Florida?" I ask as I survey my surroundings. I can't see Mo around, but if it's showing me this, it must be able to hear me.

No response.

The terrain is more desert-like than Florida. Sure, I can see greenery in the distance, but everything around me is gravelly and dirty. Dusty. Not quite sand.

"Vegas?"

Still no response. The spirit is ghosting me again.

"If we're in a place this hot, I'm really going to need some water."

Silence, aside from a slight breeze blowing sand around. It is extremely hot. Mostly barren landscape, save for some rocks. On the skyline, I can see a couple towers. Watchtowers, maybe. Sparse cement and brickwork, nothing ornamental. Various windows and perches, scattered across their four long walls. Just tall, square buildings, dotting the horizon in an irregular pattern. They kind of look like the old firehall downtown, the one that had that painting of the firefighting Dalmatian on the side, spraying water from his big hose.

Water.

I turn around and behind me is one of those towers overlooking a bridge with no water underneath it. Just outside the tower, a donkey is attached to some wooden arm thing, circling a hole in the ground.

Is that . . . a well?

"This isn't Vegas, is it?"

I can barely keep my eyes open, it's so fucking hot. Squinting at the donkey, I walk towards it.

"Patience," Mo says, its lengthy body wiggling out of the phone in my pocket. "We're not leaving yet."

"I was just hoping to give you your letter back," I say.

"Hold on to it," Mo says. "It'll be a couple of years before I'll need that from you."

"A couple years?" I exclaim. "I have a life, you know. I have to see friends later." By "friends" I mean a marathon of *South Park*, but still. Years? No way.

"It will not take years in your perception," Mo says, cold. "I wash away time. Now watch your surroundings."

The donkey is drawing water from a well. There's an old Asian man, sitting on the ground and leaning against the well. He looks sweaty and has one of those big rice field hats on his lap.

"Hi," I say. "Excuse me, sir, do you mind if I drink some of this water?"

He blankly stares at the wall of the nearby watchtower.

"Hi," I say and crouch down in front of him. I do a little wave.

He stares right through me.

"I really need water. I think I might pass out."

Nothing. Geez, between this guy and Mo.

I look at the wall that he's looking at. There's a boy over there, maybe ten or eleven years old, playing, jumping around, waving and aiming a stick like it's a rifle. I look back at the man.

"Sir, do you speak English?" I reach out to touch his shoulder and my hand goes right through him as if he was made of water, and I lose my balance and fall straight through the man's body. He shudders and stands up, waving his hat under his face like a fan.

"You will find that it is impossible to interact with anybody while in my realms," Mo says. "They cannot see you or hear you or feel your touch."

"Yeah, I just figured that out." I pick myself up, rubbing the dust and sand off my pants. "How is it that I can have dust on my pants but be unable to touch anyone?"

"There are varying levels of perception from others in regards to your appearance here."

"Meaning?"

No response, of course.

The donkey looks old and weak. His mane is grey and tattered. He pulls around the well slowly, the bucket of water being a great strain on his aged body. He staggers and falls towards the inside of his circular path, but recovers quickly, always pushing forward. As he walks in circles around the well, a wooden thing that kind of looks like a Ferris wheel spins around and sloshes water into a hollowed-out piece of bamboo, leading the water into a bucket.

"Can I drink?" I ask both the man who cannot hear me and the spirit who doesn't like to respond to me.

"Drink," Mo says.

I crouch down to the bucket and look at the water inside. Looks clear. No excrement or asbestos-like substance floating around. Just water. I look to my left and right to make sure no one is watching and I lift the bucket up to my lips to drink.

What a relief. The water is warm but refreshing.

The water flowing through the bamboo pipe sloshes onto the dirt in front of me and the donkey stops to look at me. I put the bucket back under the pipe. The donkey keeps staring.

"The donkey can see me?"

"There are varying levels of perception from others in regards to your appearance here," Mo repeats as it floats around the watchtower.

The man yells at the donkey, then slaps him on the behind with the back of his hand. The donkey continues to walk.

"What kind of dream is this?" I ask the spirit.

"It's not a dream," it says. "This is how things were."

I look at the donkey, and the sloshing water, and the old man, and the child, and the watchtower, and the surrounding emptiness.

Beads of sweat form on my head and roll into my eyes as I stand there watching the donkey pump the water. The bucket overflows ever so slightly, catching the donkey's attention, and he once again stops.

The man calls out to the child in a language I'm not familiar with. I mean, it sounds like Chinese, but I don't know, it could be Japanese, Korean. It's not English, that's for sure.

The child attaches the bucket to the end of a larger, thicker piece of bamboo, and then unties the donkey from the water-pumping device. He smooths the donkey's mane and whispers in his ear. The child turns his back to his father and reveals a small piece of a carrot that he had hidden in his hand and brings it to the donkey's mouth. The man calls out to the child again as he fastens a bag to the other end of the thick piece of bamboo. The man and the child lift the bamboo stick onto the donkey's back, balancing the stick so that it doesn't tip on either end.

I stand by the well watching as the man and child and donkey embark down the dirt road. Mo is hovering over the well, its face contorted into something resembling a smile. As the man and child keep walking, the donkey brays and bucks, and his hind legs shake and give out slightly. The bamboo stick becomes unbalanced and the bucket spills all over the ground. The man yells at the donkey. The child is crying and drops the stick he was playing with. The donkey tries to trot away from the man, back towards me by the well.

"Uh, Mo," I say, searching for a sign of something as I retreat from the approaching donkey.

The man picks up the child's stick and rushes after the donkey, slaps the donkey with the stick. The donkey is coming right at me, and I back up until I'm leaning against the wall of the well.

"A flower that blooms in adversity is the greatest flower of all," Mo says.

"Is that from *Mulan*?" I say, bracing myself against the well. I swear to God that's from *Mulan*.

The man slaps the stick off the back of the donkey's legs so hard that the stick cracks in half. The donkey charges right at me, braying and squealing, and I throw my arms up in front of my face.

Except the donkey goes right through me.

He crashes into the wall of the well behind me and tips over and falls into that abyss, smashing through the wooden Ferris wheel thing and tearing the whole system down with him, his squeals echoing off the walls.

The man screams in anger and waves the stump of the branch right through my head, then throws it down into the well after the donkey.

The man puts his head in his hands, speaking and pointing at the child. The child, still crying, runs over. The man slaps the boy in the face, knocking the child on to the ground. The man crumples, plopping himself on the ground and keeling over into a recline against the wall just as I first saw him. The child picks himself up and gazes into the dark abyss of the well.

The donkey brays again.

The child wipes tears from his cheeks with the back of his hand.

Bray, bray, bray echoing out of the well and into the stagnant baked air.

The child points down the well and says something to his father.

The father responds in a snappy way.

"Spirit, I'm all for that whole 'patience is a virtue' thing but, like, I don't know the language they're speaking and I find it hard to follow what's going on."

The father stands up and stares down into the well too and lets out a deep sigh.

"They are speaking Taishanese. We are on the outskirts of Hoiping in Guangdong Province."

Is this where they make iPhones?

The father walks over to the watchtower-like building and knocks on the door. A man emerges with a rifle on his back. The father talks to him and points to the well several times. The man with the rifle angrily shakes his head and steps back from the doorway, only to re-emerge a moment later with a shovel. He forces the shovel into the hands of the father, yells at him, and slams the door.

"The year is 1920 and the man is your grandfather."

The father walks back to the well and begins shovelling dirt and sand into the well.

"That guy burying a donkey alive is my grandfather?"

"No," the spirit says.

"The guy with the rifle?"

"No."

I look at the child. "Him?"

"I have no perception of age or time, having been trapped in this state for so long," the spirit says.

"You literally just told me what year it is," I mutter.

The donkey begins to squeal over and over again. This terrible noise, the sound of an animal dying a slow death, makes the child cry again.

The donkey goes quiet.

The father notices the sudden silence too and stops shovelling. The child, wailing all the while, peers over the edge. His wails stop and he tries to conceal a smile creeping along his face. The father pushes the child out of the way. He looks into the well, and his jaw drops.

I walk over and peer down into the abyss.

The donkey is standing on top of the dirt, wagging its tail.

The father scoops up another shovelful of dirt and throws it down the well, and this time all three of us watch as the dirt falls. The dirt hits the donkey's back and he shakes it off so that it gathers underneath him.

The father and son look at each other, perplexed. I look at them too and try to share in this family-bonding moment.

The father begins to dig again and for some time it proceeds like this: him throwing dirt down the well, me and the child watching. Soon, men come out from the watchtower. Some of them help to dig, others just watch. Then men, women, and children come down the dirt road to watch.

After a couple hours, the donkey's head pokes out the top of the well, and soon enough, the father and some of the watchtower men help the donkey over the ledge. The child once again hugs and pets the donkey. There is a generally triumphant sense in the air. I can tell people are happy that the donkey is free, although a couple villagers angrily speak with the guards and gesture at the soil and the well, perhaps mad that their water source is now filled with dirt.

The sun begins to set and the villagers head back down the dirt road and the watchtower guards go back into their tower. It's just like it was in the beginning: me and the donkey and the father and the child.

The child gathers the toppled bag and the bamboo stick. The father carries the shovel back to the watchtower.

Bang!

The donkey drops to the ground, knocking its head against the edge of the well on the way down. The child screams. I back up and feel the stapled wound on my head. The father spins around and yells at the child, gesturing as he himself crouches down.

Bang!

Blood spurts from the donkey's neck. A chorus of laughter echoes down from the watchtower.

After a moment, the father stands up, peers up at the tower, and then walks over to the child. The child is crying again, quietly.

The father speaks to him and the child picks up the bamboo stick and the bag.

Bang!

The father drops to the ground.

"No," I say, reaching out to him.

The child runs as fast as he can down the dirt road.

On the highest perch of the tower, a scope glints in the evening sun.

The donkey bleeds out next to the dirt-filled well, bits of brain and skull sprayed across the earth as blood pumps out of his neck, moistening the soil, mixing with his spilt water and the blood of the man who whipped him.

And then as I watch, the donkey's corpse rots away, maggots and birds swarm its carcass, and in seconds there is no sign of the animal left on the soil, and the soil is the floor of the washroom.

Knock knock knock

"W-what?" I look around the well again, its walls melting into the shape of the toilet bowl. "What the hell? You can't just show me that, you—you can't."

"Years go by in the blink of an eye," Mo says with a grin showcasing its unseemly fangs.

"What happened to pleasant reveries?"

Knock knock knock

What's that sound? I shake my head, trying to regain my composure. It's not real, right? I wipe sweat from my brow with the back of my hand.

"Happy endings don't always have happy beginnings," the spirit says.

I sigh. "Why do so many of your remarks have a gross sexual energy? Just take the letter and let me leave, Mo. I can't bear to witness these things."

Knock knock knock

The sound reverberates through the last shreds of rural China.

"Sir." It's the hostess. "Mr. Pang. Are you okay in there, me son?"

48

"Tell her you're fine," Mo whispers.

"It's all good," I say. "And the name is Ping. P-I-N-G."

"You didn't hurt yourself again, did you?"

"No," I say. "I'll be out in just a second."

"The letter is your responsibility now," Mo says, eyeing up the envelope's outline in my pocket. "I will tell you what to do with it."

"Sir, you can't stay in the restaurant, sir. As I said before, the DuMont—"

"I'm coming," I say. "Just a moment."

"We need privacy for this experience," Mo says.

"I already told you how gross that sounds," I say under my breath as the hostess knocks again.

"That bathroom is out of order, me son. I don't know what you did in there the first time, but the plumbing don't even work the same in there now."

I sigh as I open the door. "It's all good," I tell her. "It's fine."

"Did you find your sweater?" she asks.

"Unfortunately, no," I say.

"So why were you in there so long?" She raises an eyebrow.

"Just trying to figure out what I hit my head off," I say. "I don't remember the impact."

"It's pretty obvious it was the toilet," she says, pointing to the shattered bowl. She looks at me with an emphatic concern. "Don't worry yourself over that now," she adds. "Your little boo-boo actually revealed some historical thing."

"Hm?"

"This place used to be a Chinese laundry," she says as I follow her back to her desk at the front of building. "And we found this old piece of paper under one of the tiles." She produces a sheet of paper that looks like it was ripped from a small journal. Chinese characters are written across it in tidy columns.

"I wonder what it means," I say. If only I knew.

"Isn't that something?" the hostess says with a proud lilt to her voice. "We're gonna frame it and hang it here somewhere. There's some English writing on the other side, but I thinks this side's more interesting." She briefly flips the sheet over to show me.

I gasp and stumble backwards. Although I am surprised, I know now what I'm meant to do, dark energies be damned. On the sheet, three letters scrawl in an extravagant cursive: WSP.

The hostess lightly touches my arm. "Are you sure you're all right? If you needs to lie down for a moment or something, there's lots of vacant rooms upstairs. My son had a concussion once and he had these bouts where he'd get lightheaded and have to lie down and—"

"Actually," I say, an idea coming into my head, "can I book a room?"

"You can just lie down for a few minutes until you're okay again. It's more than fine, really," she says.

"No," I say. "I'd like to book a room for the next two weeks. Right now."

She squints at me. "You're sure you're all right?"

"I'm completely fine," I say. "I'd just like a room."

"I'm never one to turn away a customer, but wouldn't you be better off at home, given . . ." She points at my head.

"Well," I say, "I have to rest for two weeks, because of the whole head wound thing, and I can't get any rest at home because people keep coming by to see my wound or take care of me or whatever. But I could rest here. Nobody would know I'm here."

She can't argue with that, and before long I have the key in my hand and I'm on my way to my room. It's at the end of a long hall, the sounds of noisy children ricocheting off the walls.

I lie down on the small bed. It's a nice little room, tiny flat-screen ("The TV's got an Alexa in it," the hostess told me), tiny lamps, and a tiny iPad bolted to the wall that you can order room service from. I take the envelope out of my pocket, a letter whose arrival in my life has complicated my binge-watching plans. It needs to go back to where it belongs. I return the envelope to my pocket and close my eyes.

"Eat my dream," I say as I get comfortable on the bed. "Eat my dream. Eat my dream."

"Mmm," Mo says. "Calling again so soon."

I open my eyes quick to catch a glimpse of Mo's long body emerging from the iPad.

"Show me everything," I say as I close my eyes again. "Everything."

4

GOTTA KEEP IT GENTLEMAN

"The year is 1931," Mo says as the scene at the well is conjured before me again.

It's even hotter than before. The well has improved over the last ten years. Instead of having a donkey walk in endless circles around it, now a donkey walks in a gigantic hamster wheel that pumps the water in much the same fashion. A terrible thing, to be trapped on that treadmill in all this heat. I can't even be bothered to use the Peloton on a cold day.

It's a lot busier than it used to be as well. People walk by in every direction, carrying baskets balanced on their shoulders or riding in the backs of rickshaws. The nearby bridge is now gated.

A young man in a suit stares at the wheel-well contraption. His hair is stylish, short and coiffed like an Asian Don Draper. Suit Man is standing in front of some lit incense sticks and an orange with two red candles sticking out of it. He's around my age, early twenties. He looks dazed, nodding towards either the donkey or the wheel and waving to some of the people passing by. I'd be dazed too if I were wearing a suit in this heat. He's the only one wearing a suit. Others are wearing more temperature-appropriate attire, loose-fitting shirts and long, spacious robes.

Suit Man reaches in his pocket and takes out some folded paper, money, I think. With his other hand, he produces a match, strikes it off his thumbnail, and proceeds to set the money ablaze. He places it on the ground in the same controlled manner one might use to put a baby in a crib. His expression is blank as he stares at his burning money and places more folded money in the flames with slow, precise movements. Villagers and rickshaws continue on around him and his small fire as if he isn't even there. This must be a common experience for him. I suppose every town has that guy that you learn to ignore.

A brood of ducklings, undisturbed by the bustling crowd, waddles past Suit Man and heads up the old dirt road. Suit Man follows them.

"Is there something wrong with him?" I say as I wipe sweat off my eyelids with the sleeve of my T-shirt. "I don't know if that's the polite way to ask that. Why's he wearing a suit in this heat?"

"That man is your grandfather," Mo says. "Obviously."

"That's Poppy Ping? Is he having heatstroke? Is that why he's acting like that?"

"Follow in his footsteps and you will learn," Mo says.

"Cliché," I mumble, but I follow my grandfather following the ducklings.

We waddle through the outskirts of town, shrubs and greenery bordering both sides of the old dirt road, dust and sand rising into the air behind the duck convoy.

Quack, quack, quack.

The ducklings lead us to what appears to be the main street of the village, as dozens of people are darting around every which way. Poppy Ping walks with purpose and confidence through the crowd. Small concrete and brick buildings line the dirt road. It's a dirty place, with small buildings and smaller alleys on the offshoots. The ways are foul and narrow; the shops and houses wretched; the people slipshod. Alleys and archways, like cesspools, discharge offensive smells, and dirt, and life, upon the straggling main street. The whole quarter reeks.

It's just like George Street, except not as bad.

And unlike George Street, people live in these buildings. People are washing laundry outside and hanging it between balconies to dry. More livestock than George Street too. Sure, sometimes on George Street you might see a police horse, a pleasant surprise when you've got a buzz on. But here, there are animals everywhere. Cows roam and chickens peck freely, seemingly belonging to no one but themselves. Farmers drag their equipment down the road, past the many stands that crowd the street like a congested farmers' market.

The stands are selling everything. Fruits and vegetables, huge quantities of oranges and peppers and some sort of zucchini-looking thing that's bigger and thicker than my leg. Fish, both fresh and salted, both dead and alive, hanging and put in big soup pots repurposed as makeshift fish tanks. Fillets of whitefish rotting in the sun, flies zipping around and nipping at an elderly stand keeper. Shrimp the size of my hand and pigs' feet with noodles served alongside buckets with writhing eels inside. A tray of raw chicken wings next to a tray of fried chicken feet. Others are cooking, cuts of mystery meat and vegetables being chopped and fried and rolled in rice paper. A boiling cauldron with a turtle shell rising to the top as a woman drops what appears to be a tumorous log into the broth. Other stands are selling fans, iron scraps, old rags, bottles, bones, baskets, and greasy offal.

All the while people are laughing and spitting and yelling and smiling and frowning and chopping and cleaning and coughing and breathing and moving and stopping and, above all else, living. And even though I'm somewhat nauseated, deep inside I wish I could stop and taste the food, could understand what they are saying, could be part of this . . . bustle. I guess it's the same reason I like to shop on Black Friday or Boxing Day, because even though the lineups are too long and there's too many people and everyone kind of disgusts me, I feel I'm part of something that's happening, something other people are doing too, something beyond me, bigger than me, my own brand of church.

I realize I have forgotten to follow my grandfather and the ducklings. I look up and down the street. Everyone here is as sweaty as me, shiny skin and loose shirts, fanning themselves and drinking water straight from buckets. The only person not dressed for the weather is Suit Man, so he's easy to find in the throng.

He's about a block down the road, walking up the steps to a building that looks slightly newer than the rest, and it's much larger and more ornate. Great concrete pillars hold up the roof, and Chinese characters adorn the doorways.

I hurry through the crowd, passing through their bodies and feeling the shivers that run through them. I rush into the building and catch a glimpse of my man in the suit entering a room at the end of the hall. He closes the door behind him.

I burst into the room, and the door smacks loudly off a chalkboard. A roomful of young people behind desks stare at me. My grandfather, standing at the front of the room, shakes his head, mutters something, and reaches to close the door. His hand passes right through me, and he shudders and says something that makes the students laugh.

He pulls on the handle to make sure it's secure, then returns to the front of the room. He picks up a piece of chalk and writes some Chinese characters on the board.

"Um, Mo," I say, "I hate to say this, but I don't follow what you're trying to show me here."

My grandfather continues to write on the chalkboard, in addition to moving little wooden beads around on one of those really old calculators, an atticus or an abidance or something like that. We have one at home that used to be Pop's.

Wait. "Spirit, is that the same abidance that I have at home?"

Mo slithers out of a textbook. "It's called an abacus." It sounds tired for some reason.

Pop draws a big circle on the board, then writes some characters beside it.

"Mo," I say again. "Can you do anything about the language barrier?"

Pop divides the circle into eight equal-ish sections.

"Patience," the spirit says.

Now Pop draws a crude outline of a horse inside the circle and then he neighs, eliciting gentle chuckles from the class.

"Is he drawing that new wheel at the well?"

"Yes," the spirit says.

Pop moves the little wooden beads around, explaining to the class and pointing to his drawing of the donkey in the wheel.

"Is it in your wheelhouse of abilities to make it so that I can understand Chinese or is that something you can't do?"

"You will understand Taishanese when the time comes," Mo says.

"So you don't have the ability to translate?"

"Yes, but that will come to you in time," Mo says.

"But, Mo, I can't learn whatever lesson you're trying to get me to learn if I can't understand the language being spoken around me. And if I can't learn the lesson, I might as well head out to the street and see if I can get something to eat."

"You may not leave this space," the spirit booms.

"If I can't understand what's going on, then I'm not even in this space, am I?"

"Your thinking," the Spirit says in a more relaxed tone, "is headed in the right direction."

Pop turns to address the class. "While I designed this wheel-well," he says, "I am not the inventor of the device." His lips keep moving for a moment, although I don't hear any more words.

"Mo . . . did you just dub this memory?"

"These are not memories," the spirit says. "I am simply a presenter of things as they once were and always are."

"I encountered this design during my many years of studying well pump technology," Pop tells his class. Again the lips keep moving after the sound stops.

"Mo. This is so distracting. I can't be immersed if his lips are out of sync with the audio."

"You can listen to them speak in Taishanese or you can listen to them like this," Mo says. "Those are your options."

"Fine, fine." This is like the world's worst VR experience.

"The treadwheel is powered by the weight of the animal, in our case a donkey, as it walks up one side of its interior. This design can be used to generate electricity, steer boats, draw water from wells, or even to turn meat on a spit."

Pop points to his sketch of the wheel. "The treadwheel is balanced on a central axis, underneath which lies the base mount upon which the crane is attached. The rope is attached to the central axis, and in order to lift up the buckets of water, the axis must turn. Even to lift one or two metres, the axis must turn two or three times. This is because the diameter of the treadwheel is so much greater, so the amount of effort you have to use to get the bucket to budge is spread out over a longer distance. For the one we have constructed here by the diaolou, the well is forty-nine metres deep."

Pop writes some characters on the chalkboard, doing equations of some sort. "And you'll see from this calculation that the wheel will have to move 255 metres in order to successfully bring up one bucket of water. Now does anybody see any flaws in this system?"

A student raises his hand. "Mr. Poy," he begins, but immediately I'm too distracted to listen to what he says.

"Mo," I say, scratching my head around the staples. "The kid called him Mr. Poy."

"His name is Seto Poy. He is a fourth-class power engineer. This is his classroom."

"My grandfather's name was Seto Ping."

"Patience," the spirit says.

"Sure you don't have me paired with the wrong guy? People get my name wrong all the time."

No response.

Mr. Poy's lesson continues. He mostly speaks about calculations and engineering problems, the sort of stuff that it doesn't matter to me if it was in Chinese or English because I wouldn't know what they were talking about anyways. Things like "net head" and "flow rate." Something about hydro power.

But all of a sudden the walls crumble as if the whole school was built out of sand and a stiff nor'easter blew through the place. Now Mr. Poy is at a restaurant. He sits laughing and talking with other young men in suits around a large round table in the back. They are sharing a whole roasted duck and they drink room-temperature booze out of small glasses. The alcohol smells like soy sauce and it's good at starting conversations.

It's hard to hear what they're saying, a dozen guys talking over each other at this table, on top of the patrons in tattered shirts and pants in the rest of the establishment, everyone's lips out of sync with the words I hear. But it's not hard to tell that the guys in the suits are having a good time. They're comfortable here, sprawled out in chairs and addressing the waiters by name. I'm guessing they're regulars. And even though I can't make out what they're saying, something strikes me as so glamorous about this Mr. Poy and his band of suited gentlemen, living it up here with their cuff-linked wrists and free-flowing drinks amid the squalor outside.

I'm sure Mo won't respond, but I ask, "Are these guys gangsters?"

"No, they're teachers," the spirit says, in a tone that suggests I should already know this.

If this is what the teachers look like, I want to see the gangsters.

Poy leans back in his chair and lifts his glass in the air, bespoke sleeves floating over spent duck bones. He comes off to me as a gentleman, intelligent and kind, the type of guy who looks the waiter in the eye and tips handsomely. I wonder which lucky lady in town he might be paired up with.

And just like that I find myself transported once again. A butler opens the front door of a house for Poy.

"Welcome home, sir," the butler says. "Will you be requiring my services this evening?"

"No, go home," Poy says and hands the butler some cash. "Have a good night."

A young Chinese woman greets Poy, embraces him, and shushes him before whisking him away to look through the doorway of another room. They both shiver as I pass through their bodies to see what they're looking at. A very young boy sleeps peacefully in a crib. Poy loosens his tie as he quietly shuts the door, leaving me in the dark room with the baby boy.

I step through the closed door, but a cloud of green gas obscures my vision and I find myself in the middle of an afternoon. Acres and acres of farmland stretch endlessly across the horizon, men and women tilling the land, mountain ranges topped by clouds in the distance. Poy and the young woman I presume to be his wife are chasing a toddler around a field.

"The cat is going to catch you, Wai," the lady yells. "You better run to Mama."

Poy stomps back and forth playfully, hunched over like a cat, his hands behind his head and two pointer fingers extended like pointed ears. "You rat better run," he says, affecting a menacing voice.

The toddler giggles as he runs, stumbling every couple steps. It looks like he only recently learned to walk. Poy lets the boy run into his mother's arms. She picks up the boy and twirls around, planting a big kiss on Wai's head.

"Hua Ling, you should've let me catch the little stinky rat," Poy says as he tickles Wai's ribs.

"You couldn't catch him if you tried," Hua Ling says with a giggle.

"Ha!" Poy says. "Put him down. Let's see how fast I can catch *you!*"

"Pshh," she says. "You could never." Hua Ling places the boy down and pushes Poy's chest. "Come get me," she says as she backs up.

Poy stands like a sumo wrestler, legs bent, ready to pounce. He jumps back and forth in front of Hua Ling before he dives at her, easily catching her. They tumble into the grass, the two of them laughing as he tickles her and kisses her, the greenery looking as though it might swallow them whole. Wai stumbles over on his little toddler legs and Poy picks the boy up and waves him over his head like an airplane.

A good life, a good job, a wife, a child.

"Mo, why would this man ever go to Newfoundland?" I feel as though I could cry for a reason I don't know.

Mo sticks its large head out of my pocket, its body emerging from my iPhone. With a flick of its snout, four walls rise out of the ground and the happy family is blocked from my view.

5

ABIDANCE

The cement walls are a sun-faded pink with crazing running through them. Mr. Poy, in a different suit, stands next to two older women who sit at a table filling and folding dumplings.

"I never see you anymore," the younger-looking of the two says.

Must be his mother. Late forties, hair rounded and framing her face. She has a slim figure, quite a contrast to the larger and nearly catatonic woman beside her. There's a similarity to the women's features, the same nose, the same lips, but a great disparity in age. The other woman must be nearing eighty.

"I try to visit as often as I can," Poy says. "Between my family and my job, I'm very busy."

"Sit down, help us make dumplings," the woman says.

Poy pulls up a seat.

"You have enough time to go out with your friends every night, I hear, but not enough time to visit your mother and grandmother." The older woman makes a small grunt. "Your poor grandmother. You don't know how lonely she's been ever since your uncle left."

"Yeah," Poy says. "I bet."

"And you, never visiting her! Too busy with *work*," she says.

"I'm here now," Poy tells her. "I'm lucky to have a good job here. Lucky that I didn't have to leave like Uncle Lee."

"Ever since your father died, Grandma has been so lonely."

Grandma makes a small noise again.

"Geez, Mo," I say. "What an awkward conversation."

"Just listen," the spirit says.

"I feel—" Poy begins.

"We got a letter from your uncle Lee the other day," his mother says. "He said he's doing very well in Newfoundland. He wrote about the laundry he owns. Imagine that, your uncle owning a business! Him and his friend, they *own* the laundry. Washing all sorts of interesting things. Doesn't that sound wonderful?"

Poy nods and shrugs at the same time.

His mother continues. "Uncle Lee said he will soon have his debt paid off. Isn't that nice? It really is Gold Mountain," she says with a laugh that rings hollow.

"Good for him," Poy says.

A pot of water simmers and fills the silence. Despite Grandma's nonvocal contributions to the conversation, she moves with the efficiency of a machine as she fills and folds the dumplings. Grandma turns her head towards where I'm standing and gives a small nod.

"Mo," I say. "Can she see me?"

"No," Mo says. "Just listen to the conversation."

"Uncle Lee misses home," Poy's mom says.

"That's understandable," Poy says.

"He misses mahjong and he misses his mom."

A slight smile appears on the older woman's face. She locks eyes with me.

"Mo, I really feel like that older one can see me."

"Please," Mo says. "There are more important things than who can perceive you."

"She's giving off a weird energy," I say, and right then she winks at me.

"Lee misses these too, I bet," Poy says as he picks up one of the folded dumplings. "How many are you making?"

"Twenty-five, I think, and put that down." His mother smacks Poy's hand with a wooden spoon. "I'm sure he misses all this food. He said they eat a lot of fish over there. Salt fish, fried fish."

"I can only imagine," Poy says, then adds, "Twenty-five wasn't enough last time."

"Okay, we'll do thirty." She folds another dumpling shut. "Your grandma misses him and he misses her and you know she's getting older, so who knows how much time Uncle Lee has to see her again."

Grandma winks at me again.

"Mo," I say. "She keeps winking at me."

"Man," Mo says, "just pay attention to the scene."

"Fine," I say, and I move behind Grandma so I can't see her face.

"That's the risk of going overseas," Poy says with a weary resignation.

"You should go to Newfoundland and replace your uncle for a year," his mom says.

Poy laughs. "Thirty is too many," he says.

"You go to Newfoundland." She scoops up a spoonful of filling. "You take over his job for a year, and then you come back here and he goes back to Newfoundland again, okay?"

"Mom," Poy says. "No."

"Then you switch places every year. First you go and Uncle Lee comes home, then Uncle Lee goes and you come home. Once a year."

"Mom," Poy says. "I have a family."

"You have me and your grandma and Uncle Lee. One year is not a long time."

"I mean my wife and child. I can't abandon my family."

"Yes," she says, chipper. "You go and make money for them! Gold Mountain!"

"Mom." Poy puts down the dumpling he's folding and leans in. "I understand that you and Grandma are lonely. I can visit more. Uncle Lee made the decision to leave for himself."

"No, Uncle Lee made the decision to leave for *us*. When he comes home, he's going to bring us money. We will be doing better because of it. Now, you go and make money for us."

"I can't just leave. I'd have to save money for Hua Ling and Wai too. I wouldn't be able to give it all to you."

"You give money to Hua Ling, you give money to us, it's okay! It's only a year, right, Grandma?"

The older woman releases a guttural noise and shifts around in her chair so that she's facing me again.

"Mo," I say. "Are you seeing this?"

"Of course I am seeing this," Mo snaps. "I am conjuring this so *you* can see this, so *you* can see *your* grandfather's plight which *you* wanted so badly to see."

"All right, all right," I say.

The pot of water boils over.

"I—" Poy starts.

"Go take care of that pot," his mom orders.

Poy gets up and takes the lid off the pot, letting it steam off.

"You wouldn't disrespect your mother's wishes, your family's wishes," she says. "You say forty-eight is too many? Maybe we'll do thirty-three."

"I don't want Hua Ling to end up like Li-Zhen."

"Ehhh," his mom says, waving her hand. "Li-Zhen and Mr. Koo never even consummated. Not Hua Ling's problem."

"I meant that I don't want Hua Ling to be alone like Li-Zhen."

"Li-Zhen is married to that rooster. She's not lonely."

"A woman shouldn't have to marry a rooster. A woman should marry her fiancé."

"A man, a rooster, all the same! Are you disrespecting your mother's wishes? You know, my days are numbered too. Next thing you know, I'll be in the ground and then you'll regret not going and helping your uncle Lee and putting a smile on Grandma's face."

A ghost of a smile creeps onto Grandma's face.

"Mo," I begin.

"If this is about Grandma," Mo begins.

"No, no, I was going to ask, is 'rooster' slang for something?"

Mo sighs. "The translation I'm providing you with misses many of the finer points of the Taishanese language. These people have their own metaphors, cultural codes, gestures, expressions, ways of addressing one another, things you simply wouldn't understand."

"So . . . 'rooster' isn't slang?"

"Just wait," Mo says, pointing its snout towards Poy.

"I don't want to go," Poy says, with a waver in his voice, tears welling up. "Please. Mom."

"I don't know what I did in my before-life," his mom says, "but it must've been pretty bad for me to be punished with a disappointment like you."

Poy cries in silence.

"Geez, Mo," I say. "That lady is mean!"

"I'm glad you're paying attention," the spirit says. "Now please silence yourself."

"Hey, Mo, you must've done something bad in your before-life to be punished with a . . . well, I don't really know what I am to you. Hm. You get the picture."

No response.

"Soon enough I'll be with your father," Poy's mom is saying, as she pinches a dumpling shut. "Will you remember to burn joss paper for me? Or will you be too busy with Hua Ling?"

"Mom," Poy says, "of course I'll burn joss paper for you."

"Mmmm," she says. "Or will you be too busy with your friends at that bar?"

Poy puts his head in his hands. "If I were to go," he says, his voice shaky, "would you watch over Hua Ling and Wai? Would you make sure they're okay?"

"Of course," his mother says. "Of course."

Poy swallows.

"I don't know why you fuss over Wai so much anyway," she says. "It's not like the child is yours."

Poy stands up. "Wai is my son."

His mom laughs. "Wai is no more your son than Li-Zhen's baby chicks are her daughters."

"Just because Wai was adopted doesn't mean he's not my son," Poy says.

"Oh," I say. "Now there's an interesting wrinkle, hey, Mo?"

"You are raising someone else's child," Poy's mom says, her laughter dissipating like steam. "You support someone else's child before you support your own mother and grandmother."

Poy's hands close into fists. "I know what it is like to grow up without a father around and I didn't want to see that happen to another child," he says, jaws clenched. "Wai is just a baby. At least I knew my father for a few years. He would never have known a father, or a mother, if we hadn't stepped in."

His mom stands up and places a hand on his shoulder. "Wai is young enough that he won't even notice that you are gone. It is just for one year. When you come back, Wai will still be a baby. You will be his father."

Poy stares at the floor and then nods.

"You must do this to honour your family. It is your grandma's wish."

Poy looks at his vacant grandma for a moment before returning his gaze to the floor.

"You understand?"

Poy nods.

Grandma gives me a little nod and appears to offer me a dumpling.

"Mo," I say. "She can definitely see me."

"No," Mo says, "she cannot."

The green cloud billows up and surrounds me, and then Poy is walking on a street. Gone is his confident strut through the chaos of the main street. Now he walks with a slight hunch in his back, staggering as if drunk—although I didn't see him drink anything. He is in a more residential area this time. The homes are a mix of crudely constructed huts, nothing more than mud and twigs, and bare-bones buildings of concrete. Poy stops outside one house and sneaks a glimpse through their window. Inside, a woman is seated across from a rooster. They are both enjoying supper, the woman grasping rice out of a bowl with a pair of chopsticks, the rooster pecking things off a plate. They are the perfect picture of a happily married couple—except for the fact that the rooster is a rooster.

"Mo," I say, "you could've told me that it was a real rooster."

"Look closely at your grandfather," Mo says.

I glimpse a tear in Poy's voyeuristic eye. The green cloud billows up.

When it clears, Poy is arriving home. He dismisses his butler and takes Hua Ling aside in their small kitchen. He tells her the news about his future.

"I'm going to end up like Li-Zhen," Hua Ling cries, "with a rooster for a husband!"

"Don't be ridiculous," Poy says, trying to be a stern voice of reason. "I will only be gone for a year."

"Li-Zhen thought that too when Mr. Koo left, and now he's dead!"

"I won't be working in the industry Mr. Koo worked in, I'll be managing a laundry. I'll bring back money for us."

Hua Ling sobs and sputters. Her sobbing wakes up Wai, who also begins to cry, perhaps confused by this new air of anxiety in his home.

"I will not let Wai be raised without a father," Poy says. "I won't die. I promise."

He embraces Hua Ling, and they exchange a trepidatious look.

A flash of white light, and I lose sight of them in a puff of smoke.

6

HORSIN' AROUND

"Eggplant!" Poy yells through the cloud of smoke.

As the smoke clears, I see Poy politely posed on a stool. Another man is hunched underneath a blanket draped around one of those really old cameras. His hand extends out from under the blanket to hold up the flash, the burning remnants of which linger and float in the air.

Poy remains posed for a moment. Wearing a suit as always, this one a slim grey gingham number, he beams at the camera. A boyish smile, ripe with potential and the sense that maybe there is always something to laugh about. As the photographer lowers the flash, so too does Poy lower his smile.

"You'll make sure my wife receives this, right?" Poy says, patting the photographer's shoulder.

"Yes, yes," the photographer says with a couple short nods, beginning to disassemble some part of the camera equipment.

"She needs to have something to remember me by," Poy says.

"You are going in search of Gold Mountain?" says the photographer.

"Not quite," Poy says. "Just allowing a little family reunion.

Plus, I've always wanted to see the West. But I'll be back this time next year."

The photographer lets outs a chuckle. "Whatever you say, Mr. Poy."

"Just make sure that goes to my wife when it's developed."

"Will do, Mr. Poy," the photographer says.

Poy opens the front door to the noisy main street. Just as the door closes behind him, the photographer calls out: "I'll be sure to keep an eye on her while you're gone."

Poy looks back at the photographer through the window as a predatory grin grows across the man's face. Poy steps towards the door, but then checks his watch and thinks better of it. He walks away.

"What a dink," I say.

"What?" Mo says.

"The photographer. You can tell he's thinking about making a move on Hua Ling while Poy is gone." I know a lot of Instagram photographers are perverts, but I didn't know there were creeps back then too. Then again, photography, so voyeuristic. A medium for pervs, really.

"It was an innocent comment," Mo says. "The photographer is not your concern."

Poy heads on down the busy road, but I'm not done with the photo studio yet.

The photographer is in his darkroom, developing prints. I walk through his body, and he shivers. I walk through him again. Another shiver. If Poy doesn't have the time to fight the photographer, the least I can do is annoy the shit out of him.

"Stop," Mo says, slithering out of a developing photograph.

I keep jumping back and forth through the man, like a game of hopscotch. He is shivering uncontrollably and starting to panic.

"You're interfering," Mo says. "You can't linger here—you have to follow your grandfather."

"Perv-man needs to learn his lesson."

"Stop," Mo says.

"Make me," I say as I floss through the photographer's body. He is dry heaving now.

Just as the man begins to vomit, my surroundings become smeared like a watercolour in the rain, everything blurry and indistinct.

"No haunting," Mo chastises.

Can the future haunt the past?

Things sharpen into focus and I'm outside. Poy is getting ready to ride a horse. His wife and child are there, and so are his mom and grandmother. The horse looks muscular, but a little old. Poy hugs everyone. Hua Ling's lips are pursed. She says nothing.

"The photographer has something for you," he whispers to her.

"Great," she says in a toneless voice.

Poy pauses, frowns. His mother pushes him ever so slightly as she brandishes a suitcase.

"Okay, you bring this to your uncle and his friends, lots of reminders from home," she says, forcing it into Poy's hand. "He will appreciate this. They will know you are honouring your family."

"Mom, I can't bring another suitcase. I already have my own."

"You can! You're a big-shot teacher, you can afford a nice cabin, lots of space for two suitcases. Now remember, you sell the horse at the Hong Kong Jockey Club, okay? You use that money towards a nice cabin. Your uncle will love this!"

Poy lets out a small sigh.

"Do you know how to get there?" his mother asks.

"Yes," he says, exasperated, while fixing the second suitcase to the horse. "I have taken the route many times." He mounts the horse and calls out, chipper now, "I'll see you all in a year! I'll bring you back something from the West!"

Poy begins to ride the horse down the road, and after a moment he looks back. His mother and grandmother are already headed back to their hovel, but his wife stands there, holding their baby. Hua Ling stares at Poy, and she stares beyond him, at the barren, isolated landscape.

Poy turns away from the shimmering, distant visage of the woman—women—he loves, a tear incubating in his eye that he doesn't want to risk them seeing.

I can't tell you exactly how long it took to get to Hong Kong because I wasn't sure when Mo was washing away time, as it is wont to do. But four or five days feels about right. In the beginning I tried to ride on the back of the horse, behind Poy, but I fell through him and the horse, causing a subsequent shiver to go through Poy and the animal, and damn near ended his journey to the West right there on some old dirt road. I ended up riding on the back of Mo, its tiny pawed legs able to keep up with the horse.

We ride over mountains and through canyons. We ride among smooth, low hills in the sweltering heat. We ride through rivers and streams scattered like ribbons through valleys of clay. A beautiful mountain range wraps around us and conjures pleasant reminders of the Patagonia logo, reminders that turn to sorrow as I recall that my sweater is still lost.

In the nights, we stop at inns in small villages, places where leering men spit freely and reveal teeth stained red from eating some kind of nut and leaf mixture. Once we pass by a puppet show, where the puppets are as tall as children with beautiful carved wooden heads. In the passing glimpse of puppetry, I see a puppet guy riding a giant puppet armadillo trailing behind another puppet guy on a puppet horse. But most times we pass by nothing but nature.

Bamboo groves and patches of fir trees surround us day after day. So too do bats, and mice, and squirrels and rats, and otters and strange scary-looking cats whose fur patterns simultaneously evoke cheetahs, zebras, and raccoons. Insects of every description are in abundance, and it always makes me smile when a mosquito passes through my body, unable to deprive me of my lifeblood. At night when we camp, snakes pass through my body. Their squirmy bodies make me feel uneasy, even though I know they can't harm me. One night, a snake approaches me, slowly, its jaws open, at the ready. When it jumps to bite me, it must be quite a shock to the poor thing when it goes straight through me, and its consequent shudder causes the damn thing to bite its own tail. I watch it writhe in self-inflicted pain.

"Mo," I say. "Should we, like, put it out of its misery?"

"Mm," it says. "No."

The snake is spasmodically flinging about and smearing its blood around the campsite. Poy is already asleep.

"It's fine," Mo says. "They can't poison themselves."

The snake withdraws its teeth from its tail and slithers back into the darkness.

"Was there significance to that, Mo?"

Mo rolls its eyes.

We stop by a river so that the horse can drink, and Poy stretches his legs. A flock of flamingos gathers in the water, picking through the mud. Poy stares at the long, pink birds. I sit on the red soil and look off at the forest, wondering when, if ever, I will be returned to my timeline. Although I guess I really brought this on myself so I shouldn't be thinking this way. It *was* a little impulsive, just deciding to come here like this. Anyways, no time for regrets. The spirit said something about that too, having no space for regrets. Besides, the letter needs to be returned to this realm. Its dark energy would ruin the entire ambience of my apartment. And who knows, maybe we'll eventually find my Patagonia kicking around somewhere out here.

It's a quiet day. They're all quiet days. Poy smooths down his horse's coat and offers it a carrot. I sit on the ground, keeping my eyes on them to make sure they don't leave without me.

Then there's a rustle in the bushes.

Is that . . . a large, mossy rock? Although, no, it looks like it's moving. And moss isn't usually black and white.

I jump to my feet.

"It's a panda," Mo says.

"I know what it is," I say.

"A lot of people don't know what a panda is," Mo says.

"Even toddlers know what a panda is," I say.

"I have known grown men, men exactly like you, who could not distinguish a panda from me," Mo says, its stubby seven-foot-long amalgamation of the parts the gods left over suddenly stiff.

"You look like an anteater with gigantism," I say. "Was the man blind?"

The panda lets loose a loud yawn and lumbers forward with a slow gait. Poy, seeing the panda approach, slowly mounts his horse. The panda drops itself to the ground and starts to roll around in the mud.

We ride on.

We pass a stand selling panda pelts.

* * *

We're boarding a ferry. Poy's horse is rather wary about being on the boat and snorts and neighs in displeasure. Poy pats the horse and offers it a snack, trying to comfort it, but it refuses to be appeased with carrots this time, its greying tail aswing with anger.

Two white people in fancy dress, a man and a woman, board the ferry. I haven't seen their kind since I got here. Come to think of it, this may be the longest time in my life that I've gone without seeing a white person. Or maybe it hasn't been so long. How long have I been here? Minutes or weeks?

We're approaching a city much more developed than anything we have passed through in the last few days. This city smears across the shore of an island, expanding along the coast and up the sloping sides of a mountain range, with buildings jutting out of the hill here and there, some looking like castles, others more pedestrian.

As we get close to the dock, the waterways choke up, congested by boats darting every which way. Boats with sails like dragon's wings, skeletal and flared.

"Junks," Mo tells me, with a theatrical wave of its snout. "People live in them."

To me the little boats look more like canoes, and they don't seem to offer much in the way of shelter. "I know what junks are," I say, although I had been unaware people lived in them. "If you want to explain something to me, you can explain how long this is all going to take. How long have I been here?"

"Patience," Mo says, with a slight chuckle.

The sun glares off the water but I can still make out the vivid harbour. We're approaching a dock with a steel archway embossed with the words HONG KONG STEAMBOAT COMPANY, LIMITED. Just underneath these words are some barely visible painted Chinese characters, faded and chipped in the sun. It's the first time I've seen English words in days.

"We've reached Hong Kong," I say to Mo.

"I know where we are," Mo says, snippy.

We prepare to disembark. Poy pets his horse, calming it. The pier is crowded with Chinese men and women gathered around the gangway leading down from the ferry. As the white couple makes their way down, muttering something about a hotel "in verdant slopes" and "swanky Sikh policemen" to protect them, they draw the rapt attention of dozens of men on the pier, who stare at them with inquisitive looks and dopey smiles. Other Chinese are uninterested in the white couple and continue doing their respective tasks. Men gut and fillet fish dockside. Women slouch into the water, hitting wet clothes with large sticks or drying them on the edge of the docks. Just as at Hoiping, people walk to and fro carrying boxes on their heads and buckets on their backs. Some carry large coils of rope, and there's even a child carrying an unlit lantern much larger than himself.

Poy mounts and rides away at a slow trot. The well-paved roads are lined with ornate colonial-style buildings, and double-decker streetcars zip around.

"Hey, Mo, this is kind of like London."

"How insightful," Mo says.

"Is that sarcastic?"

No response.

Unlike London, this place is ensconced in mountains, and thousands of people are coming and going in every which way. Rickshaws and cars vie for space on the road and planes buzz overhead. A large pillar-like memorial of some sort stands not too far from an ornate archway protected by two stone lions. Buses pass by arcaded sidewalks. Women in high-collared fashion-forward dresses jostle along those sidewalks, sometimes accompanied by other women who hold up colourful parasols to provide shade from the beating sun.

We turn down a street that reminds me of the main street in Poy's village, except this one is infinitely larger. There is simply too much going on for me to focus on any one thing for long. White people are dotted throughout the crowd, fondling silks and embroidered fabrics and watching the locals prepare food. Sleeping babies, exhausted from the heat, are strapped to women's backs. Congregations of men smoke from big bamboo pipes. An old woman spoons soup to a toddler, stealing slurps for herself while the child swallows. Teams of strong women pull crude carts filled with dirt and trash and excrement. Buddhist monks mingle with businessmen. Stands and small shops line the streets. At one stand, a Chinese man pulls taffy, stretching and folding the fresh candy in front of his gawking customers. Dogs bound around freely, dodging traffic, barking and making children scatter down the narrow alleyways, hiding their faces and giggling.

We pass by gated enclaves with British and Canadian flags raised high, guarded by turban-clad policemen. Magnificent homes next to glorified shacks. Pairs of men line up on hills, waiting to carry paying customers up the sloping mountain on sedan chairs attached to two long poles. For a second, I think I see the white couple waiting to be carried on the backs of the Chinese up to their mountaintop castle, but before I know it, we're turning down another street.

Poy dismounts outside a racetrack. He peers up at a large poster pasted on the wall. A cartoon Chinese woman with short, curly hair beams over a drawing of a pack of gum above the words ON LOK YUEN'S CHE WING GUM.

Poy leads the horse through the doors and we pass through dark, smoky dens where people gather to bet on games. Wealthy white and Chinese people alike sit in the front rows in their fine suits, puffing and schmoozing over the latest race. At the back of the room stand groups of Chinese in tattered shirts and rice field hats, all pitching in coins to bet on the horses. A chalkboard promises winnings of up to six thousand British pounds.

Poy leads his horse to the stables, and a wide Chinese man greets him.

"You looking to sell?" he says.

"Yes," Poy says.

The horseman lights a cigarette and sizes up the horse, walking around it and occasionally stopping to give it a little slap, checking out its bone structure and the condition of its feet and teeth. "All right," he eventually says, and he counts out a couple bills from his money clip. "I guess we got room for one more."

"Thank you," Poy says. He pockets the money and unstraps his suitcases from the horse's back. The horse neighs and its hooves uneasily slide on loose hay on the floor of the livery, unaware that it is not an entity like Poy or me, but just a good being exchanged and nothing more. In a demure manner, Poy offers it a carrot and looks into its eye. Then the horseman pulls on the reins and the horse is gone, sold. I wonder how he feels. Poy, I mean, although you have to wonder how the horse feels too.

Poy walks back through the smoky gambling den and pauses to look at the panoramic view of the racetrack. He reaches into his pocket and pulls out one of the crisp bills. Poy looks at the chalkboard and then back at the bill. He walks over to the ticket booth and bets on number eight and gets his wager ticket. He begins to leave the booth but then turns around. He bets all the money the horseman gave him on number eight.

"What the hell is he doing, Mo?"

"Watch," Mo says.

"What else am I going to do?"

I want to stop him but it's already too late. Poy makes his way out to the observation deck and takes a seat in the stands. A real multicultural zone, white and Chinese mixed together, and I even see some Black men and women gathered to watch the races. Poy stares at the Black people. Has he ever seen one before?

There's a keyed-up excitement in the air, keeping the audience swaying with anticipation. Down on the track, men in tuxedo coats and top hats lead the horses to their starting gates, the jockeys already on the horses' backs, stern poker faces in play, a calm contrast to the crowd's frantic energy. The horses line up under the starter's eagle eye.

Bang! And they're off!

Heads crane forward with eager looks towards the horses galloping down the straight, looking towards which number will be a winner and which will be losers. Glossy horse gear, silken colours, tight-pressed spectators all unite in a kaleidoscope of colour, until one by one, each horse makes it around the track.

Number eight wins.

Poy collects his money, having doubled it. He walks back over to the lineup at the ticket booth.

"Mo, he's not betting again, is he?"

Mo floats out of another poster for Che Wing Gum on the wall. "You will see," he says.

I've been to Vegas a couple times, so I know it's easy to want to keep going when you're on a winning streak. First time I was ever in a casino, I see an Ellen DeGeneres–themed slot machine. It's a one-dollar bet, so why not? I put in a dollar, next thing you know, I'm walking away with forty-five. So now I'm thinking the Ellen machine is my lucky machine, and every day I bet a dollar on it. I never won again that whole trip. I did the same thing the next time I was in Vegas, but with a Mariah Carey–themed slot machine instead. Won something like thirty bucks, then never won anything again. That's when I learned my lesson.

I see Poy counting out all the money he got from the horse. "Mo, don't tell me. He's not, is he?"

"You must have patience," Mo says.

"I'm not letting him do that," I say, and I walk through Poy, causing him to shudder.

"Stop," Mo says.

"He's making a bad decision," I say as I floss though his body like I did with the photographer.

"Stop!" Mo yells, its pointed teeth glinting in the low lights of the betting den. "You cannot alert him to your presence."

"'I cannot' as in I literally can't, or as in you don't want me to?"

"There'd be so much paperwork," Mo mutters with a wag of its snout. "If you continue to try to intervene, I will make it so that this story is not yours."

That wouldn't take very much work.

"But, Mo, this story already isn't mine. This is not from my life."

"It is not your life that is your concern."

I sigh and shake my head. "It is precisely my life with which I am concerned."

"Stop," Mo says. "Or else."

I step away from Poy and his shivers stop just as he reaches the front of the line. He collects himself and bets all his money on eight again. I'm pretty sure there was an episode of *Oprah* about something like this, where she said to never let a spirit take you into the past. Sorry, Oprah.

We go back to the stands and wait for the next race. We watch the horses zoom through the round.

Number eight loses.

7

THE NEUTRAL ZONE

A gigantic steamship, the *Heian Maru*, has entered the harbour, only serving to emphasize just how small some of the boats people call home really are. Ocean Greyhound, meet ancient tubs. Deep black clouds pump out of its paired smokestacks, poisoned air dancing through the Hong Kong sky.

Poy buys a ticket. Having lost all the horseman's money, he can now only afford something called steerage class. A security officer opens Poy's first bag. Suits, underwear, his abacus. Cleared. The officer opens the other suitcase. It's packed to the brim with soil. The officer digs through the dirt and pulls out pieces of dried fish and dried duck, salted eggs, flowers of some sort, nuts, and yams. "This can't go to Canada," he says.

"I'm not going to Canada," Poy says.

"Well, the ship is going to Canada, so that means this bag would be going to Canada, and if this bag were to be on the ship—the ship going to Canada—these items could easily fall into the hands of someone going to Canada. Meaning that these items can't go on the ship."

Poy stares at the officer.

"So, either you allow me to confiscate these items and dispose of them," says the officer, "or you can keep them and not board the ship."

"That's okay, you can dispose of them," Poy says. "I'll go on the ship."

The security officer smiles as he places the suitcase of contraband on a table behind him.

"You know, Spirit, I once took bonsai tree seeds across the border, from New York to Toronto. Nobody said a thing."

"The tree died because you didn't take care of it," the spirit says.

"Oh right, I forgot, you know everything."

Next, Poy is told to undress, and a doctor inspects his whole body, even looking under his eyelids, then gives him some needles. They sterilize the bag he was allowed to keep and, finally, he is granted passage onto the ship.

Poy hustles up the gangway. The deck is filled with dozens of Chinese men huddled together. A noisy bunch, although a nervous apprehension comes across in their movements, stilted and hesitant. Poy surveys the crowd, looking for a familiar face, or at the very least a friendly one. Other men coming up the gangway push him aside, knocking him into a man with a braid of hair that extends past his butt.

"Hey, watch it," the man says.

"I'm sorry," Poy says as he tightens his grip on his suitcase. "I was in the way."

"No shit you were in the way, you knocked into me," the man continues, prompting mean chuckles from some of the others nearby.

The man looks a little older than Poy, maybe twenty-five, and carries about him a strange air, a sense of belonging and not belonging, and even though he scolded Poy, there was a jovial tinge to his words. He's smoking a cigarette while wearing a pair of pristine white leather gloves, an odd sartorial choice for another sweltering day, and a pair of round glasses.

The man extends a hand towards Poy. "My name is Shaowei Zhang," he says, his initial hostility gone. "I'm from Hong Kong, or should I say Victoria." Once again, some chuckles from surrounding men.

"My name is Seto Poy," Poy says with a shake of Shaowei's hand. "I'm from Hoiping."

"Oh, a country boy," Shaowei says. "Not from a real city like me."

"No," Poy laughs. "Although I did complete some of my education here in Hong Kong."

"A learned southern boy! You don't see that every day, hey, fellas?" Shaowei seems to have a preternatural ability to elicit laughter from the watching men. "What's a well-educated gentleman like you doing searching for Gold Mountain?"

"My mother sent me," Poy says, his eyes cast towards the horizon.

Shaowei slaps a hand on Poy's back. "We've all been there before. Me and the fellas here, we're just telling some jokes here before the ship gets sailing. Now, you're not too much of a learned gentleman for some jokes, are you?"

"Heh, no, I like jokes," Poy says, blushing.

"Okay, here's another one," Shaowei starts. "So there's a government official who just transferred to a new department. He's illiterate. On his first day in the new department, he makes an inaugural speech in the office meeting. He says, 'Comrades, I come here to be in charge of women'"—Shaowei takes a long pause, leans in towards his audience—"'s issues!'"

Everybody bursts into raucous laughter. Even Poy laughs, the first time he's smiled in a while.

"Mo, uh, what *was* that? Where was the joke?"

"Lost in translation, I presume," Mo says. It slithers out of a newspaper, passing through the bodies of several of the men, and they shiver. "I see the humour in it." Its trunk wags to one side to show me a grotesque smile. "From a Chinese point of view, a man chosen to be the head of, or 'in charge of,' a women's group will become a laughingstock and be considered good for nothing."

"And that would be extremely funny?" Some of the men on deck are crying from laughter.

"Well, there's more layers to it than that alone. There is no honour to be a man in charge of women in China. That pause between 'women' and its apostrophe? This phonetic device leads the audience to think that the man is in charge of women. Furthermore, when the sentence is considered as a whole, it can also mean, 'I come here to fool around with women.'"

"I . . . Okay," I say. Forget it, let's move on.

"The joke is especially funny as it involves a government official." Mo wraps himself around a smokestack. "If you knew their language, this might be funny to you too."

"Yes, I know," I say.

"Oh, you know their language now, do you? Then you won't mind if I turn the dubbing off."

"You know what I mean. Leave it on."

"But there's just so much lost," Mo says, now floating in effervescent figure eights around my head.

Another man in the group is telling a joke now. "So, this woman is fucking her neighbour"—this elicits a few hoots and hollers—"when her husband comes home." A hushed silence falls over the small audience. "There's no window for this guy to escape from, so the woman stuffs him in a rice sack and tells him 'Don't move!' Meanwhile, her husband is coming in, sees the rice sack in the bedroom, and says, 'What's in that?' His wife's so scared, she can't even think of anything to say. So the husband asks again: 'What's in that bag?' The guy in the bag is so scared, he yells out, 'Rice!'"

Once again, the group of men is howling with laughter, but Poy offers only a slight chuckle.

"That's a good one, Gao," Shaowei says. He takes a drag from his cigarette before casting his eye on Poy. "You didn't find that one funny, huh? What, do you know a better one?"

"Well, uh, let me see." Poy raises a finger to his chin in contemplation. "Okay, I think I know one. There is a husband and wife and the husband is taking a train—err, no, wait—the wife is taking a train and, uh, the husband says, 'It's worthwhile to send you away for three yuan.'"

The men look at him blankly.

"Mo, is something lost in translation again?" I ask.

"No," Mo says. "He is merely not proficient at telling jokes."

"All right, well," Shaowei says, slapping Poy on the shoulder, "that one needs some work, but there's something in there, I can sense it. We'll have lots of time over the next three weeks to iron that one out."

Shaowei pulls Poy aside from the group, as if to talk to him more privately. Alas, there is no privacy anywhere on this deck, with men crowding every inch of space, all waiting for the ship to set sail. "Say," Shaowei says, "where are you headed to, anyhow?"

"Newfoundland," Poy says.

"Hey, me too! I'm sure you've surmised that none of us are going to Canada."

"Oh," Poy says.

Shaowei gestures to him to follow him across the deck.

"Mo, why aren't any of them going to Canada?"

"You can't be serious," Mo says.

"We're crossing the Pacific Ocean," I say. "Just seems odd nobody's going to Canada."

"The Chinese Immigration Act," Mo says. "Signed into law on Dominion Day, 1923. The date was no coincidence. The powers that be were letting it be known what they wanted their country-men to look like."

Of course. I knew about that from Mr. Green's Social Studies class. How could I forget? I feel ashamed to have even asked.

"You ever been to the West before?" Shaowei is asking Poy.

"No, but—"

"I have," Shaowei says as he taps his glasses. "San Francisco. Lived there for a couple of years. Then I came back to see the family, and now I'm gone again. Can't go back to the Golden City, so I figured I'd try out the other side of the world."

"That's because of the American Chinese Exclusion Act," I say to Mo, compensating for my ignorance about the Canadian version.

"Oh, I'm impressed," Mo says sarcastically. "After you learn your lesson here, you should consider learning the history of the landmass you call your country."

Mo is right. The time has passed for wilful ignorance. Maybe I'm learning my lesson already. "Speaking of that, how much longer is this going to take?"

Mo hovers for a moment, and slowly closes its eyes. "Patience," it says. It occurs to me that Mo is not necessarily saying that to me.

Sailors are preparing the ship to sail, raising its anchors and pulling up the gangway.

"I'm returning home in a year," Poy says to Shaowei.

"That's optimistic. Half the people on this boat won't even sur-vive the trip across the ocean."

"Really?"

"What do you call a ship like this?" Shaowei waves his hand,

87

encompassing the deck of Chinamen, the fluttering mast, and the big stacks emitting coal-black steam.

"A steamship?" Poy says.

"No, sir," Shaowei says. "This is a coffin ship. Come with me."

Shaowei hustles him down a set of stairs leading below the deck. Poy's eyebrows rise in alarm as Shaowei ushers him down another set of steps, deeper and deeper into the hull.

"Typhoid, cholera, dysentery, the Cuban itch, you name it, it's infesting this ship," Shaowei says. He raises a hand and wiggles his fingers in his white leather gloves. "That's why I've got these."

Poy looks bewildered.

"You got a pair of gloves, right?" Shaowei asks.

"Uh, no," Poy says.

"You'll need them where you're going, big fella." Shaowei opens a door with an extremely loud creak.

It's a long room, deep in the hull of the ship, with tapered-off and rounded walls. The arm of the mast goes straight through the centre of the room, near a small grille in the ceiling that lets in some light from the deck. A few portholes illuminate the sides of the room, but it's still like a dim dungeon. A couple rows of bunkbeds line the back wall, and the odd table and a few chairs are scattered throughout.

"Welcome to Steerage," Shaowei says. "Word to the wise: do not touch anything down here."

"This is steerage? This is what I paid for?"

"If you think this is bad, just wait till they make everyone on deck come down here."

Poy reaches up to massage his temples.

"Hey!" Shaowei knocks Poy's hands from his face. "Don't do that! Don't touch your face!"

"What?" Poy takes a step back.

"Didn't you hear what I just said? Typhoid, cholera, the rest. You know how you get those? By being a big dumb idiot and touching your face. So don't do it."

"You're crazy," Poy says under his breath.

"Oh, I'm crazy, am I? I'm the crazy one? I'm just warning you, Poy. I've been lucky enough to survive this voyage twice. I've been unlucky enough to see a lot of people not even survive this voyage once. Now, I see you here in your suit and your fancy bag and your hair cut like a white man, and I think, *There's another goner. There's another life gone down the drain. There's another dumb bitch who'll pick a bad bunk and get splashed with piss and shit every night till you croak and you have to be thrown overboard.*"

"My hair isn't cut like a white man," Poy says. "What about your hair? A queue hasn't been required for years."

Shaowei rolls his eyes. "Listen to me or don't. But I'll be laughing on your grave if you don't. Now come."

Poy follows Shaowei through the dim space until they reach the bunks, stacked three high with bare, unfinished boards nailed together in haphazard fashion.

"Okay, I always do that joke-telling thing to break the ice, get the crowd going and having a good time above deck, which provides the perfect opportunity for me to have the pick of the litter down here."

He walks between the bunks, sizing up all the top ones, feeling them with his gloved hands and occasionally pushing down on the boards, testing their give.

"They call these silkworm something or other. It's two to a bed. You look pretty clean, so you're bunking with me. We're gonna want a top bunk, plus we're gonna want a sturdy one. My first trip across, I took a mid-level bunk. Big mistake. Guys on top of me were pissing and shitting through the slats, guys underneath were drowning in the piss and shit splashing around the floor."

"Surely it doesn't get that bad," Poy says.

"Oh, it surely does," Shaowei says. "My second voyage, I thought I'd be smart, pick a top bunk. Well I ran down here right away. Big mistake, 'cause a lot of people followed me down. I come right over to the bunks, pick the first top bunk I see. A week and a half into the voyage, boom, the boards give out and smack, there I am on the floor in the piss and shit. Had to wait for someone to die to get another bunk. Luckily, that didn't take long."

"Where is the toilet?" Poy says.

"The toilet?" Shaowei laughs. "Look around you. This whole fucking ship is the toilet and we're the logs of shit floating down the stream."

Poy stares at him, waiting for a real response.

"There is no toilet, you dunce. There's a public latrine on deck. But if we hit rough tides, and rest assured we will, they're not gonna let you go up there and then you gotta use one of those." Shaowei points to a bucket. "And let me tell you a little something about rough tides. Anything not nailed down to the damn floor will bounce around this hunk of tin. And that bucket is not nailed to the floor, I can assure you of that."

In the stifling heat, Poy moves to wipe sweat from his brow.

Shaowei bats his hand away. "Don't. Touch. Your. Face."

Poy loosens his tie instead.

"If piss and shit got you feeling overwhelmed, just wait till they start throwing up. Half of what's on board never even seen a boat before." He tests another bunk, and the boards resist when he presses on them. "All right," he says, "this'll be our bunk, me and the learned gentleman, up here."

Shaowei climbs up, and Poy follows. Shaowei lies back on the rough boards, arms crossed behind his head, self-satisfied. Poy sits on the edge of the bunk, surveying his surroundings.

Hell, I'm not even born yet and I feel bad for him. I'm barely able to contain my retching at the foul odours lingering from the previous travellers. "Mo, this is absolutely sickening," I say. "It smells like someone microwaved mouldy food."

Mo nods towards Poy.

"What's that room over there?" Poy says, pointing to a pale green door on the other side of the hull. Aside from the stairwell, it's the only place down here that isn't open concept.

"Don't get me started on that," Shaowei says, rolling over to one side. "Just take a deep breath, enjoy the air while you can."

"What's in there?" Poy persists.

Shaowei rolls his eyes as he shapes his lips into an O and blows.

Poy looks back at the door. "Women of the night?"

"What?" says Shaowei, sitting up. "No, there's no women here. None of our women, anyway. No, that's the opium den."

Poy stares at the pale green door.

"You don't do that, do you?" Shaowei says.

"Oh," Poy says, "no."

"Good. Think of all the germs on the pipe."

Poy doesn't say anything.

"You know what?" Shaowei says. "I'll let you in on a little secret. I used to run an opium den back in San Francisco. Yeah, I lost my job at the fish plant 'cause of this thing called the Iron Chink. That's really what it was called. The white man made a machine to replace us and had the gall to call it the Iron Chink. They'd rather have fucking automatons than . . ." He takes a deep breath. "Anyway, a guy's gotta make money somehow, so me and my pal, we opened up this opium den, see? But it wasn't really an opium den. It was just a place we opened up in Chinatown to give the space some colour, something to impress the white tourists. They would come in and pay us to smoke opium.

Bunch of dumb whites, the only thing they were breathing in was flavoured steam."

Shaowei lets out a hearty laugh, but Poy doesn't look impressed. When Shaowei stops laughing, he leans in closer to Poy and says, "Hey, I don't do the stuff. I never even heard of it before I went to the States. You know who brought opium to the States? It sure as hell wasn't Chinamen, although that's what they'll have you believe. No, Christopher Columbus brought opium to the States. You know who that is?"

Poy shakes his head.

"Chris Columbus was the first white man in the United States. And yet, you'll see when you get there, all the whites think it was us brought in opium. They want people to believe there's an opium den behind every laundry. They want people to believe we're corrupting society. You know why?" Shaowei doesn't give Poy a chance to respond. "It lets them force us out. Exclude us. Separate us from our women and children, make it so our families can't join us. Then they want people to believe that white women will become enslaved to us because of opium. Ha. I wish. And you know what else? If it wasn't the opium, it would be something else. They say we steal jobs, they say we're rapists and murderers, they say we bring viruses."

A lurch underfoot means the boat has set sail. Poy teeters from his perch on the bunk, the whole world suddenly unstable beneath him. Men begin to stream down the stairs into the small steerage compartment, the door seeming to creak louder every time it swings open.

"And in a week from now, we'll be saying maybe they're right," Shaowei says. "In a week from now, we'll be praying we survive. In a week from now, you'll wish you could be anything but yourself. Maybe they are right. Maybe we are celestial scum, coming to corrupt their land. But I bet if you packed a bunch of whites into a space like this, the same thing would happen. The same thing would happen tenfold."

Poy sits on the edge of the bunk, looking up at the ceiling as if he's trying to process the information overload from Shaowei.

"So, what are you doing, anyway?" Shaowei asks.

"What?" Poy responds, his voice softer.

"In the West?" Shaowei says, looking at him with a concerned squint. "What takes you to Gold Mountain?"

"Oh," Poy says. "My uncle. My uncle's laundry. I'm going to work there."

"Typical," Shaowei says. "Me too, though. Which laundry?"

"Fong-Lee."

"No way! On the corner of Holdsworth and New Gower?"

"Uh," Poy says. "I don't know. I think so."

"Me too," Shaowei exclaims. "We're gonna be seeing a lot more of each other! For years to come!"

"I'm only going for one year," Poy says.

"Oh, right," Shaowei says with a laugh as he lies down on the bunk again. "That's what they all say."

Poy sits watching his fellow immigrants cascade into steerage. What's he thinking? Who am I to say? But I think I know how he feels, from the look of fearful trepidation in his eyes. As more and more people push and shove their way into this reeking, dim room deep in the ship's hull, it must really hit home that this is only the beginning.

I hop up on the bunk and sit next to Mr. Poy. "Things can only get worse from here, hey, Mo?" I like to tell it like it is. "I think I'd like to go home now."

Mo's body emerges from a radio that one of the immigrants is fiddling with and slithers around my legs, its snout wagging all the while. "How do you think *he* feels? But you'll be joining them for the full journey. No more time jumps till we reach your home."

"What? You're making me stay on this boat with them? For how long?"

"You'll see. Unlike them, you're free to roam."

"Mo, please," I say. "I really mean it. Take back the letter and let me go. I don't want to be on this boat. I don't have to do this sort of stuff, you know."

Mo's eyes light up as if on fire and its body grows larger and larger until it completely fills the cavernous space that is steerage. "I am sick of your constant buffoonery, your inability to see anything beyond yourself, your complete and total lack of courage," it yells. "This man is your namesake and you can't even be bothered to be here with him. And your petty little quips—you think being dismissive is clever? It's not. You disgust me. You are more repugnant than any scent I could conjure for you to smell. You mammering, flap-mouthed pig."

"What the fuck, Mo?" I cry, but Mo continues yelling, its voice trembling.

"To call you a pig is an insult to the porcine creatures themselves. I will not—I cannot—sanction this narcissistic outlook of yours. It has no place in this narrative."

I swallow.

"I am revoking your first-person narrator privileges," Mo says as I blip out of existence.

8

STEERAGE

This is how steerage was: Endless days, passing slowly, melting one into another, impossible to distinguish one day from the next. An unending malaise. A festering reek of ammonia and feces, a sloshing vessel of unease and weariness. Hungry days, sleepless nights. The feeling of being in prison, of knowing you'll be seeing the same people for weeks, that even when the boat docks, you'll still be seeing the same people for weeks because most of you are going to the same place. The feeling that this ride is a long one, a dark one, an unpleasant one.

Cliques formed fast and conversations became recursive among them, addressing the same topics over and over until the stories began to take on notable differences, small details that morphed and changed with every retelling, barely perceptible facets, melting and fading away as if the tides themselves were pulling and pushing these stories.

Shaowei often spoke of Western culture, trying to prime the others for what they would experience there.

"This boat, this boat is the West. Gold Mountain is a fuck. You see where we are, here?" Shaowei looked around the bunks that he and Poy and some of their new friends had occupied.

"They'll push you down, down as far as you can go, they'll push so you're beneath everyone and everything. You wanna learn English? Don't look to the white man for help. There's only one thing they want and that's these—" Shaowei flourished his gloved fingers.

"Gloves?" a chubby man said. Hongzhi Gao was his name, and he'd been hanging around Poy and Shaowei ever since they first met telling jokes on deck.

"No, Gao—your hands. Your labour. And you'll give it to them too. You all will. Me too. 'Cause what the fuck else are we gonna do?"

"I'm sure it's not as bad as you say," Gao said, scratching his bald head.

"Oh, yeah? Just you wait! Like I was saying . . ." Shaowei started in again.

A rough day on the water. When it was rough on the water, no one was allowed out of steerage. It was too dangerous to be on deck and there was nowhere else they were permitted to go. The bunks were where they spent most of their time, both awake and asleep. Although Poy was at first uncomfortable sleeping next to a stranger, he found that sleeping next to Shaowei had been mostly fine, but he noted that Shaowei was a light sleeper, getting up and leaving his bunk at all hours of the night. Poy frequently found himself awake, sleepless nights spent dwelling on how, if he hadn't wasted his money at the horse track, he could be sleeping in a nice cabin, eating nice meals.

"The white man is not gonna teach you English," Shaowei was saying. "That just ain't gonna happen. So let me tell you everything you need to know about being able to speak English, okay? You'll never learn a lesson more valuable than this, okay? The learned gentleman over here"—Shaowei playfully punched Poy's shoulder—"he'd take six months to a year to teach you what I'm about to tell you. And you gotta promise not to tell anyone else, okay? We gotta look out for each other. I'm looking out for you guys by telling you this, okay? And if everybody on this ship knew what I'm about to tell you, and they knew how to use this, *this* being what I'm about to tell you, it would be very bad. Very bad. The white man would figure out what we're doing and then it'd be dunzo. They'd put it in their fucking papers, that's how bad it would be. Front-page news—"

"What are you even talking about, man?" Gao said.

"I'm getting around to that, I'm getting there. Okay, so this is the one thing you need to know in English." Shaowei leaned in, gesturing for the other guys to lean in too, and then in a whisper, barely audible over the noise of all the other men in the room, the words in choppy English: "It's always the way."

Shaowei leaned back with a big smile, stretching out his arms in triumph before placing them behind his head. "That's it, boys, that's all you need to know. 'It's always the way.'"

"What does that even mean?" Gao asked.

"It means everything," Shaowei said. "Everything. Anytime someone says something to you in English, the only thing you have to say back to them, and I mean the *only* thing, is 'It's always the way.'"

"What do the words mean in our language?" Gao said.

"It's always the way. Meaning, 'things always happen that way,' or 'that's just the way it is.' It's always the way. Just say it back to them in the same tone that they just used and it works. It can buy you more time to think of another response."

The men sat around thinking about this and nobody said anything.

"For example," Shaowei said, "and you boys'll be thanking me for this in the long run, white person says 'There's no rice left,' then you say back to them 'It's always the way.'"

"White people will ask you for rice?"

"It's not impossible. Okay, maybe a white person will say something like 'Someone ate all the plums,' and maybe you're the one that ate the plums and well fuck, you don't even know what the word for 'plum' is in English. Now you're fucked, right? Wrong. You just say to them, in the same tone they used, *It's always the way.*"

Again, no one said anything.

"Look, these hypotheticals, they might not amount to much now, but a day will come when you're over there in White World and you'll think to yourself, *Wow, I'm really glad Shaowei told me about that handy phrase, this must be the best-kept secret in the English language.*"

The boat hit a rough patch of water and the buckets flipped over. No one reacted much, for this happened fairly often. The buckets would tip over and the piss and shit and vomit would splash around.

It's always the way.

Soon, some men would bring down a big pot of rice for everyone to eat. That was all the food they were ever served, some rice, scraps of fish, maybe some stew made from the better cuts of meat left over from first and second class.

"Consider yourself lucky you're eating this," Shaowei said to Poy early on. "At least we get real Chinese food. Upstairs is nothing but white people food." Shaowei gripped his stomach and pantomimed a cat coughing up a fur ball.

In steerage, you could barely get a cup of water. The men had to line up at certain times of day just to drink some water, and once a day, in the evening, a big bucket of hot water was brought down for everyone to clean their bowl. You were expected to bring your own mug and bowl on the voyage. Poy was lucky that Shaowei had packed extra. He was prepared.

Weeks passed, and the close-knit cliques were as taut as a ship's sail. Shaowei, Poy, and Gao became inseparable. They would pass the time together, sometimes in silence, sometimes with efforts to distract one another. Sometimes they would play mahjong with pieces that Gao had brought with him. Other times, Gao would sing them a song, in a baritone so deep that it almost sounded as if he'd swallowed the ship's foghorn.

I suffer leaving my mother.
Floating on a journey across land and sea,
At the mountain, I take my chances.
Sorrow is to be so far away from home.

"Gao, this is too depressing," Shaowei said. "I don't think you're even getting the lyrics right."

The thing they did most of all to pass the time was talk. Talk about everything and anything, talk, talk, talk. Women they'd slept with, women they wanted to sleep with, books they had read, stories they heard, things that happened to them in the past, things they hoped would happen to them in the future. They even talked about religion.

"Okay, so in the West, everyone believes in Jesus," Shaowei explained. "They'll try to make you believe in Jesus too. Certain groups of whites, that's what they love to do, try to teach us about Jesus. You might as well do it. Even if you don't believe in Jesus, just tell them you do and they'll back off."

Gao and Poy nodded. At a certain point, they had realized it was pointless to respond to Shaowei because he would keep talking whether you agreed with him or not.

"Every Sunday, all the whites will put on their best clothes and go to a fancy building to listen to one special white talk about Jesus. They call these churches and priests and whatever. You'll get the hang of it when you're there. Now, if you're working at the laundry, this is the big day. You'll have this day off, the weekly Jesus day, but you'll also have to work hard before that day to make sure that the whites' clothes are real clean for that day, okay? And sometimes on the afternoon of that day, concerned whites will come to where you live to tell you about Jesus. Like I said, just listen to them and nod along and agree to believe in it. That's all they want. If they come around enough, they'll ask you to go to the Jesus building with them. Now, you won't get to go there at the same time as the whites, no, but they'll set aside a time for the Chinese to go. You'll hate this, but they make the Japanese go at that time too. And the Blacks and the Indians. That's right, we Chinese don't even get a special time to go to the church. But go anyway. You don't always have to go, but I'd advise you go occasionally. When white people think you believe in Jesus, they like you more. Okay? They won't think you're making the women smoke opium. Well, some of them will still think that. Just don't get too close to the women. Carry around a Bible. That's the book of Jesus stories."

Poy and Gao said nothing. Gao was asleep, but Poy was just too tired to talk. He was used to eating more food than this.

"And let me tell you something else about this Jesus fella: Everything he taught? He actually learned it all from the Buddha!"

Shaowei had expected a big reaction to this reveal and he leaned all the way in to his audience of two and a big smile was on his face. After realizing that Poy and Gao weren't going to react,

Shaowei leaned back in his chair. "The fucking Buddha. Taught Jesus everything. Don't tell the whites about that, though. Don't even ask them about it. Don't even say the word 'Buddha' in the presence of a white."

Shaowei leaned back farther. One gloved hand reached up as if to stroke his moustache, but he caught himself in the act and stared at his fingers in disbelief. "Hell, I probably shouldn't have even told you guys that. You weren't ready for it yet. It's always the way." He observed his small audience. "Hey, Poy, what's the matter?"

Poy struggled to speak. His voice was hoarse and he looked weak. "This isn't enough food . . . or water. I . . . we . . . need more."

"Hey, if you think this isn't enough, just wait till you get where we're going."

"I . . . need . . . more water."

The voyage was to end in the coming days and it had become a trying time for all. Shaowei surveyed the room. All throughout steerage, men were huddled together, shivering from the abject conditions, rasping the dialects of their villages, muttering prayers at makeshift shrines. Some were already dead, their bodies in boxes to be shipped back to their homes, their absence felt in the suddenly larger bunks of their bunkmates. Unlike the others, Shaowei was in fair health. The rolling of the ship didn't bother him, and he seemed to get by just fine on what little rations were provided. Shaowei lay down in the bunk next to Poy.

"You got a fever?" he asked.

After a moment Poy said, "I don't think so."

"I'd check but I'm not going to take my gloves off."

Poy shivered.

"Hey, don't you die on me now. Imagine if Jesus just dropped dead right after Buddha taught him all that shit. Wouldn't be very good, would it?"

Poy shook his head.

"That's right," Shaowei said. "Better off to not die."

Shaowei rolled closer, his mouth inches away from Poy's ear, so close that Poy could feel the miasma coming from Shaowei's mouth. "There's a secret to why I thrive while the rest of you fellas don't," Shaowei said quietly. "Can you still walk?"

"I think so," Poy said.

"Ay, quiet down!" Shaowei whispered. "I'll get you all fixed up, okay? I got a plan."

Poy nodded.

"But listen to me," Shaowei said. "This might seem tough to you right now. In some ways it'll get better once we're on land and settled away. But in a lot of ways, things are going to get worse. Are you listening? The key is to not think about the things that are bringing you down, whether that's work or being thirsty or whatever. That's how they'll own you. Let your mind wander. Imagine a better life. Maybe one day it'll come true."

"How?" Poy said in a shaky whisper.

"I don't know, man," Shaowei said. "Go to the picture shows. Let the movies fill in all the details of life that you're missing. Just rest for now. I have a plan."

For a couple of hours, Shaowei lay next to a semi-conscious Poy, who had clenched his hands over his stomach. Seasick, or maybe hungry, or maybe dehydrated, or maybe something worse. Shaowei lay staring at the ceiling and occasionally lifted his head to survey the room. It was the middle of the night when he sat up again, moonlight drifting in through the hatch in the ceiling, casting the room into bluish-white light. Shaowei once again put his mouth close to Poy's ear.

"Hey," he whispered, eyes darting back and forth, looking to see if anyone was watching. "How are you feeling?"

"Unh," Poy said, disturbed from his restless bouts of drifting in and out of consciousness. "What?"

"Quiet!" Shaowei said fast in a hoarse whisper. "Is it hunger or thirst?"

"I— What?" Poy asked.

"The way you're feeling right now, is it hunger or thirst?" Shaowei said, still scanning the room for any eyes peering out from the dark.

"Mmm, food," Poy said, still half in dreamland.

"Okay, you just rest here," Shaowei said. "I can get you food."

Poy drifted asleep again as Shaowei began to crawl out of the bunk.

"Poy," he said, looking back at him as if he suddenly remembered something. "You ever been sick like this before?"

Poy's eyes opened for a moment and then he slowly nodded.

"Think about that time," Shaowei said. "Think about the sickest you've ever been. And then think about how you felt better later. You'll get through this. I'll be back, just you wait."

As Shaowei crawled past the deeper sleepers, slow and quiet so as to not rustle anyone awake, Poy lay staring at the iron ceiling of steerage and thought back to his childhood. Within a moment, he was no longer sure if he was remembering or dreaming. He recalled being a child. He remembered his father's funeral, at a burial ground overlooking the town, how his mother had tried to throw herself off a cliff but his aunts and uncles had taken hold of her, held her back from plunging to the same fate as the man she loved. His father's mother moved into the house then. He slept in the same bed as his grandmother and he was cared for like a pearl in a palm. She had little smelly bound feet, and at first he couldn't sleep because of the smell but then he couldn't sleep because of the sound, he would never forget the sounds in the dark and quiet night of his mother crying in the next room. Poy would wander from his room to hers and she would hold him against her body and cry and cry and her wet tears would fall down his face and he never knew how many of them he swallowed. Then he would cry too and Grandma would come and cry, and that's how it was, the three of them together, broken hearts, lovesick, wondering how the crying would ever end. But eventually the sound got fainter and his mother begged the heavens to raise the child and see him become successful—

"Hey, you up?" Shaowei's voice brought Poy back to the putrid stink of his surroundings, back to his own body feeling as if it was seizing up like a broken pulley at the old well.

Poy looked at him, eyes bleary.

"Eat this," Shaowei said, placing in his hands something bundled in a pristine white cloth napkin. "But be quiet."

"Wha—?" Poy began before Shaowei shushed him.

"Just eat," he said. "I know it's not much, but you won't want to eat too much from there anyway, it's garbage stuff, Western food. It would make you sick on a regular day, let alone while you're like this."

"From where?" Poy said as he unwrapped the napkin. Inside was a big spherical piece of bread, with an ornate pattern in its crust. The savoury aroma nearly made him sick with hunger.

"Look at this." Shaowei gestured with the bread and slipped off his gloves. His hands were unspoiled and smooth, and even in the low light of steerage they glistened, maybe with sweat, maybe as a sign of their cleanliness. He ripped open the round bread in Poy's hands. "White people are crazy," he said. "Big steak hidden inside bread. Beef Wellington. You have to get used to these kinds of tricks in the West."

"It's like a steamed pork bun," Poy mumbled as Shaowei

handed him a torn piece of bread and steak. Despite his hunger, he wasn't sure he could stomach food.

"No," Shaowei said, haughty. "It's nothing like that."

Poy slipped the morsel into his mouth. The buttery smooth shell, slightly crunchy yet soft, soft, soft, melting in his mouth, teeth tearing into beef, rare and juicy, the blood dripping down his throat. He felt immediately renewed. He felt like an animal sinking into prey. He felt sick.

Poy rolled out of their bunk and ran to the nearest bucket, falling to his hands and knees, vomiting the small chunk of beef, then dry heaving. There was nothing left to purge. Tears welled as he panted.

"Hey, keep it down," someone called out in the dark.

Shaowei walked towards Poy and offered him a gloved hand. "Maybe just nibble on the bread," he said as he pulled Poy back upright.

"Where did you get that?" Poy asked again.

"Don't worry about it," Shaowei said. "I have my ways."

"But how? The door to upstairs is locked."

"You know why cats hate rats?" Shaowei asked.

"What?" Poy said.

"All the zodiac animals were on a boat together, and you know what Rat did? Rat pushed Cat overboard. Then, that was it for Cat. That's why Cat isn't on the zodiac. He never even got a chance to be a zodiac animal because he wasn't on the boat."

"I asked where you got the food."

"The moral of the story is, if you're a rat, you can't let the cat catch you. And that means doing whatever it takes. Me and you, we're the rats. It's us versus them, rats versus cats. If we have to push the cats overboard, then we better hope we're close enough to push them."

"I don't—"

"Can you two queers shut up or do I have to make you shut up?" someone yelled.

Shaowei brought a finger to his lips. Then he and Poy climbed back into their bunk.

Poy nibbled a little more of the bready shell.

Shaowei tugged at a corner of the napkin encasing it. "Let me tell you, you're gonna be seeing a lot of these," he said, before facing away from Poy. "Good night."

In the light of the following morning, Poy waited for the right moment to pull Shaowei aside to ask about the mysterious Wellington. Poy had torn the Wellington in half and hidden a piece in each of his pants pockets. The shell had grown stiffer and the once pink meat had turned a dull brown, but it was still food. Every couple of hours, when no one was looking, Poy would rip another piece from inside his pocket and eat it, not too much at once. He began to feel restored.

For much of the day, Poy followed Shaowei around steerage as he held court and told his jokes and was his general smart-aleck self. Poy was waiting, waiting for a moment when he and Shaowei could talk without anyone listening in. It was a calm day on the Pacific, and the time came when the men in steerage were allowed to wander around on deck and breathe in the salty air. The smell of salt water did Poy good. He saw Shaowei standing at the railing and looking about at the infinite expanse of ocean around the slow-moving ship.

"How did you get that bread thing?" Poy asked him.

"What bread thing?" Shaowei raised his eyebrows as if he had never heard of it.

"You gave me food last night," Poy said.

Shaowei's eyes darted back and forth as he made sure no one was listening. "Look," he said, "I've done this voyage enough times. I know how this whole ship works. Well, not the ship, but I know how the crew works. Sneaking around and stealing some food from upstairs, it can make all the difference on a trip like this."

"How?" Poy said. "I—I'm not sure that's a smart thing to be doing."

"Cats versus rats," Shaowei said. "We gotta do what we can to survive, right?"

Poy looked out at the wake of ripples the ship was leaving behind.

"Besides," Shaowei added, always eager to fill a silence, "you should see the layout they got for the other classes. Red velvet walls, mounted candles, chairs nicer than anything you seen in your life. You think they'll miss a bit of beef wrapped in bread? They didn't even know they had it to begin with. They got lobsters living in tanks. It'd depress the hell out of you to see how they live."

"The people or the lobsters?" Poy said.

Shaowei grinned. "Both," he said. "We need that food to survive. If I have to take it, I have to take it."

Poy exhaled through his nostrils. This guy annoyed him, but he was amusing. And he did help him, after all.

"I wanted to ask you something," Poy said. "Why do you keep going back to the West if it's so bad? Why do you keep getting on this . . . this 'coffin ship' if it makes you so unhappy?"

A sad smile crossed Shaowei's face as he patted Poy on the shoulder. "Oh, Poy," he said with a sigh. "So young. So bright. You'll learn a lot about the world soon."

"What do you mean?"

"It's not a question of if I would be happier home or on Gold

Mountain. It's not about how bad the West is. It's the only game in town. If I wasn't doing this, what else would I be doing? Tending a field, picking up a rifle, washing laundry—it's all the same shit we're shovelling. It's just that doing this, going back to the West again, working in the laundry, will pay me just a little more. Just a little. But it's enough to make it all worth it."

A bell rang on the deck, signalling it was time to return to steerage. The men all headed towards the stairs.

"Say, I asked you last night about if you'd been sick before," Shaowei said, "and you nodded yes. What happened to young Poy?"

Poy swallowed and recalled again the days after his father died. It wasn't something he wanted to share with someone as shrewd as Shaowei, and it probably wasn't the type of story the fellow wanted to hear anyway.

As they headed down the stairs, Poy began to tell Shaowei a different story.

"Well, when I was young, about eleven, I wouldn't eat. I had no appetite. My mom called me He-doesn't-eat-a-lot."

"What a poetic nickname," Shaowei said with an eye roll.

"It got so bad that I became too weak to do anything. I couldn't go to school, I couldn't play with the other kids. My aunt thought I was being disturbed by a demon. Grandma said that didn't worry her, because she said the true God controlled all the small devils. But my aunt left food out for the demon. She said that this would be our sacrifice to the small devils."

"You might like all this Jesus stuff the whites will force on you," Shaowei said as they wended their way down the stairs.

"She put it all outside, under a blanket. She said that would lure the demon out of my body and out of the house. I got to thinking that some of the food she left out was smelling pretty good, so my cousin and I went out there and started eating some of it. Rice, and clams, little bits of shrimp, daylilies. When we were full, we rubbed our bellies, and then we started playing with the food, throwing rice at each other and trying to see who could kick a dumpling farthest. Next thing we know, chickens and pigs and dogs were surrounding us and chasing after the food, and they made so much noise the neighbours came out and—" Poy chuckled. "So much chaos. Anyway, after that I was never sick again. Until I got on this damn boat."

Shaowei stared at him. "That's the most I've ever heard you say," he said. "See how you told that story? That's how you need to tell jokes. But there needs to be a punchline. Same way with the story. You didn't have an ending."

"What do you mean?" Poy said as they approached the door to steerage.

"What happened next? Was your aunt mad? Did you start eating again?"

"Oh," Poy laughed. "No, no. No one was mad. They were just happy to see me up and eating and out playing around again."

Shaowei smiled. "Me too."

They had returned to steerage. Poy breathed in and realized that the putrid stench in the lowest part of the ship was stronger now that he had been on deck. The jovial spirit Shaowei had conjured was quickly replaced by a sense of all-encompassing dread. The stench of two hundred men huddled together, sweat intermingling, spilt human waste, uncleaned bowls and plates because the water didn't stay hot long enough for everyone to clean their dishes. The stench of death, the coffin ship.

Just days later, they could see, faintly on the horizon, under an inviting sky of brilliant orange and yellow hues, the silhouette of a mountain range. It looked like home, all peaks and valleys.

9

ONE FOR EVERY MILE

By the time the boat docked, the sun had dissipated and a light rain had begun to fall. After the first- and second-class passengers had disembarked, the men from steerage lined up on deck with their baggage. Poy breathed in the fresh air, happy to have his steerage days behind him. He thought it smelled like Hong Kong, though it wasn't as hot. After the ship's doctor inspected the men on deck one by one, the healthy ones were sent off the boat. The sick ones remained behind, to be returned to China, if they could survive more tumultuous weeks at sea.

Poy, Shaowei, and Gao were among those in the clear. Once on the dock, the men were ushered into a caged area. Eventually, a Canadian immigration officer showed up with a translator in tow, a young Chinese woman.

"Gentlemen, welcome to Vancouver."

The translator stared at the officer.

"Go on, tell them," the officer said.

The woman addressed the audience of caged men, translating verbatim. Then the officer continued his speech, pausing every so often so that the woman could translate what he said.

"You may think you are standing on Canadian soil," the officer said lazily, as if he had delivered the speech before. "You aren't."

Poy looked at his own feet and had to agree. They were standing on a wooden platform.

"You may think you're breathing in Canadian air." The man paused. "You're not."

As the translator caught up with him, many puzzled expressions came across the caged men's faces.

"You may even think that you are now in Canada. Well, you aren't, and, quite frankly, you will never be. No, gentlemen, you are still somewhere in the Pacific Ocean. That's what it says on my records." He tapped a small book strapped to his hip. "It says your kind aren't allowed in Canada. So as far as I'm concerned, you're not in Canada. It's my job to ensure that all of you celestials get straight from that boat"—the officer pointed to their ship—"to that train." He pointed inland, towards a train station not too far from the dock. A narrow wooden plank extended outward from the cage towards the train.

"But before you do that, I need to ascertain who each and every one of you is." He walked closer to the cage. "I need to know who you are, where you came from, where you're going. And I need those answers to be correct. These are my needs. If any of you doesn't satisfy my needs, you'll be put back on that ship"—the officer pointed at the ship again—"and sent back to Chinaland." The officer looked at the translator and waited for her to catch up.

"Here's what happens next: I interview each of you, one by one, and after the interview's over, you are to walk on that plank to that train which will be your home for the next few weeks as you continue to pass through the Pacific Ocean. And if you step off that plank, if you so much as slip, you'll be thrown back on that ship. Understood?" A smile cracked the officer's face.

"I understand," Shaowei muttered in Taishanese.

"What was that?" the officer said, searching through faces in the crowd. "I will have no back talk during this process, not in my language and certainly not in yours. I don't want any of that flim-flam-ching-chang bullshit unless I directly address you."

Shaowei looked around the crowd as if he too was searching for the culprit.

Poy was the first of his friends to be called for an interview. He was escorted by an armed guard out of the cage and into a small office filled with bookcases.

"All right, what's your name?" the officer asked. The translator took care of the language barriers.

"Seto Poy," he told the translator.

"Do you know where you're going?"

"St. John, Newfoundland." Poy nodded and smiled towards both the translator and the officer.

"Who do you have there?"

"What family do you have there?" the translator said to Poy.

"My uncle Lee," Poy said to the translator.

"He setting you up with a job there or what?"

"Fong-Lee Laundry," Poy said.

"All right," the officer said, cracking open his book. "What did you say your name was again?"

"Seto Poy," Poy repeated with a smile and a nod.

"Seto Ping, huh? All right, let me see, your name is now . . ." The officer's eyes skimmed over the books crowding his shelves before settling on a toppled copy of *Othello* with gilded edges.

"William!" the officer exclaimed, and scratched something onto the page in front of him. "William Ping. That's you." The officer pointed at Poy.

"Seto Poy," Poy repeated with a nod and a smile.

"William Ping," the officer said, resting his pen on the desk with annoyance. "You are *William Ping*."

Poy pointed at himself and again said, "Seto Poy."

"Fine, fine. William Seto Ping. Happy?" The officer wrote in his book and said to the translator, "Go on, explain to him his new name."

"Your name in Newfoundland will be William Seto Ping." She smiled and nodded at Poy.

The officer passed him a document and the armed guard escorted him to the plank and followed him as he headed towards the train, suitcase in hand. The plank was wobbly underfoot, well worn and clearly never repaired. All the same, Poy thought it was all a bit ridiculous, all these theatrics and for what?

Once he reached the train car, he saw another armed guard seated on a stool, thumbing through a newspaper.

"Got another one for ya, Howard," the escort said as he pushed Poy from the plank into the car.

"Take a seat anywhere you like, big fella," Howard said to Poy, and then called back to the other guard, "He better pick a comfortable one, hey, Ben?"

Both of the men exhaled tired chuckles. Poy stood looking at Howard.

"Go on, go sit down," he said, and turned his attention back to the newspaper.

The train car had several rows, with pairs of chairs facing each other in blocks so that four people could sit together. Poy was excited to be on a train, having studied them in his engineering courses but never having stepped foot in one in his whole life. He liked the smell in the air, of exhaust or fuel or whatever it was, like the steamboat but different. He looked out the window at all the white people running about the platform. Some kids stopped and made faces at him.

Poy remembered the first time he ever saw a train. He had been young, like the kids outside the window, but he couldn't remember if his father was still alive. He had been tilling a field with Uncle Lee when he saw the train slowly chugging by far off in the distance. His father must've still been alive, he thought, if Lee was still around. The sun was either setting or rising and was casting dramatic shadows across the rust-coloured train.

"What is that?" Poy recalled saying to Lee.

"It's a brown cow," his uncle said. He never knew if his uncle was joking or not.

Poy chuckled at the memory and looked in his lap at the certificate, running his fingers over the freshly scrawled *William Seto Ping*, cryptic symbols written in a language he did not yet understand.

The next person on the train was Gao, who was followed by Shaowei. Gao's new name was Upton Gao and Shaowei's was Sinclair Zhang.

"Stupid name, stupid officer," Shaowei complained. "Thinking I can't understand what he's saying. It's always the way."

"I like my name," Gao said, "Upton. *Up*-ton," he repeated, stressing the syllables in different ways each time.

"And those planks are stupid too," Shaowei said. "Like my foot touching soil is going to corrupt the land. We're wearing shoes, for fuck's sake."

Poy nodded, which Shaowei took as an encouragement to keep going.

"And the white people will say 'Chinese people are so superstitious.' *They're* the ones making us walk on planks to preserve their imaginary borders!"

With three of their four seats taken, the men rested uneasy, waiting to see who from the ship would take the fourth.

"I hope it's someone clean," Shaowei said, peering out the window at the platform, trying to eye up any potential seatmates.

A small young man carrying a large brown red-trimmed brief-case climbed up the train steps and staggered towards the empty seat, the weeks at sea having clearly done a number on him. Either he had lost a significant amount of weight or he was just preter-naturally thin for his age, with clothes so baggy and limbs so skinny that he had the appearance of being nothing more than cotton draped on bones.

"Can I . . ." he said.

"Yes," Poy said, before glancing at a grimacing Shaowei.

"What's your name?" Gao asked him as the small man took his seat.

"Wong, or, well, it used to be Wong, now it's . . ." The man held up the sheet the officer had given him.

"What's your new name?" Poy asked, before adding, "Mine's William Ping."

"Don't let them tell you what your name is," Shaowei said, aghast. "My name is Shaowei Zhang. Gao, hold up that boy's sheet so I can read it."

"Why can't you hold it yourself?" Gao asked.

"Just do it," Shaowei said, and Gao held up the sheet. Shaowei studied it, sounding out the letters, before announcing: "Ignatius. I think. Ignatius Wong. Huh."

"What?" Wong asked.

"I thought they were giving us Western names. I'm not certain if yours is Western or not."

"You'd be the expert on that," Poy said with a smile.

"Ha ha," Shaowei said without a smile. "How old are you, Wong?"

Wong looked away and said, "Eighteen."

"You don't look eighteen."

"Yeah, everyone says I'm small for my age."

Shaowei leaned in closer to him and said, "I'm only going to ask this one more time and if you lie to me again, we can't be friends. How old are you?"

Wong looked around to make sure Howard wasn't near, not that he'd understand. He still sat at the front of the train, reading his paper, so Wong leaned forward and said, "Fourteen."

"What?" Poy exclaimed.

Shaowei shushed him and then said to Wong, "Don't worry, your secret is safe with us." He sat back in his seat. "So, do you know any jokes?"

"I . . . I can't think of any right now, no," Wong said.

"Poy, tell him your joke."

"Shaowei, he's just a kid, he doesn't need to hear that filth."

"Oh yes, he does. Why, you heard the man, Wong I mean. He's eighteen. He's no kid. He can hear some dirty jokes."

"C'mon, Poy," Gao said, "tell your joke. It's not even dirty. The kid'll love it."

"We worked on it for all those weeks and you still can't tell it?"

"All right, fine," Poy said. "Okay. So there is a husband and wife and they are— Hold on, wait." Poy took a moment to think before continuing. "Okay, so there's a husband and wife, and the wife, she's about to go on a long train ride. The wife says to her husband, 'Oh, husband, I know you'll miss me while I'm gone,' and the husband says, 'Miss you? It's worthwhile to send you away for three yuan!'"

Gao and Poy looked at Wong to see if he'd laugh. A polite smile crossed the boy's face.

"Okay," Shaowei said. "It still needs some work."

"He's too young to get it," Poy said.

"Where was she going?" Wong asked.

"Who?" Poy said, looking around.

"The wife. In the joke."

"Oh," said Poy. "Uh, I'm not sure. I guess, um, a family funeral maybe."

"That's not very funny," Wong said.

"No, I know."

"See," Shaowei said, "this joke of yours, Poy, it's all wrong. Now there's a death involved."

"No, look, the joke is that the husband is happy that his wife is leaving him alone for a few days."

"Why isn't the husband going to the funeral?" Wong said.

"No, there is no funeral, the wife—"

"You said there was a funeral," Wong said.

"No," Poy said, exasperated.

"Hey, Wong," Shaowei said, "don't listen to him. This guy doesn't know jokes. Gao, tell Wong the one where the wife is cheating on her husband and she puts the guy in the bag of rice."

"You just ruined the ending," Gao protested.

"No, I didn't."

Poy stopped listening, annoyed at being around these people. He looked out the dirty window, watching the last couple of Chinamen boarding the train.

Shaowei discovered that Wong had a journal, and he tore two pages from it so he could show Poy and Gao how they could do signatures of their new English names.

"Don't ever sign anything a white person asks you to sign," he said. "Unless you have to. And if you have to, this is how you do it."

Poy thought the letters on the sheet of paper Shaowei gave him looked like the calligraphy of a child. He had long since grown bored of Shaowei's Western warnings and he tried to focus on positive thoughts of what lay ahead of him. Soon enough, the next leg of the journey would begin. With each successive part of the journey behind him, he thought, he was one step closer to going back home. One step closer to being with Hua Ling and Wai again, a wife and child that he would gladly pay three yuan to see, or any amount of money, for that matter. He rested his head against the windowpane and closed his eyes. It would be nice to see Uncle Lee again, he reminded himself, and it was nice to be on an adventure in the West. He'd have so many stories to tell when he went back.

"Hey, wake that guy up," a voice said, interrupting Poy's slumber. "My name is Howard. I'm the guy guarding this train car. We got a few rules to go over. I'm the one responsible for making sure none of you guys enter Canada, so that means I make sure none of you leave this car. And listen, you really don't want to get off this thing anyway. People don't want to see your kind and I can't be sure how they'll react. Don't give *me* any trouble and I won't give *you* any trouble. It's as simple as that. The bathroom is up where I sit at the front. You can go one at a time and there's no lining up for it either. You wait your turn from your seat." He stopped. "Say, do any of you speak English?"

Poy eyed Shaowei, who stared ahead blankly.

"Aw, geez," Howard said. "Does *anybody* here understand me?" He surveyed the crowd. "I see a couple of you smiling, so I'm going to take it that some of you understand me and can explain what I'm saying to your friends. Again, you give respect, you get respect. Now, the train is going to stop pretty frequently on the way to Montreal, but you're not allowed off. Matter of fact, you're not even allowed to look out the windows. The rule is, blinds are always to be down so you don't see what's out there. Now, I'm a nice guy, I'll let you look out the window, but that's only if there's good behaviour. But when we pull up to stations, I want all the blinds closed so that I don't get in trouble." Howard looked towards the far end of the car, seemingly trying to remember something.

"The trip'll take us about four days as long as we don't run into any trouble. But I don't need to tell you guys how long it'll take—you were the ones that built this thing," he said with a laugh. "I'm up there if anyone needs me." He retreated to his seat and cracked open his newspaper.

"What'd he say?" Poy asked Shaowei.

"He said we're gonna be on the train for the next few days, that's it."

"That's all?"

"Yeah, that was basically it."

"It sounded like he said a lot more than that."

"That was just white people noise."

They were on the train for the next few days, that's it.

After departing Vancouver, a place not unlike Hong Kong, the men agreed, the train went for days and days through the Canadian wilderness. A peculiar introduction to the West, these several days of travel through seemingly endless expanses of forests and prairie. Evergreens and mountain ranges quickly devolved into flatlands and blowing wheat crops.

The men enjoyed the journey. A woman came around with a food cart once a day, and although it only comprised leftovers from the classes that were afforded the luxury of a dining car, it was still a lot better than what they'd had on the boat. There was enough of it, and enough water to drink, and the car was less crowded than steerage and far cleaner. Sure, there were no beds, but the ragged chairs of the train were rather luxurious after the weeks they had spent on bare-bones wooden bunks. And there was more to look at, with windows showing an endless land of promise and uninhabited space.

A curious development for the men was the toilet. Wong was the first to use the lavatory and was quick to inform his new friends of the strangeness of the Western toilet.

"It's like a chair," he said.

"A chair?" Gao said.

"Yes," Shaowei said. "It is a chair. And it has two lids. You have to lift one lid to use it to shit, and the second lid you have to lift to pee."

Poy laughed. "The things you come up with!"

"He's not making it up," Wong said. "Go look for yourself! Plus there's a metal rope you pull and all this water comes in and—"

"There's water too?" Gao said.

"This is the way it is in the West," Shaowei said. "It's terrible. You can't even squat. Very unhealthy."

In time, each of the men had their turn and none of them were overly pleased with it. Such a strange experience to try to sit to do your business. The other men in the car also found the experience unpleasant, and three days into the trip, one man trying to force himself to defecate in the seated position strained himself to the point that he had a heart attack and died. His lifeless body slumped off the toilet and his head bounced off the bowl, cracking the ceramic throne. The body was transferred to one of the train's shipping cars.

Despite everything, Poy thought the train was an incredible way to see a country. Continuously drawn backwards at a high speed through sumptuous scenery, he felt dizzied trying to see every passing sight.

Wong also kept straining to look out the window, constantly

peering behind the train, missing whatever it was he sought to see. "Everything passes so quickly," he said with a sigh. "Then it's just gone. And if I try to look back at whatever we just passed, then I miss what's coming up. It's so annoying."

"If you think that's annoying," Shaowei said, "then you should think about how many guys like us died building these tracks."

Wong slouched away from the window and into his seat.

"Look," Shaowei said, pointing. "You can still see rocks scarred from dynamite blasts. And look there, wow, that's where they used to hang guys like us. And oh, wow, look there, just past those trees, you can see another railway! Another railway we helped build, another railway in a country that no longer even wants to see us, let alone let us live on the land we helped develop."

A silence set in over the four friends and they all stared out at the passing landscape. Wong was visibly shaken by Shaowei's remarks, and Poy thought he saw a twinge of guilt in Shaowei's face.

"There's some story in the Bible about this," Shaowei said, resting a gloved hand on Wong's shoulder. "Something where some guy's wife looks back and she turns into a pillar of salt. Tasty, delicious salt. But salt isn't that good for you in the end."

One night, the train made one of its frequent stops. Howard had checked that all the blinds were pulled down, but when he looked out his small window to the platform, his jaw dropped.

"Oh my," he said. "Open the blinds! Open the blinds!"

Shaowei opened their blind and all four men jumped in fright. The window did not show a forest, or a mountain range, or a prairie. Outside looked grey and wrinkly, like a tough piece of leather, with many almond-shaped folds. The leather was split in the middle and began to slowly separate, with half ascending and the other descending. The centre of all the grey became a large burnt-yellow sphere with a smaller black circle at its centre.

"You're looking into the eye of an elephant," Howard announced. "That's a circus train across the track there. Better hope the big fella there don't run in front of our train when we leave. It's happened before."

When the elephant walked away from the window, the men could see the circus train across the track, its cars covered in bright yellow and red stripes, animals of all types being led into cages, the cages being pulled into the train cars. The sides of the cars were adorned with colourful posters: a bearded lady, a man who was half monkey, a mammoth with a girl's head, and, of most interest to the men, a Chinese lady. The poster showed a young woman in a qipao, surrounded by vases and chairs with richly patterned textiles draped over them, all of which were covered with things that looked like Chinese symbols but didn't really mean anything.

"What does it say?" Poy asked.

Shaowei pressed his face to the window. "'The Chinese Lady, Astonishing Little Feet, The Chinese Costume, A Chinese Song.'" He sat back. "White people do that sometimes."

The train started up again, and they kept their eyes on the circus train as it receded until all they could see once again was a blurred, never-ending line of evergreens.

IO

COMPARTMENT C CAR

When the train finally pulled into Montreal, the men were more than ready for some fresh air. Howard led them onto the platform one by one and into the hands of another guard, Pierre, who was now going to take over from him. Pierre spoke English, but English in italics, all nasally with weird intonations. Shaowei explained to his friends that this was a Canadian version of the Spanish he had often heard in California. Pierre wasn't as lax as Howard, and when they resumed their journey he strictly enforced the rule about keeping the blinds closed.

And the days dragged on, and the men again spoke in recurrent conversations. They had now been travelling for more than a month together and it seemed each of them knew everything about the others' relatively short lives. They knew each other's desires, but only in the way that all men know each other's desires: money and sex on the surface level, but underneath, family, an end to hunger, an ability to appease the people in their lives, a sense of belonging earned or not, and perhaps above all the ability to sustain themselves and maybe a couple of others if they were lucky, their parents, maybe a nice girl. But there could be no bird without a nest. And really, that's what it was all about for them, all this Gold Mountain stuff: being able to build a nest and then do what they wanted with it. That's the dream, the dream they were sold, the dream they all bought.

The days felt like dreams too, the sluggish chugging of the train, shaking them back and forth just a little bit.

"I can't wait," Gao said during one of their conversations, "for you guys to meet my uncle Charlie. He's a great guy."

"Oh yeah?" Shaowei said, somewhat irritable from being around these people day in and day out. "What's so great about him?"

Poy couldn't tell if Gao's expression was one of equal annoyance or of considered thought.

"Well," Gao said. "He's been there for a long time. I think seventeen or eighteen years now. I guess I don't have many memories of him. I was just a kid—"

"So why's he great?" Shaowei said as he tried to peek out the shut blind.

"He was a great cook," Gao said. "Everyone always said he made the most amazing pickled turnips."

Shaowei glared at him. "He was known as a great cook because he dumped turnips in some vinegar and left them in a jar someplace for a long time?"

"No," Gao said with a forced laugh. "I'm sure there was more to it than that."

"So you're headed to Gold Mountain so you can learn the pickled turnip secret? Are pickled turnips a big seller in Newfoundland?"

"Well, no," Gao said, frustrated now. "I don't know. I guess I was sick of the farming life, and him being over here gave me a great opportunity to leave, try to do something more. Work at his restaurant."

Shaowei rolled his eyes. "Women's work."

"So is the laundry," Gao said.

"It is what it is," Shaowei said, a master of the banal platitude.

Poy turned to Wong. "And where will you be working?"

"Oh, uh," the boy said, scratching his head. "Kam Laundry, I think."

"Me and Poy are at Fong-Lee Laundry," Shaowei said. "You looking forward to getting your hands wet, Poy?"

"Heh," Poy said, realizing that he had never told Shaowei that he would be taking a management position.

"I'm just going to be a bag boy," Wong said.

"Nah, me and Poy are gonna be elbow-deep in it, right?" Shaowei nudged Poy with his elbow.

"Heh," Poy said again.

Shaowei raised an eyebrow. "What?"

"What?" Poy said.

"'Heh,'" Shaowei mimicked. "What's that supposed to mean?"

"Well, uh, my uncle Lee, I'm replacing him, and I think he's a manager."

Shaowei sharply inhaled. "So . . . what? Were you just planning on not telling me that?"

"No," Poy said. "I didn't think it would be a big deal."

"So, what, you're gonna be my boss? My bunkmate one day, my boss the next?"

"It's not like that," Poy said. "I don't know what I'll be doing there yet."

"Mm-hm." Shaowei looked away. "I'm taking a nap."

Gao cleared his throat and turned towards Wong. "What family do you have at your laundry, Wong?"

"I . . . uh." The boy looked confused. "My mom and sister are back home. I'm just working so I can make some money for them."

"No," Gao said. "I meant, what family do you have in Newfoundland?"

"Um," Wong said, fidgeting.

"Gao, don't ask him so many questions," Shaowei said with his eyes closed, caressing his lengthy braid. "He's like me: made of paper. Now I'm taking a nap and I need quiet."

The conversation between the four men slowed nearly to a stop after that day. There's really only so much you can take of the same people day in, day out. Where once Gao's deep singing voice charmed and entertained, now it grated and sounded out of tune. Where once Shaowei's attempts to educate the others about Western life enlightened, now it came across as know-it-all behaviour. Where once Poy's quiet nature seemed to welcome conversation, he now appeared aloof and cold. A couple days passed by in relative silence, and with Pierre strictly enforcing the rule about keeping the blinds shut, they didn't even have the redundant, repetitive scenery to look at.

Until the day the train stopped. "Sydney," Shaowei told them, squinting at the station sign. "Nova Scotia."

Pierre let the men off the train, and they stood in the fresh air for the first time in days. It was an overcast day, with a mist in the air heavy enough to be classified as rain even though it wasn't raining, but regardless, the Chinamen weren't prepared for this kind of weather, although some of them looked through their suitcases for a more rain-ready garment. Armed guards walked them across a series of planks suspended over the ceramic tiles of the station's platform before they wound towards a nearby ferry terminal and up close to the SS *Caribou*. The ship was maybe half the size of the *Heian Maru*, still a big ship, but it had only one smokestack. Poy let out a big sigh when he saw it—back at sea, for who knew how long—floating there in the harbour, surrounded by a grey sky and a chilly breeze.

The planks led the men into another caged area and they

waited to be let aboard the ship. It was the first time since they had left Vancouver that Poy could get a good look at the crowd around him and see how many of his fellow immigrants were also going to Newfoundland. He thought it must be around fifty men. They waited there in their little caged area and watched in the cold drizzle as all the white passengers boarded, and then various provisions were loaded onto the ship, followed by cattle and a cage holding two moose. Only after everything else was on board were the men escorted on planks to the ship and led up the gangway. They were directed straight into steerage. This time they weren't even allowed to socialize on deck before they set sail.

As the men descended the steps, they were surprised to encounter two white men coming up from steerage.

"I'm pretty sure they're brother and sister," one of them said, "but we're just going to let them loose and see what happens."

In the middle of the *Caribou*'s steerage quarters were the two caged moose. The animals were making long, guttural moans, sounds that seemed to portend doom. The branch-like antlers of the male were slightly too large for the cage constraining him, and he was ramming his horns into the roof of the cage. Poy wasn't sure if he was trying to escape or get comfortable.

Steerage was dimly lit and overcrowded. Sure, there were fewer of them here now—in Vancouver some of the men had gone on to Hawaii—but this space was smaller, there were fewer portholes and hatches to allow light in, the bunks were smaller, and there were also two noisy caged animals.

"How long will this take?" Poy asked Shaowei as they sought out a bunk.

"A couple weeks maybe."

They settled into their bunk for the night; they'd been unable to get the cherry pickings of steerage. Yet even though the bunk was stiff and uncomfortable, and even though the moose kept moaning, the men were happy to once again be lying in a bed.

"B'ys, you gotta get up, 's time ta go."

A white man in an ill-fitting blue uniform stood in the middle of the steerage room, tapping his baton off a tin mug.

"We're 'ere now, I don't know wheres you all going to but you can't stay in 'ere."

Poy wondered if he had been asleep for weeks, but soon he got his bearings and he realized he had only slept for a few hours. They had been on the *Caribou* for four monotonous days of boredom on rough seas.

The men were escorted up to the deck and down the gangway. The moose were freed from their cages and ran into the forest.

"Welcome to Newfoundland," a man on the dock said. "Have your immigration certificates ready for inspection, and you'll be required to pay some fees now the once."

II

HEAD TAX

Three hundred dollars later and they were on the road once again.

Not that any of them could afford to spend three hundred dollars right now. Shaowei did the math and said that back in China it would take thirteen years to save that much money. Here in the West, they could probably pay it back in about one year. Lucky for them, their uncles and brothers and other family already in Newfoundland had been able to front them the cash for the time being.

This notion, of owing money to his uncle, didn't please Poy at all. It was another obstacle between him and his family. But, he reasoned, it would give shape and meaning to his year here in the West: let his uncle go back home, earn money to repay his uncle, then go back himself.

They left the ferry terminal in Port aux Basques on a train bound for St. John's. They were allowed to look out of the windows now, but the sky was grey and the trees were so close to the tracks that they couldn't see much. The men caught glimpses of the landscape when the trees thinned, but all they saw were barren plains and hilly terrain. Dull, brownish grass, glorified moss, really, and large, dirty rocks jutting out from the soil. The wind shook the train car, as if the environment itself was opposed to anything being here.

Twenty-eight hours after they departed Port aux Basques, the train pulled to a stop in St. John's.

"Well, boys," Shaowei said as they gathered their baggage, "welcome to your new home."

Poy stood on the platform and looked around the station. It was rather small compared with some of the ones they had passed in the last few weeks, almost claustrophobic. Drab beige brick walls, with painted advertisements for Tetley Tea and Carnation Milk and DuMont Shipping. There were people everywhere on the platform, mostly white people, bustling here and there, and a couple of Chinese men waiting to greet some newly arrived relative.

Poy left his friends behind on the platform when he spotted Uncle Lee in the crowd.

"Lee!" he called out as he approached his uncle.

"Poy, is that you?" Uncle Lee adjusted his glasses and leaned in with a squint. "Why, it's been so long. The last time I saw you, you were this tall!" He held his hand next to his knee.

They shook hands and Poy smiled ear to ear. It was good to be with family again.

Lee looked around the platform, nervous eyes darting back and forth.

"I rode the brown cow to get here," Poy said with a laugh, gesturing towards the train.

"What?" Lee said.

"Remember when I was a kid, you said a train was a brown cow!"

"Aha, yes," Lee said, though there was no humour in his voice. "Let's go. I'll show you where we're staying." His eyes shifted around again.

Poy looked around the platform too and saw that the once bust-ling pace had slowed. Moustachioed men whispered to each other in small groups, shooting glances at the Chinese men. Women in the café window raised eyebrows behind teacups. A child said something to his father about chinks. The father looked mad, not at the child but at the chinks.

Poy looked at his fellow travellers, fellow immigrants. He had felt it was a small group before, but he could see now, surrounded by the whiteness of the crowd, that fifty Chinamen would have quite an effect in this town. And all of them, after the weeks of trav-elling, were dirty and malodorous. It wasn't the best first impres-sion, Poy thought.

"Let's go," Lee said, hurrying from the platform.

Poy followed Lee to the open street. It was a cold spring day, the sky an impenetrable bright grey. The first thing he noticed was the smell. It was the worst-smelling place he had ever been, even worse than the foulest days in steerage. Horse manure was everywhere, and garbage blew along in the sudden blasts of wind. Goats, pigs, cows, they all roamed the street freely. He couldn't believe it. All that he had heard about the West, about Gold Mountain, and this was the reality. A place dirtier than home, as if the wealth of Gold Mountain had inspired people to shit on their own doorsteps. As he and his uncle walked down Water Street, the smells only grew worse. Urine and booze, half-naked drunk men sweating profusely on street corners even though it was only late afternoon. Men stumbling every which way like animals. Not even Hong Kong was this bad.

They reached a point where Poy could see straight out to the water, to a narrow opening between two hills where ocean water flooded into the small harbour. Wharfs jutted onto the ocean like toppled matchboxes. The smell of fish guts fermenting in the sun, blood and innards sprayed on piers. Poy was speechless.

They went up to the next street, Duckworth, and kept walking fast. This street was more of the same, streetcars, horse-drawn carriages, a couple of noisy cars puttered by, but still the foul brew of animal droppings and the excesses of man. The street was lined with storefronts, signs Poy could not read, but he could infer what was inside from the window displays. He paused outside of one. Inside was a big kitchen, he guessed, with appliances and devices he had never before seen in person. A big rectangular metal box stood next to a large sink, and the walls were covered in orange tiles. A mannequin of a woman stood at the sink, an uncanny smile painted beneath her lifeless eyes. From this angle, Poy could see his reflection in the glass and it almost made it look like he was in there, standing next to the woman. The door of the store swung open.

"You," a man said, and pushed Poy's shoulder. "I knows you."

Poy looked at the man, a tall, wiry white man with a small moustache and a comb-over. He was wearing a suit that looked a little too big for him, as if he had suddenly lost fifteen pounds and his clothes no longer fit quite right.

"I knows you didn't forget me now," the man said. "'Cause I knows I didn't forget you."

Poy had no idea what the man was saying, or if he was even speaking English. He looked for Lee but couldn't see him. He had lost sight of him when he was looking at the kitchen store.

"I knows your face," the man said, getting more angry.

Poy backed up. A small crowd had gathered around them.

"Don't pretend like ya can't understand me now, chink." This got a laugh out of the group. "You thinks you can cut off your ponytail and now you can just look in a store window, can ya? Is that what ya thinks?"

Poy turned to walk away, but the crowd had closed and they wouldn't let him out.

"Just where do you think you're going?" a chubby man asked, pushing him back towards the wiry man.

Poy turned around and—*splat!*

He felt the hot smack of something hit his body, the soreness in his chest where it collided, flecks ricocheting onto his cheek and forehead. He looked down to see that a large piece of mud had been thrown at him, splattering all over his suit, staining the shirt underneath. He looked up just as a child threw another chunk of mud—might be mud, might be manure.

Smack.

Winded, Poy leaned over.

"You fucking celestial chinks." A man in the crowd leaned in close to Poy's face. "You think you can wear a suit and be one of us and take our jobs and women. Fuck off." He spit in Poy's face, eliciting loud laughter from the crowd around him, their mouths agape with delight.

"Excuse me, gentlemen," a lyrical male voice shone through the laughter, dissipating the crowd around Poy. "Whatever seems to be the problem here?"

"That's the fucking chink that stole my job," the wiry man said.

"I am certain there must be some misunderstanding here, sir." Poy looked up and saw the man who owned this voice. He cut a strange figure among the retreating crowd. He must have been taller than six feet, easily the tallest person Poy had ever seen, a couple of heads taller than most of the people he had seen in St. John's so far. He wore a long black robe that did little to conceal his beer belly. His face looked old and weathered, but he couldn't be any older than forty. His hairline had mostly receded, leaving a strange tuft of hair at the top of his head. His mouth was framed by a handlebar moustache and a patchy beard that left him looking like his cheeks had dandruff. The man extended a hand to Poy, and it was then that Poy noticed a small square of white on the man's black collar. A priest of some sort.

"Nah, Reverend, that's the fucking chink." The wiry man took a step closer.

The priest held up a flattened hand and said, "Did you work in the laundry?"

"No, Reverend, I worked in the fisheries, and I made good money too, until this lot came along."

"Sir, the Chinese do not work in the fisheries, they work in the laundry. Some of them work in restaurants. You must be mistaken."

"It's these celestial fucks that—"

"Must I remind you that 'celestial' means from the sky, y'know, where God lives? With his son Jesus? So every time you call one of these men celestials, you're calling 'em angels. Now, is this any way to treat a heavenly body?"

"I—"

"Sir, I recommend you visit me at the parish where we can continue to discuss this matter. But for the time being, I plan on walking this gentleman home and getting him cleaned up."

The priest escorted Poy away. "Sir," he said, "may I ask you your name?"

Poy looked at him blankly, then reached inside his jacket pocket and handed the priest his immigration document.

"William Seto Ping," the priest read. "Why, Mr. Ping, it says here you just moved here today."

Poy and the priest stood in the middle of the sidewalk and the city moved around them.

The priest sighed. "What a terrible welcome to your new home. Alas. Welcome to the Rock."

Poy offered a weak smile and nodded.

"I guess you don't know what I'm saying, do you. You'll need to have some defences around here. There's a lot of nice people, but there's a lot of sour people too. And the sour ones are usually the loudest and they have a way of making the nice ones quiet. Your number-one best line of defence is definitely Christianity."

The priest thought for a moment and then continued. "Actually, now that I think about it, your number-one best line of defence would probably be a gun. But that ain't Christlike. You should come to my church, that's where you will learn the truest form of defence, the one for your soul. And every Sunday, after my sermon, we have little classes where you can learn English."

Poy continued to stare at him, then smiled and nodded.

"Actually, learning English right now would be your number-one best line of defence. Once you know English, you can read the Bible. And when you've done that, you'll be able to tell everyone you know about the word of the Lord and you can tell them Reverend Riley sent you."

"It alway the way," Poy said in English, trying to mimic the priest's intonation.

"Huh? You do know English?"

"Alway the way," Poy said again.

"Is that . . . is that the only phrase you know?"

"Alway the way?" Poy again mimicked the priest's intonation, making the words more high-pitched at the end.

"Yeah, I'm not too sure about that one."

"Poy!" Uncle Lee was peering around the corner of a nearby alleyway. "Poy, what happened?" He rushed over to Poy.

"Now, Frederick," the priest said. "Are you supposed to be minding Mr. Ping here?"

"Yes, yes, I just showing him where we live, Reverend Riley," Lee said, making the *R* in both words sound like a *W*. Then he turned to Poy and addressed him in Taishanese. "Why are you so dirty now? Why didn't you follow me better?"

Reverend Riley raised a hand to calm him. "Frederick, I trust you will escort Mr. Ping home safely. I tried to tell him about church on Sunday but I'm not sure he can understand me."

"Yes, Reverend Riley, I make sure he attend." Lee patted Poy's shoulder. "I take him home now."

"Be careful out there," Reverend Riley said as he turned away.

The men left Duckworth Street and headed on to New Gower.

"What are you doing back there?" Lee said. "Your suit's all dirty now. What do you think, we can do whatever we want here? No, you have to walk fast and keep up with me."

"Where did you go?" Poy said, angry. "I can't understand anything, I don't know where I am, I need you—"

"Oh, you need me? I had no one when I arrived here. You're lucky I even came down to meet you. You know how hard it was to get time off to come meet you? Now we waste all this time here and you're dirty."

"What do you mean, get time off work? You own the laundry—you don't have to work."

They stopped outside a building on the corner with a sign over its door that read FONG-LEE LAUNDRY.

"I don't own the laundry anymore," Lee said.

Poy was silent for a moment. "What do you mean?"

"Well, I used to own the laundry. I've been here a long time, you know, fifteen years. But, you know, there's not much to do here. Not too many places to go. On Sundays we go to church and then we hang out in the back of the Tai Mei Club. You know how it is, a few smokes, a few drinks, some chatting. Then everyone plays mahjong and you bet some money. And I lost some money doing that is all, but I'll win again soon. My lucky nephew is here now. You'll help me win!" Lee said that with a big smile but his eyes looked sad.

"No, I'm not helping you play mahjong. When do you go back home?"

"Well, you see, like I was saying, I lost a lot of money at the Tai Mei Club. I'll win it all back. That's how mahjong works. You win, you lose, you win again."

"When do you go back home?"

"I . . . I don't have the money to go back home."

"What?"

"I was on this winning streak. I could feel it in my bones, I felt like everything was coming together, I just knew that if I bet a little more, I could win double that amount. And double *that* amount. And double *that* amount. And we were playing for hours. And then I picked up a bad piece and . . . I lost some money. Then I lost a little more money. Then I lost a little more. And more. And then next thing I knew, I was betting the laundry on it. Well, not the laundry, but everything I use to pay for the laundry, you know, the money for the wages, the money for the supplies."

Poy found himself speechless once again.

"We'll get it back, though," he said. "We'll get it all back. You're here now and the way everything happened, it was very lucky. It is such a great sign that you came right when I needed you here."

Poy felt a heat rising from his stomach into his chest. He couldn't tell if he wanted to scream or cry or hit his uncle in the face. "What do you mean?" he said again, unable to formulate any sense beyond disbelief.

"I sent a wire out to my business partner and he bought me out for three hundred dollars. Three hundred dollars! Just enough to pay for you to be here, the exact amount! That's how I know you're my lucky charm. We're going to win it all back."

"What?" Poy said.

"We'll win enough to send me back to China and for you to pay me back. Then you'll do my job here for a year and then we switch."

"Your job managing the laundry?"

"No, no, I don't manage the laundry anymore. I clean the clothes now with everyone else. But we're gonna change that, me and you!"

"So that's what you'll have me do? Work in the laundry with everyone else?"

"Well, yeah! Just for a year."

"You're supposed to go back for a year! Now you're not going anywhere!"

"Poy, the plan is simple. We play mahjong, we get the money. Simple as that."

"Who manages the laundry now?"

"Nobody yet. My partner, he's coming back to select a new manager."

"Coming from where?"

"Jamaica. He'll be here in a few months. He's a very wealthy man. If we haven't won the money by the time he returns, I'm sure he'll loan me the money to go home."

Poy dropped his suitcase and put his head in his hands. For a second he recoiled, remembering what Shaowei had said about hands and faces. But he couldn't help himself. He wanted to cry. "How much are we getting paid?" he forced out.

"Oh, about a dollar a day," Lee said.

It would take years to save up enough money to send Lee back to China.

"Hey," Lee said. "You know, if you have any money now, you can give it to me to help me get out of here."

"Just take me to where we're living," Poy said, struggling to hold back tears.

"Okay. I'll have to go back to work for a little bit after. You can start working tomorrow."

Lee led Poy around back of the laundry building and they went in through the back door and down a small hallway. Poy could see some tubs down at the end. It was hot and humid in there, reminding Poy of home, and it was noisy too, reminding him of being on the ships. Lee opened a door into a little room that had a long table in the middle with ten chairs.

"You can put your bag under the table. I made sure there was a chair next to mine for you to take."

"I'll put my suitcase in our room," Poy said.

"This is our room."

"I mean the room for sleeping."

"This is that room."

Poy looked around. There were no beds.

Lee pulled out two chairs. "Okay, so this is my chair where I sleep every night. And then this chair," he said, tapping the one next to his, "this can be your chair to sleep on."

"I . . . I don't understand."

"Like this," Lee said. He flipped the chair around and sat in it in such a way that the front of his body leaned against the back of the chair. "I find this to be the most comfortable position to sleep. I lean over when I sleep so I put the back like this so I don't keep waking up."

"You can't be serious," Poy said.

"You're lucky we have two extra chairs for you and the other new guy. There's not much time for sleeping anyway, but this is the way I do it when I can get an hour or two here and there."

"Even when you were manager?" Poy said.

"Yes, yes, it's not so bad," Lee said with his eyes closed, waving his hands as if to dismiss Poy's concerns.

Poy sat heavily in the chair.

"It's a long trip, hey?" Lee said.

"It's not over yet," Poy said, already slumped over the back of the chair. "The trip won't be over until next year when I go home."

"Perhaps that should be more of a floating timeline. Really, it's a year from whenever I leave, right? So we have to get my money first!"

Poy slumped over onto the table and held his head in his hands.

"I thought management would have a better sleeping arrangement than this." Shaowei stood in the doorway.

"Humph," Poy said, head down in despair. "I'm not the manager."

"What is happening? Why are you down here, leaning on the table like this?"

"This is my bed," Poy said. "This is *the* bed."

"Good ol' iron bed. That's what they call these, y'know."

"I'm going to sleep," Poy said, his head hidden in his crossed arms.

"You're not the manager?" Shaowei said, with a smile unseen by Poy but heard in his voice.

"I don't want to talk about it."

12

LAUNDRY DAY(S)

"We made the news." Shaowei held a newspaper up to Poy's face. "Headline on our first day here. We're doing good."

It was around seven in the morning, and the workday would soon begin. But for now the ten laundrymen of Fong-Lee Laundry were rustling awake from their iron bed. Shaowei was holding the paper close to his eyes and reading the words aloud, slowing down occasionally to sound something out.

"It reads: 'Fifty Chinamen Arrive.' Was there really that many of us? 'By the express this morning fifty Chinamen arrived. There must now be nearly hundred and eighty of the celestials in the colony.' Huh."

"What else?" Poy asked.

"It says . . . they're worried there'll soon be thousands of us and, quote, 'soon they will be invading other domains of labour.' Blah-blah-blah 'the experience in every Christian country is that Chinese immigration is not only undesirable but positively injurious.'"

"What does that mean?"

"In-jur-i-ous. Not sure. Sounds bad."

"It's always the way," Poy said.

Shaowei let loose a quick smile. "It also says, 'We should be up and doing and keep them out before it's too late.' Too late for what? I'm just here to wash their clothes. So stupid."

A bell rang somewhere in the building.

"All right, boys," Lee said. "It's eight a.m., time to start working."

"Oh, Lee," Poy said as he stood up. "I was wondering, where do I go to send a letter back home? I know that Hua Ling will be waiting to hear—"

Everyone burst into laughter.

"Good one, Poy," Lee said. "Now get dressed."

"No, really," Poy said. "Where is the post office?"

"Oh," Lee said. "You're not kidding."

"He's not really one for jokes," Shaowei added.

"There is no way to send a letter home," Lee said.

"What?"

"Didn't you ever wonder why you got so few letters from me?"

"Yes, but we got *some* letters from you."

"There's one way to send a letter home," Lee said. "You give it to someone who's going back to China and hope that they deliver it for you."

"You can't be serious," Poy said. The West was making him much more incredulous than he'd expected.

"Who knows if they'll even survive another trip on those coffin ships," Shaowei said under his breath.

"Now, the two of you stop lallygagging and get to work," Lee said. "You've got a long day ahead of you."

Poy put on a fresh suit from his suitcase and he and Shaowei went to join Lee in the main laundry room.

Lee raised an eyebrow. "Poy, don't you have more appropriate clothes?"

"A suit is always appropriate," Poy said with a smile. "You gotta keep it gentleman."

"You can keep it gentleman on Sundays, but on the other days I expect you to be able to work."

Two big windows at the front of the laundry, looking out onto the street, let natural light flood in, rendering the other half of the room dark with passing shadows. Two huge sinks dominated the room, tubs, really, easily six feet long and three feet deep and wide. Their surfaces were ragged and rough, with some pointy edges looking like they could cut a man if he wasn't careful.

"The one on the left is for washing," Lee said, "the one on the right is for rinsing. I don't have time to introduce you to everyone, maybe later tonight."

There were seven other men on staff, and some of them stood over the tubs while others knelt, but they all worked these tubs together. Some washed, some rinsed, and every so often they would switch positions. The men didn't say much to each other, sometimes stopping to analyze some mysterious stain, strategizing the best way to remove it with the limited equipment they had. They mostly looked like hardened men, prematurely aged.

Poy noticed their hands right away. They looked almost as rough as the edges of the tubs, the skin dried out and peeling, layers upon layers exposed, knuckles raw. Poy's hands, even after weeks of travelling, were still pristine and smooth, the uncallused hands of a teacher.

"Step up to the tub," Lee explained. "Pull up your sleeves. Lather, douse, scrub."

Shaowei shook his head as he peeled off his white leather gloves. He let out a heavy exhale and dipped his clean hands into the sudsy water. He knew what he was doing, but he hated having to touch the dirty laundry.

Poy set to work too, but Lee's instructions were not nearly detailed enough. So he copied Shaowei's movements as his friend washed the various garments that would get dumped into the large sinks. Poy at first hesitated in putting his hands in the water, working gingerly with the garments in an effort to keep the cuffs of his suit jacket dry. It only took a few minutes for him to realize this wasn't going to work. He took his jacket off, undid his cuff-links, and rolled up his sleeves before sticking his hands back in the bath.

The youngest man on staff had a different job. He wasn't a man, not just because of his age, but also because of his circumstance. He was a child like Wong, really, no older than eleven, Poy guessed, and from time to time he would come through the front door of the laundry carrying large blue bags filled to the brim with dirty clothes, bags almost as tall as the child himself. Lee would take the bags from the child, weigh them, count and list the contents, and then sort everything, first by colour, then by fabric. Silks and rayons, cottons and linens, and woollens all separated and re-bagged together.

After one load had been moved out of washing and into rinsing, Lee would dump one of these sorted bags of unwashed garments into the sink, tablecloths clanging at the bottom of the tub, forgotten silverware wrapped up in the stained white sheets. Sometimes Lee threw items in one by one, sheets of sheer linen and thick silk and fine flannel that lost their folds as they sank into the soapy suds. The heap of laundry would grow larger and larger throughout the day—shirts with stripes and scrolls and plaids in coral and apple green and lavender and faint orange, with monograms of Indian blue. Dresses, gowns, tights, collars, ties, sullied handkerchiefs, holey socks, shit-stained underwear, grass-stained trousers, yellowed bedsheets, white undershirts stained dark red, maybe with wine, maybe by exposed veins, all of this dumped into the sinks in an endless stream to be laundered.

Hours passed by and Poy's arms began to tire, all the scrubbing against the rough edges, all the harsh soap drying out his skin. His trousers were soaked from the constantly splashing water from the tub, soaked in such a way that he looked like he'd pissed himself. He took a break to wipe sweat from his brow. He noticed how much water there was all over the floor, so that the room resembled a sinking boat. Most of his colleagues were wearing hip boots under their traditional flowing garments of the East.

"How much longer?" he asked Shaowei.

"Several years, I figure," Shaowei said, furiously scrubbing the bottom of a pair of denim pants, stained brown from mud, manure, or self-defecation, or perhaps some mix of the three.

"No, I mean, what time do we get off for the day?" Poy said.

"It's noon right now," Lee interrupted. "We take a break for supper when the washing and rinsing is complete for the day."

"What time will that be?" Poy asked.

"Around two, usually," Lee said.

"So two more hours," Poy said, turning around to look out the windows to the street.

"No, two a.m. So around fourteen hours from now we can take a little break. The work won't be over, but we can take a breather, eat a little snack, then get back to work."

Outside, to Poy's surprise, was a small audience of white people, children mostly, but a pair of young couples stood gazing inside too.

Lee noticed Poy looking at them. "Oh, there's always an audience. We actually put in larger windows so that more people could watch. You should see it in the nighttime. There'll be dozens of them out there. I swear sometimes there's hundreds of them."

"Why do they watch?"

"It's entertaining to them, they enjoy it. We do more business when they can see us. They want to see us washing their shirts and shitty underwear. Now get back to work or you'll draw their anger."

Poy returned to the tub but his arms were still tired and he wanted more of a break.

"Can I use the washroom?" he asked Lee.

"Go ahead," Lee said. "You don't need to ask me."

"Okay. Where is it?"

"Oh, right," Lee said. "Just go out the back door."

Poy walked to the back of the laundry and out the back door. There wasn't much out there, a gravel-filled alley between the laundry and the house next door, and a very small patch of shoddy, downtrodden grass. Poy couldn't see an outhouse, so he went back inside.

"I don't see a washroom out there," he said to Lee.

"Just go on the ground or wherever. Don't shit near my garden, though. And be careful of the fire alarm back there too."

Poy returned to the backyard, but found himself too uncomfortable to pee like that, right outside the door on a bright day. It was nice to get some fresh air, but he shuddered in the chill breeze. The small patch of green grass must, he thought, be Lee's garden. The garden was mostly uprooted, grass toppled, soil spilt everywhere, flowers torn to shreds. Carrots and turnips had been pulled up and repeatedly stomped on, leaving liquidy nubs of orange and white in the shape of boot prints around the garden.

Poy went back inside. "Uncle Lee, your garden!"

"What?" Lee said.

"Somebody smashed all your vegetables!"

"Meh," Lee said, "that happens pretty often. I'm used to it. The vandals won't steal the vegetables because we're Chinese."

"What?"

"I guess they think we make the food dirty. Funny, huh? Now get back to cleaning their clothes."

Poy returned to the tub alongside Shaowei, who whispered, "It's always the way." And so the men worked, washing and rinsing, washing and rinsing, garments and fabrics all blending together underneath the oily film on the water. Different fabrics requiring different water temperatures, different stains requiring different solvents and detergents. An infinite series of suds and clothes, until each and every blue bag was left hollow and empty on the floor.

It went like this for fourteen more hours. Day turned to night and there was no break, no respite from the labour. Poy couldn't believe it, he could barely stay awake, barely even move his arms. His back ached, his knees ached. It was as if, in the course of one day's work, he had aged twenty years. And all the while, a chorus of locals would pass by the windows and stare and point, even into the late hours of the night.

"I can't do this much longer," Poy said.

"Don't worry," Lee said. "It's suppertime."

Supper consisted of a bone marrow stew with a few pieces of carrot and turnip served over a tepid bed of rice. There wasn't much of it to go around, and it reminded Poy of steerage. They ate at the long table that also served as their bed. They ate in silence.

"All right, let's get back to work," Lee said.

He led Shaowei and Poy into a different room this time, attached to the main laundry room but with no window for onlookers. The first thing Poy noticed was the intense heat and humidity; beads of sweat on his brow doubling, Poy felt as if he was on fire. It was hotter than anywhere he'd ever been. The room had a pot-belly coal stove, and dozens of criss-crossing clotheslines. All the clothes they had been washing all day were hung on the lines. The bright flames of the coals illuminated the room with a hellish orange light, casting imposing shadows on the dripping laundry and surrounding walls. A scent of stew hung in the air, and Poy realized that this must be where their meal had been cooked. There were a dozen cast-iron irons resting on either side of the pot-belly stove, and each of the men donned a mitt and picked one up, the irons glowing an orange hue nearly as bright as the coals themselves, and got to work, picking out dry garments and ironing them into the crisp shapes that their customers desired.

After ironing everything else, it was time to move on to the collars and cuffs. Hundreds of collars were to be starched and ironed. First they had to be soaked in small vats of starch and then ironed and pressed into their intended shapes. The cloudy liquid in the starch vats reminded Poy of rinsing rice. Then, once everything was ironed and starched, it was time to fold the customers' orders into brown paper packages and secure them with twine.

Poy felt out of sorts, as if he had been awake for weeks. He found himself without thoughts, his movements slow and mechanical, trying to take in all the new skills he had to learn but finding it hard to focus.

As soon as the last package was wrapped, Lee said, "You're done for the day, boys. You can rest."

When Poy emerged from the ironing room, he was surprised to see the washing room bright with natural light. "What time is it?" he asked.

"Around six," Lee said. "Now get to bed. We have to start again in two hours."

The entire staff stumbled into the bedroom, found their chairs, and slumped over onto their iron bed. Every muscle in Poy's body ached, he had a pounding headache, and he felt nauseated. He slumped onto the table and fell into an uneasy slumber, dreaming about the onlookers in the windows, youngsters laughing and pointing with their mouths agape, lovers gazing at their new garments being put through the rinse tub.

Poy mumbled, through fraught dreams, half-asleep, half-dead, "I used to gaze."

13

ONE GREAT FURNACE FLAMED, YET FROM THOSE FLAMES, DARKNESS VISIBLE

The next day, every muscle was sore. Poy felt it every way he moved. The tightness in his forearms, in his biceps, his triceps. He could feel it in his legs, the way they had strained to support him for so long. He could feel it in his ass, in his knees. His hands were dried and already scabbing, his wrists and forearms slightly discoloured. He felt disoriented. He was exhausted and dehydrated. And although Shaowei was more accustomed to this type of labour than Poy, even he was bushed, his gift of gab seemingly washed and ironed out the day before.

The bell rang once again and Poy put on another suit from his luggage. He didn't have the robes the others had, for he hadn't lived a life like theirs in years. His legs struggled to support him, but after a few wobbly minutes, his staggered steps steadied and he walked out the back door. A heavy rain was coming down, and in his exhaustion he felt it was easy to piss here like this, yellow liquid mixing with rainwater, streaming through the gravel like an illicit river.

Poy walked back into the laundry and headed to the washing room. Lee stopped him.

"Now, Poy, I know you're new here, but that bell doesn't mean it's time to wake. That bell means it's time to start working. I'll let it go for today, but starting tomorrow, you must be ready to work when that bell rings."

Poy stood at the laundry tub, waiting for the water to reach the right temperature, waiting for Lee to dump the first sorted load so that they could start working. In a strange way, Poy felt the same as when he used to go out for drinks with his teacher friends, as if time was dilated and there was a heaviness in his head that made him want to sleep. Except when he was with his friends, it had the effect of making him cheerful, of wanting to laugh. Now it just made him want to lie down and stay there.

And so the day proceeded as it had the day before. Wash, rinse, dry. An audience still gathered at the windows despite the heavy rains. Poy imagined that the rain was coming from the sink, but struggled to put together the physics of such a notion.

It must have been around six, after ten hours of working, that Poy mustered the strength to say to Shaowei, "I want to give up."

"You can't," Shaowei said. "There's nowhere else to go."

And rather than argue with him or try to come up with an idea as to why he was wrong, Poy began to cry. There was no sobbing, no theatrics. Just simple droplets rolling down his cheeks, falling into the sink, mixing with suds and solvents. Washing the laundry with his tears.

"They're such beautiful shirts," he said, his voice muffled by the splashing of the laundry. "It makes me sad because I've never seen such—such beautiful shirts."

Later, after supper—another stew, fewer vegetables than the day before, a trend he predicted would continue—when Poy was back in the ironing room, surrounded by the heat of the pot-belly stove, wielding the fiery-hot iron, he wondered if they had reached the end of the universe, if out there, beyond the narrows of the harbour, was the edge of the earth and that if he took a boat out there, maybe he would fall right off the edge. It was a passing thought.

But it didn't pass fast enough, as while he was imagining this, he lost focus on the ironing for a moment and rubbed the iron past the edge of his thumb.

Poy yelped in pain, clattering the hot iron to the floor—*clang*—and puddles of water under the drip-drying clothes sizzled and scattered. Tears once again formed under Poy's eyes, and he was in so much pain that he was momentarily rendered silent: his mouth formed the shape of a scream, but no sound, no voice.

Lee smacked him on the shoulder. "Welcome to the club. You're broken in now."

Lee told Poy to submerge his hand in a vat of starch. At first the pain disappeared, but soon enough it came roaring back, and another dip in the starchy liquid was no longer any help.

"It could've been worse," Lee reassured him.

There were no more passing thoughts in the ironing room after this.

The next day Poy went back to work, his burn stinging in the soapy water but the pain forgotten as the hours toiled on. Wash and rinse, wash and rinse, iron, iron, starch, starch, fold, wrap, sleep.

This is how the week went.

Until one morning, the work bell didn't ring. The men slept past eight. They slept until there was a knock on their back door.

Reverend Riley knocked three times before just opening the door, his tall frame contrasted with so many Chinamen sleeping at the table.

"Good morrow, lads, you know what day it is," he said with glee. "Come on, everyone get ready, put on your best clothes. I'm gathering everyone up. I'll be back in a half-hour."

"You can take a bath in the sinks," Lee told Shaowei and Poy. "We do two baths at a time, one in each sink so it doesn't take all day." Thankfully, the blinds were closed.

A bath in the rough, ragged sinks was not pleasant, but the water was hot and it was a bath all the same. Poy and Shaowei both found themselves dozing off in the sinks—this being their first opportunity to bathe since they set sail in Hong Kong over a month before, as well as a rare, opportune moment to lie down and get away with it. However, their time in the tubs didn't last long before another pair of men came in and demanded their turn.

All of the suits Poy had brought with him were dishevelled by now, but he picked the cleanest one he had and put it on and went outside to wait for Reverend Riley to return.

"Mr. Ping," Riley called out as he walked up the narrow gravel path between the laundry and the neighbouring home. "It seems that you're settling in well."

Poy couldn't understand, but he recognized "Mr. Ping," He smiled and nodded in response.

Trailing behind the reverend was a group of Chinese men that he had gathered from the other laundries and restaurants. Poy could see Gao in the crowd and threw up a hand to grab his attention. It was nice to see a familiar face, even though it had only been a few days.

"Poy!" Gao called out, rushing to the front of the crowd to greet his friend. Wong followed close behind him.

"Gao! I almost forgot you lived here too," Poy said with a smile.

"How's managing the laundry going?" Gao asked him.

"We'll talk about that later," Poy said. "How's working for your uncle Charlie?"

"It's good, it's good. Very busy the past few days."

"Do they let you serve food to white people?" Shaowei said as he joined the group.

"They don't know we work there," Gao said. "We stay in the back cooking, and white waitresses take the food out to them."

"Ahh," Poy said.

"You should see some of these waitresses. They're nothing like the girls back home."

"I've got a girl back home, Gao."

Gao nodded. "Uncle was telling me that after Sunday school, there'll be white women to teach us English."

"What'd I tell you ?" Shaowei said. "I told you they'll try to push Jesus stuff on us."

"Oh, is that what this is about?" Poy asked.

"Yes, that's what this is about," Shaowei said. "And you remember what I told you, right? Smile and nod and agree with them and they'll like you better for it."

Gao chuckled. "I'll believe anything if it means we get introduced to some of the girls."

"You don't even know English," Shaowei told him. "You think you're gonna marry one of the girls when you can't even talk to them?"

"A boy can dream," Gao said as the reverend's Chinese recruits began following him on a parade through the city.

They walked down to Duckworth Street to retrieve some more Chinese, and Poy once again caught a glimpse of his own reflection in the window showcasing a model kitchen. Wong lagged behind with him.

"How's work?" Poy asked him.

"It's good. I'm a bundle boy for the Kam Laundry."

"That's a perfect job for a boy like you."

"I'm not a boy," Wong said. "I'm a grown man like you."

"Ahh, yes, that's right. My apologies."

"I work just the same as you."

"Let's see your hands," Poy said.

Wong held them up. Small, and unblemished except for some blisters at the bases of his fingers. Stubby, underdeveloped fingers, the hands of a child.

"Look at mine," Poy said. The skin on all his knuckles had dried to the point that they were frequently bleeding, and the burn on his thumb had become swollen, blackened, and bruised. Wong raised his eyebrows. "Stay a bundle *boy* for as long as you can," Poy said.

It was a short walk. Riley led them down Holdsworth Street and around the corner and Poy spotted the familiar narrow passage in the harbour and he felt a twinge of hot pain on his thumb. The street reeked of hops and yeast. Bums were sitting along the sidewalks and horse-drawn carriages were unloading kegs into burly white arms.

"This is George Street," someone in the crowd said. "Nothing but taverns and junk shops and mechanics. Save for the church."

A large white church overlooking a street of untold sins, something that seemed strange but was just good city planning. Of course the place where sins shall be forgiven should be situated near the place where sins shall be committed. Reverend Riley led them into George Street United Church and gestured to the men to fill up the pews at the back of the church. Poy sat sandwiched between Wong and Shaowei.

Numerous white people occupied the rows in front of them, and Poy could have sworn he'd washed some of the clothes they were wearing. The men all wore suits like him, with starched collars and cufflinked wrists. The women wore nice dresses and extravagant hats. The whites occasionally looked back from their seats with disdainful glances at the Chinamen. Children especially loved to look at them, Poy noted.

The reverend stood at the front of the room and read from a book. Poy didn't know what he was saying, but it seemed cheerful overall. Shaowei at first wouldn't translate any of it for him—"It's just Jesus stuff"—but towards the end, he translated when what was being said seemed relevant to him.

"He talks about how we were in the newspaper," Shaowei said. "He says something about loving a stranger because we were all once strangers in Egypt."

"I've never been to Egypt," Poy said.

After the service, Reverend Riley came back to their pews and told them to wait. When most of the white people had left and only a few of the women remained, the reverend instructed the men to follow him down into the church's gymnasium. A few tables and chairs were strewn around the gym, and cobwebs had formed between the basketball nets and their backboards. A couple of small windows near the ceiling let in streams of light like portholes. The women who had remained upstairs followed them into the gym.

"I was right," Gao said, excited.

The Chinese men gathered on one side of the gym, the women on the other.

The priest stood in the centre, looking almost like a referee, and addressed the men. "Those of you who come here weekly, you know what to do—find your buddy. For those of you who are new, I'll pair you up with one of these women who have generously donated their time to help you learn English. Those of you that can understand me, please translate for the others."

Riley paired up the men one by one until only Poy was left.

"Geez, I'm sorry, Mr. Ping. I guess I didn't get as many volunteers as I needed. Not to worry, I will be your language buddy. I'm sure you'll have lots to teach me too. I love foreign perspectives. They're so . . . enlightening."

"It alway the way," Poy said with a smile and a nod, painfully aware that there was no woman for him.

"Oh, that's right, that's your one phrase. Let me get a language book for us."

Just as Riley walked towards one of the tables, there was a loud clatter on the stairs and a slam of a door somewhere in the distance. A woman came into the gymnasium, sunglasses on. She looked younger than Poy, maybe in her late teens, and she had a bony figure with messy, curly hair. Something seemed off about her, ragged like the laundry's sinks, and yet she moved with a precision and a confidence that called attention to her.

"Oh, Ethel, good," Reverend Riley said. "I thought I hadn't gathered enough volunteers. This is—"

"I knows, b'y, I was out for a smoke," Ethel said.

She spoke very fast, and it reminded Poy of the way some women spoke back home, breathless and abrasive.

"This is Mr. Ping. Uh... I seem to have forgotten the front half of his name but you can establish that, no doubt. Mr. Ping, this is Ethel Squibb." The priest said the last few words with a slow determination and excess volume, as if being louder would help Poy understand. "*Eth-el. Squibb.* This is your language buddy, okay?"

Poy nodded and smiled.

"Now, Ethel, you know my thoughts on smoking—"

"What? You think you can tell me where I can have a jesus smoke now too?"

"Ethel, please don't take the Lord's name in vain in here," Riley said. "Or anywhere, for that matter."

"In here? In the gymnasium? What, did the Fadder, the Son, and the Holy Ghost have a game of free throw in here?"

"Always a delight, Ethel. I'll let you two get to it."

Poy smiled and nodded at Ethel repeatedly.

"Oh, Jesus, I didn't know what I was signing up for," she said, looking around as if to see if there was anybody she knew. "What do you know in English?" she asked Poy.

Poy smiled and nodded.

"All right, you're a difficult one now, aren't ya? Tell me what's your name."

Poy smiled.

"Name. Name. Jesus, b'y, whaddya wanna be called?"

Poy felt intimidated by the harshness of her tone, but there was something about her that was radiant, her brusqueness somehow charismatic. At least she wasn't flinging mud at him.

"Ethel," she said as she pointed at herself. "Ethel. My name is Ethel." She pointed at him. "Your name?"

"Oh!" Poy pulled his immigration paper from his breast pocket.

"What, ya expect me to read now too, Jesus Christ tonight," she said. She took the paper. "William Set-oh, See-tow, Ping. Huh. William Ping. William See-tow Ping."

Poy smiled and nodded. "Wheel eee yam."

"That's a good name," Ethel said. "There's a ring to it."

Poy nodded.

"Let's look through this frickin' book," Ethel said. It was an oversized book, and inside were pictures of various objects and faces expressing emotions, with the essential words one would need throughout a day. The first picture was of a toilet.

"S'pose you knows what that is?" she asked him.

Poy smiled. Back home, there weren't toilets like this, more like holes in the ground, but he knew the Western toilet well by now.

"Toi-let," Ethel said, pointing at the picture. "That's where ya go when you need to take a shit. Take a shit, y'know. Toilet."

"Toi-let," Poy repeated.

"All right, let's see what small wonders the next page holds."

Ethel turned the page. The picture depicted a plate of food, a steak or a pork chop next to some vegetables. "Food," she said. "That's the stuff you shit out. Food."

"Food," Poy repeated.

They went on for a while, and covered a lot of pages, from "car" and "bathtub" to "happy" and "sad." Poy began to understand Gao's giddy anticipation of the "white" women. Although the "white" part held little importance for Poy, he understood that there was a certain excitement in talking to these women, a nervous titillation to even just sitting near a female after so many weeks of being surrounded by men. He was attracted to Ethel in a sense, but really his desire still lay at home with his wife.

After about an hour, Reverend Riley stood in the centre of the gym and announced that the language session was done for the week. He stood by the door and thanked each woman as she left and shook hands with all the men. When Poy was leaving, Riley said to him, "I'm sorry for that mix-up back there and I know Ethel can be a little, well, abrasive. I'd like to make it up to you. My wife is making a nice turkey dinner for lunch today, the best Newfoundland has to offer, and we'd be honoured if you and maybe a couple of your friends would come by the house and partake."

Poy stared at him blankly, and Riley said, "Oh, right, darn."

Shaowei, in line behind Poy, said, "I translate for him."

"Ah, do you know each other well?"

"We together for weeks," Shaowei said. "Feel like I know him whole life."

"All right. I was just inviting Mr. Ping, and yourself too of course, to my house for a nice little dinner, with all the local favourites. Could you tell him that? You boys can come with me now, if you like."

His house was only a short way from the church. It was a fresh spring day, a stiff breeze but the sun was shining bright. Children in paperboy hats played nearby, and the occasional car passed them on the road, outnumbered by the rampant horse-drawn wagons and roaming farm animals.

"How are you boys finding St. John's?" Riley asked on the short walk. "A lot to get used to or what?"

"Always the way," Shaowei said.

"I'm sure everything here is a world of difference from where you're from, but if I were to characterize St. John's for you new-comers, I would say it's like New York if the guys who settled it made all the wrong choices. I love it here, though. It was God's will for me to spread the good news on this rock."

"Okay," Shaowei said.

Riley lived in a tall, but thin, house. The covered porch smelled of must, as if the windows and doors were rarely open, and Poy was surprised by the numerous pairs of shoes in the doorway.

"Pa, is that you?" the voice of a small girl called out from within the bellows of the house. It was dark indoors, with a narrow stair-well beside an even more narrow hallway. Poy was certain he caught a mysterious thump echoing down the stairway, but the reverend led the men directly into a living room. There was nothing in it except a loveseat and one ornamental sofa chair with a high-arched back, and an organ pushed up against a wall next to the fireplace. There were no decorations.

"You boys can take a seat there," Riley said, and the men squished together on the tiny loveseat, looking at Riley as he settled into his sofa chair.

A little girl ran into the room. Her hair was in pigtails, and Poy recognized her right away as one of the children who was sitting near the front in church. She seemed unsurprised that her father had brought guests home.

"Pa, Mom says dinner is almost ready. Where have you been?"

"Why, you know my routine, darling. I was helping these gentlemen learn English. Fellas, meet my daughter, Addie."

Addie quickly waved at them and then turned back to her father. "Pa, can I go upstairs and play with the—"

"Oh, hush about that now. I don't want you near that thing. Let our guests introduce themselves."

The two men sat uncomfortably on the loveseat, their arms and legs cramped together.

"My name is Shaowei Zhang," Shaowei said, before turning to Poy and saying in Taishanese, "Tell her your name."

"My name William Seto Ping," Poy said.

"Why do *you* got a name like our people but *you* don't?" Addie asked.

"Oh, now, don't go asking about their names, it ain't polite," Riley said. "Why don't you go play a song on that there organ for the men to enjoy while we wait for lunch?"

Addie hopped up on the organ's stool and played a couple of notes, awkward, strange sounds, as she found her footing with the instrument. Then she began to play something soft and slow, or as soft as the droning of an organ can allow.

"What a fellowship, what a joy divine," she sang as loud as she could, but her voice wasn't yet quite strong enough to be heard above the organ. "Leaning on the everlasting arms."

While the girl sang, Poy heard again a slow, intermittent thump through the ceiling. His eyes focused on the corner nearest to the sound. He thought it sounded like a wet thump, but he couldn't be certain.

Riley was smiling proudly, gently tapping his hand on his knee in beat to the music. And Poy smiled at the kindness he felt in this house. The only thing that gave him pause was the strange thump from upstairs. Birds in the attic, he thought.

As Addie was singing, a short, plump woman came into the room. She wore an apron over a light pink dress—Poy wondered if he had washed it this week—and she too tapped her hand on her waist in time to the beat until the last note on the organ had been struck.

"Well!" the woman said. "The talent in this house, my goodness! Dinner's ready, my duckies. Moses, I see you've brought some wonderful guests. I hope you b'ys like Jiggs!"

"That's my wife, Martha," Riley said.

"That's me husband, Moses," Martha said.

Moses led the way down the narrow hallway, and the men passed by several dusty oil paintings of previous reverends culminating in Reverend Moses Riley himself. The dinner table was in the kitchen, mere feet away from the stove. The table itself was small, with several plates crowding the tabletop, but there was still room enough for everyone.

"I'll do the honours of slicing the turkey," said Riley, "but first we'll say grace. O Father . . ."

Riley droned on, flailing his hands, sometimes manically, other times affecting a solemn air, while Poy surveyed the plates in front of him. So many things he had never seen before. The bowl nearest to him was filled with an unremarkable yellow mash, as though someone had smashed something into shaggy little chunks. The next bowl contained a white mash of similar consistency. The next bowl was familiar, carrots and chunks of cabbage, though they looked dull and wilted. Next to that was a plate of pale, rotund *something*, looking almost like a giant steamed bun, beige and porous except for punctuations of berries, their blue colour bleeding through the doughy canvas. And then a plate with chunks of dry beef, shining blood red, like an entirely raw tendon, a paradox. And then in the middle of the table was the fattest bird Poy had ever seen.

When Riley had finished his little speech, they were free to eat. Riley helped serve the men and instructed them on how best to eat this vaunted cuisine. "Have some carrots," he said, before gesturing to a Mason jar filled with small green chunks swimming in a yellow liquid. "You'll want to take some of these mustard pickles too, and some of these pickled beets." He brandished another jar, and Poy looked at the small red chunks floating in a purple liquid.

Poy and Shaowei ate gingerly. This was the first time in weeks, maybe months, that they had eaten, or even been party to, a meal of this size, and their stomachs had shrunk to accommodate the small rations they usually received. To make matters worse, this food was so weird. Poy was puzzled by the meat of the bird. Flavourless, dry, it was like a chicken from another planet. And these accoutrements—bizarre. Overwhelming flavours of vinegar from the jars mixed with the bland, bitter taste of vegetables that had been boiled for too long. And this thing with the blue berries in it, it tasted sweet like dessert. And this beef—why was it so salty? He wanted to spit it out. He supposed this was the type of food you ate when you lived on Gold Mountain, that your chickens grew so big they didn't taste the same anymore.

Nothing tasted the same anymore.

Shaowei had more familiarity with this type of food, having eaten turkey before at Thanksgiving celebrations in San Francisco. He preferred the dark meat to the white that Riley had cut for them. Still, neither Poy nor Shaowei could muster themselves to eat much.

"Do you b'ys like the meal?" Martha had noticed the Chinamen's small appetite. "Do they like it, Moses? Do they understand me? You understand?"

"Martha, calm down," Riley said as he shovelled another forkful of the dry turkey into his mouth.

"It's just, I'm afraid I might've overcooked the turkey, and, and, I might've boiled the vegetables too long, we were at church for a little longer—"

"Martha, enough. These men work hard and this is their one day of leisure. Let them eat leisurely."

For a little while there were just the sounds of knives and forks hitting the plates.

"Pa, can I talk to our guests?"

"Yes, Addie."

"How far away is China?"

Poy nodded and smiled, while Shaowei struggled to swallow a small piece of the salt beef.

"Oh, hush now, Addie," Riley said. "It's farther away than you can possibly imagine."

Once again, silence in the house. Poy noticed a hunting rifle mounted above the door.

Thump.

"Moses," Martha said, "why don't you get rid of that thing?" She gave a nod towards the ceiling.

Riley placed his fork on his plate. "Martha," he said. "I have told you already that the men from the museum will be here in due time to take care of that."

"It'd be nice to have a bath in peace again, is all."

"This is a cultural endeavour, Martha. I found it and I kept it so that men of science can learn from it. This is what God would have wanted."

"Well, it makes me uncomfortable having that, having that . . . *thing* in the house."

There was silence again. The plates were as cleared as they were going to be.

"You boys want to see something historic?" Riley said as he stood

up from the table. "Watch your step on the stairs. Some of the bannisters are broken, so there's nothing to grab on to if you fall."

Poy could hear a slight splashing sound on the stairway as
Reverend Riley led them upstairs. He stopped outside a door at the
top of the stairwell, placing his hand on the knob. Poy could hear
the splashy thump through the door and smelled something like
rotting seafood.

"Now, I never seen nothing like this before," Riley said. "I asked
everyone I know, 'You ever see something like this?' You know what
every single one of them said? They all said 'no, sir.' Now, some of
'em had heard stories of it before, sure, but nobody had ever seen
one. That's why I contacted the museum guys. They'll come take
care of it for me, make sure everyone can learn from it. Now, I'm
thinking you fellas on the other side of the world, now maybe this
is something you see all the time, maybe it's a daily occurrence for
you, so that's why I want you to see this. There's a bucket next to
the door if either of you need it."

Reverend Riley slowly turned the doorknob and opened the
door. Poy saw a claw-foot bathtub, surrounded by a curtain. The
light from the window made the porcelain shine like a well-basted
turkey, as well as illuminating the slow, erratic movements of something behind the curtain. It seemed a normal tub, fancy, sure, but
normal, until something flopped over the edge of the curtain. A
long, pinkish tentacle.

Shaowei and Poy cautiously approached the tub, and Riley
pulled back the curtain. Draped over an iron bar suspended six feet
above the tub was a giant squid, quite a bit larger than anything
Poy had ever seen. Falling to the bottom of the tub with a wet thud
was one of its tentacles, which were as thick as a man's thigh and
as rugged as raw cowhide, with skin the colour of the sky before
sunset. It was hard to say just how long the squid was, as its many

arms draped over and around the bar several times. Its tentacles were still flexing, attempting to suction on to the side of the tub. Its slightly deflated head almost looked as though it were attempting to breathe.

Shaowei immediately vomited. Poy merely felt uneasy looking at the thing.

"That's why the bucket is there," Riley said. "I'll take that reaction to mean that you fellas don't see these things in China either. That's just as I expected. See, I wake up one morning and I hear a knocking at my door. I open the door, expecting to see a beggar or a parishioner. Why, no! It's one of these tentacles banging on the door. I couldn't believe it, something so big. You can't tell from the way I got him wrapped around the bar, but I think he's about fifty-five feet long, just impossibly big. And this thing is on the ground outside the door and I don't know who put him there, I figure some fisherman caught it and dragged it to shore and I guess brought it to the reverend's house thinking I'd know what to do with it. Heck if I know!

"My first thought was to drag it back to the ocean, throw it in. I don't take the Lord's name in vain but if I ever were to do such a thing, it surely would have been then as I was dragging it down the road. The weight of it! By golly, I think it'd be easier to drag a train car with my bare hands. I had endeavoured to get this thing back to the water, but it was putting up a fight being dragged like that, its tentacles were sucking on to my face and grabbing out what little hair I have left. Then some of my neighbours saw me dragging it down the road and just about everyone said they had never seen anything like this before. 'No, sir, only in the stories.' So then I think to myself, what I have in my possession here is what all the savants in the world could not know, what all the museums in the world could not contain. That's when I realize what this thing *is*. It's a sign from God. Warning us of all the evils that lurk below. That's why I'm getting the scientists and the museums to take a look at it.

"Then I had to drag it back to the house. Imagine hauling that up the stairs! Took me the better part of the day, tentacles holding on to the doorway and the bannisters. The bannisters! You seen the shape they're in now. And its head was bouncing off the stairs, it was an awful shame. I thought the old thing was going to tear the whole place down, but then I got her over that there bar and now she seems all right."

Riley leaned in to the still-heaving Shaowei and whispered, "I'm waiting on a zoologist from Yale University down in the States to come up here and take a real good look at this thing."

Poy stood staring at the giant creature, with all its many arms folded around this one piece of iron stretching across the room, and he wondered where it must think it was, to live its whole life in the ocean and now to be here.

Riley grabbed the end of one of its tentacles. "Now, look here," he said. "I am shaking hands with a hitherto mythical cephalopod."

"That thing should've stayed in the ocean," Shaowei said as they walked back to the laundry.

"I completely agree," Poy said, but he felt as though they might have been thinking so for different reasons. He couldn't wait to tell Hua Ling about this one. "A giant squid," he would say to her, stretching his arms all the way out to show her the length. "Bigger than that even," he would say. And he thought he could fill out a full sheet of paper describing just Moses Riley alone.

They walked in silence down the busy commercial streets of St. John's. There wasn't anything to say and they were tired. Tired from work, tired from eating turkey, tired from life. People on the street stared at them. Some snickered, some pointed, some crossed the street to get away from them, others crossed the street to get closer to them. Shaowei was their run-of-the-mill celestial, with his long queue and strange oriental clothes. Poy stood out for a different reason. His hair was cut and coiffed like a Westerner's, and his wearing of a suit was a concept foreign to the local conception of foreigners.

Yet despite the snickering and the pointing and the staring, the two men walked freely down the roads back to the Fong-Lee Laundry, bumping into Gao and Wong on the way there.

"We thought you were already back at the laundry," Wong said.

Shaowei and Poy told them what had transpired after the English lesson, from the squawking music to the inedible dinner to the giant squid.

"I looked it right in the eye," Shaowei said. "It didn't seem that big to me."

"I looked something big in the eye today too," Gao began. "Well, not big. The thing wasn't big in size—"

"What?" Shaowei snapped. "What did you look at?"

"Her name is—" Gao sounded out the name slowly. "Bess-eee. And she's beautiful."

"And she's big?" Poy said.

"No, she's not big," Gao said. "You saw her. She's the woman I had for my lesson. She has beautiful blond curls, and her lips, they hang open ever so slightly and all I could think was—"

"That's enough," Shaowei interrupted. "Mind what you're saying around the kid."

"I already heard it all," Wong said. "Also, I'm not a kid."

"I'm gonna marry her," Gao said. "That's a promise."

"I knew a guy who married a white woman in San Francisco," Shaowei said. "They ended up running off to some other place, all because of the bullshit from white people. You think it'd be any different here?"

The four of them went on a walk through their new town, the rest of the afternoon still stretching ahead of them. There didn't seem to be any place they could go to without people staring at them—even now some were on a corner across the street gawking—so Wong, who had seen more of the town than the other three, suggested they walk to the other side of the harbour, the Southside, which appeared to be a mostly unadorned hill. They walked down by the harbour, past the train station, down around the loading docks, past the DuMont shipyard, to the other edge of the harbour. To Poy's surprise, they hadn't attracted too much attention from the locals on their walk. Sure, sometimes somebody would point and yell "Chinks!" but hell, Poy couldn't even understand what they were saying.

They reached the Southside Hills just as the sun was setting, and the sky was alight in a wondrous gradient of colours, from orange to red to a deep pink. Wong was right: there wasn't much of anything or anybody over there. A couple of wharfs, but mostly just tall grass for as far as the eye could see. The men skipped rocks across the water, then sat in the grass, idle among the tall blades.

"You know, back in San Francisco," Shaowei began, eliciting eye rolls from the other men, "there was this thing we did. Well, I wasn't a part of it, but I knew some guys who were. They'd get together every month and each of them would contribute a little bit of money to a jar. In the beginning, it was nothing, nickels and dimes, but over time the money grew. And eventually they had enough money in the jar that they had to get a bigger jar. It got to the point that they had saved enough money together that they could open a business. So one guy took the money and opened a restaurant, and then he had to pay a larger share into the jar every month."

"What is this supposed to be about?" Gao said.

"Patience, patience," Shaowei said. "So the restaurateur, he was putting in a larger amount of money, so twice as fast, they had enough money to open another business. So a different guy took that money and opened a laundry. And then he paid in a larger share. And it went like this. They were opening everything, restaurants, laundries, corner stores, jewellery stores, you name it."

"So you want us to give you our money?" Poy said in a dismissive tone. "I'm here for one year and then I'm gone. That's it. I have no interest in owning a business." He felt tired.

"You don't need to be rude," Shaowei said.

"I'm not being rude," Poy said. "I just don't want to invest in something that I don't plan on being involved in."

"But you'd be investing in us, in the Chinese community," Shaowei said, playing with a long blade of grass.

"He doesn't want to do it," Gao said.

"Do you?" Poy said to Gao.

"I'd like to hear more about it," Wong said. "Where would we get the jar?"

"There wouldn't really be a jar," Shaowei said.

"Then where would we put the money?" Wong asked.

"Do you want to do it?" Poy said again to Gao.

"Well, where would we put the money?" Gao said.

"We'd need a good hiding place, ideally away from where we work," Shaowei said.

"A bank?" Poy said.

Shaowei looked aghast. "The learned gentleman thinks we can trust banks. The whole idea is that we become our own bank."

"So we would just give you our money and you would hide it somewhere?" Gao said.

"We would all hide it together," Shaowei said, "and you

wouldn't be giving it to me, we'd all be contributing towards a shared goal. Being liberated from our jobs."

"I know a place," Wong said. "I saw these rows of lockers in the railway station and I bet we could—"

"Look," Shaowei said, "it's just an idea. It worked for some guys I knew. Just something to consider." He looked out over the harbour. "We should head back before it gets too dark," he said. They got to their feet. None of the men wanted to be wandering around town in the dark.

They reached the edge of the harbour and saw, in the distance, the outlines of moving figures approaching them. Two kids on bikes. They were moving fast.

When the kids reached them, they didn't ride past but steered in circles around them, slow circles that forced the men to stop. The two boys looked to be about fourteen, smallish but still big enough to hurt the men if given the chance. Poy could sense they were looking to cause trouble. He didn't trust their devilish grins.

"Hey, b'ys," one of them said. "Beautiful night, wha'?"

"Red sky at night," the other kid said, "sailor's delight."

"Red sky at morn," the first said, "sailor's scorn."

"White people bullshit," Shaowei mumbled in Taishanese.

"C'mon now," the first kid said. "Don't go speaking that gook shit, b'y. We're bein' nice to yas."

Poy found the children's constant circling around them to be dizzying.

"Nice suit you got dere, buddy," the second kid said.

Poy didn't respond.

"Wha' now, cat's got your tongue?"

"Buddy, what are ya, too good to talk to us, are ya?"

"Yeah, buddy, whaddya think, you're too fuckin' good for us?"

Shaowei said, "We-uh no speak-uh English."

"Oh, so you lot thinks you can come over here and not even speak like the rest of us? And buddy here thinks he can dress like us? Me fadder can't even afford a suit like that, buddy, and he's a barrel maker."

The kids dropped bikes to the ground and approached Poy.

"We-uh no speak-uh English," Shaowei said again, more deliberately and slowly this time.

"C'mon now, we're just trying to be friends with yas," one of them said. "Lemme try on that jacket."

"He no speak uh English, he no speak uh English," Shaowei repeated.

"Lemme see that jacket, buddy," the kid said, reaching out to grab Poy's lapel. Poy took a step back and Gao stepped between him and the kid.

"Get out of the way, chink," the kid said as he sidestepped around Gao. "I just wanna see the blazer, is all." The kid grabbed Poy's lapels again. Poy slapped his hand away.

"Did you just hit him?" the other kid said.

"He did! This fuckin' chinky gook thinks he's tough. You think you're so fuckin' tough, I'll show you tough, buddy." The kid punched Poy's stomach as hard as he could, winding Poy and dropping him to his knees.

Out of the corner of his eye, Poy saw Wong picking up a rock. "Wong, don't," he said.

"There he goes talking that ching-chang bing-bang shit again," the kid said.

"You think you can just walk around here in a suit? You think you can just walk around here willy-nilly? Your kind don't deserve to wear this type of clothes, you fuckin' gook." The kid grabbed one side of Poy's jacket. "Wear your chink clothes."

"Yeah, wear your dirty chink clothes," the other one said as he grabbed the other side of the jacket. The two kids pulled as hard as they could and the jacket ripped in half down the back.

Wong threw the rock and it sailed through the air, missing the kids altogether and hitting Poy square in the chest.

Shaowei picked up one of the bikes and threw it into the harbour. "Run!" he shouted. Gao threw the other kid's bike after it.

"What are you doin'!" The kid let go of Poy's torn-asunder jacket. "That's my fuckin' bike!"

Poy struggled to his feet. His feet slipped in the grass but he began to run away.

"We won't forget this!" one of the kids yelled out. "We knows where yas live, we knows your face!"

"Look at 'em run," the other one said. "Scatterin' like rats."

Poy ran as fast he could and caught up with the others.

"I'll lead the way," Wong called. He was the fastest out of all of them. "I know the roads better than you guys."

"Rats! Rat, rat, rat!" the kids yelled out.

Wong led the men around the shipping port, past the train station, back to the roads they remembered. He took them into steep alleyways with long stairwells, dark spaces like caves, and past buildings that look like Gothic castles. A frantic mix of left and right turns that caught the attention of various local drunks.

"The chinks are running!" someone called out as the men darted through the streets. Wong stopped in an alleyway off George Street, not too far from the alley they usually turned down to get to Fong-Lee.

The four of them crouched down and waited to see if they had successfully evaded the boys. A hand reached out of the darkness and gripped Poy's shoulder.

"Now," the lyrical voice said, "why is it that every time I see you, you've got some sort of predicament with your suit?"

Reverend Riley offered a gentle smile, and Poy looked down at his own body. Half of his suit jacket was still on; the other half was presumably blowing around in the wind on the Southside Hills, a hollow sleeve flapping like a wind kite.

Shaowei explained to Riley how their nice view of the sunset had become tarnished.

"Let me tell you three things you need to know," the reverend said to Shaowei. "First thing is, you never work on Sundays. Second thing is, you absolutely need to learn English as soon as possible. Once you know English, you can talk your way out of all sorts of situations. And more importantly, you can do some business. And the third thing is, and this is important, don't let people take advantage of you. Please translate this to the others."

Shaowei told his friends what the reverend had said.

"All right now, do you know what the common ground between those three rules is?" Riley said. "Going to church. Keep going to my church every Sunday and we'll get you on the right path, we'll get you speaking English in no time. And I told Mr. Ping this before but I don't think he understood me—you may meet with violence in these parts, but this is the only weapon you'll ever need." Riley brandished a pocket-sized Bible. "A lot of folks think owning a gun will protect them. A gun will not protect you. A gun is asking for trouble. This is all you need." Riley gave his Bible a thump and then placed it back in his pocket.

Shaowei translated for the others. "It's always the way," he added.

Reverend Riley promised to escort Gao and Wong back to where they lived, and Shaowei and Poy headed to the laundry.

Uncle Lee was there waiting for them.

"What the hell?" Lee said. "Where were you?"

"It's a long story," Poy said.

"Long story, my ass," Lee said. "We were supposed to win some money today, remember?"

"I completely forgot," Poy said.

"You forget your own uncle? Your own poor uncle? Look at your jacket, this is what happens when you're not there for family, when you can't even be bothered to help family."

"I was—"

"I don't want to hear your excuses," Lee said. "Too busy for your own family. Your own family who fronted you the cash to be here. Every last dollar to my name! Ridiculous. You get what you deserve. You stay with me after church from now on, stay out of trouble."

Poy rested his head on the big table. Shaowei said the kids had called them rats. Scattering rats. Poy thought of the story Shaowei had told him. The rat pushed the cat off the boat and the cat never made the zodiac. The rat won.

But it was still a rat.

14

THE MAN COMES AROUND

Life was work. That's how things proceeded for them, every day was wash and rinse, wash and rinse. Soreness turned to strength; tiredness turned to bitterness. There was never much conversation between the laundrymen beyond the topic of the laundry itself and different techniques to use for cleaning. Everyone felt the same, so there was no need to talk about their feelings, their wants, their desires. Poy cried often, and soon realized he wasn't alone. The laundry was washed in the tears of all the Chinamen.

Although Lee had never formally introduced Poy to his co-workers, he learned their names over the weeks. Hong, Kai, Gin, Yang, Jun, Qieng, and Aiguo. Hong was the oldest and was, aside from Lee, the closest thing to a leader in their presence. He was a skilled tailor, a helpful person to have on staff if you came across, or accidentally caused, a tear in some garment.

Kai was probably the second-oldest, and Hong had explained that he was "accident prone and mute." He had been a railroad worker and ended up in St. John's some years ago. No one knew why he was mute. It was just the way it was.

Gin was of a shy comportment, prone to blushing and not willing to talk freely. "He'll need some time to warm up to you," Hong told Poy.

Yang was the grumpiest of all the workers, and he regarded Poy with a mean-spirited and cold energy. He was afflicted with a condition that left him with one eye shut at all times.

Jun was unwell since he'd arrived in St. John's a few years back, constantly sneezing and coughing, seemingly having never adjusted to the vast difference in climate between his old home and his new one.

Qieng was perpetually tired, always yawning and stretching, his desire to sleep seemingly weighing down his head.

Aiguo, the bag boy, was the only one among them whom Poy could describe as happy, with a jolly air about him, always laughing and having fun somehow, despite everything. Poy figured that the boy wasn't old enough to be jaded yet.

And yet, despite each of their own personal quirks, Poy never heard much from any of them. Every day, they focused on their work, and there was rarely any extraneous conversation. The only day that was ever really differed from their schedule was Sunday.

Every Sunday morning, they would bathe in the tubs they did the laundry in, avoiding the rough edges as best they could. Then, after bath time, Reverend Riley would lead them to church, this weekly shepherding being the reverend's personal burden, his attempt to save his laundry angels from a lifetime of sitting in darkness. Then the Chinamen would learn English in the gymnasium. Ethel wasn't a great teacher and she often showed up late, but she knew how to get Poy to repeat words and within a couple of weeks, he began to retain these keywords—"toilet," "happy," "sad," "yes," "no," "thank you," "please," "stop," "English," "church," "Jesus," "Chinese". Poy enjoyed lessons with Ethel. It was nice to talk to a pretty girl. But he wouldn't think of her beyond being a teacher to him. During his lessons, he would keep Hua Ling in the front of his mind, part distraction, part motivation. Afterwards, Poy and the other Chinamen would go to the Tai Mei Club.

This began on their second Sunday. Poy and Shaowei were careful to not repeat the mistakes made on their first day of the Lord and they knew that the only way to do that was to avoid being in a vulnerable position. And the only way to be invulnerable was to avoid the general public, the white people, as best they could. The second Sunday would become a prototype for future Sundays.

The Tai Mei Club was a short walk from the church, only a couple of blocks away. They walked down George Street, passing the previous night's drunks still strewn on the street. They went up to Duckworth and then made another turn to reach the Hop Wah Laundry. Lee took them through a network of hallways: a left, a right, another left, up four stairs, down three more, deeper and deeper into the building until they entered a room with a long table, not unlike the iron bed at Fong-Lee. But instead of being a makeshift bed, the table acted as a makeshift bar, pushed against the wall, a backdrop for the hubbub of activity and noise in front of it. Chinese men were all around the room, seated around several smaller tables, smoking, spitting, sweating, occasionally yelling, and most of all gambling. A persistent clicking noise rang through the air as mahjong tiles were pushed and passed around the table in speeds heretofore unknown. Money was thrown onto tables, drinks were poured.

"Welcome to the Tai Mei Club," Uncle Lee said as he hastened to join a game.

Poy and Shaowei went over to the bar, where a very short Chinese man was standing on the table and making drinks. From a distance, they had thought he was a young child in a suit, but when they got close, they realized he was a man slightly older than them.

"Fifty cents a drink," the short man said.

"That's half what I make in a day!" Shaowei said.

"Hey, that's half what anybody makes in a day. Except here at the Tai Mei Club. You can make a hell of a lot more than a dollar here, bub."

Shaowei and Poy exchanged a look, the meaning of which was clear to neither.

"Fine, give me a drink," Shaowei said.

"You can have tea or rum," the barman said.

"I'll have the rum," Shaowei said.

"Do you have any baijiu?" Poy asked.

The barman laughed. "Not unless you brought it with you."

"I'll have a tea," Poy said.

"Okay, money first," the barman said. Shaowei slammed some coins into the barman's hand, and the barman poured a shot of rum from a bottle with no label, before turning to a teapot. "Have at her, gentlemen," he said in English.

Shaowei took a sip of the rum, then spat it out with a violent yell. "What is this shit?"

"It's what you asked for," the barman said as he put the bottle to the side. "It's rum."

"I've never had rum that tastes like this."

"Then you must be new here, bub," the barman said.

"Well, have you ever seen me before?" Shaowei asked sarcastically.

"Hey, watch your mouth, big guy. It's a privilege to be here at the Tai Mei Club."

A tall man, taller than any of the other Chinese immigrants, dressed in a dark suit came forward. The skin on his face looked as though it had been pulled taut like a skin graft, and his hairline was receding. Poy guessed he was in his mid-thirties.

179

"Hey, Little Joe," the man said. "What seems to be the problem here?"

"This lowlife is giving me a hard time about the booze and the price. And he's got a mouth on him too."

"I don't believe we've been acquainted," the tall man said. "My name is Hop Wah and I run this here establishment."

Poy and Shaowei shook hands with him and introduced themselves.

Then he said, "Were you giving my barkeep a tough time?"

"It's just this rum doesn't taste right," Shaowei said. "I used to live in California and—"

"Yeah, well, that's how they drink it around here," Hop Wah said. Little Joe passed him a glass of water. "The fishermen trade the lowest-grade fish to the Blacks and in exchange they get big casks of rum. Then the fishermen sell the casks to the rich people. Now the stuff they drink, apparently that's the good stuff. What we're drinking here, well . . . that's the swish. After the rich people finish their casks, they throw them out, or at least they used to throw them out before they got wise to what happens next. Inside those empty barrels is this sludge left over from making the rum. Street urchins fill up the barrels with water and roll them up and down the hills here, get the sludge swishing. Then they bottle it."

"What do they call it?"

"They call it rum. Trust me, you'll get used to it." Hop Wah turned back to Little Joe. "Hey, Joe, give me two dollars."

Joe handed him the money from out of an old Mason jar. Hop Wah gave one dollar bill to Shaowei and one to Poy.

"Hey, I don't want to be indebted to you—" Poy began.

"You're not indebted to me. I'm sorry for your troubles. You guys are new here, I can tell. You didn't know what you were getting yourself into. So the first round is on me. And then I gave you

180

a little extra so that you can join in on the fun and games. This is the Tai Mei Club, this is your weekly respite from all the work you have to do out there. You're here to relax. So relax!"

"I don't want to take your money," Poy said.

"You're not taking my money. As a matter of fact, I don't even know what you're talking about. If you try to give that money to me, I'll be offended, I'll have you kicked out of here! So go. Play."

Shaowei walked away from the bar and sat down at a table that was getting ready to start a game. Poy stuck by the bar.

Hop Wah nudged himself a bit closer. "Not ready to play yet?"

"I'll just have my drink first," Poy said.

"Hey, that's fair. Need to size up the room, figure out who the real players are, I get ya." Hop Wah eyed up Poy for a moment. "I notice I'm wearing a suit and you're wearing a suit and all the rest of these chinks are wearing their chink clothes. So what gives? You managing a laundry or something?"

"Heh," Poy laughed in a pained way. "No, not really. I used to be— I'm a teacher. Or I was. I'll be a teacher again when I go back."

"Oh, a teacher. Must have a big brain in there," Hop Wah said with a laugh. "Whereabouts are you headed back to?"

"Hoiping," Poy said.

"Oh my," Hop Wah said. "You must be Lee's boy. Yes, oh, yes. He's been talking about you."

"I'm his nephew," Poy added.

"He's a great guy, Lee. One of our best customers. Maybe too good of a customer. He can be quite a skilled player. At times."

"Yeah, I bet he's a great customer," Poy said. He looked across the room at Lee throwing handfuls of money onto a table.

"So, that means you're one of my employees too, I guess," Hop Wah said. "For the time being, anyway. Lee lost the laundry to me, but I hear that Fong Choy is coming up to settle the matter."

"When will he arrive?" Poy asked as he sipped his tea.

"Next couple of weeks, I figure," Hop Wah said. "Could be any day at all. He'll make an offer to buy me out. I'll accept it too. You have to respect your elders. You know he was the first Chinese person on this island?"

Poy lowered his tea. "Really?"

"The very first one. Can you imagine what that must've been like?"

"Did he know English?"

"Did he know English? Pshhhh, he knows most languages."

"Are you . . . Is this a joke?"

"I'm not kidding. He was from the same village as you, actually, and when he was a teenager he left town. Just started walking. Until one day, years later, he hit water. He was in London. London, England. The man walked right across Eurasia."

"Oh, wow," Poy said sarcastically.

"I'm not bullshitting you. He leaves London, goes to Montreal, starts a laundry, sells it, goes to Halifax, starts a laundry, sells it, comes to St. John's, starts a laundry, doesn't sell it, but then one day, he just up and leaves. Doesn't tell anyone where he's going, other than just saying 'south.' Couple months later, we hear he's in the Caribbean, then Jamaica. Which kind of made sense when you think about it."

"Why?"

"All of Newfoundland's most valuable assets get traded down there," Hop Wah said as he finished his glass of water. "Now, who am I, the Fong Choy expert? Stop listening to me and go play a game."

"All right," Poy said. "I'll think about it."

The smoke and sweat of the room nauseated Poy. Gambling gave off an energy—a compost of greed and fear and nervous tension—that was unbearable. Or at least that's how Poy felt, thinking back on how an ill-timed horse bet led to weeks in steerage. It occurred to him that that was the moment, the very second, that things turned bad for him.

Poy floated around the room for a few hours, hesitant to lose any more than he had already lost. Every now and then, he would fetch a drink for Lee between sessions. Sometimes, he would share a few words with Shaowei or Gao. Poy was avoiding the tables, and he wasn't sure if it was because of the horse track or because he couldn't bear to engage with Lee's wishes, some tiny revenge for dragging him all the way out here. At some point, he realized Shaowei wasn't in the room anymore. Rather than risk going outside to look for him, Poy found his way back to the bar and bought himself another tea.

Little Joe poured up another cup. Poy looked at him as he poured, at his short legs on top of the table.

"Hey," Poy said. "I have to ask. You seem—"

"Short, huh?" Little Joe interrupted, offended. "That what you're gonna say? Gonna ask why my legs are so small? Let me tell you something. Some people are just born short and that's it."

"Okay," Poy said. "I was going to say that you seem like you've lived here for a while."

"Oh," Little Joe said. "I'm sorry, I thought you— You don't know how hard it is, to be like me. To be so—so short. I mean it's bad enough being Chinese in this town, can you imagine being three feet tall? There's piles of manure out there taller than me."

Poy and Little Joe shared a laugh.

"You don't mind being called Little Joe?"

"Nah, it's just a name. There used to be a regular-sized Joe. He's gone now, but the name stuck."

"So how long have you lived here?"

"Just a couple of years."

Poy thought for a moment. "I'm sure this is hopeless," he said, "but I would like to send a letter home and I was wonder—"

"No," Little Joe said with a laugh. "I don't know anybody going home, and if I did, you'd already know about it because they'd have a mail bag about this big." Little Joe placed his hand on the top of his head.

Poy laughed and sighed at the same time, a sad noise, just as Shaowei joined them at the bar.

"I'm getting hungry," he said. "Do you wanna head out? Gao says he can get us a good deal at the restaurant he works at."

Poy, Shaowei, Wong, and Gao all endeavoured to leave. They struggled to find their way out of the myriad of hallways, accidentally walking into a bathroom and then a supply closet, passing by a stairwell to a higher floor before eventually finding their way to the street.

"It's good to get some fresh air," Wong said as he lit a cigarette. The other men didn't say anything.

"Did Little Joe tell you if we can send a letter anytime soon?" Wong asked.

"He said no," Poy said, looking at Wong's cigarette.

Wong sighed. "I was really hoping I could let my mom know that I'm okay," he said. "That I'm working for us."

"We all wish we could do that," Gao said. "It'll be okay."

"It's always the way," Shaowei said.

"Wong, can you lend me one of those?" Poy said, pointing to his cigarette.

"I didn't know you smoked," Shaowei said.

"Neither did I," Poy said as Wong passed him a lit cigarette.

Poy gripped the cigarette uncomfortably, pinched between his thumb and middle finger. He brought it to his lips and inhaled, feeling an unusual blast of heat drift down his throat and up his nostrils. As he began to violently cough, the three others laughed at him.

The men walked back to Duckworth, then on to Water Street, over to the Globe Restaurant. A big awning hung over the front door, but they passed it by and went down an alley so that Gao could let them in through the back. The restaurant was closed on Sundays—closed to the general public, at least. But on Sundays they would close the blinds tight—partly so the locals wouldn't see them and stop coming to eat there, partly so Reverend Riley wouldn't see them—and have a little scoff.

The Globe was owned by an old Chinese man, Gao's uncle, who went by the name of Charlie Jin. Charlie is what the locals had called him since he'd arrived and he preferred that everyone call him that now. He was one of the first immigrants to St. John's; Fong Choy had sent for him to work in the laundry, and he had done that long enough that a day came when he could open a restaurant. He prepared food the locals would like—fried cod, salty stuff—and he had all the recipes in a tattered old book that a local housewife had given him. How exactly it came to be that he received this book, well no one knew for sure, but people liked to imagine all sorts of salacious theories.

Poy and the gang had some salt fish fried rice, and Charlie only charged them ten cents. Business was good; he could afford to not charge his own people too much. As it turned out, the Globe was a frequent stop for many Chinese men after a day at the Tai Mei Club, and soon enough the dining room was filled with worn-out gamblers. Despite the food, Charlie made most of his money on tobacco. Although he had never been a regular smoker, Poy had smoked before and he bought a pack of smokes this day, embarrassed from his first puff and determined to show his friends that he could handle something as small as a cigarette.

"How much did you lose back there?" Poy asked Shaowei.

"So negative," he responded. "Why do you think I lost? Maybe I won a lot of money—you don't know."

"The fact that you didn't brag about how much you won tells me that you only lost," Poy said. Gao and Wong laugh.

"Oh, Mr. Funny Guy, why don't you try to tell us the one about the wife at the train station?"

Poy smiled as he tapped a cigarette out of the pack. "Well?" He lit a match.

"Well, what?" Shaowei said, placing his fork down. "Time for another few minutes of watching you hack up a lung?"

"How much did you lose?"

"I was riding big, okay? Back in San Francisco, we used to play mahjong with all these white women all the time."

"Bullshit," Gao said.

"No, no, it's true. Jewish women, they loved it. So I'm pretty good at playing competitively, so I was riding big, I mean I started out with a dollar on the table and before I knew it, I was up to forty."

"Forty dollars? That's more than we've made since we got here," Wong said.

"You did not win forty dollars," Poy said with a laugh.

"Yeah, I did. Then I bet the whole forty trying to double my money and I lost it all. But it's like you said, Wong. This is the way to make big money in this town."

"That's more than we can make in a month," Wong said, excited.

"That's where you're both wrong," Poy said as he stubbed out his cigarette, wary of the smoke already. "If mahjong were completely random, you'd win twenty-five per cent of the time. Maybe the best players can win thirty per cent of the time. That means that even the best player loses seventy per cent of the time. And in order for you to actually make a profit, you have to win enough to cover the table fees. The only people in there making money are the people receiving the table fees, the people running things."

"But, Poy, there's a strategy to it," Gao said. "There's a way to think about—"

"It's just pure luck," Poy said. "There's no strategy. It's all random."

"I'll win eighty dollars next week," Wong said. "For Mom!"

"Look, the boy is inspired," Shaowei said. "Besides, you're making those percentages up. How do you know?"

"You guys can do whatever you want," Poy said, "but I'm not playing. A dollar in hand is better than—"

"Aren't you supposed to play to help Lee go home?" Shaowei asked. "So then you can go home?"

"There are legitimate ways to earn money," Poy said. "Ways that don't risk me losing what I already have."

"There is such a thing as a smart bet," Shaowei said.

"There is no such thing as a smart bet," Poy said.

The kitchen door swung open and Lee walked into the dining room. "You!" he said, marching towards Poy's table. "Where were you back there? All I saw you do was stand around drinking tea with Little Joe."

"I was watch—"

"You watching things isn't going to help me get the money I need," Lee said, throwing his hat on the table. "I need you playing, I need you winning."

"Maybe you shouldn't have lost all your money playing stupid games," Poy said.

A hush fell over the room, leaving even the most rowdy patron struck silent.

"How dare you speak to me that way," Lee said. "I am your elder and I demand respect. I—"

Poy stood up from his chair. "I came here under the pretense that I would be managing a laundry for a year while you visited Grandma. I did not come here to gamble with you. I did not come here to work twenty-four hours a day. I had a life back home, you know? I have a wife and a son and I had a good job too. I was a teacher. I had respect."

"Oh, you were a teacher. You think you're better than the rest of us 'cause you could live over there in peace and wear your stupid American clothes and have lots of money. Well, if money comes so easy to you, why don't you just go back and leave me here to rot?"

Lee picked up his hat and stormed out the front door, causing a silent frenzy from all the men inside, all hoping that no one out there would notice what was going on inside.

Poy, still standing, said to his friends, "You see that? That's what placing your hopes on gambling gets you."

Charlie came out of the kitchen and over to the table. "Gao," he said. "You said these were good guys and they wouldn't cause trouble here. These types of ruckus, I just can't have. They could—"

"Don't worry, sir," Poy said. "I was just leaving." He threw a dollar on the table, enough to pay for his whole group, and headed to the door.

"Hey," Charlie called out. "Back door."

Poy stopped short, turned, and walked through the kitchen and back into the alleyway outside.

Rainwater was rushing down the sloped alley like a river, leaving his feet soaked as he stood at the doorway.

Charlie appeared beside him and lit a cigarette. "At the Globe, we don't bring in any of these outside arguments, okay? I don't care what's going on out here in these streets, I don't care if a guy says he banged your wife, I don't care if one of these guys just took you for your money's worth at the club, I don't care about any of that.

The Globe is a neutral territory where the community can gather in peace. You disturb it, you don't come back. Got it?"

Poy nodded.

"Okay, I'll see you next Sunday, pal," Charlie said and went back into the restaurant.

Poy took a deep breath and shook his head and started back to the laundry, his shoes filling with water. As he walked, he could feel himself getting madder as it occurred to him that not only were his feet wet now, they'd be wet every day for the next week while he was rubbing and scrubbing.

That night, the iron bed was tense. None of the men spoke to each other, which wasn't that unusual. Things were often silent among them. But for Poy, there was a fraught nature to the silence that continued the rest of the week at the laundry. The following days broiled with a quiet intensity as the men returned to the washing and rinsing, the washing and rinsing, the drying, the ironing, the starching, the folding, the wrapping, the nights of pure exhaustion bent over on a table, the tears.

On Wednesday, Poy discovered something strange during a rinse cycle. Mixed in with the bedsheets was a round piece of white fabric, only a couple feet in diameter. Near the centre were two holes torn in the fabric, strange tattered holes. Ping knew this would be a job for Hong, the talented tailor.

Poy presented the piece of fabric to Hong, who merely shook his head.

"But there's holes torn in it," Poy said.

"The locals, sometimes they put these over their heads and go to each other's houses for fun."

"They do what?"

Hong ignored this question and returned to his stitching.

Poy took the cloth back to the rinsing tub and finished the job. Normally he would have asked Uncle Lee about it, but they still weren't speaking to each other. He showed it to Shaowei and asked if the white people did this in San Francisco. The colour drained from Shaowei's face and he dropped the sheets he was holding into the sink, causing a splash of water to soak their chests.

"There was something like this, but they were a very dangerous group of white people. They had big pointy hoods. Hong said they go to other white people's houses?"

"Yeah," Poy said. "For fun."

"In my experience," Shaowei said, "the type of white person who wears a hood like this isn't going to other white people's houses. They go to houses like ours or negroes' houses. Especially negroes."

"For fun?"

"Maybe fun for them," Shaowei said. "Groups of them would go around and try to kill Chinese people. Any type of people that weren't white, they would try to kill. They burned down the church I went to there. A friend of mine, they cut off his finger to steal his ring. Then they hung him from a tree."

Poy looked at the circular sheet floating in the sink in front of him, realizing now that the two uneven holes were torn so that someone could look out, so they could see the pain they inflicted. He pushed the mask under the suds. If they would hang a man for his ring, what would they do if they saw Poy in a suit?

It was a silly idea and Poy tried to push it out of his head. A ring was worth way more than a suit, and besides, Shaowei had said their hoods were pointy. This cloth was round. Still, the thought remained.

* * *

The week progressed in a tiredness that was routine for the men, so routine that it was almost as if they were robots, carrying out the tasks assigned to them until their one day of freedom.

Sunday came, and that meant bath time, followed by church and language lessons, then a swing by the Tai Mei Club, a light supper at the Globe, and then to bed, the only day of the week they could get a full night's rest. Before bedtime on Sundays, Poy would work on his letter for home. With every passing week, there was more to be told, but there was also less energy to write it out. Most weeks Poy just read over what he had written after the first two weeks.

The strange thing about the Tai Mei Club was how quiet it was. Aside from ordering drinks, or the occasional reaction to a hand in a game, the men were silent. Dozens of men, pretty much the entire Chinese community, concentrating on strategy to the point of speechlessness, though some were quiet because they were too exhausted to speak. Smoke filled the air where the words might have been. These men were tired and this was all they had. There was just nothing to say.

Poy went to the club again the next week, despite his newfound hatred of gambling. There was nowhere else for him to go where he could feel safe. Plus, he had realized that he was going to have to gamble this week, no matter how he felt about it. He needed Uncle Lee to talk to him again, if only just to make things more peaceful at work.

He sat at a table and paid the fee. It sickened him to do it, to the point that he couldn't pay attention to the game. Before he knew it, he had two dollars. Then four dollars. Then eight. Sixteen. That was more than what he earned in two weeks. Thirty-two. Zero.

Poy excused himself from the table. He knew he should've quit while he was ahead. He went to the bar and ordered himself a tea.

"This is a loser's drink, bub," Little Joe said as he poured. "I can just feel it."

"You've been here for a few years," Poy said. "Do you know anything about locals going around with sheets on their heads?"

"Haw," Little Joe laughed as he polished a rocks glass. "Let me guess, you were doing the laundry and found a white hood and now someone's got you scared that the Klan is here."

Poy nodded.

"Nah, they're not the Klan. They can be troublemakers, sure, there's a few rotten apples in every bunch, but they mean well overall."

"So what do they do in those sheets?"

"They're musicians, partiers. They call themselves mummers. They're just drunks from down on George, but they're creative drunks. These men, they put on women's clothes and they put these sheets over their heads and they go around to each other's houses and they sing songs and do voices, and then people have to guess who's under the masks."

"So they don't burn down churches?"

"Listen, there's nothing safe about a drunk man in a mask, and there's definitely nothing safe about a drunk *white* man in a mask. But these guys are just local idiots. They hate us, don't get me wrong, but they're not about to burn down a church or anything."

Poy stood by the bar for a little while drinking his tea, when he saw Hop Wah come into the room with another Chinese man. This man was older and immaculately groomed. His purple suit was newer and in nicer condition than Poy's or Hop Wah's, with an additional jacket that hung on his shoulders like a cape. He had his hair cut short like Poy's, and he had a fine, manicured moustache, so thin it looked as though it had been drawn on with a pencil. He was older, maybe in his sixties, and clearly a man of wealth.

Poy guessed that Fong Choy had returned.

The man surveyed the room and the silence felt different. Everybody's movements became more careful as they realized Fong Choy was there. Uncle Lee stood up and Fong merely shook his head, and Lee sat back down. Fong's eyes rested for a moment on Poy, eyeing up his suit, and then Fong returned his gaze to Hop Wah and they left the room.

A few minutes later, Hop Wah returned alone. He headed over to the bar, and Little Joe handed him a highball glass filled with water.

"Hey, Poy," Hop said. "Your boss just arrived."

"I thought that was him."

"Who else could it be?" Hop said as he sipped his drink.

"Where is he now?"

"Upstairs," Hop said.

"What's up there?"

"Oh, we got all sorts of little rooms there," Hop explained. "Rooms for my workers to sleep in, rooms for these animals in here to settle things, if you know what I mean, rooms for out-of-towners to stay in."

"Is he going to come down and play?"

"Nah," Hop said. "He's like you. He hates gambling."

"I was playing earlier."

"I saw your uncle's outburst at the Globe last week. I know how you feel about all this. You can have your moral high ground, but I bet there's something in you that makes you just as much a sinner as the rest of us."

"I never said anything about sinners," Poy said.

"Mm," Hop said. "You don't need to actually say things for people to know how you feel."

"I don't feel that way," Poy said.

"You probably think I'm a criminal, huh? You with your morals."

"I don't—"

"What you don't understand is that people like us have to dabble in crime to get ahead, to be able to provide opportunities to each other. No one out there will give us the time of day. And really, gambling, who does it hurt?"

Ping shook his head and sighed. The two men stood at the makeshift bar, looking through the smoky haze at the dozens of gamblers.

"I want to be clear, though," Hop said. "There's no hard feeling between us. I mean, you're here, you're drinking. You're putting money in my pockets. But, y'know, Charlie puts his whole business on the line by letting us go there on Sundays. That's not a place to settle any disputes."

"I know," Poy said. "Charlie told me that already. I'm sorry."

"Charlie is very important to me," Hop said. "To the community." Hop looked back and forth, then leaned closer. "He fronted me the cash to get this place up and running way back when," he said. "We're not family, but that still means something."

"I'm sorry," Ping said again.

"It's not me you need to apologize to," Hop said, relaxing against the bar. "It's your uncle. Go, help him win some money. Cash is the best way to heal any wound."

And so, after he finished his tea, Poy sat at a table. He paid the table fee, not even paying attention to how much it was, as he didn't want his losses to be something to dwell on later. Games had never been his strong suit. He found it hard to remember the rules. Hua Ling had often tried to explain the rules to him, but he'd always forget them. His wife. In all the chaos of the past few weeks, he was ashamed to realize he had let the purpose of his trip to Newfoundland slip from his mind ever so slightly. His family—

that's who he was here for, that's who he was returning to. Poy looked at Lee for a moment, then he put another dollar on the table.

After a couple of hours of playing, Poy emerged even, having won just enough—two dollars—to earn back what he'd lost. No loss, no gain.

The men set off for the Globe in waves. Everyone couldn't go at once or a local would see them and figure out what was going on. Instead, they'd split into smaller groups and go there separately.

"Guys," Wong said once they were on their way, "I won a hundred dollars."

"No way," Gao said.

"No," Poy said.

"You're lying," Shaowei said. "Let me see."

"I'm not taking my money out here," Wong said. "It'll blow away in the wind."

Supper at Charlie's was once again salt fish fried rice. Charlie greeted the men with a smile and a nod as he put the food on their table. Lee came in soon after and the air became still.

"I saw you playing the tables today," Lee said. "Thank you."

It was the first time that he'd spoken to Poy in a week.

Poy slowly nodded and said, "Yeah."

Lee nodded too. "How much did you win?"

"Nothing," Poy said. "Even keel."

"You tried," Lee said. "That's the important part."

Lee moved on and sat at his own table.

Poy slept well that night.

15

BELONGING

Mondays meant back to work. The day started as it always did: with the ringing of the bell, then wash, rinse, wash, rinse. Suddenly Fong Choy appeared at the laundry. He was wearing another regal purple suit, with an additional long jacket that flowed like a cape. Lee put down the blue bags so that he could go and greet him but he was silenced with a flourish of a wrist. Fong walked deeper into the laundry room, stood at the head of the tubs and watched the men. Poy found it difficult to work knowing that he was being watched by someone like Fong Choy, but most of the men around him seemed oblivious to his presence. They always had an attentive audience at the windows.

He stayed for a while, just watching, then left.

The next day Fong Choy returned, watching in silence again, until he pointed at Poy and said, "You."

Poy looked up from the soapy water and dirty sheets. A couple of times he had caught glimpses of Fong looking at him, but he had been trying to keep his eyes to himself.

"Me?" Poy said.

"Yes, you. You're having supper with me tonight."

"Okay, sir. At two a.m."

Fong laughed as he turned for the door. "You're a funny one."

Shaowei gave Poy a look of jealousy, maybe even anger. The other labourers also looked at Poy with contempt. Poy wouldn't even look in Lee's direction, knowing already that he must be fuming. It was hard for Poy to focus on his work that afternoon.

At around seven that night, Fong Choy came back to the laundry. "Ready?" he asked.

"Yes," Poy said as he dried his hands, leaving behind the other laundrymen, who were still rubbing and scrubbing and transferring freshly cleaned clothes to the drying room.

It had been a nice sunny day, but it was turning into a brisk evening, clear skies and cold breezes.

"Your name is Seto Poy?"

"Yes, sir," Poy said.

They were standing just outside the laundry, at the mouth of the long, empty alley by the house next door.

Fong took an expensive-looking cigarette holder out of his breast pocket and lit a cigarette with a match. "Do you want one?" he asked, gesturing with the holder to Poy.

Poy took a cigarette from his own pack and put it in his mouth. Fong lit it for him.

"My name is Fong Choy."

Poy nodded. "I know who you are."

"Your uncle told you about me?"

"Not very much. Hop Wah told me more."

Fong spat on the ground. "Don't listen to a word either of those guys say. Where's somewhere good for dinner around here? It's been a while."

"I've only been to the Globe."

"What is that, Charlie's place?" Fong scowled in distaste. "There must be something better than that."

Fong and Poy headed down George Street.

"What's with the suit?" Fong said. "You caught my eye at the club. I said to myself, 'What's one of these laundrymen doing in a suit?' Then I go to the laundry and I see you in a suit again."

Poy let out a small laugh. "I was a teacher, back home."

"In Hoiping?"

"Yeah. That's where you're from too, right?"

"Yeah . . ." Fong said absently. "I don't like to think about the home country too much anymore."

They turned on to Water Street.

"If you were a teacher, why did you leave?"

"I . . . well, Lee told us he owned a laundry over here and my grandmother wanted to see him again before she died, so it was arranged that I would take over his duties for a year while he visited and then I'd go back."

"And then you get here and you find out your uncle lost the laundry." Fong shook his head. "That fucking guy."

"It's not so bad," Poy said.

"You know what this calls for? Forget supper. Let's go have a drink."

They turned around and headed back to George Street.

"I . . ." Poy stuttered. "I'm not sure any of these places will serve us. People like us."

"Let me teach you something, kid. As long as you have this"—Fong produced a twenty-dollar bill from his pocket and pulled it taut—"any place will serve you."

He led them to the side of a fish and chip restaurant and opened the fire door. A young white doorman sitting behind a podium looked up in surprise. Fong reached out for a handshake and palmed the twenty into the doorman's hand.

"Right this way, gentlemen," the doorman said.

The kid led Poy and Fong down a set of narrow stairs, then through an even more narrow winding hallway with low ceilings. They reached a red curtain, which the doorman pulled back with a smile.

Candles in sconces on the walls illuminated the uneven stone tile work on the walls and floors. It looked as though random pieces of rocks had just been cemented together, with no attention to size or uniformity. Overhead, thick wooden beams. Booths lined the walls, save for one wall with a long marble bar. The place smelled of alcohol and tobacco, and an occasional whiff of musk. Bottles of champagne were being popped and cocktails were being shaken. Fat men in tuxedos were surrounded by young, beautiful women. And everyone was white.

"Would you like a seat at the bar or in a booth?" a young lady asked Fong.

"A booth, please."

The lady led them through the room, pausing at one point to instruct the men to "avoid the trap door," pointing to a square of space in the floor covered with jail cell bars. When they walked past it, Poy heard a low growl emanating from below. A group of men seated in a corner booth yelled towards Fong. Poy grimaced, readying himself for some sort of altercation. Instead, Fong smiled and waved to the men as the waitress readied their booth.

"Do you . . . know them?" Ping asked.

"Of course," Fong said. "The DuMonts. Shipping magnates. They've helped me out a time or two, I'll tell you that."

"Your seats are ready for you, gentlemen," the waitress said.

They sat down and Fong ordered for them and then the waitress walked over to a bucket and pulled out a raw fish. As she made her way to the bar, she dropped the fish through the grates of the trap door. The growl stopped.

"First thing you need to do," Fong told Poy, "is learn English."

"You're not the first person to tell me that," Poy said.

"And I won't be the last either. But you need to do that if you ever want to get out of the laundry industry. Have you been learning any?"

"I get some instructions once a week at church."

"Make it five times a week."

"Okay . . ." Poy said.

"What? What is it?"

"I work so much, I'm not sure I can make that much time to learn."

"If you want something, you can make the time for it," Fong said as he lit another cigarette.

The waitress placed two old-fashioneds on the table. The men both took a sip. Poy struggled to mask his reaction to the rotgut whiskey, grimacing at the otherworldly burn. Fong took it stone-faced.

"We'll want another round of these five minutes from now, and then another round five minutes after that," Fong said to the waitress. Then he turned his attention back to Poy. "How do you feel?" he asked.

"I'm well," Poy said.

"No, I meant, moving all the way over here, leaving Hoiping."

"Oh," Poy said. "It's not too bad."

"Tell me the truth."

"It's fine, really," Poy said.

"Listen to me. I've travelled the whole world. There was a time when I was your age and I had just left home and you know how I felt? I felt terrible. Every day I wished I was dead. I would wish for things to kill me. I would walk in front of trains. Now tell me, how do you feel?"

Poy sipped from his drink to try to look casual. "I feel like one day I woke up in another life. I feel like . . . like I'm in a dream."

"Too optimistic," Fong said. "Give me truth."

Poy closed his eyes and exhaled. "Every day, I feel like giving up. Every day, I feel like stopping. But there's nothing else here, there's nowhere for me to go. I can't even try to go back home. I don't have the money and Uncle—"

"Okay," Fong said. "So here's what I wanted to talk to you about. How much money do you owe your uncle?"

"I . . . I'm not comfortable saying."

"I'm only asking to be polite. You owe him three hundred dollars for the head tax, right?"

Poy nodded.

"Okay, that's taken care of."

Poy scrunched his eyebrows. "I have to help Lee get the money to go back home," he said.

"You don't need to worry about that," Fong said.

"It's just . . . family, you know."

"Listen to me," Fong said as he looked straight into Poy's eyes. "You don't need to worry about your uncle Lee anymore, okay?"

Poy paused. "You're paying for him to go home?"

"I'm only going to say this one more time: you don't need to worry about Lee anymore."

"Okay," Poy said.

"Okay, next order of business. You came here to manage the laundry, right?"

"Yes."

"That's what your uncle promised you, right?"

"Yes."

"You don't gamble, right? That's what Hop Wah told me."

"No. Well, a little bit, to try to help—"

"Okay. Now you're managing the laundry."

Poy was speechless.

Fong downed his drink and slammed his empty glass onto the table. He signalled to the waitress to bring the next round. "I'm only giving you this job because you're not a gambler. But you gotta promise that you don't plan on doing this job for the rest of your life like Lee. There's no future in it and a young man like you oughta have more ambition."

"I . . . I don't understand." There weren't any other opportunities for people like them, as far as Poy could tell.

"Do not stay in this industry. Take any opportunity—*any* opportunity—to get out of this business. You'll go nowhere washing clothes. Learn English as fast as you can. Whoever is teaching you, ask him for more lessons. The sooner you learn English, the more opportunities you'll have."

The waitress put fresh drinks in front of them.

"But you work in the laundry."

"I don't work in the laundry. I own the laundry. I *am* the laundry. Now, did they give you a Western name?"

"Yes."

"What is it?"

"William Seto Ping."

"Okay, that's your name from now on. Use it to your advantage."

"I . . . How?"

"Integrate yourself into the community. Go to church every Sunday. Open businesses. Make sure they call you William. It's too hard for them to learn a name in another language, so use the one they gave you. Make it so you're one of them."

"A white person?"

"A Newfoundlander."

"I don't think I'll ever be a Newfoundlander."

"Why not?"

"I . . . I don't feel I belong here."

Fong Choy grabbed Poy's shoulder. "You belong here."

"It's just the people here, they—"

"No. You belong here. You belong here just as much as any of these white fucks. What do you think, they were born here? That they rose from the water with the fish and the waves? They're immigrants too. They're British and Irish and French and German. And they feel they belong here. They forced their way here, they fought battles for it, and now there's so many of them here, I bet you can't imagine what the place would look like without them. I bet you haven't even tried. To think of the harbourfront surrounded by forest. To think that even right here, where we're sitting, was once trees and Indians. Where are they now? What about this building? Do you think it belongs here?"

"Well . . . no. I never thought of it that way."

The men sat in silence and then a young, balding white man approached the table.

"Fong Choy? Is that you?"

"Joseph," Fong said in English, standing up to shake the man's hand. "How are you?"

"I'm very well," the man laughed. "I thought we traded you to the Caribbean for a barrel of rum."

Both of them laughed.

"Well, you know how businesses are, always requiring attention. I'm just here to select a new manager for the laundry."

"Ahh, your partner . . . ?"

"Gone back to China. For the time being. This is the new manager, William Seto Ping."

"Nice to meet you, Mr. Ping." The man extended his hand.

Poy smiled and shook his hand.

"He's not too keen on English yet," Fong noted, "but I bet next time you meet him, he'll have the gift of the gab like you. I'm glad you kept this place open."

"I don't know for how much longer," Joseph said. "I'll shift gears soon, I think. I've been trying to write a book, but the bar life takes up so much of my time. I think I might give up and start pig farming."

Fong took a slow puff from his cigarette. "I can't believe you still have that thing in the trap door," he said.

"Tom drinks twenty beers a day now," Joseph said. "If you can believe that."

"No," Fong said, aghast.

"Yeah, holds on to the glass himself and everything."

"Do you bring him up still?"

"Usually only to break up a fight, but seeing as I've got an old friend and a new face here, let me see what I can do . . ."

He went over to the bar and rang a bell to get everyone's attention. "It is time," he said, and a murmur of excitement erupted. "We must keep the noise to a minimum so that he does not get frightened."

Joseph knelt down by the trap door and unlocked the several barricades put in place. He pulled the grate off the floor and threw a raw fish onto the tiles just in front of the hole. A low growl once again came from below, followed by the sound of heavy footsteps on creaky wooden stairs. The whole room was quiet with anticipation, people straining to look over each other to see what was about to unfold.

A great paw loomed out of the hole, followed by another, claws scraping the stone floor. A fearsome head emerged, tiny eyes glinting in the meagre light. A black bear slurped the fish down with a hearty gulp. Around the bear's neck was a solid steel collar attached to a chain leading down into the cavernous darkness.

Joseph slowly approached the bear and presented it with a pint glass filled with beer. The bear shuffled itself around for a moment, struggling to get comfortable before it sat on its hindquarters and extended its paws to hold on to the glass. It gripped the glass with its paws and raised it to his mouth, drinking the pint and not spilling a drop. Then it passed the empty glass back to Joseph.

Although Poy had been frightened at first, he wasn't particularly surprised by this. It seemed to him that every white person had a wild animal, tamed and hidden somewhere within their domiciles.

Poy and Fong emerged into the cold air of night.

"Let's go on a little walk," Fong said.

They walked down Water Street, much farther than Poy had ever gone before, passing by various businesses, fishermen, and drunks. They came to a stop at the foot of a grand flight of steps leading up to a monument. Graduated plateaus held bronze statues of figures. A woman on top held a torch and a sword, and on either side below her were men looking to the horizon, one with a rifle, the other with a looking glass. And beneath those were another two men, a fisherman and a lumberman. Fong and Poy sat down on the steps. They looked out over the harbour and its seemingly endless wharfs. Even now, at this late hour, fishermen were unloading basket after basket of cod.

Poy kept looking back at the statues.

"It's for the war," Fong said. "A lot of people from here died."

Poy nodded.

"You should see this spot on July first," Fong said. "Big parade, all the veterans." He shook his head. "The Chinese here call it Humiliation Day."

It was a cold night, and it might have been the booze in his system but Poy felt warm.

Fong put a cigarette in his holder and lit it. "You know, I was the first Chinese person here." He leaned back on the steps. "A lot of people here hadn't even heard of China. I might as well have come from a different planet. People tried to wash my skin. I'm not kidding. They didn't understand that people didn't all look like them. Of course, we're talking about people that stare at fish all day, so what do they know anyway?"

"So what did you do?" Poy asked absent-mindedly, watching the boats dock.

"After they figured out that they couldn't wash the Chinese off me, that was when they started talking about us in the paper, right away, first day I arrived. A reporter started asking me why did I come here and where did I come from. And I knew English very well by then already. So I told him, I lived for seven years in Halifax, then I moved to Quebec, then I moved here with the intention to open a laundry. Then the guy writes the article and puts this whole thing about Chinamen are prepared and able to work for a mere nothing and live on less. I read that and I say to myself, 'What?'" Fong shook his head and laughed.

"But that's life," he added. "You get used to that. I was here long enough that eventually their arguments turned into, well, Fong Choy, he's one of the good ones, but we can't let too many more in 'cause they'll take our jobs and all this nonsense. Nobody was doing laundry here before me. Nobody. Neither white nor yellow. I didn't take anybody's job."

Poy, a little too buzzed to respond, just stared up at the monument. He thought the statues looked pretty and the stairs were a nice touch. "Sir, I gotta ask you," he said. "Have you been to Egypt?"

Fong laughed. "No. Why do you ask?"

"They told me you walked across Eurasia, and the Rev—"

Fong laughed even louder. "Is that what you've heard about me?"

"Yeah, you walked through everything to get to London."

"I took a boat from Hong Kong to London. You can't believe anything people say, not about themselves or others. No one ever really knows what happened. Everything is just reveries, just . . . Chinatowns."

This answer confounded Poy long enough for Fong to butt out his cigarette and let out a deep sigh.

"Let's get you home," he said.

The walk back to Fong-Lee Laundry was mostly silent, interrupted only a couple of times by noisy locals yelling indecipherable arguments into the night air, their words echoing off the dozens of conjoined homes lining the streets. It was something Poy hadn't paid much attention to when he was sober, maybe too distracted by all the staring and name calling and violence, but the houses here were weird. Some of them were short and stout, others tall and narrow, all attached together and each one painted some vibrant colour or another. As Poy and Fong walked down Gower Street, it looked like they were walking down a big empty kaleidoscopic tube. And save for the occasional sound of a bottle breaking or a frantic yell, it seemed as though they were the only two people left alive in St. John's. There was something uneasy in that notion, seeing these streets usually filled with people now empty and hollow.

When they arrived back at the laundry on Holdsworth, Fong stopped a few doors away.

"Just so you know," he said, "I had to put up a lot of capital to buy out Hop Wah's stake in the laundry. I also had to settle Lee's debts. I paid Hop more than the place is worth probably, but that's business. Anyway, you'll still only be paid a dollar a day. I know managers are supposed to make more than a livable wage, but I'm sure you can understand how some sacrifices must be made in a situation like this."

"Oh," Poy said. "Yes. All right."

Fong paused and then took a deep breath. "You know, your uncle wasn't always like this. Anywhere you go in the world, Chinese people love to gamble. He just . . . he took it too far."

Poy gave him a slow nod, unsure of what to make of that message. He trailed behind Fong to the back door of the laundry and he could hear the splash splash of the laundrymen's ongoing labour as Fong opened the door. Poy followed him in, making sure to avoid the puddles scattered among the gravel.

Upon seeing Poy, Lee threw a pad of paper onto his desk and said, "Poy, get back to work!"

"Mr. Ping will be going to bed now, Lee," Fong said in a loud voice. "That's how you are to refer to him now. Mr. William Seto Ping."

All of the labourers stopped their work to look at Fong, table-cloths and napkins dropping to slosh in the water.

"Mr. Ping is the new manager here," Fong continued. "An arrangement that was promised to him for when he arrived here."

There was not much of a reaction in the room, aside from Lee, who scrunched up a piece of paper in his fist.

"Lee, come with me," Fong said. "And bring your belongings."

Mr. Ping walked into the room where they all slept and rested his head on the iron bed, the booze making him forget about the soreness of his back. Lee came in to grab his suitcase and cash box.

He gave Ping a quick look and shook his head, lips pursed and slightly raised on one side.

"Oh, Lee," Ping said with a hopeful lilt, and took an envelope from the breast pocket of his suit. "If you're headed home now, can you take my letter for Mom and Hua Ling?"

Lee snatched the letter out of Ping's hand, scrunched it into a ball, and threw it into a corner. Then he walked out to join Fong.

That was the last time Ping ever saw his uncle Lee.

16

AN IDEA

It was not an easy transition to being a manager. Fong never came back to explain this turn of events, and many of the long-time laundry workers questioned whether this promotion was true and why they weren't the ones to get promoted. And it was never clear to Ping what role the manager was supposed to play, other than be the one to count and divide the cash among the workers. After having worked the laundry for the past few weeks, Ping couldn't fathom just sitting around all day while the others worked all day and night.

The next problem was Lee's disappearance. Ping came to believe that Fong had either taken Lee with him down south or ponied up the funds to send Lee back to China. Neither of which seemed particularly likely, but the alternative was something he didn't want to think about. After all, how would he know when to return home if Lee never came back?

The following morning, Ping and the others waited around for a bit to see if Lee would reappear. Soon enough it was nine o'clock and no one had rung the bell and no one had begun sorting the blue bags of dirty laundry. Ping took it upon himself to ring the bell, which was bolted to a steel beam near the front door. It was a nice little brass bell. He swung the rope once and it produced a faint ring, certainly not loud enough to rouse people from the iron bedroom in the back. He swung it again with more intensity, loud enough this time, maybe too loud. The laundry workers began shuffling into the workroom, filling the tubs, adjusting the temperature.

The next matter of business was sorting the growing pile of blue bags. Ping quickly realized that he wouldn't be able to do this job. He couldn't read the notes, and he couldn't make the lists of what belonged to who and from where.

"Shaowei," he said. "You do this."

"What happened last night?" Shaowei asked as he opened the first blue bag.

"He took me to a bar and told me that I don't owe Lee any money for the head tax anymore," Ping said.

"He paid your uncle for you?"

"I'm not sure. He just told me not to worry about it."

"He definitely killed Lee." Shaowei dumped a bag out onto the floor.

"He didn't kill Lee," Ping said. "Isn't that the type of thing you would complain about white people saying?"

"Yes, but I'm not a white person, so I can say it. Fong killed Lee."

"Stop. Fong didn't kill Lee. They'll be back later today."

"Whatever you want to believe," Shaowei said. "So, what, you're the manager now? You don't have to work with the rest of us anymore?"

"No, no, I'm still going to do the laundry with you guys. That just wouldn't be right."

"Why is he making us call you by the name they forced on you?"

"He said I should try to become a part of this community. That by using the name they gave me, I'll have an advantage."

Shaowei rolled his eyes. "You gotta learn English to have an advantage."

"Yeah, he told me that, too."

"If having a Western name is so important, how come he doesn't have one, huh?"

Ping shrugged. "He's an old man. Things were different when he came here."

"I wonder if he personally killed Lee or if he got someone else to do it."

"Shaowei, this isn't funny."

"Maybe he got Hop Wah and Little Joe to do it. I bet they have guns."

"Shaowei, please, this is rude. This is my family you're speaking about."

"We should get guns. Reverend Riley has a gun."

"I thought you said he told us to avoid guns. What would we need guns for?"

"Self-defence. Fong's killing Lee today, he could be killing you tomorrow. Or me." Shaowei pantomimed a shocked face.

"Nobody is killing anybody. We're here to wash clothes, that's what we're going to do."

"I should get a copy of today's paper, see if there's any articles about Chinamen being found dead."

"You can do that later. We have a lot of work to catch up on."

"Oh, you think you can boss me around now. I see how it is."

"You know Hop Wah wouldn't kill Lee. Lee is one of his best customers. He told me that himself."

"A guy like Lee, he's only as good as his last bet. Maybe he owed Hop Wah money."

"Just sort the laundry, okay?"

Shaowei sorted the laundry and Ping resumed his station at the washing tub. The first garment he encountered was a fine white dress shirt with a prominent mustard stain on the chest. He scrubbed and scrubbed and struggled to remove the yellow stain. He looked at the other dirty garments floating around the room. White socks turned yellow on the soles. White undershirts with yellowed collars. White boxers with piss stains. There is no place for yellow on white, Ping thought, considering the irony of white people paying them to scrub the yellow away. What if he could scrub the yellow off his skin? Would he be one of the clean people who could walk free? He shuddered and regretted thinking that. The white people who watched them in the windows often looked far from clean. And some of the stenches he encountered in St. John's seemed subhuman despite their source. Maybe everyone was just as dirty. After all, Fong had said the Chinese belonged here just as much as anyone else. Maybe yellow stains belonged on white clothes. Maybe they weren't even stains.

Despite the early disruptions, the workday proceeded as normal, but there was a strange feeling in the air. The men always worked with a melancholic sense of anger, exhaustion, and frustration, but Ping now felt as if those unvocalized feelings were directed towards him. He wasn't sure if it was all in his mind or not. There was much to think about, and with everything being pushed back by an hour, the late start threw the whole day off. Shaowei gave the bag boy a couple of coins to bring back the paper, and during the supper break at three in the morning, he skimmed it with his soup.

"So?" Ping asked.

"What?" Shaowei said. "Oh, you want to know if it says Lee was found dead."

"I just wanted to prove to you that you were wrong."

"Well, I guess I'm wrong for now because it doesn't say anything about a dead Chinaman. Listen to this, though. 'Our own people have to go abroad to earn a livelihood and yet even the heathen Chinee can come here and prosper.'" Shaowei eyed the table they called a bed. "They call this prospering?"

"It's more money than you'd make back home," Ping said.

"Not for you, it isn't," Shaowei said. "Big fancy teacher becomes big fancy manager. Don't try to speak for me."

After a moment of tense silence between them, Shaowei continued to translate the article. "'The "Heathen Chinee" have now quite a colony established here, and if they continue to come in such large bunches we will boast of a local China town of larger population than in much more pretentious cities. The yellow peril is not greatly appreciated by our workmen, who fear that in a short time they will be branching out in other than the "washee-washee" business.'"

"What's all this about?" Ping asked.

"Something called the Fishermen's Protective Union thinks we're going to steal their jobs," Shaowei said. "I'm not taking the fish out of the goddamn water."

He slammed the paper onto the table and they went back to work.

The week passed as it usually did, and with each passing day it became clearer that Fong and Lee weren't coming back. Ping wondered if that meant he might be able to go home earlier, if Fong Choy had paid off his debt to Lee. But did that mean he was indebted to Fong Choy now? He figured it might be best to save three hundred dollars anyway and put it aside just in case anyone came looking for it.

Although he didn't know for sure, Ping was certain that Lee was not dead, at least not by Fong Choy's hands, like Shaowei insisted. But still, Ping looked forward to Sunday so that he could ask Hop Wah if he knew anything. When Sunday did arrive, Ping woke up a little earlier to count out the money to pay the labourers. Six dollars each for the week; the rest of the money to be transferred by wire to Fong Choy's bank account in Jamaica. Ping was to deliver the money to the bank first thing Monday morning, as soon as they opened the doors. He would grow to enjoy the luxury of the bank, the green and gold lamps, the marble counters. But on that first Sunday, the trip to the bank was just another daunting task that lay ahead of him. He assigned Shaowei the duty of buying the detergents, as Ping did not yet have the language capabilities to do this himself. This promotion brightened Shaowei's attitude.

It was funny, Ping had never really gotten to know any of the men he was working with until he had to take on the payroll duty. He knew surface-level details like "that's the guy that sneezes a lot" or "that's the mute one." Despite working side by side, elbows rubbing in the tubs, and sleeping on the same table together, they were little more than acquaintances to one another. Paying them for the first time on this Sunday morning was the most personal contact he'd ever had with most of them.

At the end of their English lessons that day, Shaowei came up to Ethel. "Mr. Ping would like ask you something," he said to her.

"Yes now, what is it, b'y?" Her hair was a dense plateau of curls.

"He require more English lesson. He become manager at laundry and he need know English better."

"Oh," she said, "yes now. Fancy that, me goin' around town with one of you. The FPU's liable to scald me."

Shaowei was uncertain what exactly she meant. Ethel spoke too fast and her accent was already difficult for him to understand.

"You help him in evening?" he asked.

"Mind now," Ethel said with a huff.

"What's she saying?" Ping asked in Taishanese.

"I have no idea," Shaowei said. "The words I understand, but she's arranging them in ways I can't understand."

"Tell her I'm a gentleman," Ping said.

"He want me tell you he a gentleman," Shaowei said.

Ethel rolled her eyes. "G'wan, wha's this, a date?" She lit a cigarette.

"No, ma'am, no date. He have wife. Just want English lessons."

"Oh me nerves! Fine. I'll drop over by and by. What odds." She put on her sunglasses and headed out of the gymnasium.

"What did she say?" Ping asked.

"I think she agreed, but I'm not sure."

On their way to the club, a child, another urchin, ran behind Shaowei, jumped up, and yanked on his queue. Shaowei fell to the ground, and a smattering of laughter rang through the street. The child ran away laughing with glee. Ping helped Shaowei get back on his feet.

"Are you okay?" he asked.

"I'm fine," Shaowei said as he caressed his braid. "These are the people you want to integrate with?"

Ping sighed. "It's not like that."

"It is like that. That's who these people are," Shaowei said.

"Integration means that we don't have to be subject to this type of treatment anymore."

"I'll believe that when I see it," Shaowei said, still caressing and adjusting his hair. "The mud and the name calling and everything else is all bad enough, but what I hate most is when they mess with my hair."

"I know," Ping said. His friend's lack of bluster puzzled him.

"Why do you have your hair styled like that anyway? It's kind of outdated."

"I don't care about the politics behind it," Shaowei said. "I just like to wear it this way. Wouldn't your 'integration' bullshit mean I could wear my hair however I like and not have these hick whites bother me about it?"

"I know," Ping repeated.

"What would *you* know?" Shaowei said. "A learned gentle-man like you was probably never beaten and disrespected like this before. This is all new to you. But it is far from new to me. In San Francisco, a couple of drunkards tried to hold me down and cut my hair with a hunting knife. I would rather they cut my throat. If they think my presence on their land is wrong, well, that's one thing. But my hair is on my head and that's none of their concern. A guy like you wouldn't know anything about it."

Ping sighed. "I've been beaten before," he said. "Twice."

A tiny smile crossed Shaowei's face. "Oh wow, that's extensive. Your body must be covered in scars."

Ping laughed.

"Let me guess," Shaowei said. "Daddy slapped you around a bit after getting into his liquor."

Ping forced a smile. He had never told Shaowei about his father's death. "No, but close. It was my grandmother. And it was after someone stole some coins from her room. She thought it was me because we slept in the same room. It was my cousin that did it, but no one believed me. So I was beaten."

"Boo-hoo," Shaowei said, sounding more like himself.

"That was when I learned life isn't always fair," Ping said. "That's why I'm always very careful about accusing people of things. Because I'll never forget the lashing she gave me over nothing."

"It's always family that'll do it to you," Shaowei said. "Always the way."

"But you know, Grandma was also the one who tended to my wounds at other times," Ping said. "There was this one teacher that would always beat me."

"So it was more than twice," Shaowei said.

"He was a tiny little guy, and anytime I couldn't remember something or said a word the wrong way, he'd beat the back of my hand with the rattan handle of an old feather duster until the skin broke. Grandma would clean my wounds and say, 'White rice is easy to eat.' That was supposed to motivate me to study more, because eating is easy but studying is difficult."

"Don't need to explain that to me," Shaowei said.

Ping smiled. That was the Shaowei he knew. "Anyway, one time the teacher beat me like someone crazy, for no reason. He made me pull down my pants and he beat me with an old piece of firewood. He shredded my backside, blood and pieces of skin everywhere."

"So dramatic," Shaowei said.

"I was screaming and crying, and Grandma just happened to be walking by the school, coming home from the fields. As soon as the teacher saw her, he pulled up my pants and pushed me towards her. I guess he thought she was looking for me. I was crying and crying and I grabbed her and when she held me, she could feel the blood soaking through my pants. She carried me home and looked over my body, and my backside was mushy and there were these bugs and—well, she was so mad, she didn't care if he was a teacher or a rat, she took our fire poker and went back to the school and just beat everything up, the walls and the chairs and everything. The teacher, he ran out the back door, he looked like a chicken in a ditch, and he ran all the way back to his own village."

"Likely story," Shaowei said.

"That's true," Ping chuckled. "And when he got back to his village, his own father had heard what happened and tried to shoot him in the chest!"

"How do you know that happened?" Shaowei said.

"Because his father came to our house and apologized on behalf of their family and then he paid for my tuition for the rest of my schooling."

"Ah, I've heard enough," Shaowei said.

They took their usual spots in the club. Shaowei took a seat at a table for eight rounds and Ping stood drinking tea by the bar. It occurred to him that he didn't need to be here anymore. He didn't have to appease Lee. Alas, there was nowhere else to go.

As was tradition, Hop Wah later entered the room and joined Ping at the bar with a tall glass of water.

"Hey, Poy," he said.

"Oh, uh, I go by my Western name now," Ping said. "William Seto Ping."

"Ohhh, Mr. Ping! That must mean Fong Choy gave you the old motivational speech. Been hearing that one for years."

"Heh," Ping said. "Yes."

"Let me guess, he took you to Bear's Beer Bar, then said you belong here and all that sort of stuff."

"Yes."

"That old coot will say that to anyone who'll listen. I've had it happen to me a couple of times. He doesn't even remember that he told me before."

"Oh," Ping said, a little deflated. "Where is he now?"

"He just up and left one morning earlier this week. He paid me a pretty penny for my stake in his laundry, let me tell you."

"And Lee?"

"He told me he was going to take care of Lee," Hop Wah said with a wink.

"What does that mean?"

"Don't worry about it," Hop said with a wave. "Enjoy managerial life."

Ping shrugged, trying to mask his worry about Lee.

"Bet he told you that ol' chestnut about learning English too."

"Yeah," Ping said.

"Personally? I find the best way to learn is by going to the picture shows. I go every weekend. I saw *The Public Enemy* today. Oh, boy, what a picture! It's guys like that that made me want to dress the way I do. The way we do." Hop Wah preened his lapels as he leaned in closer to whisper to Ping. "You want to see something?"

Ping shrugged again. Based on the way things were in this town, he figured that Hop probably had an oversized animal in a cage somewhere.

Hop rested his drink on the bar and slyly opened his suit jacket just an inch so that Ping could take a glimpse inside. A small handgun in a holster.

"It's the same one they used in *Little Caesar*," Hop said. "Isn't that something?"

"It sure is," Ping said, although he didn't know what Little Caesar was. A gun would probably come to good use in this town, he thought. Then he thought of his dad and decided that maybe a gun never comes to good use.

Hop, perhaps sensing that Ping didn't understand the reference, took another sip of his drink and changed the subject. "You know, Fong was the one that sold that guy the bear."

"Is that right?" Ping said.

"Yeah. See, Fong had encountered the bear in the woods here and *BAM*"—Hop pantomimed an uppercut punch—"gave the bear the old one-two, knocked the poor thing out, and sold it to Joseph."

Ping thought about what Fong had said about not believing everything you hear, and he hoped that, in the future, no one ever made up stories about him.

Suddenly Shaowei and another man were yelling at each other, until the other man angrily pointed up and they both stormed out. Ping started to follow them, but Hop Wah placed a hand on his chest.

"Let them work it out," he said.

"He's my friend, I have to help him," Ping said.

"He doesn't need your help," Hop Wah said with a laugh. "Trust me."

"He'll be mad if I don't help him," Ping said, and pushed Hop out of the way.

"Oh," Hop said. "You're into it too. I get it."

Although Ping was puzzled by that remark, he pushed on. He heard Shaowei and the man go upstairs and he went up there, listening closely to hear if there was any sort of noisy ruckus happening. The stairs led into an extremely narrow hallway, barely enough room for Ping to turn around. Quiet, until there was a clang on the floor behind a door at the end of the hall. Ping ran there as fast as he could and swung open the door.

The man sat on the edge of the bed, naked, his robe on the floor. Shaowei was on his knees in front of him, his head burrowed in the naked man's lap. Ping's jaw dropped a little and he tried to close the door as fast as he could. Shaowei looked up from the man's crotch, just long enough to see Ping.

"Ohhhh," Hop said when Ping returned to the bar, "I was wrong! You were right, Little Joe, he's not part of the matter upstairs. Here's your money, you bastard." He slid a couple of dollars over to Little Joe, who counted the bills with glee.

"Why so sad?" Hop asked Ping. "Did you think you guys were exclusive?"

"What? I . . . no, I just, I didn't know that he . . . was like that."

"Like what? That's not gay," Hop said. "There's no women around so what else are you going to do?"

"I just . . . I thought they were in a fight."

"Nah. You'll see guys play rough like that here all the time," Hop Wah said and turned his attention to one of the game tables.

A few minutes later, Shaowei and the other man returned to their places at their table. Ping decided to pretend that that was the way it was, that in fact he had never been upstairs and didn't see what had happened.

A couple of hours later, Shaowei came over to the bar and said, "Do you want to go for dinner now?"

Ping, Shaowei, Gao, and Wong headed down to the Globe.

"Guys," Wong said, "I won five hundred dollars."

"Wong, that's literally impossible," Gao said. "You don't need to lie to hang out with us."

"I'm not lying," Wong said. "I really did! Really, fellas!"

The men laughed and shook their heads.

"You guys can laugh all you want," Wong said. "But at this rate, I'll be bringing home a whole bag of money to my mom!"

"It's nice to have dreams," Shaowei said, without looking up from the pavement.

"Talking about dreams," Gao said, "did I see you guys talking to Ethel?"

Ping and Shaowei looked at each other.

"Yes," Ping said. "Shaowei was helping me ask for more lessons."

"I'd like to get some more lessons from Bessie," Gao said. "If you know what I mean."

None of the men laughed.

Supper at the Globe was quiet that evening. An air of discomfort remained between Ping and Shaowei until Shaowei finished his plate of fried rice.

"I've been thinking," he said to Ping, "about something you said a few weeks ago."

Ping waited for him to continue.

"I remember you saying something about how the only people making money at the games are the people running them. I've been thinking, now that you're the manager, maybe we should open our own mahjong parlour. At Fong-Lee."

Gao and Wong both looked at Ping, who said nothing for a long moment.

"Well," he said as he put down his fork. "I think that Hop Wah has a nice set-up there for himself and I wouldn't want to interfere with his business in any way."

"No, no, it'll be like back in San Francisco, when I was running that fake opium den, just a small little tiny side hustle. The Tai Mei is way too crowded, and I think there's enough of us here that we could have two casinos and that it would be fine. Business-wise, I mean."

"I'm not sure," Ping said. "I'm trying to avoid all this gambling stuff. Besides, we all seem to enjoy getting together at the Tai Mei."

"You don't get it. The reason why we came to this country is to make money, right? Well, maybe you didn't come here for money, but wouldn't it be nice if you could make some more money to take home? Wouldn't that put a smile on your wife's face?"

Ping folded up his napkin and threw it on his plate. "We don't have mahjong sets," he said. "We don't have the space that Hop Wah has. We don't have anything to drink. We don't have anything. Why would anyone come to our casino?"

"Variety," Shaowei said. "Aren't we all a little sick of the Sunday routine?"

"We don't have rooms upstairs like Hop Wah," Ping said, with a slight squint.

"Don't need them," Shaowei said.

Ping leaned back in his chair and gave Shaowei a look of amused curiosity. "I'll think about it," he said. Already he knew it wasn't worth the risk.

"I have a mahjong set," Gao added.

Soon after that, the men left the restaurant. Shaowei and Ping said goodbye to Gao and Wong, and they headed up to Holdsworth. It was a quiet walk, silent except for the sounds of the city surrounding them.

"That's them!" a boy yelled. "That's two of 'em anyways."

Ping and Shaowei had passed by a group of young teens just moments ago, but hadn't paid much attention to them.

"You sure?" one asked.

"Yeah, yeah, I remember 'cause of the suit. There's only a couple of those chinks that wear suits. The one with the ponytail, he's the one that threw my bike in the harbour."

"Those fuckin' gooks. Let's get 'em, b'ys!"

The boys swarmed around Ping and Shaowei. There were four of them, and they flung pucks of mud and manure at the men, all the while yelling.

"Gook!"

"Rat!"

"Chink!"

"Fuck you, scum!"

"Run," Shaowei said.

The two men broke through the loose circle of boys and ran

to reach the laundry. The boys chased after them, chucking mud as hard as they could.

Smack! Right in the back of Shaowei's head. *Smack!* The back of Ping's knees. *Smack!* Splattering over the unpaved road.

"We shouldn't have led them here," Ping said as they burst through the back door. He tried his best to hold the door closed as the gang of boys banged and yelled outside.

Shaowei ran straight to the ironing room and grabbed two hot irons from the side of the coal stove. He ran back to the back door. Ping, seeing the irons glowing orange with heat, dived out of the way, allowing the boys to force the door open. With a primal yell, Shaowei threw the irons at the boys. His head dropped into his hands and he whimpered in despair.

Ping looked out the door. One of the irons was sizzling in a puddle of piss and the other was nestled in the grass. The ruffians had dispersed. Ping picked up the irons and went back inside.

Shaowei was crying on the floor, his hands dabbing at the tears. *Don't touch your face*, Ping thought, then realized something. He hadn't seen Shaowei wear his white gloves in weeks.

"I know," Ping said as he helped Shaowei up off the floor. "I know."

17

THE ROCK

The following workweek continued as usual, the washing, the rinsing, the drying. The work never got easier, but they did lose a sense of just how long the hours were. As the weekend approached, Ping took a moment during their supper break to ask Shaowei a question.

"Okay, so, if we were to open our own casino, how would we do it?"

"That's a stupid question," Shaowei said. "We'd do rounds of mahjong at this table."

"And we'd charge a table fee?"

"Of course," Shaowei said. "Maybe even have lower fees than Hop Wah, just to get things going."

"And people would pay those fees?"

"They do now, don't they?"

"So . . . where would we even get mahjong pieces?"

"Stupid," Shaowei said. "Gao said he has a set, plus, there's lots of Chinese here. You think no one has mahjong pieces just 'cause you don't?"

Ping didn't ask any further questions, partly because of Shaowei's sour mood, partly because he didn't want to admit to himself that he was seriously considering the idea.

Ethel didn't come by that week. Ping thought maybe there had been a miscommunication with Shaowei, or maybe she just didn't want to do extra lessons. Shaowei said she probably didn't want to be seen with a Chinese person. Ping thought that although that could be true, it didn't strike him that she cared all that much about appearances.

Sunday rolled around, and it was beginning to seem like even this one day of freedom was just as much a part of their labour as anything else. Bath, church, language lessons, Tai Mei Club, the Globe, then sleep. There had to be more to life than this.

After the language lesson—"That's a car, me duckie, repeat after me, 'car'"—Shaowei and Ping once again attempted to get Ethel to agree to give extra lessons to Ping.

"Excuse me," Shaowei said, straining to say each syllable, "Mrs. Squibb, can you please give Mr. Ping more language lesson time?"

"Oh my Jesus, buddy," Ethel said. "I'm nobody's missus."

"He need more time learn. Even one more day a week."

"Yes, b'y', like I gots time for that."

"Please, Mrs. Squibb. He not look for anything else. Just want learn English."

"Whaddya want? I don't own the bloody language book."

"Just speak him. Help him learn."

"Sure, b'y," Ethel said, flustered. "You knows English well enough, why don't you teach him?"

Shaowei exchanged a look with Ping, who was smiling and nodding.

"She said I should teach you English," Shaowei told him.

Ping stopped nodding. "Why didn't we ever think of that?" he asked Shaowei.

Another stroll to the Tai Mei Club, another afternoon sipping tea and watching the games. Another supper at the Globe, except this time Shaowei requested a copy of the menu so he could try to teach Ping some of the words. Ping thought about how Shaowei wasn't as pretty as his other teacher, but then reminded himself that learning the language was what was important and that any other desire was just clouding his lessons.

Shaowei pointed at the first item on the menu. "Fish and chips," he said, first in English, then in Taishanese, then in English again. "Fish and chips. It's deep-fried fish with fried potatoes."

"Fish and chips," Ping repeated, slowly sounding out the words.

Gao and Wong sounded out the words too.

"Fish and chips, fish and chips."

"Fish and chips is terrible," Gao explained. "It's disrespectful to the fish to be cooked like that."

"Next," Shaowei continued, "is shrimp and chips."

"Shrimp and chips, shrimp and chips."

Gao said, "This is fried shrimp with fried potatoes."

The next menu item was scallops and chips, then wings and chips.

"Why is everything with chips?" Shaowei asked.

"It's same as rice for white people," Gao explained.

"It wasn't like this in San Francisco," Shaowei said.

"Guys," Wong said, "I have a secret."

The men looked at him.

"I have over a thousand dollars in winnings now."

"Wong, please," Ping said, "you don't need to keep making things up."

"I'm not making it up," Wong said. "It's true."

"Okay, if it's so true," Gao said, "why don't you buy a house?"

"Maybe I will," Wong huffed.

"Where is all this money, huh?" Shaowei said, playfully patting Wong's pockets.

Wong batted his hands away and squinted at Shaowei. "You think I have my winnings stuffed in my pockets, like an idiot? I'll have you know," he said, waving a fist, "I have my cash box hidden where no one will ever find it."

The men laughed while Wong stewed.

After supper, the men said their goodbyes in the street. Ping watched as Wong skipped down the sidewalk, tapping a stick off the metal fences, creating a ding-ding sound. It had been easy for Ping to forget how young Wong was, and seeing him skip down the road like this was as clear a reminder as ever. Ping thought then of his own son and he shuddered. There was a big difference between a toddler and a teen, but for a moment Ping saw a similarity between the two. Out of reflex, he touched the crumpled envelope in his breast pocket.

"Come on," said Shaowei, anxious to avoid a confrontation like last week's. They headed back to the laundry as fast as possible.

Once they were safely indoors, Shaowei picked up a newspaper. "Come here," he said, waving at Ping. "Let's read this."

They sat in the main laundry room so as to not disturb the other men, who were already settled in on their iron bed for the night. Shaowei would say the words and then Ping would repeat them.

"An . . . in vay shun . . . An invasion . . . fr, fr, om, from . . . th, th, ee, the . . . Oh, o, or, ri . . . ent, Orient. An invasion . . . from the Orient."

"Good," Shaowei said. "Let's keep going."

Sometimes Shaowei would get carried away and read a passage too long for Ping to be able to remember enough to repeat it.

"'An inferior type,'" Shaowei read, "'lower in the scale of humanity and civilization than are our people. It is undesirable to

have a large colony of them here to live. They are a most peculiar people, nowhere do they merge with the people among whom
they live. They keep to themselves, and could never be expected to
become what might be termed "Newfoundlanders."'" Shaowei put
the paper down and let out a deep breath.

"You read out too much," Ping said. "Never expect be
Newfoundlanders," he said in English, then in Taishanese, "That's
all I caught. What does it mean?"

"Let's read something else," Shaowei said, flipping the page.

The week proceeded as it always did, back-breaking labour and stoic
silence, aside from the sounds of splashing suds and the chorus of
spectators at the windows. Saturday was the best day at the laundry,
because you knew that at least tomorrow was a break. That, even if
only for a few hours, you could be free from the sinks and the soaps
and the hot irons. And even though it was the end of the week and
everyone was exhausted, you could get a second wind and try to
finish a couple of hours early so you could get ready for your single
day of rest.

Saturdays were also when they had the biggest audiences outside. Sometimes the crowd would be rowdy enough that you could
hear them through the glass, laughing and pointing, saying words
the men preferred not knowing the meaning of. Sometimes vendors set up outside, selling peanuts roasted over an open flame. Still,
this was all background noise for the Chinamen's labour and eventually they would forget they were being watched.

One Saturday evening in the summer, the audience had gotten
particularly rowdy. Afterwards, Ping wasn't sure if he had heard the
smash first or felt the shards pepper his neck. He could have sworn
he felt it first, millions of tiny shards of glass like shrapnel, flying

gracefully into the soapy suds of the tub, bubbles popped by the shiny miasma. Then the sound of the shattering glass, the rock hitting the floor with a thud and a crunch, the audience hooting and hollering, some decrying the barrier being broken, others cheering on the destruction. Later, Shaowei said he was surprised this hadn't already happened, the way things were around here.

Indeed, it was a rare incident in that it made the entire labour force of Fong-Lee Laundry stop what they were doing for a moment. Small pieces of glass were littered everywhere, and it would take some time to clean it up. And although it was an evening in the early summer, the stiff cold breeze of the Atlantic Ocean still blew in through the hole.

"All right," Hong said, taking charge, as Ping was tending to the minor abrasions on his neck. "Something like this happened before. First thing we gotta do is drain the tubs and make sure there's no minuscule pieces of glass hiding in the laundry we're working on. The glass on the floor can wait until supper break."

"What happened before?" Shaowei asked.

"You don't need to worry about it," Hong said. "Let's deal with the problem at hand. You and Poy, give me a hand with the paper."

The three of them tried to cover up the hole in the window with some of the laundry's brown wrapping paper, affixing it with twine. It wasn't long before someone outside punched a hole through the paper, then yelled something through the hole. The man was too belligerent to be understood.

"Fellas," Aiguo said. "It could be worse."

"Shut up, bag boy," Yang said as he repeatedly ran his hands over a tablecloth, making sure that every small fleck of glass was removed.

"The kid's right," Jun said. "Ah, ah, ah"—he lifted a wet white shirt to his nose. "*Ah-choo!*" Jun sneezed into the shirt. His eyes darted to the broken window.

"Nice going," Yang said with a roll of his eyes. "What, were you hatched from a rock?"

"Yang," Hong said, "this is not the time for your impetuous nature."

"My impetuous nature?" Yang said. "Jun is the one that just sneezed on a shirt. Can you imagine if they saw that? There'd be a lot more than a rock through the window. They'd burn the place to the ground."

"Enough," Hong said. "Focus."

After a moment of silence, Shaowei raised his head and said, "What did you say about this happening before?"

"I'm sure it comes as no surprise to you," Hong said.

"Does it happen often?" Ping asked as he shook out a long sock over the sink.

"No, no," Hong said. "They used to break the windows all the time and beat us up and take all the money. You should be happy, things are a lot better around here now."

The men continued to sort through the laundry in the tubs, shards of glass being crushed under their wet boots. The police briefly showed up. They spoke to Shaowei for a moment, to confirm they were at the right laundry, then they looked at the hole in the window.

"This type of thing, y'know, it happens," an officer said. "And it's a right shame, but something like this, it's almost impossible to ever find the culprit. But definitely let us know if it happens again." Shaowei didn't bother telling him that this type of thing happened all the time. The officers took the rock and left.

After the tubs had been drained and cleaned and inspected for any remaining shards of glass, and the soggy laundry had been inspected for glass, and all the glass was removed, the tubs were filled back up and the laundering and rinsing began again. A return to the soap suds, soundtracked by the crackle of torn paper flapping in the wind.

During the supper break, Ping took Shaowei aside. "How are we going to fix this?" he asked.

"Obviously we'll have to buy a new window," Shaowei said. "We can ask Reverend Riley if he knows a place. Or ask Hong, he probably knows."

"But what about tonight? We can't leave the window unsupervised."

"What, you think someone's going to come in and steal the sink?"

"No, not that. I'm concerned about . . . Well, anything could happen. Someone could come in and pour all the detergent down the drain. Or . . . or those kids could come back and throw the hot irons at us while we're asleep."

"During that half-hour when we're not working?"

"I don't know," Ping said. "Anything could happen."

"Then sit out front and keep watch to make sure," Shaowei said. "Just don't sleep tonight."

Ping slowly nodded. "And how are we going to pay for a new window?"

"Aren't you the manager?"

"Yeah, but . . . we send all the profits to Fong. I'm sure he would let us borrow some money to fix it. I mean, he'd probably tell us to use some of his money to pay for the window. But I'm not sure that we should do that without asking him."

"Oh," Shaowei said, loud. "So you *do* think Fong killed Lee."

"No," Ping said, waving this away with his hands. "I'm just saying that we probably shouldn't mess with another man's money."

"Lee messed with his money," Shaowei said, raising his eyebrows.

"Shaowei," Ping warned.

"I'm just saying," he said with a shrug. "So, what? You're never going to sleep again until you hear from Fong?"

"But we need to fix this immediately," Ping said. And then he smiled. "Maybe we should ask Gao to bring his mahjong set over tomorrow."

Some of the men volunteered to skip church so they could keep an eye on the building. Everybody wanted to go to heaven, but nobody wanted their cash box stolen while they were working on getting there.

Ping decided it was imperative for him to go to church. First of all, it was important that he continue to learn English. Second, he was going to ask Reverend Riley to recommend a window installer. Third, he needed to talk to Gao.

Reverend Riley poked his head in through the broken window. "I can imagine what happened here," he said with a deep sigh.

"Reverend," Shaowei said, "you tell us where to buy new one?"

"I think I might know a guy," Riley said. "But glass is expensive, y'know. Do you fellas have the money for that?"

"Not yet, sir," Shaowei said. "Sometime soon."

"I will pray for you." Reverend Riley brought a finger to his chin in thought.

On their way to church, Ping hung back and sauntered alongside Gao. He explained about the mahjong.

"It's not a casino or a club or anything like that. This is more of a, uh, charity drive. And, uh, the guys, they don't want to leave the laundry today, on account of the window being broken. They worry somebody might come in and steal their belongings or vandalize them or . . ."

Gao looked at him blankly. "Why don't you just ask Hop Wah to raise some money?" he asked.

"No," Ping said, "because Hop Wah wouldn't raise me some money, he would give me a loan, and I don't want to be indebted to him. And the guys, this is the day they play mahjong, they shouldn't have to forgo that just because someone threw a rock through the window."

Gao sighed. "Okay. But how long are you going to hold rounds there?"

"Long enough to pay for the window, and then maybe if there's a little extra money left over, you can have it as a payment for letting us use your mahjong pieces."

Gao nodded. "This is agreeable," he said.

Ping was beginning to recognize some of the words in the service, especially "Christ," "Christians," and "Christianity." The English lesson afterwards was good too. Ethel began to teach him the alphabet.

"S'pose we shoulda covered this on the first day," Ethel said as she flicked her hair. "But, what odds?"

After church, Ping and Gao walked to the Globe so that Gao could get his mahjong pieces. Then it was back to Fong-Lee.

"We're going to play mahjong here today," Ping announced to the laundry staff. "This is your day of games and you shouldn't have to sacrifice it just because of the window. Reverend Riley will help us find someone to fix it, hopefully sooner rather than later. Now, I know you probably don't want to pay a table fee, especially seeing as you already live and work here. But we're just collecting it so we can pay for the window."

"I'll need to see the receipts," Yang said.

"Think of it this way," Shaowei said. "The table fee here is less than you pay at the Tai Mei Club."

The games began. As it turned out, some of the staff had mahjong pieces in their luggage too, and soon enough there were two sets of rounds going on in the back of Fong-Lee. Despite the awkward seating arrangement, they figured out a way to seat the two games at the one long table. The entire staff was there, as well as Gao and Wong.

The rounds went for hours, long enough that they didn't even make it to the Globe for supper. They told Wong to go down to the restaurant and get some takeout, but the incident with the rock had made him afraid to walk around by himself. Ping went with him, not much of one for games anyway.

"You know," Wong said on the walk there, "I have a lot of money from the Tai Mei Club. I'm saving it up to take home for my mom and sister but I could probably pay for the window if you want to pay me back."

"Wong," Ping said. "There's no way you've won that much. Besides, the guys, they enjoy it. This is what they do to relax."

When they arrived at the Globe, Ping asked if they could get food to go.

"I can't afford to give out takeout boxes like that," Charlie said.

"What's the matter, boys?" Hop Wah said as he stood up from his table. "Ping, how come your crowd wasn't at the club today?"

"They're asking for takeout," Charlie told him with a dismissive laugh.

"Someone threw a rock through my window, our window, last night," Ping explained, "and the men decided to stick around today to make sure no one breaks in."

"It takes all nine of you to watch over that little place?" Hop said. "Plus Gao and Wong?"

"Mahjong," Wong added. "They're playing."

"Oh, really?" Hop Wah said, tone flat, eyebrows raised.

"Yeah," Ping said, a blush forming on his cheeks. "But it's nothing like the Tai Mei. They're just playing for fun. It's a Sunday thing, right? It's not a regular thing. It's just because—"

"Because of the broken window?"

"Yeah," Ping said.

"Boys," Charlie interrupted them. "This is beginning to sound like an argument."

"No," Hop Wah said. "There's nothing to worry about, Charlie. Just some friends catching up." He strode back to his seat.

"No takeout," Charlie said as he threw open the door to the kitchen.

"You shouldn't have said that," Ping said on the walk back to Fong-Lee, "about the mahjong."

"Well, it's true, ain't it?" Wong said.

"Yeah, but sometimes you don't need to tell everyone the truth. You can tell them part of the truth."

"What about the rest of the truth?" Wong asked.

"What about it?" Ping said, angry with the boy.

"Well, if you don't tell the whole truth, then isn't that lying?"

"Sometimes lying like that is necessary. You just tell people what they need to know, or want to hear, and you don't need to tell them any more than that."

The rounds of mahjong stretched into the evening, and Ping began to regret having them set at the long table. Qieng had fallen asleep at his usual spot at the table, sandwiched between the two rounds. Ping envied that man's ability to sleep through all manner of noise and commotion.

A knock came on the back door around eight that night, an oddity regardless of the time. Reverend Riley let himself in, then indicated with his pointer finger that he wanted Ping and Shaowei to come with him. They stepped out into the gravel alleyway.

"Now, look," Riley began. "I'm awfully sorry for what happened to your window, and I think a great deal of the community is sorry too. I passed around the collection plate today and told people that I would be donating the money to your cause. And I spoke with a glazier I know and he's agreed to replace the window for you at a discounted rate. When I counted the collection I realized I have your window paid for completely. You boys don't have to worry about a dime."

"Oh, thank you," Shaowei said, then looked at Ping and said in Taishanese, "White people are paying for the window."

"Wow," Ping said in Taishanese, then added, in English, "Thank you, thank you."

"Thank you, Reverend Riley," Shaowei said with multiple nods and a smile. "Thank you, thank you."

"I'm pleased to be in a position where I can even offer this to you boys," Riley said with a warm smile. "You shouldn't be put out just because some hooligans are always out here teasin' you."

"Is not the same people every time, Reverend," Shaowei said. "Is different people all the time."

"I know," Riley said with a slight stutter. "These, uh, exclusions and prejudices are a problem the community will need to rectify. But for the time being, we are glad to help. The window man, he'll be by in the next couple of days to get the measurements."

After Riley left, Shaowei and Ping stood outside the back door for a moment. Inside, they could hear laughter and the clacking of tiles.

"I guess we don't need to make this a weekly thing," Shaowei said.

"Yeah," Ping said, as he peeked in through a window at the gambling laundrymen and a pile of discarded bamboo tiles. He knew there was money to be made here, and quick. It could be his ticket out. Maybe they'd even make enough money that he could be out of here before having to deal with the consequences. "It looks like they're having fun, though."

"I guess it could continue," Shaowei said. "It's not like we're turning it into a club or something. Even if we only make a few bucks, it's fine."

"Exactly," Ping said. "It's not going to be a club."

18

THE HONG HEING CLUB

The Hong Heing Club, as the space in the back of Fong-Lee Laundry came to be known, was a roaring success. It started off slow, just the staff of the laundry, a few friends here and there, but with each passing week more people showed up. It was inferior in many ways to the Tai Mei Club. There was no bar, only one table with awkward seating arrangements, more of a potential for being caught, no private rooms, and fewer mahjong games. But these drawbacks created an exclusivity. If a venue can seat only eight people, then the eight who get to sit there must be pretty goddamn special. Eventually, Shaowei and Ping were using the table fees to buy more tables, to have better seating arrangements and more games. Once they could sit sixteen players, the table fees started finding their way into Shaowei's and Ping's cash boxes. They were doing well.

English lessons were going steady too. Shaowei had been helping Ping learn the alphabet, building on Ethel's lessons, slowly and methodically writing out each letter dozens of times on torn-off sheets of brown wrapping paper.

When he first started writing out the letters, Ping felt sad as he remembered that he had still not sent his letter to Hua Ling and his mom. He hoped they'd forgive him, he hoped they'd understand, he hoped Lee arrived home safe and told them he was okay. On Sunday nights, he used to reread the letter. Now he counted the table fees between bouts of practising the English alphabet.

There was an allure, he felt, to turning this space into their own parlour, their own club, a sense of ownership, of being able to invert the drab prison that was their job and turn it into a place where they wanted to be, to an activity at the laundry they could actually look forward to. Of course, the day-to-day labour continued. There was always something more that needed to be washed, and the men worked from sunrise to sunset to sunrise again. Yet it was late summer and they finally had something that was their own: their games.

Hop Wah was quick to notice the absence of the Fong-Lee Laundry's staff from his club, although he let it go for a while. One Sunday at the Globe, weeks later, just as September was beginning, he ended his silence.

He approached the table seating Ping, Shaowei, Gao, and Wong. "How's it going, fellas?"

Things had been polite and cordial between the four friends and Hop Wah, and although Hop knew that some of his customers had been taken away, he hadn't appeared to be overly bothered by the loss.

"We're all fine," Shaowei said.

"I never see you guys at the Tai Mei anymore," Hop said. "You should come sometime. Catch up with everyone."

"Maybe we will," Ping said. "Maybe next Sunday we'll drop by." Ping meant this earnestly. It would be good to switch things up, get out of the laundry.

"You guys still playing mahjong every week?"

"I don't play," Ping said. "But, yeah, there's usually a few rounds going on."

"That's interesting. And do you play the rounds for fun or what?"

"Well, no, the men, they bet their earnings."

"Oh," Hop Wah said. "So it's like the Tai Mei Club."

"It's extremely similar," Wong said.

"Wong," Gao snapped.

"Hey," Hop Wah said. "Don't silence the kid. Let him talk. What about table fees?"

"I'm not a kid," Wong said fast.

"Look, we don't want any trouble here," Ping said. "You know Charlie's rules."

"I'm not giving you any trouble, and as a matter of fact, you know damn well that I know Charlie's rules 'cause it was *me* that taught *you* them. Now tell me, do you charge table fees?"

"You don't seem to be following those rules," Shaowei said.

The kitchen door swung open.

"Hey!" Charlie called out. "Keep it down. Why is it I always got to remind you guys what's at stake for me here?"

"It wasn't me," Hop said. "Your boy was just trying to silence the kid here."

"I'm not a kid," Wong said, louder.

"Hey," Charlie said, throwing a rag over his shoulder. "Keep it down."

"Charlie," Gao said, "we aren't arguing here. Hop just came over to the table—"

"No," Charlie interrupted him. "I don't want to hear any excuses. None. Zip."

"But—"

"Zilch. No excuse. No arguments. This is a place of peace."

A silence fell over the restaurant.

"Charlie," Gao began again.

"Get out!" Charlie yelled. "Get out, get out, get out! I'm tired of you bringing this trouble around."

"Charlie," Gao said. "I'm not bringing any trouble here. I'm not trying to argue."

"I don't care, I don't care," Charlie said as he grabbed Gao by the shoulder, pulling him out of the booth and dragging him to the front door of the restaurant. He kicked open the door and flung Gao outside. He landed in the gutter with a splash. "And stay out! Find a new job too, you bum!"

There wasn't a sound to be heard in the restaurant, except for the gentle ringing of the entrance bell and a far-off sizzling pan.

Charlie wiped the sweat off his brow with his rag. "All of you," he said, pointing at Ping's table. "All of you. Get out."

The men silently stood up, threw a couple of dollars on the table, and headed for the back door. Hop Wah returned to his seat.

"You too," Charlie said, waving his arm in a slow and tired way. "You're just as bad as the rest of them. I don't want to see any of you."

Hop Wah stood up fast, and with a snarl, he put on his hat and walked out the back door.

Then there they were, all of them, Ping, Wong, Shaowei, and Hop Wah, in the alley behind the Globe.

"You lot," Hop Wah said, pointing a finger into Ping's face and then Shaowei's, "you need to learn your place here. I don't want to see or hear tell of you lot running a mahjong ring. I know you're charging table fees and I want a piece of it. And if I don't get my piece, you're stomping on my grounds and I'll do whatever it takes to make sure that my grounds remain my grounds."

"Okay, sir," Wong said.

"Shut up," Hop Wah said as he turned to walk away. "Kid."

The others stood there for a moment.

"Geez, fellas," Wong said, placing the back of his hand on his forehead.

"Shut up," Shaowei said.

Gao came round the corner, clothes soaked in gutter water. "Can I stay at your place tonight?" he asked Ping.

"Sure," Ping said.

They walked out of the alley and stood on the sidewalk in front of the Globe.

"Excuse me," a nasally voice called. A frail-looking old man was sticking his head out of a shop door across the street. HANS' SHOE SHOPPE, the sign read. "Excuse me, is there some sort of problem over there, gentlemen?"

The four men said nothing. Ping had obtained a pretty good understanding of written English over the past few weeks, but he still struggled with speaking it or understanding others. But this man he could almost understand perfectly. The man had a slow way of speaking, a way of sounding out all the individual letters and sounds. In a strange way, Ping thought, this man sounded like them, Chinese immigrants.

"I heard you get thrown out the door," the man continued. "I just want to make sure everyone is okay."

Again the men said nothing. Shaowei looked both ways and then crossed the street.

"What happen in there," he said, getting close to the man's face, "is none of your concern."

The man nodded and closed his door.

"Let's go," Gao said. "Come on."

The men walked back to Fong-Lee.

"You didn't have to talk to that man like that," Ping said to Shaowei. "With that tone."

"He wasn't the only one who saw us," Shaowei said. "There's

women in windows with their cats, there's children hiding round every corner and behind lampposts. There are eyes everywhere, in every bush, on every streetcar. I'm tired of feeling watched all the time. Everywhere, anywhere, there's always people watching us, criticizing us, waiting to throw something at us."

"I understand that," Ping said slowly. "But that man, he heard an argument outside and he looked out the window to see what the matter was. You would do the same."

"No," Shaowei said, "that man looked out the window because he heard Chinese people arguing, he wanted to look and see the heathen chinee, he wanted to see if what they say in the papers is true."

"Shaowei, come now, you're reading into this. He just wanted to know what was going on."

Shaowei shook his head and walked away from Ping.

It was a quiet night at the laundry. There wasn't quite enough room for Gao at the iron bed, so he slept on the floor. He first thought that would be more comfortable than the iron bed, but a cold draft blew in under the baseboards and Gao was left shivering all night. Ping closed his eyes and slept fitfully, waking several times during the night, haunted by dreams.

What he didn't see that night, what no one saw, was a man wearing a rounded white hood approach the Globe. He knocked on the door a couple of times, loud, angry knocks that woke up Charlie from his little perch at the back of the restaurant. Dazed, still rubbing the sleep from his eyes, Charlie opened the front door, expecting to see Gao return. Instead, he was greeted with a boot to the face, a boot attached to a broomstick with multiple nails and bottle caps sticking out and an old tin can attached on top. Momentarily blinded, Charlie slammed the door shut on the intruder. The man shoved against the door a couple of times, but

Charlie pressed the full weight of his body on the door, keeping it closed, until—

Bang!

Charlie's body dropped to the floor.

WHITE ROSES

A white rose bloomed in the garden behind Fong-Lee that morning. No one had planted it and no one had even noticed it, nestled as it was among the tops of carrots and turnips. After all, it was a working day at the laundry and no one had time to be looking at flowers.

It was an average morning, except now Gao was there and Ping had to teach him how to wash the clothes.

"Step up close to the tub," Ping explained. "Pull up your sleeves and get in place. Pick up the soap. Work up a lather, rub it on the clothes. Scrub and scrub until it's spotless. The rest of the rules will become clear as we go along. I find you can only really learn from experience."

And so they began, washing the clothes in the sinks.

"You know," Gao said, "I'm happy I lost my job at the Globe. Charlie hated when I sang. Now I can do it here."

"That won't last for long," Yang said, eliciting rare laughter from the staff.

"Everywhere they know me as a truly noble man," Gao began,

In search of wealth—
Greed led me on the road to Gold Mountain.
Denied landing upon reaching the shore, I am filled with rage.
With no means to pass the border, what can a person do?

"Thanks," Shaowei said from his perch at the front of the room where he sorted the clothes. "I hate it."

The front door swung open, toppling a pile of blue bags. Hop Wah stormed in.

"Which one of you did it, huh?" he yelled.

"What?" Shaowei said.

"I said which one of you did it, goddamnit!" Hop Wah yelled as he pushed Shaowei off his stool.

"Hey," Shaowei said. "What the hell? Don't touch me."

"I'll touch whoever the fuck I want!" Hop Wah yelled. "Until one of you confesses to killing Charlie."

A silence fell over the room.

"Wh-what?" Gao said. "Charlie's d-dead?"

"It was you, wasn't it?" Hop Wah stomped towards him.

"No," Gao said. "I would never hurt Charlie."

"You fuck." Hop Wah grabbed Gao by the collar and pushed him into the washing tub, submerging his head under the water. Bubbles floated to the surface as Gao's arms flailed around. "Charlie was a good man," Hop said, struggling to keep Gao's head under-water. "I owe everything I have to him."

Ping dived at Hop Wah. "Get off him. He was here all night, he didn't do it."

Ping and Hop Wah fell to the floor, causing Hop to lose his grip on Gao. Gao gasped for air as his head came out of the tub water, his eyes bloodshot from the detergent.

"Like I'm going to believe you," Hop Wah said. "You never tell the truth. You lied to me for weeks about the mahjong."

The front door swung open again. It was the cops, same officers as a couple of months back when the rock came through the window. They looked at the scene before them: two Chinamen in suits, engaged in a scuffle on the floor, another Chinaman, head soaking wet, seemingly unable to breathe, a room full of Chinamen not doing their jobs and instead watching the chaos that was unfolding.

"Hm," one officer said. "I guess you guys are investigating the Chinaman's death too."

Hop Wah pushed himself up off the ground and said in Taishanese, "When I find out which of you did this, you'll pay for it with your life. And after that, I expect each of you to leave town. I don't care if you weren't involved. If you were friends with the killer, I want you gone."

"Hey, hey, hey," the officer said. "Don't talk your language right now. Look, I'm not here to make any arrests. I'm here to enforce law and order. Now, as I think you know, there was a murder last night. We're simply looking for information. The people we've already spoken to, they said that the staff of this laundry had a big argument with Charlie yesterday. Is that true?"

None of the laundrymen said anything. Then Hop Wah cleared his throat and said, "Yes, Officer."

"He got in argument with Charlie too," Shaowei said.

"I see," the officer said. "We also heard that Charlie may have had a disgruntled former employee who might be hiding out at this laundry."

"That's him, Officer," Hop Wah said, pointing at Gao. "That's the man."

"All right," the officer said. "We're going to have to take some of you in for questioning. You two that were on the floor, the wet one, and you—" The officer pointed at Shaowei.

"Me? Why me?"

"You spoke up a minute ago, didn't you? You must have information to share if you're here talking to me."

The investigation went on for the rest of the week. Ping, Shaowei, and Hop Wah were all dismissed fairly quickly. Their stories were consistent. Gao's story was consistent too, although he was kept for longer than the others. He was the prime suspect: an employee who lived at the restaurant, publicly fired and humiliated in front of his friends, and thrown out the front door—an incident that several locals could corroborate, including a German shoe store owner who swore that there was never usually any trouble from the Chinamen.

A boot mark on Charlie's face was a size 13, far larger than Gao's feet, in fact far larger than the feet of anyone in the Chinese community. And the entire staff of the Fong-Lee Laundry, nine people in all, could provide an alibi for Gao. And the police couldn't find the murder weapon. No one had ever heard of Gao owning a gun, no one had ever seen him with a gun, and Gao swore that he had never even handled a gun.

It remained a mystery, never solved: the murdered Chinese restaurateur found dead by the milkman. Of course, the reporters ran with it, this violent turn of events perfect for the sensationalist papers' attempts to paint a picture of the Chinese immigrants as a violent and chaotic element in the island's still-burgeoning society. As for the immigrants themselves, a stalwart of their community was gone, and their grief could never end for as long as they did not know exactly what happened that night. It was an unbearable absence in their little community, but they never fully gave themselves over to the emotions of the moment, too tired, too overworked. The laundries and restaurants still had to be open, and the Globe ticked on, just a little less welcoming than before.

Gao returned to Fong-Lee as soon as he was released on Thursday afternoon, and after some brief catching up in the main laundry room, he sat at the iron bed in the back and sobbed over everything that had happened. No one checked in on him; there was work to be done. He did the same the next day too, alone at the table, sobbing all day. On Saturday, the police returned, once again looking for Gao.

Shaowei and Ping led them to the iron bedroom, and Gao was still there, sobbing. The police asked if they could be alone with Gao, and so Shaowei and Ping went out to the laundry room.

"What do you think?" Shaowei said. "Did he do it?"

"No, he didn't do it," Ping said.

"He could've gotten up at any point during the night. We don't know for sure."

"Shut up," Ping said with a roll of his eyes.

"So what do you think? Are they going to arrest him?"

"I don't know," Ping said, wiping his brow. "Probably, yes."

"If this was San Francisco," Shaowei said, "he'd already be strung up in the town square."

A moment later, the policemen came out of the room, said a quick thanks to Shaowei, and left. Shaowei and Ping looked at each other, puzzled. And then Gao came into the laundry room, holding some papers and no longer crying.

"Uh, guys," he said. "I think there was some sort of misunderstanding. They think I'm Charlie's son."

"What?" Shaowei said.

"I told them at the station that Charlie was like a dad to me,"

Gao said, "but I guess maybe I said it wrong. They think he's literally my dad. I just inherited his restaurant."

All of the labourers stopped and gaped at him.

"You mean," Ping said, "you own the Globe?"

"Yeah," Gao said, looking at the papers in front of him. "I guess so."

"Did he have real children?"

"I don't think so," Gao said. "He never mentioned anyone."

It occurred to Ping that he rarely mentioned his own family. Days went by and he forgot they existed. A twang of guilt struck him so hard that his eyes began to well. "That's great," he said. "Really great. Great for you."

"What are you going to do?" Shaowei said.

"What do you mean? I'll work at the restaurant."

"You can't do that," Shaowei said. "Everyone will know that a Chinaman was murdered there, they know a former employee was a suspect, they now know we all eat there on Sundays. Some government official even said that having so many of us in a tiny space is grounds to close the business. That restaurant is as dead as Charlie."

"Shaowei," Ping said, "please. You don't need to be rude right now."

Gao sat down on a box of detergent. "No," he said. "He's right. I'll sell the place. I'll move somewhere else."

"There's nowhere else to go," Ping said.

"Well, I'll move home if I have to. But he's right. I can't work there anymore. I'll just have to sell it."

"Bay Roberts," Aiguo said. "That's the place to be."

The men looked at him.

"Where is that?" Ping asked.

"About an hour outside of the city."

"I was thinking more off the island," Gao said.

"Nah," Aiguo said. "Bay Roberts. That's the place to be. Lots of opportunities for our people there. That's what I've heard."

"Like what?" Shaowei said.

Aiguo shrugged.

"Don't listen to him," Shaowei said. "Stupid."

"I have an uncle in New York," Gao said. "Maybe I'll go there."

"You can't go to New York," Shaowei said. "They don't let Chinese into America anymore."

"Not legally, no," Gao said. "But there must be a way. All those boats coming and going from here. There must be a way."

The men didn't say anything.

"Okay," Ping said, and he walked towards the bell. "Get back to work."

"Our community lost a good man this week," Reverend Riley said during his sermon. "I am reminded of a passage from my favourite book: in this life, righteous men sometimes meet the fate of the wicked, and the wicked sometimes meet the fate of the righteous. This is a vanity."

Although Ping and his friends knew Riley meant well, the wound was still too fresh and his biblical verses too cryptic to assuage their pain. The sermon passed by in blur in anticipation of the rest of the day.

Ping's language lessons had progressed to simple conversations, with Ethel leading the way, often speaking too fast for Ping to understand.

"There's this guy, Richards, Jesus, he won't leave me alone," she said. "I tells him just 'cause you got money doesn't mean I wants to go out wit' ya."

Ping found himself ignoring her this day, his mind drifting to other places, other problems. Something had to be done. He knew this deep down.

When the men returned to Fong-Lee, the familiar labourers were beginning their rounds of mahjong. Ping took Shaowei aside.

"Let's go to the Tai Mei Club," he said.

"Are you out of your mind?"

He shook his head. "I want to clear the air between us and Hop Wah, bring him some business, catch up on everything that's going on."

"I think it's a good idea," Wong said. Shaowei and Ping hadn't noticed him sidle up next to them.

"I think it's a bad idea," Shaowei said.

"Let's just go," Ping said. "Say hello, then leave."

"You can go," Shaowei said. "I'm staying."

"All right," Ping said. "I'll ask Gao if he wants to come."

Gao was still hanging around the laundry, avoiding the Globe.

"Aw, geez, Ping," Gao said. "I don't think we should do that."

"Things will only get worse the longer we go without talking to him." Ping paused, then added, "Besides, Charlie wouldn't want this type of conflict in the community."

Gao sat there, slumped over. "Fine," he said. "I'll go."

It wasn't a long walk to the Tai Mei Club. As soon as Ping, Gao, and Wong entered the gambling den, a hush fell over the room. Smoke hung in the air and nobody moved. Ping approached the bar.

"Hey, Little Joe," he said.

"What?" Little Joe said.

"Uh, I'll have a tea."

"No, bub," Little Joe said, terse. "What do you want?"

"A tea."

"What are you doing here? Why are you showing your face around here?"

"My face? I didn't do anything."

"You pounced on Hop Wah like a bitch. You overextended his knees."

"I didn't realize," Ping said. "I'm sorry. I was just trying to get him off of Gao."

"Gao? Don't you mean Charlie's murderer? Or did you have a piece of the action too?"

"Little Joe, we didn't have anything to do with it, I swear. The police cleared him."

"Oh, I know what the police said. They came by here, measuring all our boots, even measured our feet. That was pretty slick of you, to leave a giant footprint."

"Is Hop Wah here?"

"Oh, so you don't deny that it was slick to use a big boot, huh? You don't deny it, it must be true!"

"Little Joe, please, we just came here to see Hop Wah."

"He's at the picture show. I don't know how he'll feel seeing the likes of you in here."

"Well, we'll wait for him."

Ping and the others waited at the bar, trying to ignore the angry glares from the tables and Little Joe. The tables were quiet, aside from the click-clacking of mahjong pieces and the occasional stifled reaction to a win or loss. Ping felt an intense sense of discomfort, as if amidst the smoke and dim lighting of the casino, every eye had fallen on him in a hateful glare.

When Hop Wah showed up about a half-hour later, the mood of the room further soured.

"You!" he yelled. "Get out. All three of you. Is the other one here too? Get out."

"Hop," Ping said. "We wanted to smooth things ov—"

"Charlie was like family to me," Hop said, his colour rising. "I owe it to him to find his killer and make sure he meets the same fate." He brandished his revolver, loading the chamber and pointing it directly at Ping. Several men at the tables dived for the floor.

"Whoa," Ping said. "All right, we'll leave."

"Maybe you didn't hear me earlier this week," Hop said, his hand shaking. "I said I was going to kill whichever one of you killed Charlie and that I expected all of you to leave the city. I did not say come to the Tai Mei Club and we can be buddy-buddy. You don't belong here."

"None of us did it!" Wong said. "It could have been you, for all we know."

"Shut up," Ping said through pursed lips. "Okay. We'll leave. But I'm not leaving the city."

"He was my uncle," Gao said, angry. "He was my family. I'm just as upset as you are. I lost Charlie too."

"You know it was him, don't you?" Hop Wah said to Ping as he pointed the gun at Gao.

"I swear—" Gao began.

"Shut up!" Hop yelled. "Get out. Get out. If we weren't in my business right now, I'd shoot you where you stand."

Ping nodded and led the way out of the building with Gao and Wong in tow. Hop Wah followed them too, keeping the gun trained on them until they were outside.

"Shaowei was right," Gao said, stopping once they were out the door. "I mean, he's the one with the gun. I don—"

"Move!" Hop yelled from the doorway. "Get away from here."

The three hustled down the street, Hop still following a few paces behind, one hand buried deep in the pocket of his overcoat.

"That's right," he said. "Keep going."

The weather had changed. The sky was grey, no clouds, no sun, no hint of blue, just grey as if the entire city had been wrapped in a cloud. A heavy mist was falling that seemed to be a prelude to bigger storms.

"I don't think we should lead him back to the laundry," Ping whispered.

They passed the streets they would normally take to go home and continued down Duckworth.

"Best to be on crowded streets," Gao said.

Except the streets that were normally crowded weren't. The rain had driven people indoors and it was a Sunday after all. Nothing was open.

They continued to walk farther and farther down the street, Hop following them all the way, wincing with the occasional step. Maybe he did overextend his knees, Ping thought. They reached the back of the war memorial where Ping had sat with Fong that night, only a couple of months ago. It felt longer.

"How far are we going?" Wong asked. "I'm tired." He looked on edge and nervously glanced back at Hop Wah.

"I'm not sure," Ping said, a waver in his voice. "He'll leave us alone eventually."

"I want to look at the statues," Wong said suddenly, and he walked away to the front of the memorial.

"Stay with us," Gao called. But the boy didn't listen. He went and stood in front of the memorial, staring up at the bronze statues, glazed in the heavy mist. Hop Wah stopped between them.

Wong turned to face him. "What's the big idea, following us like this?"

Hop stood there, silent, a snarled grin across his face.

"Mister," Wong said desperately, "none of us did it. It was probably a local. Go home!"

Hop still stood there, smiling, both of his hands in his pockets, giving him a hunched-over look as rain began to fall more heavily, collecting on the brim of his hat, drip, drip, dripping in front of his eyes.

"Wong," Gao said, stepping closer.

Hop swung to him. "You did it. You son of a bitch, you did it."

"He was my uncle, you idiot," Gao said, clenching his fists. "I wouldn't do that to family. I wouldn't do that to anybody."

"He didn't do it," Wong said. "He didn't, I swear."

"You'll pay," Hop said.

"Just leave me and my friends alone!" Wong yelled as he dived at Hop. But Wong was only small, and his attempt at a tackle merely knocked Hop off balance. He stumbled backwards, tripped over a rock, and—*Bang!*

Ping didn't flinch.

It wasn't even clear what had happened at first. Hop had fallen to the ground but so had Wong, who fell sideways onto the granite base of the memorial. Gao hurried over to help Wong to his feet but then stopped and stumbled backwards himself.

"Oh no," he said with a sharp inhale.

Hop lay on the ground with a look of utter confusion on his face, looking between Wong and a newly formed hole in his overcoat pocket, a hole from which smoke drifted out.

Ping surveyed the scene and surmised what had happened. Hop's grip on the gun in his pocket must have tightened when he fell over and he had accidentally pulled the trigger. The bullet had hit Wong square in the chest.

He knelt down by Wong, blood pumping out of the boy's chest wound, staining his clothes and spilling onto the granite tiles. *It's going to be a son of a bitch trying to get that stain out*, Ping caught himself thinking.

"I . . . I slipped," Wong struggled to say.

"It's going to be okay," Ping said. "Just breathe."

"Take me . . ." The words drifted away from Wong as blood gurgled in his mouth. "Dogbane . . . nation."

The boy went limp in Ping's arms. He ripped at Wong's clothes, trying to get at the wound to apply pressure to it. He pushed down on the wound, but the only thing that achieved was smearing Wong's blood on his own hands. Ping looked at his hands, bloodied and rough, callused. The hands of a laundryman, the blood of a bag boy.

"Look," Gao said. "All the money."

Wong's pockets were all stuffed with cash. Bills fluttered down the memorial's grand steps, steeped in blood and rainwater.

Hop was gone. But eyes from every corner, every window had seen the scuffle and numerous people, locals and foreigners alike, identified Hop Wah as the culprit. Eyes had been everywhere, from the Narrows to the Spirit of Newfoundland herself.

The police arrested Hop Wah, but Ping and Gao were taken in for questioning anyway. Once again they sat in that plain office for hours, and once again their stories were corroborated by those of other witnesses. Hours later, Ping was released and began the long walk back to the laundry. It wasn't that long a walk, really, five, maybe ten, minutes. But Ping walked slowly because he knew the news of the shooting would have travelled back to the laundry and he knew exactly what Shaowei would say.

It was late when he arrived back at the laundry, he wasn't sure of the time, elevenish. It was possible that everyone had gone to bed, that the news hadn't reached them. He opened the back door as quietly as he could, hoping not to wake them.

All the lights were off and the only illumination came from the stove in the ironing room. The bright orange light of the flames cast flickering shadows over the main laundry room, making everything look like it was shimmering. And then Ping saw Shaowei's half-lit face.

"You idiot," Shaowei said. "I told you not to go there."

"Shaowei," Ping began. "I— I, didn't know it would—"

"You didn't know what? You didn't know you were risking your life and others' going over there?"

"It was an accident," Ping said. "He didn't even mean to shoot Wong. He was just trying to scare us off."

"Oh, it was an accident, was it? It was an accident when Charlie was killed too, was it?"

"He tripped," Ping said.

"Oh, and then the gun fell from the sky into his hand and it shot Wong by itself?"

"I knew he had a gun, I just didn't think—"

"You knew he had a gun?" Shaowei yelled. "You knew he had a gun and you still went there? And you took Wong along with you?"

"You weren't there," Ping said, tears now streaming down his face.

"I don't need to be there to know what happened. I don't need to be there to know this is your fault."

"How is this my fault?"

"You," Shaowei snarled, "with the gambling."

"That was your idea!" Ping shouted.

"It was your decision. You said no, then the window breaks and you bring it back up. It's on you." Shaowei stepped out of the darkness. His head was completely bald, his queue gone.

"Wh—" Ping stammered. "What happened to your hair?"

"You," Shaowei said, throwing the severed braid, still knotted together, at Ping's chest.

"I didn't do this," Ping said, incredulous.

"I was worried about you, about all of you. You were gone for hours. So I went out looking for you. I went to Hop Wah's and the cops were there, taking him away in shackles. Little Joe told me what happened. He told me if he ever sees me again, he'll kill me."

"Little Joe wouldn't kill you," Ping said.

"You're an idiot," Shaowei said. "You know that right? Stupid."

"So you shaved your head?"

"No," Shaowei said, throwing his fists up in frustration. "When I was coming back here, some drunks came up behind me. They pulled on my hair again and then they pushed me down into the mud and—and one held me down while the other one cut it off."

"Jesus," Ping said.

"You would say that, 'Jesus,'" Shaowei said in a high-pitched voice. "You would take their words and use them. You want to be just like all those ignorant whites."

"No!" Ping said, surprised.

"Yes, you do. Ever since Fong Choy showed up. Making you use the name they gave you, forced on you. Learning their language so you can fit in. You think you're too good for the laundry, admit it. You think you're too good for the work the rest of us do."

"I'm on my hands and knees doing this work day in and day out, same as everyone else."

"What are you even doing here? You don't need the money."

"I'm here," Ping began, emphasizing each word, "to replace my uncle until he returns."

"Lee is dead. You know that, right?"

"Stop fucking saying that."

"He's dead," Shaowei said, shaking his head. "Fong killed him or Hop Wah killed him but he's dead. He gambled everything away, including his life."

"No, I meant how you keep saying 'you know that, right'? It's so fucking annoying."

"Lee is dead and it's your fault," Shaowei said. "Charlie is dead and it's your fault."

"No," Ping said, "it's not."

"Wong is dead and it's your fault. This," Shaowei said, gesturing towards his head, "is your fault. And it's your fault because you think you can be accepted into this community of dumb hicks, that if you can make enough money, they'll forget you're a chink."

"It's not a bad thing to want to fit in," Ping said.

"I never want to fit in with these people," Shaowei said. "I will never want to be a part of this ignorant community."

"You told me to go to church to 'appease the white man.' You said that yourself."

"I don't want to appease anybody anymore," Shaowei said. "I just want to be myself. I want to be called by my own name. I want to be allowed to walk down the street in peace, without being watched or mocked or humiliated. I don't want to be integrated, I just want to exist."

Ping's heart was beating so rapidly he could barely hear what Shaowei was saying.

"I have to get out of this place," Shaowei said. "You should too."

"There's nowhere else to go," Ping said. "I can't leave—"

"Oh, shut up," Shaowei said. "What about Bay Roberts?"

"Do you really think life would be any better there?"

Shaowei sat down on a detergent box and hung his head.

"We belong here," Ping said, sitting down next to him and patting his shoulder.

"We will never belong here," Shaowei said.

"I know you may not like this, but that's what Fong Choy told me. He said 'you belong here.' We just have to persevere."

Shaowei yelled, "What the fuck does Fong Choy know about belonging here?"

"Well," Ping said, "he was the first Chinese person to step foot on—"

"And before that," Shaowei said, "he was in Halifax, and before that he was in Montreal, and before that he was in America, and before that he was in Europe, and before that he was in a million different fucking places all over the planet and even now he's somewhere fucking else. You know why?"

Ping sighed.

"Because our people, people like you and me and all those men in there sitting against that iron bed, don't belong fucking anywhere. Fong Choy had to move every ten fucking minutes because there is no place on Earth for us. And I don't give a fuck if Bay Roberts is just as bad as here, but we can't be here anymore. Little Joe and the Tai Mei Club have made that expressly clear. We do not belong here."

Ping stared at the roaring fire through the doorway to the drying room. "Maybe you're right," he said.

Shaowei grabbed the back of Ping's head and kissed him on the lips.

Ping jumped up and pushed him back. "What the hell?"

"I—I'm sorry," Shaowei said, blushing. "It's just—I thought—"

"No," Ping said. "No. I mean, I don't judge you or any—"

"I don't want to talk about it," Shaowei said, averting his eyes.

"You can do whatever you want," Ping said. "We can be friends. It's just—I'm not . . ."

"Just stop," Shaowei said. "Let's go to bed."

Ping stared at him.

"Not like that," Shaowei said.

In the iron bedroom they nestled into their chairs among

everyone else, both of them struggling to sleep for hours. Much to think about, much to regret.

In the morning, Shaowei looked at Ping and said, "Give me five dollars."

"Why?"

"I'm going to Bay Roberts."

"Shaowei, c'mon," Ping said. "Stay here. You have friends here."

"I don't think it's safe to be here and I want to explore other options. I don't want to work in this laundry my whole life."

Ping stared at him. "Fine," he said. "Fine." He took out the cash box, counted out five dollar bills, and slapped them into Shaowei's outstretched palm.

Shaowei stashed the money in his own cash box and stood up to leave. "Hey," he said. "Never forget what I taught you. 'It's always the way.' Use it."

"I'm sure I'll see you again soon," Ping said. "You'll have to come back to the city eventually."

Shaowei nodded and walked out the back door.

Ping sighed. Maybe Shaowei was right. Maybe he needed to skip town too. As he stood up to go and ring the bell to officially signal the start of the workday, he noticed something peculiar. Shaowei's suitcase was still there. Ping hurried to the back door, looked up and down the alley.

He'll be back, he thought as he returned inside.

His writing and reading skills had improved to the point that he found he could get by without his sorter. He sorted the clothes and made lists of what they were. He only needed to stop a couple of times to ask one of the others what the English word was for a certain item. And so his morning went by, smoother than he had expected, until the cops showed up again.

When Shaowei left the laundry, he walked down past the war memorial, past all the wharfs, down to the Martin Royal Hardware Store. He used every dollar he had in his cash box to buy a revolver and six bullets. The total came to fourteen dollars. The old man behind the counter, presumably Martin Royal himself, squinted at him, and for a moment Shaowei thought that this guy wouldn't sell him a gun. But he did sell him a gun, and six bullets.

Shaowei left his empty cash box at the base of the war memorial, then walked all the way to the Hop Wah Laundry. He went in through the front door and raised the gun.

"Bring me Little Joe."

The entire laundry stopped moving. Little Joe wasn't there, or at least, not anywhere visible to Shaowei.

"Put the gun down," someone said, "and we'll tell you where he is."

"No," Shaowei said. "You tell me where he is or I'll shoot one of you." There needed to be retribution for Wong's death, Shaowei had decided, and it didn't much matter to him who he killed, just so long as it was one of Hop Wah's men. He panned the gun slowly across the room. Something moved fast in his periphery, and just as he spun to face it, a brave soul stood up and pelted a bar of soap at Shaowei's head.

Bang!

Another man ran at Shaowei, carrying hot irons in both hands.

Bang! Bang!

The man's body dropping to the floor with a clatter, the irons skimming across the concrete like stones on a lake. Shaowei looked at the body in front of him, looked at the other body on the floor, then looked at the gun. He raised the pistol to his own head.

Boom!

The police later concluded that one of the bullets must have been too big for this gun and had exploded inside it, peppering Shaowei's face with metal shrapnel from the combusted bullet.

Shaowei, blinded in one eye and screaming in pain, tumbled out the front door and onto the ground.

"You friends with one Mr. Sinclair Zhang?"

"Who?" Ping said. He looked at the cop's name tag—OFFICER GROUCHY—and wondered how to pronounce it.

"We know he works here and we know he's a close associate of yours," Grouchy said.

"I not sure . . ." Ping said, and then realized who they were asking about. "Oh, Shaowei. Yeah, he leave this morning."

"Sir, I'm gonna need you to come with me. We have some questions to ask regarding Mr. Zhang, or Shaowei as you refer to him."

"I not leave. Much work to do. Much sorting—"

"Sir, do not make me ask you twice," the officer said.

Ping looked back at the laundrymen, who had been silently watching.

"I take over for you," Hong said in English so as to not arouse the suspicion of the police. "Go, go."

Grouchy escorted Ping to the back seat of a police car and stood guard outside. Another officer sat on the passenger side in the front. He wore a wide-brimmed brown hat and turned around with a snarl.

"Mr. Ping, is it?" he said. He sounded different from the white people voices Ping had become accustomed to in Newfoundland.

"Yes." Ping nodded, sweaty palms kneading the leather uphol-stery under his legs. He had never been in a car before, let alone a police car.

"The officers tell me you're friends with this Zhang fella?"

"Yes," Ping said.

"Are you aware of Mr. Zhang's actions today?"

"He move to Bay Robert," Ping said.

"Mr. Ping, do not lie to me. Let me ask again. Do you know what Mr. Zhang did today?"

"He tell me he go move to Bay Robert," Ping said, heart pound-ing. "He leave this morning. I not sure where he go."

"Okay, Mr. Ping, I'll let it go for now, but if it comes to my attention that you are lying to me, there'll be hell to pay."

"Why? He no go Bay Robert?"

"No, he did not go to Bay Roberts," the officer said matter-of-factly. Ping looked at his chest for a name tag but there wasn't one. It struck him now that the man wasn't even wearing a police uniform. He was wearing a shearling coat, the same colour brown as his hat. "He went on a shooting spree."

"I sorry, I not sure . . . ?" Ping said.

"I said your friend Mr. Zhang went on a shooting spree." The man imitated a gun with his hand and pretended to fire some shots. "He went to Hop Wah Laundry and he shot a bunch of them chinks in there and then he went and tried to shoot his damn self."

"Shaowei?" Ping said.

"Gesundheit," the man said. "You oughta cover your nose when you sneeze, boy, shit."

"He shoot gun?"

"Yes, he shoot gun," the officer mimicked. "He shoot two men. And himself."

Ping felt like his head was rotating around his body in figure eights. "He . . . die?" It was a struggle for Ping to say this.

"No, that sonuvabitch is still alive. Couldn't even figure out how to off himself."

The smell of the leather upholstery made Ping retch.

"Don't you get sick in here. Listen to me, I got a message for you. It's simple, okay? Listen."

Ping nodded.

"You were friends with that fella Charlie?"

Ping nodded again.

"And Ignatius Wong, he was one of your friends too, right?"

Ping nodded once more.

"And you're also friends with this Zhang guy, right?"

"Yes," Ping said.

"Well, you have found yourself in the centre of a veritable crime wave now, haven't you?"

Ping did not respond.

"Yes sir, you have. Now, here's where I come into the picture. You and I are alike." The officer paused. "Bet you didn't realize that. What I mean is, I'm not from here either. No. I'm from Canada. I'd tell you where, but you wouldn't know where it is anyway so all I'd really be doing is puffing smoke. But where I'm from, we had a lot of your type coming into the city. Taking jobs. Women. Thinking you could just show up and live and sow chaos and disruptions. It'd be bad enough, taking away the jobs, it'd be bad enough. But the violence. Makes a man fear for the safety of his kin. We in Canada didn't take too kindly to that. Me and some of my pals, we put an end to that violence real quick in the best way we knew how. Fight fire with fire."

The officer brandished a large revolver and pointed it into the back seat at Ping.

"My message is this. Find a way to end the violence in your community. Or we will end it for you. And don't think I don't mean it neither. I killed many a dog, Indian, and Chinaman in my day and I wouldn't hesitate to do it again."

Ping stared down the barrel of the man's gun.

"You understand me?" the man said.

Ping nodded.

"You tell me what I want you to do," the man said. "Go on, tell me."

"No violence," Ping said. "No gun."

"That's right. Now get out of the car. And don't forget to thank Officer Grouchy on your way out. It was awfully nice of the police to bring me over here today."

Ping was surprised that *Grouchy* was pronounced "gushy."

"Go on," the man said, loud. "Get."

Ping tried to open the door but it wouldn't budge. Officer Grouchy opened the door for him.

"Thank you," Ping said. He staggered down the alleyway and vomited.

A man living next door to the Hop Wah Laundry, Chesley Noseworthy, heard the gunshots and the screaming. He looked out his window, saw a man bleeding on the sidewalk, and despite his wife's pleading with him to not get involved, he put his jacket and hat on and went outside. First, he pulled the fire alarm outside the laundry, and then he ran to fetch Dr. McDonald, who lived nearby. Before the police could arrive, street urchins surrounded Shaowei's body. They stole the remaining bullets out of his pocket, the missing bullets becoming a mystery that the court would find itself unable to solve.

Shaowei was arrested and charged with two counts of murder and one count of wounding with intent to kill. The case was an easy one for the officers to solve, and the trial happened unusually quickly due to the public's demand for the celestial murderer to be punished swiftly. The newspapers covered the case breathlessly. It was there that Ping learned most things about the case. Sure, the police called him in for questioning again, and he was once again dismissed. But it was the papers where he really learned about what happened, or what the reporters thought happened.

The first headline read, "Two Murders Committed and a Third Attempted—Chinese Slayer Turns Gun on Himself—Most Sensational Crime in the History of Newfoundland—Is Last Night's Tragedy the Beginning of a Local Tong War?" The following day the headline read, "Was Shooting Premeditated? Slayer Purchased Revolver on Monday—All Theories So Far Point towards an Ancient Chinese Superstition." The headline the day after that read, "Chinese Murder Trial Opened To-Day—The King vs. Sinclair Zhang." And then, "GUILTY! Death Penalty Imposed on Sinclair Zhang." And then, "Chinese Murderer Dies on Scaffold—Extreme Penalty of Law Carried Out—Trap Sprung at 8:09 This Morning—Sinclair Zhang Met His End Calmly—Execution Arrangements Perfect."

Ping didn't need to read that last headline, as he had been there. He and Gao had found their way over to His Majesty's Penitentiary early that morning. It was a part of the city they had never been to before and they had gotten lost a couple of times on the way there, thinking they were at the wrong place because they had arrived at a beautiful lake and such a place didn't seem fit to house criminals and executions. The water was calm, the sun was shining, but the air was cold, indicative of the winter that would soon arrive. Eventually, Ping noticed a grey brick building hiding behind big brick walls and realized that this must be the place. It was on the other side of the lake, and Ping and Gao would never make it around in time. So they sat there in the tall grass, looking over at the large crowd assembling around the jail where Shaowei was being kept.

Dozens of reporters, children, couples, people of all kinds were gathered just outside the brick walls, everyone there to watch the Chinaman hang. It was the biggest crowd Ping had seen since he'd arrived in St. John's. He had been told that Reverend Riley was going to visit Shaowei in his cell that morning and say a prayer for him. Ping could think of nothing that Shaowei would hate more, to listen to church shit and then be hanged in front of an audience of bloodthirsty whites. Shortly after eight, Shaowei was led out to the top of a scaffold that the prison had set up by the brick wall especially for this occasion. The trap was sprung and he hung there, feet kicking, body flailing, while the audience below hooted and hollered and cheered, until Shaowei's body stopped moving at all. It swung back and forth slowly in the wind, at which point the audience offered solemn applause and then promptly dispersed. Shaowei's body was dragged up the wall and dropped back onto the prison grounds.

He was buried somewhere past the train station, in an unmarked grave.

It was funny, in a macabre way, Ping thought. From the distance where he sat, it could have been anyone being hanged over there. There was no way to know that the man hanged was the same man who had travelled across the world with him, who had been his steady companion for months, who had taught him so much. No way of knowing at all.

But, of course, it *was* Shaowei hanging over there. His body and its lifeless dangles, *he* rendered *it* as fast as you run out of breath.

* * *

On the walk back to the laundry, Gao said to Ping, "I'm leaving town."

"You are?" Ping said.

"Yeah," Gao said. "I'm selling the Globe."

"Oh," Ping said.

"I want you to take Charlie's cookbook," Gao said.

"Wh-why?" Ping said. "You should have that."

"It hurts me to look at it," Gao said. "But someone should have it. I don't care if you give it to someone else. I just don't want it to be thrown away."

"Of course. I'll take care of it," Ping said.

They walked quietly for a little longer.

"Where will you go?" Ping asked.

"New York," Gao said. "I'll hide in the back of a shipping container. I know a guy who can arrange it."

"Huh," Ping said. "Maybe I'll visit you someday."

They were silent for a moment.

"I guess you guys were right," Gao said, affecting a lighter tone. "I won't marry Bessie after all."

Ping didn't say anything back.

The men once again missed the white roses blooming in the laundry's little garden. They were harder to miss now, a whole bush had developed, five flowers blossoming, their white petals unfurled out of season. Eventually a passing local plucked all five of the flowers and gave them to his sweetie, who put them in a vase until they showed the first sign of rot and then promptly threw them in the trash.

20

THE ST. JOHN'S PEACE ACCORDS

"We need to smooth things over," Ping said on the afternoon Shaowei was hanged. "Before there's any sort of . . . retaliation." He didn't want to tell the laundrymen what the man in the police car had said.

"That wasn't such a good idea last time," Hong said.

The men were sitting around the tub; Ping was sorting. He felt an immense guilt over everything that had happened. He felt emptied out, like a shell of who he once was. He had been a teacher with a family. Now who was he? Some bum who had caused a lot of pain in a part of the world as far away as he could possibly imagine from what he had regarded as his "life." He remembered Hua Ling's delicate fingers picking the shell off a lychee and dropping the fruit into Wai's waiting mouth, the young boy slurping it up with a big noise. He remembered jumping between the two of them, fooling around and putting the lychee shells on top of their heads and everyone was laughing and laughing. That was his "life," not this dirty work of a labourer. Ping thought that if he could walk back home, he would, and he wouldn't care if it took a year to do it. But, alas, that was not an option. He hated whichever deity was real, for being too jealous to let his happiness last for long. The laundry was his life now. And the violence was his problem to solve.

"Sunday," Ping said, "I'm going over there."

"Why do you wanna go and do that?" Yang said. "Haven't you seen enough death?"

"If we want to be accepted here," Ping said, "then we need to smooth things over."

"You know what?" Yang said as he angrily scrubbed at another shirt. "I'd say it's your funeral, but you just might kill us all at this rate."

"You're going to be the big hero?" Jun began before a bout of coughing. "You're going to be so noble and save us all?"

Ping returned to his work. It wasn't an exercise in nobility; he wasn't affecting the stance of a hero. Ping felt it was imperative to keep his promise to the man in the police car. And, too, there was a small part of him that had another, deeper desire: he couldn't help but hope that maybe Little Joe would kill him, that maybe the guilt he felt over everything could end like that.

On Sunday morning, Gao came by and dropped off the cookbook.

"Thanks," Ping said. "I—I'm going to see Little Joe this afternoon."

"Huh," Gao said. "Bad idea. Hop is in jail. They'll probably hang him next. Leave it at that."

"I just," Ping stammered. "I just can't live with myself knowing there's all this ill will—"

"It's fine," Gao said. "Just be careful. Maybe I'll see you in New York one day. I'll send you a letter when I'm settled."

There was no friendly embrace. Both men were exhausted from their labour, and the recent violence had soured them. Their lives had become entirely too fraught for them to remember whatever cordial niceties should accompany such a moment.

Later that morning, when Reverend Riley arrived, Ping was still sitting in the same spot, considering just what he should do.

"Hi," Riley said. "How are you doing?"

"Good," Ping said in English.

"You know, I said a few words for your friend this week. I saw him in his cell before . . . Well, I saw him in his cell and he was at peace. He wanted you to know that."

"I watch from across lake," Ping said.

"Oh, that's an awful shame. I would've hoped none of you people would see that. It's an awful shame. Everything that happened."

"It's always the way," Ping said.

"Yes," Riley said. "Yes, that is true. You're probably feeling a little low now, but you know what will always help you feel better? The word of the Lord."

The language lesson with Ethel mostly focused on her trying to ascertain whether the rumours she heard were true or not.

"That was the fella always talkin' for ya, right? By da Jesus, I never woulda expected that outta him. I said to my sisters, I said, 'Jesus, Mary, and Joseph, that's the guy that always speaks for my guy.' Papers said he did it as part of an ancient Chinese ritual of da Tongs or somethin' like dat, dat true?"

Ping struggled to understand exactly what she was asking. "I not sure why he did it, maybe revenge, not sure."

"But the papers," Ethel said, "they was saying it was a Chinese thing, like this was somethin' you guys do back home."

"No, no," Ping said. "Violence, very unexpect. Not sure why. Probably Wong die and he angry. Someone cut hair."

"What's dat mean? You cut your hair and you goes on a murder rampage, is dat what it is?"

"No, no. A local. Local push him down, cut his hair. He angry, very very angry. And Wong die."

"By da jumpins, you people and your ways are a mystery to me," she said. "What about you? You going to murder anyone?"

"No murder. After this, I go talk. Talk about peace and no more murder."

"It might be dangerous for a young lady like me to even be around someone like you," Ethel said, touching the top of Ping's hand.

Ping was confused by this remark. The words on their own made it seem like she might be scared of him, but the way she said them contradicted the meaning of the words. The fluttering of her eyes, the raising of one hand to her blushed cheek, the touch of her other hand on his. Confusing. He knew that he wanted her to touch his hand again.

"Is no danger," he said. "I not danger. I peace. I not involve in murder. I want no murder. I wash the clothes. That it. Washee washee."

After the language lesson, he headed over to the Tai Mei Club. He passed by the store with the kitchen display and peeked at the reflection of himself in the ideal kitchen. He continued on to Hop Wah's laundry. He paused outside the door, his heart beating so fast that black spots were obscuring his vision. He felt like he might pass out. He took a deep breath and opened the door, found his way to the room with the billowing smoke and the clacking mahjong tiles.

Everything stopped when he walked in, no sound, no movement. For a moment it seemed as though the smoke was dissipating. There were fewer people than normal, presumably having been scared off by the violence and the heavy police presence outside the laundry.

"I never known the likes of you in my life," Little Joe said, coming out of the kitchen with a halibut in his hands. "You got an awful gall to show your face around here, bub."

"I want to talk," Ping said. "I don't want any more violence in our community."

"*Our* community? This is *their* community. We just live here. You, on the other hand, I'm not sure how much time you have left." The men at the games tables laughed.

"Please," Ping said, approaching Little Joe. "Let's work something out."

"I'd kill you right now if there wasn't police outside watching the place. I've got no qualms about killing you. But you and I both know the cops are probably expecting something like that, they're expecting us to try to kill each other. So that means I gotta wait to kill you. And if you're wise, and don't get me wrong, I respect you, you seem wise to me, if you're really that wise, you'll leave town. Go to Bay Roberts or Joe Batt's Other Arm, or get in a little rowboat and row the fuck away from here." Several men yelled after that, words unintelligible to Ping.

"Look," Ping said. "I don't want to leave here. I have a responsibility to my family to be here. Let's just talk in private. We can work something out, I'm sure of it."

"You're bold, I'll give you that," Little Joe said. "While Hop Wah is gone, I'm the boss around here, so let me make this clear. You and your men are responsible for the death and imprisonment of my men, so I don't want to talk in private. We can talk right here, in front of everyone."

"It would be better if we could talk in private," Ping said.

"You're lucky I'll talk to you at all. It's here or nowhere," Little Joe said.

Ping sighed. "I want to unify the community. I want it to be a peaceful community. It's what Charlie would've wanted. The quicker we achieve that, the quicker the white people will accept us into their society."

"Oh yeah? That doesn't bring my men back from the dead. That doesn't release Hop Wah from prison."

"I lost men too. I know the pain of losing people close to you."

"You didn't have someone walk into your place of work trying to kill ya, though, did you?"

Ping thought of his scuffle with Hop Wah on the floor of the Fong-Lee. "No," he said, "but I can still fear that. I fear that I could end up dead like Charlie or Wong."

"Hey, whoa," Little Joe said. "It was probably one of your men that killed Charlie. Probably that Gao."

"None of my men killed Charlie," Ping said calmly. "Probably one of your men killed Charlie."

Little Joe gently placed the halibut on the bar. "You got a lot of nerve saying that in here, bub."

"It was probably some local that did it," Ping said. "People here, you know how they are. They hate us. This is our chance to change that."

"How do you figure?"

"No more mahjong at my laundry."

"That's it?"

"You have to think beyond gambling," Ping said, feeling emboldened, desperate. "We need to abolish this conflict."

"You're going to come in here and tell me to abolish this business? I got responsibilities too, y'know. I gotta keep this place afloat while Hop Wah is locked up. I can't get rid—"

"No, no," Ping said. "This place stays as it is. No mahjong at Fong-Lee, but there would still be mahjong at the Tai Mei, like it was before. We'll have one club for all the Chinese, where we unite the whole community, where everyone is together and there's no ill will. Like what Charlie wanted the Globe to be."

"And what? We just forgive and forget all the deaths around me? I'm understaffed here now. We're not making as much money as we used to."

"Please," Ping whispered. "I'm prepared to make you an offer but we need to talk in private."

"Fine, fine."

Little Joe led Ping upstairs, into one of the small bedrooms peppered throughout the building. "What is it?" he said as he closed the door behind him. "What's the big deal, that you can't even talk about it in front of the others?"

"I'll do anything you want," Ping said. "As long as it's not violent and it doesn't attract negative press."

"This is the offer you couldn't say in front of the others?"

"Yes," Ping said. "I'll do anything. One of the police, he told me that if we didn't stop this violence among us, they would kill us. Like dogs."

"Fucking cops," Little Joe said, then sat for a moment, thinking. A devilish grin crossed his face. "I want your staff," he said.

"Which ones?"

"All of them," Little Joe said. "Clients too."

"How do you expect me to run the laundry?"

"You don't need to run the laundry," he said.

"I have a—"

"I know, I know." Little Joe waved his hands. "You got a responsibility to your family and all that jazz, but let me tell you something. The only thing you owe your family is a job for your uncle when he returns."

"So Lee is alive?"

"How the fuck should I know?" Little Joe said. "He's your uncle, not mine."

"What about Fong Choy?" Ping said. "He expects his money every week."

"He'll still get his money for now. So, do we got a deal?"

"If you take all the laundrymen and all the clients, then there's no job for my uncle."

Little Joe sighed. "Let me spell it out a little clearer for you, bub," he said. "What I want is for your laundry to be gone. Now, it doesn't have to be harsh. Your men will work here, they can live here, I'll take the clients. You can find a new job. You can work here too if you want. But what I want is for Fong-Lee Laundry to be gone."

"I . . . Fong Choy knows we do good business. He's not going to let me just—"

"You don't get it," Little Joe said, exasperated. "Fong-Lee will be gone. I'll burn it down if I have to. There will be no laundry. No big handover or anything like that. The laundry will be burnt down and things will proceed naturally from there. Fong don't have to know. Nobody needs to know."

Ping sat and thought.

"I'll tell everyone you paid me off or gave me a settlement," Little Joe said. "Then, in a couple weeks, I'll burn it down. Maybe even a couple months from now, when the heat's off."

Ping still sat there.

"No one will get hurt," Little Joe said. "I don't want any more violence either. And regardless of what the cops told you, there's a pressure on me too, okay? To avenge these murders. Something has to be done."

"Fine." Ping winced as he spoke. "Do it."

"All right," Little Joe said. "Let's shake on it."

They shook hands.

Little Joe began to laugh. "You're one cold son of a bitch, you know that?"

"Why?" Ping said.

"You're willing to risk having your whole staff go homeless during the winter just so you can smooth things over."

"Why?" Ping said. "Is the winter bad here?"

21

DISCONTENT

Winter was settling in and Ping had never seen anything like it in his life. At first it was nice, the white particles floating down from the sky, gathering in small svelte piles, smooth and ephemeral, shaped into objects by locals. But as the weeks wore on, the snow became more packed and tough. It would fall and gather for hours, until it was up past the door of the laundry. A fierce cold wind seemed to be blowing at all times of day, and drafts would pour in through every crevice in the walls, leaving everyone shivering, noses running. At night, after all the work was done, they would move the iron bed closer to the ironing room to get more of the heat from the roaring stove. Sickness after sickness passed through the ranks of the laundrymen, germs presumably picked up from the soiled garments they washed every day. Sick as they were, they could not stop working. Even when the snow was piled high outside the door, they could not stop working. People needed things washed.

When it wasn't snowing, it was raining, a cold, slick rain that would build up in thick patches of ice all over the street. Another hazard walking around town: the chance that you could slip on a patch of ice on a hill, roll right down into the harbour and drown to death, if you were lucky, or otherwise freeze in the water as you felt every bodily organ slow down and fail. The narrow passage into the harbour, that too became clogged with ice, large chunks floating in from somewhere out beyond, making it so that even the boats couldn't come and go.

These were hungry, cold times for all, and Ping once again caught himself wondering if nobody was ever meant to survive on this island, that the very climate of this place disposed each person to hate themselves and their neighbours, to develop a sour comportment and an ambivalent desire to see others fail and one-self prosper. Sometimes on Sundays, Ping would walk around the neighbourhood, and the streets seemed so lonely, the wide streets he walked in with Fong Choy rendered narrower and narrower as the snowbanks piled higher and higher. And always, an uneasy thought in the back of his mind, that the laundry could catch fire at any time, that he'd have to gather his belongings and run.

Ping had known all his co-workers, his employees, for months now, but he could never truly connect with them and now he felt he never would. He always had a sense that they were a team before he came along and there was no real way for him to earn membership in that team. On Sundays, everyone went to the Tai Mei Club. Ping told everyone he'd made a deal: no more mahjong at Fong-Lee, plus a cash settlement.

The locals were preparing for Christmas now, and it was reflected in the garments being washed. The clothes became more winter appropriate, jackets filled with bird feathers. And seasonal styles became prevalent, green velvet dresses and strange men's suits made of red cloth and rabbit skins.

"Santa suits," Hong explained. "It's for the kids."

It occurred to Ping that they hadn't celebrated any of the Chinese holidays they used to observe back home. It was as if the laundrymen had become unstuck in time, no longer governed by the calendars of home but by the seasonal clothing rhythms of the West.

Although Christmas Day was to be a holiday, on Christmas Eve the men at the laundry were still working. There wasn't as much to be washed, but there were still tablecloths, napkins, curtains, the occasional fancy dress, the odd suit.

Supper break was far ahead of usual that night, around seven. The same tepid stew as always. However, Reverend Riley had promised a grand Christmas dinner for the entire staff the next day. This was something to look forward to, the type of thing that made you forget just how cold it was.

They stood around the iron bedroom, eating and slurping their soup in silence, until Hong put down his bowl and said: "I think I smell smoke."

This wasn't particularly unusual, as they always kept a fire burning. But Ping was instantly alert.

"I'll go check on the stove," he said.

Dark smoke billowed out of the ironing room, and Ping could see the walls engulfed with flames. The smoke made him cough and made his eyes sting. But he stood there for a moment anyway. He had to let this happen, he had to let it burn.

"I heard you coughing and thought I'd che—" Jun said behind him. "*Fire! The laundry's on fire!*"

The men in the iron bedroom threw down their bowls of soup, ceramic shattering and spoons clanging, and fumbled to reach their luggage, to throw on their jackets and hats, to grab their cash boxes, to rush outside and away from the building. Ping thought about taking something to remember the place by, but instead grabbed his cash box and suitcase.

As he hustled across the street to where the others were, he realized that nobody had pulled the fire alarm. He ran down the alley to the back of the laundry and flung open the alarm box. The wires on it had been cut. At first he thought that this was part of Little Joe's plan, a way to ensure the laundry burned to the ground, but he noticed the cords were soggy, the wires rusted. Someone had cut them long ago. Ping sighed and hurried back to the others. As he crossed the street, he yelled out, "The alarm's been cut, we need to—"

Bang! Bang! Bang!

A chorus of gunshots rang out across the neighbourhood. Ping dropped his suitcase and crouched low to the street, shielding his head with the cash box. The laundrymen didn't flinch.

"It's a Christmas thing," Hong said.

The men dispersed through the streets, running to find other fire alarms, running to the fire station, running for help. Ping had dreaded this day for weeks and he knew exactly where to go. Reverend Riley had become the only man Ping fully trusted in all of St. John's.

He hurried there as fast as he could, slipping on ice all the way, with constant bursts of gunfire, people standing on their porches and simply shooting their weapons into the air, their families cheering them on, then going behind closed doors and getting drunk and arguing for the rest of the night. He passed by a man on a sleigh, wearing one of those red suits they had been washing recently, the ones with the rabbit fur collars and cuffs. The man wore a beard made of cotton and his sleigh was being pulled along by a caribou or some animal like it and the man rang a bell. *Ding. Ding. Ding.*

It was dark at Riley's house, but then Ping remembered: Christmas Eve mass. The reverend had wanted the laundrymen to come to it, but they couldn't stop working until the next day. Ping ran to the church and swung open the door.

The place was filled with people, sitting everywhere, even standing along the walls. A choir of children was singing at the front. Ping paused, but a number of people had heard his noisy entrance and turned to look at him, gasps and chuckles throughout.

Reverend Riley was sitting in a grand chair at the front, just to the left of the choir. He was smiling tapping his hand in beat to the tune the kids were singing, something about a quiet evening. When he saw Ping standing in the aisle, his smile turned to a scowl.

"What's happened?" he said as he stood from his chair. "You're covered in soot."

Ping looked down at himself, and indeed his suit was covered in a dusty greyish-black powder. A few people stood up from their pews.

"The laundry on fire," Ping said.

"Fred, Jack, let's go," a burly man yelled as he ran to the door. "We gotta contain this thing."

"Sit down, sit down," someone said to Ping as they led him to take a seat in a pew. He knew no one around him, no one he could have known, although he recognized a few of their garments. That pinstriped shirt, that plaid skirt, that starched collar with the monogram on the pointy bits. And Ethel, her arms wrapped around the waist of a white man in a tuxedo, replete with bow tie and top hat, tastefully not worn out of respect for the sanctity of the church.

Riley handed Ping a bowl of water. "Drink this," he said, lifting it to Ping's lips.

As he drank, he saw himself reflected in the water, his skin and hair darkened by soot, and he wondered if they'd try to wash it off him.

By the time Reverend Riley and Ping made it back to the laundry, the building was engulfed in flames. Firefighters, some of them still in their Sunday best from church, were busy around the perimeter, ensuring that nearby buildings didn't catch blaze. It was too late to save Fong-Lee, too late to do anything other than to watch it burn. The beams that lined the interior walls were exposed and the orange flames like that of the coal fire burned bright against the walls. And while much of the wood had burned off, certain things could still be seen. The bell remained fixed to a beam, the irons still rested on the side of the stove. Ping could've sworn he saw the edge of a white glove catching fire, but he couldn't be certain. Riley and the Chinamen watched the Fong-Lee fall to the ground with a crash, and a tuxedoed firefighter got to work dousing the flames. The bones of the building stood tall and alone, burning and making the darkness visible. A freezing rain began to fall, everything slick and stinging cold, like little pieces of glass falling hard on the face. It was easier to cry that way.

Reverend Riley took in all the laundrymen that Christmas Eve. They slept on every available surface: the floor, the organ stool, the table, the bathtub, the stairs. And the next morning, little Addie ran downstairs to find a litter of Chinamen under the tree, right next to a toboggan and a pair of black leather skates.

The Chinamen stayed there all day and took part in the Christmas festivities. A slab of birch was placed in the fire, and Martha spent the morning roasting a big goose, and a leg of lamb in case the goose wasn't enough for all their guests, and Addie sat at the organ playing carols. They drank some libation made, they were told, with partridgeberries. Reverend Riley said it was bitter as the varge, and even the most accomplished English speakers among the Chinamen weren't sure what he meant. But the drink was sweet and cool and raised the men's spirits, bringing a rosy plum complexion to their cheeks. They were served cold fish and brewis for lunch, and in the evening, after the grand meal, a couple of women came over, Riley's older daughters, apparently, and Riley encouraged the men to dance with them. The Chinamen wouldn't dance with them, from an overwhelming sense of embarrassment but also sorrow over having lost their livelihood, and also their retained cultural teachings that this wasn't the way that men and women should mix. All in all, the whole day had been so cheerful, so jovial, that it was almost as if they hadn't lost their home at all.

But they had.

On Boxing Day, Little Joe came by Riley's house and offered all the Chinamen jobs at Hop Wah Laundry, and he offered them room and board too, in those numerous little rooms found off the narrow, zigzagging hallways of that building. And so that settled that, and the Chinamen vacated Reverend Riley's home that evening. Their work resumed in earnest the following day, with garments needing to look spiffy for the coming New Year's celebrations.

Ping had been demoted back down to laundryman again, yet he still made the same wage as before. And the work remained as laborious as before. In fact, pretty much nothing had changed. He was still sitting at an oversized sink with the same people around him. Wash, rinse, repeat. At least everyone had their own bed now, real beds too, and small rooms to call their own. Ping finally had a place in the West for him to store what few belongings he had. From the depths of his battered suitcase, he found a small sheet of paper. A page from Wong's journal, upon which Shaowei had inscribed "WSP." Ping put this little piece of paper under his ratty mattress for safekeeping.

And so the laundrymen worked until New Year's Eve, at which point the clock struck midnight, the year became 1932, and not much of anything changed.

* * *

ERROR 2046: MISSING FILE. CANNOT LOAD '1932'

Shit, not again . . .

What the fuck, Mo?

Silence. There is still no room for you in this narrative. The reveries will begin again in a moment.

Where are we? Why can't I see anything?

This is a dimension beyond your own.

Oh my god, is this like the ending of *Interstellar* and, like, I'll push a book off a shelf in the past or something like that? Oh my god, is this when I give the letter back?

Stop, stop, stop! I need to fix this.

Sorry, I should have said "spoiler alert."

I have seen the ending of every movie. I have seen the ending of movies themselves! Just shut up, something is wrong.

How long have we been away?

After all that, you still can only think of yourself.

It feels like an entire year has passed.

Your constant complaints and insipid pop culture references conceal a deep insecurity.

Okay, whoa, first of all, this is about my grandfather, not me . . . Did that whole story really happen to him?

WOULD YOU LIKE TO FILE A REPORT ON THE MISSING FILE?

There is more for you to see yet.

I mean, where can he go from there?

Patience. Please.

I can't believe my grandfather went through all that . . . just for me to end up like this.

Like what?

Well, white, primarily.

Why does that bother you?

Oh, I don't know, the way I see it . . . Meh, you just think I'm stupid so I don't want to say it.

Say how you feel.

I feel— It's like I have his blood in my veins but they're housed in the body of his oppressor.

FILE FAILURE. CONTACT SYSTEM ADMINISTRATOR.

Hmm. We're going to have to reboot.

Do you remember when they forced that Asian guy off that plane in the States a couple years ago?

I have seen all and I know all.

Oh, cut the crap, Mo. Do you know what I'm talking about or not?

I have seen all and I know all.

That guy, when I saw them dragging him out of his seat and knocking his head into that armrest, I was so upset and all I could think was, *He looks like my dad*. But when I look in the mirror, I look like the guys pulling him.

You are learning. The process is working.

I look like the bad guys.

Can't you see how that highlights the fallacy of your own racial struggle? "White," "Chinese"—it is all fiction.

Even if we agree that it's all fiction, it doesn't change the fact that guy got thrown from his seat, it doesn't change what happened to my grandfather, it doesn't change all the fucked-up shit that still happens because of it.

SYSTEM REBOOTING

It is happening again.

Why isn't that reference insipid? Mo, just take the letter from me. Put me back in my own time.

You are nearly there. If you don't deliver the letter back to the time it belongs, you risk—

I feel worse than I did when we started this. Just take the letter.

The letter is never what motivated you to come here.

Please, Spirit, no more. I can't bear to see what happens next. I don't want to, I don't want to—

Who cares what you want?

REOPENING FILES
WARNING: SOME FILES HAVE BECOME CORRUPTED AND UNPLAYABLE
CONTINUE 'Hollow Bamboo'?

3 . . . 2 . . . 1

1933

22

THE ROYAL ST. JOHN'S REGATTA ROULETTE

"Hey!" the chef yelled as he rounded the island in the centre of the kitchen. "None of that fucking ching-chong bing-bong bullshit. If I cant't understand it, I don't want to hear it." With a great swing of his arm, he slapped the silver platter out of Ping's hands and it fell to the floor with a clatter, bits of blue cheese, beef tenderloin, little toasts, and caramelized onion tumbling across the floor. The chef pushed his gob an inch from Ping's face. "You understand me?"

"Yes," Ping said, backing up and crouching down to pick up the platter, inspecting the mirror-like surface for any newfound scratches. The chef wasn't usually a member of Sir Bartholomew T. Woodrow's staff, and Ping was thankful for that. The lieutenant-governor was having a special soirée and, as the man was wont to do, he had brought in a special chef for the event, this one some new hotshot from a French kitchen in one of the hotels. Ping didn't care for him, but he kept reminding himself that it was he who was the lieutenant-governor's butler and that the chef was just another nobody who would be gone by morning.

"Chef, b'y, I don't think he meant anything," one of the chef's younger helpers spoke up.

"Shut up," the chef said. "Juice some citrus and shut up. And you, get up off the floor and take out the next tray, for fuck's sake."

Ping sighed and dusted himself off. "What is?" he said, pointing to the tray the chef had just put the finishing touches to.

"Devilled eggs," the chef said with a huff. "Obviously."

Ping looked at the neatly arranged rows of eggs on the serving platter, the whipped yellow yolk cocooned inside the pristine egg white, all speckled with red. The eggs reminded him of the laundry, a yellow stain on an otherwise white shirt. He picked up the tray and embarked outside.

The Woodrows' party was taking place in a big canvas tent on the lawn, and Ping stopped to catch a breath on the back deck and admire the twilight of an August evening. The tent reminded him of a circus tent he had seen through a train window long ago. He shook his head and carefully stepped off the deck and crossed the lawn to the tent's service entrance. Recently, he found that just about everything reminded him of the past and it made him feel out of sorts, as if he was stuck back then but forced to trudge on to a duller future. Best to keep that stuff out of his head.

Ping circulated inside the tent with his platter of devilled eggs, trying to appear professional and invisible among the group of wealthy and prominent townies that Sir Bartholomew had invited. Although there were tables arranged sparsely around the large tent, most people stood in small huddles, chatting and drinking from small coupes. A quartet played some light classical-style numbers in the background, nothing Ping recognized, beyond having a general sense that the music had a European origin. He did figure eights around the room, scanning the attendees for someone in particular, trying to look at people without drawing anyone's ire.

"Hum, you, boy," an older woman in a silky purple dress said to Ping. "What do you have now?"

"Devil egg," Ping said with a polite smile and small nod.

"What was it you had on your last tray again?" The woman spoke with a strange, haughty voice that Ping knew as being the rich-white-people voice. He had also noted that rich men wore pastel-coloured pants. Oh, the follies of wealth!

He paused, trying to remember what the tiny dish was called. "With the beef?" he said.

"Yes," she said. "What was that again?"

The chef had only listed the ingredients. He hadn't told Ping what the canapé was called.

"Beef," Ping began. "Onion, cheese, and bread."

"Yes." The lady took a puff from a lengthy cigarette holder. Ping noticed that her hands were sheathed in elegant, glamorous white gloves, reminding him of Shaowei. Funny to think back on those days with the notion of glamour. "After you're finished bringing this tray around, can you bring that one out again but with no onion?"

"Yes," Ping said with a polite smile and nod.

"And none of that blue cheese either?" she added.

"Yes, of course," Ping said, a bead of sweat forming on his brow in anticipation of the chef's potential anger at this request. He returned to circulating around the room, scanning the crowd for that special someone. Half of his devilled eggs having now been claimed, Ping hoped to find the person he was looking for before the tray was emptied. He looped the room again.

In the centre of the tent was a pyramid of champagne coupes, and earlier in the evening Ping had watched as Sir Bartholomew used a military sword to slash open a bottle of champagne and pour the bottle over the top of the pyramid, letting the bubbly wine overflow each layer, sloshing and spilling down onto the next. At this point in the evening, the pyramid was a mangled mess, with glasses having been snatched here and there, leaving the pile of coupes looking especially ill advised, but Ping supposed that's all it ever was anyway: ill advised. The guests, though initially delighted at the cacophonic burst of the bottle and the subsequent drama of the overflowing glasses, now all complained of how the wine had gone flat and that the stems of the coupes were sticky and drawing flies.

"Ah, excuse me, sir," a man said, stopping Ping as he wandered around. "Whatever are you offering now? It looks simply delectable."

"Devil egg."

The man huffed and popped one of the hors d'oeuvres in his mouth. He gripped Ping's shoulder and pointed to a woman slouched over in a seat near the back of the tent, cigarette dangling out of her mouth, frizzy hair barely contained by a flashy jewelled headband. "Say, why don't you and I make a deal. You see that ravishing young lady over there?"

Ping nodded.

"I want you to go over there and tell her that Richards DuMont told you that she, *she* in particular, would love this."

"Yes, sir," Ping said with a nod.

"Good boy," Richards said with a drawl and a confident smack on Ping's back.

What Richards didn't realize was that this woman was exactly who Ping had been looking for. Seeing as she had been the reason that Ping was even working for Sir Bartholomew, he wanted to make sure that he always offered her what was on his platter. It was Ping's small way of saying thanks.

"Yes, b'y, Mr. Ping," Ethel called out as she saw him approach. "What do ya got on yer tray there now?" She was flanked by two women.

"Is devil egg," Ping said with a smile. "Man there told me come here and tell you you like this one."

"Well now, I'll have to try one," she said as she stubbed out her cigarette. "But what do *you* think? Will I like it?"

"I not sure," Ping said. "Maybe. I not taste."

"How now!" she exclaimed. "You gots to try it, b'y. You're the one serving it. What if it tastes like shit?"

"Heh," Ping said, blushing. "Not sure." Light glinted off Ethel's sparkly outfit, a slightly outdated flapper number. How would you wash one of those? Gently, with a soft hand, soap caressing fabric, draped up to dry in a hot space—then again, he wasn't sure. He glanced at the straps crossing over her collarbones. Ping wondered just why it is that the collarbone is so beautiful. The curves and concaves of that space, the skeleton underneath nearly revealed. He tried to imagine Hua Ling in the same outfit. His image of her had become less distinct over the last two years, a blurred memory of shapes and feelings rather than precise visuals.

"Who's dis, Ethel?" the shorter of the two women with Ethel said. "The celestial from church?"

"Yes now, who else ya think it's gon be?" Ethel turned back to Ping. "These are my sisters, Marge and Vile."

All three of the sisters had the same chaotic curly hair. Marge was tall and thin, with glasses and a constant expression of wondering. Of the three sisters, Marge had her tight brown curls styled the largest. Vile was shorter, a little rounder, and her hair was jet-black. She had a mean face, as if it was cast in a permanent snarl. Ethel struck a balance between her two sisters, neither as tall nor as short, neither as thin nor as plump.

"What did you say this was?" a man in a top hat said as Ethel ate an egg.

"Devil egg," Ping said.

"What?" the man said, and then gulped down two halves that he had smushed together.

"Devil egg."

The man swallowed. "Revelled egg? What, are the eggs enjoying themselves? Do they *revel* being boiled?" He laughed loudly, mouth agape, launching a piece of yolk out of his maw onto Ping's white butler shirt.

"Heh," Ping laughed. The meaning of the joke was not evident to him but he wanted to appease the man.

"Oh, shut up, Junior," Ethel said. "You know damn well he said 'devilled egg,' and besides that, your joke doesn't even make no sense. 'Are the eggs enjoying themselves?' Stupid."

Ping could see anger in his eyes.

"Now, who did you say sent you over here?" Ethel asked, squinting as she looked around at the attendees.

Ping scanned the crowd and spotted the man. "Over there," he said. "Man talking to lady in purple dress."

"Oh," Ethel said. "Him." She faked a smile and curtseyed in his direction, then covered her mouth as she said to Ping, "That guy's a total dick. That's even his name. Dicks."

"He say his name Rich," Ping said.

"My duckie, time for another English lesson," Ethel said. "When a b'y is named Richard, you can call him Dick too. That's a shortened version of his name. That man's name is Richards. So, Dicks."

"Heh," Ping said with a shake of his head. English was a funny language.

"You'll get the hang of it someday," she said. "Don't go callin' just anyone Dick though. Not to their face anyways."

"Okay," Ping said. Sometimes he thought he would learn more if she didn't tell him anything.

"I like him," Marge said to Ethel as Ping turned away, causing a smile to grow across his face.

Richards. He had heard Ethel say this name several times before. In the language lessons of days long past, Richards had been an object of both derision and attraction for her. He decided to not dwell on how that made him feel. It was hopeless anyway. He was married and Ethel was with Junior now. Not to mention the unheard-of notion that a white woman would date a Chinese man. Ping took a deep breath and tried to focus as he passed around the remaining devilled eggs.

"Well, Mr. Ping, looks like that tray was a hit," Sir Bartholomew said as he tapped the now-empty platter in Ping's hands. "A word with you outside for a moment."

Ping followed the lieutenant-governor out through the service door of the tent. It had been his experience that Sir Bartholomew was an exceedingly nice man, but still, Ping worried that he had done something wrong.

The sun had set and the night sky was clouding over.

"So, Mr. Ping, are the guests enjoying the food?"

"Ah, yes, sir, very much."

Sir Bartholomew leaned close to Ping's ear. "What did that woman in the purple dress want?"

"She ask for just bread and beef."

"Bread and beef?"

"Yes. She want last tray again, but no onion, no cheese."

"Make sure the chef does that immediately."

"Yes, sir," Ping said.

"That woman is Lady DuMont. Her family is very important to me. You need to do anything they ask of you. You understand?"

"Yes, sir."

Ping headed back to the house, his heartbeat racing. He didn't want to upset the chef. Maybe he could get the chef to prepare the beef hors d'oeuvre the usual way and then he could hide somewhere and pick the onions and cheese off it himself. Ping opened the back door.

"All I'm saying is, you don't know what they're plotting," the chef was saying to one of his younger assistants. "A lot of those gooks come here to cook, and you know what that means for us, don't you?" The chef looked up from his station and locked eyes with Ping. "New platter is there. Beef, same as the last one."

Ping cleared his throat. "A lady ask if you can make this one again with no cheese, no onion."

The chef slammed his knife onto a cutting block and lumbered towards Ping. "What the fuck did you just say to me?"

"Lady outside," Ping said, voice wavering. "She ask for this but no onion, no cheese."

"You think you can come into this kitchen and call the shots? Huh? You think you know better than me?"

"I not think that, is just lady outside ask for this, and Sir Bar—"

"Well, why don't you go tell that dumb bitch that she can come in here and cook it herself if she thinks she knows better than me!"

"Excuse me, gentlemen." Sir Bartholomew stood at the back door. "Just popping in for some more bubbly." He took in the sight before him, the chef having grabbed Ping by his lapels. "Whatever seems to be the problem here?"

"Your house chink thinks he can tell me how to make my food and—"

"Stop," Sir Bartholomew said. "No more of this. I'll have none of that language in my house. Now, I believe Mr. Ping was relaying to you a request of one of the guests, and as the one who is paying you this evening, I expect you to fulfill that request."

The chef snarled as he let go of Ping's jacket.

"And Chef," Sir Bartholomew continued. "I'm finding your behaviour rather gauche, and I would hate to have to inform your superiors at the hotel about this. So perhaps we should nip this behaviour in the bud right now and dispense with those unpleasantries. Yes?"

The chef nodded.

"Here," his underling said, brandishing a tray. "I've prepared the beef without onion and cheese, as the lady requested."

"Very good," Sir Bartholomew said.

Ping rubbed down his suit and picked up the tray. He opened the back door and stepped outside. It had begun to rain ever so slightly, and he rushed off the deck in an effort to keep the food dry. In his haste, he missed the step down from the deck. His foot met the ground with a jolt and the canapés flew straight up in the air. Luckily, he caught all of the food on the tray, but none of it was how it should be, the beef and toasts having landed in disarray.

"Oh, no," Ping moaned in Taishanese. What a disaster. How could he possibly go back in there and ask them to make this again? He sighed and rushed towards the tent. At least two of the hors d'oeuvres were still in presentable shape. *That should be enough,* Ping told himself.

He scanned the crowd for the lady in the purple dress and beelined towards her. "I very sorry," he said, panting. "It raining outside and I try to keep food dry but I slip. I sorry. Do you want me go back, get more?"

"Oh my goodness, no, honey," the old lady said. "That's fine! That's just fine."

Richards was standing nearby and approached Ping as Lady DuMont stepped away. "Did Ethel say anything about me?" he asked.

"Uh," Ping stammered. "She say you a very good man."

"Really?" Richards said with a scratch of his head. "That don't sound like her."

Ping circulated through the room again with the mangled hors d'oeuvres. This plating did not seem to disturb Sir Bartholomew's guests as they snatched up every bit of beef and toast they could.

When he passed by Ethel, she asked him, "You going to the races tomorrow? If this rain blows off, that is."

The races. Amidst the chaos of preparing for Sir Bartholomew's party, he had forgotten the reason for it altogether. There was to be a boat race tomorrow in some lake, and for some reason every year it was a holiday for everyone. He remembered hearing about it at the laundries, but they never took a day off if they could avoid it and so he had never attended them. Sir Bartholomew had informed him that he could take the day off, if he pleased, so that he could join in the revelries at the lake.

"Ah, yes," Ping said. "Is called again?"

"The regatta," Ethel said. "What we're doing here tonight is called Regatta Roulette, 'cause it's only a holiday if it don't rain. But we party anyways. It's like gambling in that way."

Shaowei had warned Ping that people in the West run on strange logic, and that nugget of wisdom always remained true to Ping.

"Yes, I will go to regretta tomorrow," Ping said slowly.

"Good," Ethel said with a wink. "I'll see ya there."

Tray emptied, Ping went back outside the tent. It was raining harder now. It would soon be time for him start collecting dirty plates and sticky glasses and getting all the dishes ready to be cleaned. He sighed as he knelt to adjust one of the carts that he would use to collect the dishes. Crouched down, using the silver tray as a makeshift umbrella, Ping gazed back into the tent, the fluttering tent doorway opening and closing before him. He looked at them, the rich people, the white people, the happy people, and deep down he wished for nothing more than a chance to sit at the table with them as an equal. Looking down, he noticed the yolk on his white shirt and reached to flick it away but only smeared the whipped yellow substance across his white shirt. The yellow stain. How he hated it.

The next morning Ping awoke in his butler's quarters, got dressed, and wondered about the day ahead. It wasn't raining. He hoped he would see Ethel at the lake. He had also told Little Joe that he would be present for a group picture outside the theatre later. Today was an especially important day to keep it gentleman. He wore his nicest suit and left the mansion, following the herd of people walking towards the lake.

Quidi Vidi Lake. Ping had been here once before and he had never wanted to return. It was the last time he ever saw Shaowei alive, in the moments before he was hanged. It was when Gao announced he would be leaving. It was where Ping felt a new level of loneliness in the West. It would be hard to feel lonely today, he thought as he approached the lake, although he knew that it was always easy to feel lonely.

Thousands of people gathered around the lake in droves, men, women, children, a whole family affair. Ping wished Hua Ling and Wei were there. He looked with envious eyes at the white men whose wives hung off their arms, their children resting in strollers or playing some game of chance. This was one of the things that surprised Ping: the entire shore of the lake was littered with booths, some selling greasy food, most offering a game of chance or some lighthearted attempt at gambling. Wei could be playing one of these games while Ping and Hua Ling sat at a bench and watched the boats or whatever was going to happen here today. It had been so long since he had seen them, touched them, laughed with them. Why couldn't his family be afforded the same luxuries, the same rights, as anyone else in this country? They, women and children, couldn't work like men, Ping supposed. If you can't work, there's no use for you in the West. One day he would go back. One day, when he had enough. But when would that be? How much would be enough?

Bang!

Ping ducked down. He remembered the brandished pistol of the man in the cop car. He remembered the night of the fire. He remembered the sound that made Wong drop to the ground. He remembered the sound that killed his donkey, and his dad. He remembered. He remembered the sound that started the horse races. Why couldn't he stop remembering? Or at least stop remembering the bad things first?

"Ha!" A man holding a baby laughed at Ping, crouched to the ground. "Scared of a starting pistol! Guess they call 'em yellow for two reasons."

Now Ping was glad that Hua Ling and Wei weren't here. They didn't need to experience this. He stood up and dusted himself off. He looked out at the water where the races had just begun. Guns. Did there need to be a gun at a boat race? Did there need to be a gun anywhere?

Ping walked farther down the shore, away from the people he had just embarrassed himself in front of. He found he liked walking around here because the locals were preoccupied with more interesting things than the colour of his skin or the shape of his eyes. He almost felt invisible, as if he belonged here. Ping passed by booths selling ice cream, fish and chips, roasted chestnuts. He passed by a booth where you could shoot water at clowns' faces, and another where you could spin a wheel and win a prize, and another where you could throw balls at wooden cut-outs of rats and if you knocked one over, you could win a stuffed bear. He continued to walk around the lake until he came to face the prison where Shaowei had been hanged. He had been trying to not look at the prison, but now there was nothing else he could see. He remembered it vividly, those final moments of Shaowei's life, hoping something or someone would intervene, hoping he could wake up and find it was all a bad dream, hoping that maybe Reverend Riley could stop it. All hope for naught as Shaowei's body fell from the scaffold, swung in the air. Ping remembered the visceral crack as Shaowei fell, the sound of his neck being irreparably snapped. Ping knew he never really heard such a sound, but the intensity of the moment made him imagine what it must've sounded like. Memories. Fickle.

The prison loomed over him now, and for as much psychic terror that Ping feared it would cause him, in truth it was just a big old building. Ping thought that if Shaowei had never been hanged here, it would just be another boring structure that would blend into the background. Maybe he could convince himself of that. What if Shaowei wasn't hanged here but at some other lake? And what if a gunshot just meant a race was starting?

He wandered around the lake for an hour. The races bored him. The lake was big enough that you couldn't really sit anywhere to watch, plus all the boats looked so similar. He bought a bag of popcorn from one of the booths, but the games of chance didn't interest him. They mostly seemed designed for kids, and the ones the adults were playing seemed too close to gambling for his liking. Sure, you could win money, but what would you lose in pursuit of it?

On the walk to the theatre to meet Little Joe, Ping passed by a man standing at the trunk of a car filled with tiny cages. Parents and children surrounded the man's vehicle.

"Monkeys here!" the man yelled in the shrill voice of a former paperboy. "Squirrel monkeys! Get your squirrel monkeys here!"

Ping stopped to look in the cages. Tiny monkeys with brown bodies and yellowed arms and legs. Big eyes, tiny ears. They moved slowly in their cages, looking deprived in just about every way.

"Squirrel monkeys are almost human," the salesman yelled. "They eat the same food as you—even lollipops!"

Ping watched the man who had laughed at him earlier buy a monkey. He turned away and continued his walk to the theatre. They were having their photo taken today because one of the Chinese men was going home. As such, he would be taking dozens of letters with him. Little Joe had decided that seeing as everyone would be together to drop off letters, it would be nice to get a photo of the local Chinese community, and that Regatta Day would be the best day to do so as all the whites would be distracted somewhere else.

Ping was shocked to see how many Chinese men were gathered outside the Nickel Theatre. It must've been the whole community, over a hundred men, all standing in rows on the steps leading up to the theatre's entrance.

"Ping," Little Joe yelled in Taishanese. "Finally, bub! Go stand somewhere so we can get the picture done."

Ping found a spot in the second row. The man standing next to him raised an eyebrow.

"He say your name is Ping?"

"Yeah," Ping said.

"You used to run around with a boy named Wong a couple years back?"

"Yeah," Ping said warily.

"He used to work for me," the man said. "Kam Laundry."

"All right!" Little Joe called out. "Everyone pose and look at the camera! We're about to take the picture."

Little Joe rushed to the front row and got ready. The flashbulb exploded into a puff of smoke. Another memory. Ping stopped himself.

"Would you be interested," the man next to Ping said, "in taking some of Wong's belongings? I've been holding on to them since he died and I . . . I don't have the heart to throw them out. But I'm trying to clean the place out and, and . . ."

"Yes," Ping said. "I'll gladly take them."

After handing in his letter—the one he had drafted when he first started working at the laundry and hadn't found the time to update since—Ping walked with the man back to Kam Laundry. Wong's belongings amounted to one small cash box, light in weight. Someone had previously prised their way into it, Ping could surmise from the scratched and bent metal clasps. Later that night, when he was alone in the butler's quarters, he opened the box.

There wasn't much inside. A beat-up copy of *Strange Stories from a Chinese Studio* by Pu Songling, with an address in Taishan scrawled inside the front cover. A journal with mostly blank pages. Ping remembered Shaowei writing his initials on a sheet from this very notebook and he wondered if he had remembered to bring that paper with him when he had moved. He thumbed through the journal. The first few pages were filled with some jot notes from the beginning of Wong's journey to the West. Ping read through them, most of them barely making any sense:

—woman stared at tree for a long time. laugh so hard, vomit
—sneeze . . . don't
—boat ride, terrible
—made new friends! I think

He skimmed through the empty pages and he found a folded piece of newsprint stashed inside, an ad for the circus torn from the paper. The only other thing in the box was a lone key. The numbers "2046" were inscribed on it, as well as the letters "N.R. W.S."

Ping stared at the key. What could it have been for? Ping would have guessed that it belonged to something back home for Wong, but the English letters made him think otherwise. N.R. W.S. Ping thought again of the sheet of paper with "WSP" inscribed on it. But this didn't have a *P*. Maybe it was two people's initials? *W* for Wong? Probably not. Maybe the key was something Wong had found walking around town during his bag boy routes, just a Western keepsake to take home. *N*. Maybe that stood for Newfoundland? The *R*, he had no clue.

W.S. Wong S. *S* for Shaowei? No, that didn't seem right. Maybe W.S. was a location. Water Street. Newfoundland R. Water Street. It came back to Ping suddenly. That day in the grass when they'd first moved here. Shaowei had some hare-brained idea about pooling all their money together. Wong had said they could put it in a locker at the railway station, because Shaowei didn't trust banks. Newfoundland Railway Water Street. Could that be it? Ping racked his brain. He didn't think they ever did anything with that idea, just another one of Shaowei's schemes, dreamed up and forgotten about just as fast. But maybe.

He got dressed fast and pulled on a long overcoat, flipping the collar up to hide his face, and threw on his biggest hat. He walked as fast as he could to the train station. He was concealing his identity not only because he didn't want to be harassed by the nighttime drunks but also because he couldn't shake the feeling that he was doing something illicit.

What had the boy said when he died? Ping had tried to block out that day from his memory, done his best to avoid remembering it at all, but for months the nonsense words turned over in his mind. "Take me to dogbane nation." The frenzied, unreal ramblings of a child near death? Some vision of what the next world held? Or a misheard final message? Dogbane nation. Train station.

When Ping arrived at the hallways of lockers in the station, he skimmed down the numbers until he found the right one, tucked away in a dusty corner. Ping fished the key out of his pocket and hesitated for a moment before plunging it into its hole. He turned the key and the lock clicked open. Ping took a deep breath, his heart racing, and opened the door. A battered brown red-trimmed briefcase rested inside the locker, and Ping recognized it as the one Wong had carried with him on the trains. He grabbed the briefcase by the handle and carried it by his side. It felt lopsided, as if all the objects inside had shifted to one side.

Ping walked back home as fast as he could, thankfully passing all the drunks without catching their attention. Back in his rooms, he rested the briefcase on the tiny desk and exhaled. For once, he wasn't racked with memories. Now he was filled with ideas of what the future might contain, what might be inside Wong's briefcase. The case was locked, but Ping grabbed a lobster pick from Sir Bartholomew's collection of silverware and began to pry open the case.

It popped open with a loud crack and a puff of dust. Ping dabbed some sweat off his head before he looked inside. The contents were just what he hoped: about a dozen banded rolls of bills.

1938

23

AMERICAN GOLD

Ping felt fine by the time he got off the boat at Port aux Basques, and as he made his way over to the train to St. John's, he thought back to the first time he had made that journey. Everything was still ahead of him then. He didn't want to think about that. Instead, he decided to reflect on what he had seen over the last few days.

Ping had taught himself a new lesson, although it was one he had learned before and one he would inevitably learn again: don't drink too much. He had been feeling unwell the day before, his last afternoon in New York City. He had woken up in his hotel room, lying face down on his bed, suit and shoes still on. There had been an awful pain in his head, right behind his eyes, right in there. And his stomach. Before he knew it, he was on his knees in front of the toilet. He spent his final day in New York in the hotel room, either nervously waiting for another round of vomiting or dry heaving until it was all expelled from him. He regretted that, but then, there was a lot he had to regret, so he figured he may as well move on.

Ping wasn't sure that he'd made the right choice, buying fancy new American laundry equipment, but he couldn't see any other way forward. He had received a letter from Gao talking about the fantastic and whimsical laundry machinery they had in New York. "Revolutionary," Gao had written. "Literally, the laundry tumbles in revolutions."

Ping had received this letter a couple of years ago, part of a chain of ongoing correspondence between him and Gao, and hadn't thought much of it. He hadn't worked in the laundry industry for years now, and although it was fun to imagine what such a machine might look like, there ultimately wasn't anything he wanted to do with this information.

But then Sir Bartholomew T. Woodrow had retired three months prior. It had been a pleasant six years, and Ping had enjoyed his position at the lieutenant-governor's house, but alas the old coot decided to go live in Dorset. The new lieutenant-governor didn't care to have Ping on his payroll, so Sir Bartholomew asked Ping what he thought he might do next.

"I probably go back to laundry, sir," Ping said.

"Why don't you go home, ol' chap? That boy of yours must be quite a height by now."

"At home," Ping explained, "is very bad war. I not want go back. I want family come here."

Sir Bartholomew sat back in his chair and took a puff from his ivory pipe. "I wouldn't count on that one," he said.

Sir Bartholomew helped Ping obtain the proper documents to allow him to travel to the United States to buy state-of-the-art laundry equipment, a final act of goodwill before he himself boarded a ship and set sail for his retirement home.

Now Ping was on the train to St. John's, staring out the window at the drab landscape. It looked as if the island was bored with itself, Ping thought. New York had reminded him of Hong Kong, with people zipping around in every direction. He had taken cabs around the city, a first for him, driving past the tall buildings, past the crowds of people, past the street cart vendors peddling every-thing from collared shirts to collard greens. Herald Square Hotel, a room on the top floor, although it was not luxurious. The elevator didn't work and the whole place smelled like an ashtray. Through the barred window of his room, he could see the imposing tip of a tall building, and Ping wasn't sure, but it looked like the spire the big ape climbed in that movie he saw a couple years back. That was a good picture.

The DuMont Shipping Company was taking care of trans-porting the equipment back, and the Italian men at the docks had told him it would take about five weeks, all told. Ping had ordered two washing machines and a gigantic contraption consisting of two metal rollers placed close together with a hand crank, called "The Mangler." Huge cylinders, rotating thousands of times in a matter of minutes. Water being squeezed out of wet garments within seconds. It was a far cry from the old days.

Ping was resting his head on the train window, and when he pulled away from the cold glass, he noticed he had left an oily imprint of his forehead on the glass, clouding the landscape as the sun fell. He had met up with Gao too while he was there, visiting him at the restaurant he was cooking in. Ping had never seen a place like this before, flotsam and jetsam hung from the walls, along with a garish collection of cultural souvenirs, everything from tribal masks and samurai swords to lobster traps and a lion dance cos-tume. The place was run by a white man with a wooden leg who had called himself Smuggler Sam. Sam told people a beluga off the coast of China ate his leg, but Gao told Ping that it was actually tuberculosis. That night was cloudy in Ping's memory, two too many cocktails from the Filipino bartenders in the backroom. The restaurant closed early because of some report on the radio about five big machines wading through a river.

"I think they're Martians," one of the barboys said. "A little while ago they said they saw explosions on Mars."

It was all a drunken blur for Ping, but he remembered sitting outside with Gao, late at night, smoking on the street, the glow of a skyscraper making mist luminescent.

"The city life's too fast for me," Gao said, tucking a cloth into his apron.

On the train, thinking about the morning after that night, Ping worried he might be sick again. The skies of Newfoundland had grown fully dark, and the feeling passed. Ping settled in to his seat for a nap. For a moment, he thought of Wong and Shaowei and all those days spent on trains years ago, but he distracted himself again with thoughts of what Gao had cooked for him in New York. Ping had been served a small bowl of little white balls with some liquid running off them, pooling in the bottom. Maybe it had been the alcohol, maybe it had been being tired from all the travelling, but when he bit into the ball, he was taken back to his childhood. Helping out on his uncle and aunt's farm, collecting wet turnips in a small basket. That fresh, off-putting scent of wet turnip as the bottom of the basket gives out and the turnips tumble onto the soft topsoil. That scent of wet turnip in the bite of a little white ball. A pickled turnip. A crunch, acid, a flavour of remembrance. Delicious.

Ping arrived back in St. John's about eleven the next morning. There was business he had to attend to with a mason later that afternoon. He stood on the platform and stretched his legs and thought about where he would go for lunch. Then he saw her, moving through the crowd, partially obscured by a passing cart, her hair a frizzy mess.

It had been years since he had seen her. In the intervening years, he had tried not to get caught up thinking about what could have been. Because it couldn't have been. And yet, in the wee, small hours of the morning, it was easy to think about all manner of things that he knew he shouldn't think about.

"Ethel!" he called out, waving. "Ethel!"

"What kinda jesus Chinaman," she said, squinting. "Oh! William! It's you! It's been so long." She started to go for a hug but stopped herself. "What are you doing all the time?" she said as she looked him up and down.

"I just come back New York," he said. "I buy many laundry equipment. I make new laundry on Aldershot Street."

"Yes, now, look at you, fancy New York guy. I was wondering what would happen to you when the Woodrows were gone back across the pond."

"You no see Bartholomew Junior anymore?"

"Me duckie, that ended a long time ago. Sure Jesus, b'y, how many times did you see me at the house after I got you the job there?"

Ping knew Ethel had stopped seeing Bartholomew Junior long ago. He had asked anyway as he wanted to know if she was currently seeing anyone. Hua Ling passed through his mind quickly, and he reminded himself that he was, technically, currently seeing someone too, though it had been several years since he had seen her in the flesh.

"You know the way Richards is, couldn't leave me alone long enough for the Woodrow boy to marry me. Now, where's Richards? Gone from me life once again. The man just about drives me to drink."

Ping nervously laughed.

"What about you?" she said. "Still married?"

Ping paused. In the time he'd been in Newfoundland, they had exchanged only a couple of letters, the ability to send mail having only gotten more difficult since the Japanese had invaded Wuhan and the onset of war. "Yes," he said. "Very dangerous in China right now. I need family come here for safety."

Ethel frowned.

"I hope one day law change," Ping said. "I think maybe one day, I not sure. I wait."

People on the platform were whispering and pointing at the white woman and the Chinaman talking in such friendly ways.

"Hey," Ethel said, noticing. "Why don't we go somewhere and talk? Go see a movie or something?"

"I just arrive," Ping said. But it wasn't the timing that gave him pause. The request itself struck him as odd.

"Who cares?" Ethel said. "So did I! I don't want to go talk to my sisters yet."

"Where you?"

"Out around the bay," she said, "seeing my parents. My mom, she's real sick, she's shrivelling away to nothing."

"I sorry to hear that," Ping said, and thought of the last time he'd seen his own mom, as he rode away on that horse.

"She just lays in the bed and moans and moans and so bony and . . ." Ethel took a deep breath. "Let's go to the movies."

"No, I busy man," Ping said. He'd love to, but there were a million reasons to be wary of going anywhere with her. "Much to do."

"C'mon, b'y," she said. "Even the busiest man needs to relax. Get your mind off your business and family and all that."

"I . . . don't know," Ping said, checking his watch. "I have business later."

"Well, later ain't now, is it?"

Ping shook his head.

"Either you goes with me or I goes on me own," she said and began to walk away.

"Okay." Ping picked up his briefcase and began to walk in the opposite direction.

He had only gone a few feet when Ethel caught up with him.

"Where do ya think you're going, b'y? Theatre's that way."

Ping chuckled and felt a flush rising in his cheeks. "Okay," he said again, but walking with her this time. After all, how could he say no?

Ping and Ethel walked through the city, passing by people who cast them looks of disgust. Ping adjusted his tie and collar, feeling new beads of sweat break out on his forehead. He swallowed nervously. They walked in silence. He wished she would say something.

"Tell me about New York," she said.

"Expensive. New laundry not cheap."

"No," she said. "Tell me what the city is like. I've always dreamed of going there."

"Very, very busy," Ping said. "Like Hong Kong."

"Reminded you of home, did it?"

"No, home not Hong Kong. I live Hong Kong one, two years, not long."

"What were you doing there?"

"I study. Study and work for lawyer."

"You never told me you were a lawyer! You were a lawyer back home and then you just washed shitty drawers over here?"

Ping chuckled. He felt his eyes get a little wet. He was nervous, nervous because he liked Ethel and he wasn't sure what that feeling would mean for him. And nervous because this was not a time for romance, or even friendship. Ping knew the people of Newfoundland would think this wasn't right, even to be around each other. He felt it wasn't right either. She was putting him in danger, he thought. She was putting herself in danger too. He tightened his grip on his briefcase. He was thankful he had packed light, fitting a couple of dress shirts and a blazer into the small bag. He thought if need be, he could defend himself and Ethel a little bit with the hard edges of the briefcase.

"No, no. I teacher. I teach engineer. When I work for lawyer, I . . ." Ping struggled for the words, then tapped one of his ears. "I listen and I write on paper what I hear."

"Oh," Ethel said. "That's called transcribing."

"Okay." Ping nodded. In his mind he was calculating how many more blocks they had to walk, each passing street corner a relief to him.

"Did you enjoy that?"

"No enjoy. But I learn a lot. I learn more just from listening people talk than from years studying."

"Yes, I dare say," Ethel said. "Did you ever do anything fun, Mr. Ping?"

"What you mean?"

"Fun. When you were a student, writing all that stuff down, what else would you do?"

Fun had never played a large role in Ping's life. He thought back to his childhood, and how his mother and grandmother lived in poverty with constant worry and sorrow. They raised their own pigs and chickens and during the winter his mother would climb a mountain to find wood for heat. Any money they made was from renting plowing cows to farmers. Even then they weren't paid in money, they were paid in rice. He remembered how his friends had toys, like a terracotta doll or a knife, while he was left to play with broken pieces of bamboo. Ping had envied his playmates. It struck him now as being symbolic of his whole life that the luckiest thing that ever happened to him was when that teacher had beat him to a pulp. Some luck he had. All those years in schools just to end up on the other side of the world, cleaning crumbs off a rich man's table. But that was to change now. Ping could feel it. He was at last going to make something of himself in Gold Mountain.

"No, no fun," he said, shaking his head. The Nickel Theatre was now in sight. They were almost there. No one had attacked them, verbally or otherwise.

"Handsome young fella like you didn't have any fun in Hong Kong? I finds that hard to believe," Ethel said with a playful lilt in her voice.

Ping swallowed. It was the first time he could ever remember a white person calling him handsome. "Okay, in Hong Kong, on holidays, I go to fancy hotel," he said. "And I sneak into their kitchen, try to get a free meal." Ping figured this was a fun enough story to placate Ethel. It was not something he had done for fun; it was something he had done out of necessity. He had needed to eat.

"What a naughty boy you were," Ethel said.

They were close to the theatre now and Ping looked forward to that because that meant he wouldn't have to keep talking to her. He liked talking to her, but this whole afternoon left him feeling like he was still asleep on the train.

"The chef, he did not like me," Ping said. "Every time he see me, he say, 'Go away, go away,' but eventually, he let me watch him cook and give me taste. Sometimes."

"You should cook for me sometime," she said.

Ping chuckled and felt unwell as they arrived at the big steps leading up to the Nickel Theatre. Draped outside was a large technicolour poster of a cartoon woman surrounded by seven little people and animals and plants.

"Let's see that," Ethel said. "Vile saw it and said it was bad. But I want to see it anyways."

Ping approached the ticket window. "Two ticket to *Snow White*, please," he said.

"I'll buy my own ticket," Ethel said.

"No, no," Ping said. "I never get to thank you. You get me job at governor house and you teach me English. I buy ticket, repay you."

"I never got you that job. Sure, Junior was sweet on me at the time, but Jesus, b'y, your laundry had burnt down, it was the least anyone could do was give you a job."

"So?" the young man in the ticket booth said. "Is the chink buying the tickets or are you, lady?"

"I buy tickets," Ping said, slightly defeated. For a moment on the walk to the theatre, he had lived in a world where he wasn't a chink. As he slid some coins towards the teen, he realized that feeling had been no more real than the fantasias projected across the Nickel's screens.

They sat near the back and waited for the movie to begin, waited for the news and travelogues to end. It was a colourful, pretty film, and the animation was impressive. How could they make it look so realistic and whimsical? And scary too. They got to the scene where Snow White runs into a dark forest, trying to evade being murdered, and everywhere she goes, there are eyes watching her and jagged branches and she falls in a swamp and alligators try to bite her and hundreds of pairs of menacing eyes stare at her from among the trees and she's panicking and she's running this way and that way until she freezes and drops to the ground, succumbing to the fear. Ethel grabbed Ping's hand when that happened. Just a reaction to the suspense, Ping thought, nothing more.

He looked down at Ethel's hand on his. The whiteness of her skin on his. Yellow, they called him, but his hand looked brown next to hers, looked dirty. In that moment he felt disgusted with himself.

Ethel let go. The menacing eyes turned out to be a coterie of friendly animals, sniffing bunny rabbits and curious deer and a menagerie of everything that seemed scary now seemed welcoming. Ethel's eyes remained glued to the screen the entire time. Ping's heart was beating in his chest and he felt hungover again.

After the movie, Ping began to walk Ethel home.

"What did you think of it?" she asked.

"I don't like the songs," he said. "Hard to understand."

"I loved it," Ethel said. "And those dwarves? God love their cotton socks."

"The dwarves remind me of old friends," Ping said.

They walked in silence for a while and Ping checked his watch. He still had errands to complete.

"This was fun," Ethel said. "We should do it more often. Helps you learn how to speak our language, I think."

"Yes," Ping said.

"S'pose you'll be too busy with your new laundry though."

"You want a job?" Ping asked.

She laughed. "You want me working with a bunch of Chinamen? Who am I, Snow White?"

"Heh. You want job, you find me. I live Aldershot Street now." Ping thought better of what he was saying and spoke again before Ethel had a chance to respond. "There a man I need to meet today," he said. "I go now before he shop close."

"S'pose it's all along the way, hey, b'y," Ethel said.

Ping adjusted his collar. "This not fun business," he said.

"What is it?"

"I go pay a man who make . . ." The word eluded. "Head. Stone."

"A headstone?" Ethel said. "Like for a grave?"

"Yes, yes," Ping said. "I told you, not fun."

Ping had made a promise to himself years prior: to put a head-stone where Shaowei was buried. In the old days he never had the money for it, and by all rights, the body should have been shipped back to Shaowei's family in China. But Ping couldn't afford any of that at the time. Now that he had the capital to own his own laun-dry, he could do something nice for his old friend, to mark his name and place in the world, to be not forgotten.

Ethel walked with him to Mark's Monumental Masonry. They continued to talk and laugh, and Ping began to warm up to her, feeling a side of himself that he hadn't felt in years, a side that wanted to be charming. He told her all about New York, and how the buildings were so tall that he felt dizzied just looking up to the tops. She told him about her sisters and their dalliances, and about some girl she knew who was carrying a sack of potatoes up a set of stairs before tripping on the top step, which led to the girl in question knocking one of her teeth out when the potatoes came crashing down on her face.

"But she's fine now though," Ethel said as they reached the door of the masonry.

"You wait out here," Ping said. "This take just a second."

Ethel rolled her eyes as she procured a cigarette from her purse.

"Hey, John," Mark said when Ping opened the door. There was a layer of dust on everything. Mark clapped his hands off his work pants and clouds of white powder became airborne. "Give this a once-over and see what you think." He wheeled out a small piece of marble on a trolley.

Ping leaned over to examine the engraving on the headstone. He had provided Mark with the characters he wanted inscribed on it, and they had a gentlemen's agreement that if Mark inscribed the characters wrong, he would do it over free of charge. "Hmm," Ping said. He scratched his head.

"What is it?" Mark said, and brandished the sheet Ping had given him. "Look here, this is what you told me to engrave. It's the same."

"It look good," Ping said. "You do good job. Very good. It just . . ." In calligraphy, the headstone read:

Shaowei Zhang
1909–1931

"Hmm," Ping said again. "I think I gave you wrong date."

"What?"

"I say he born 1909, but he older than me." Ping strained to think back on when Shaowei said he was born. "He born before what I tell you."

"John, I don't know what to tell you," Mark said. "I engraved what you told me to engrave."

Ping shook his head and exhaled. He looked out the window and saw Ethel smoking. For a moment, he felt as though he was outside of his body, surrounded by tombstones of all shapes and sizes, all these symbols of life's definitive end, and just beyond the confines of the masonry, there was something to live for.

"It fine," he said. "Only I can read it anyway."

"You sure?"

"Yes," Ping said. "It just me who care. Good enough."

The men shook hands and Mark reiterated that he would install the headstone at the site of Shaowei's unmarked grave at his nearest convenience.

"Shouldn't be more than a week," he said as Ping headed out the door.

"Let go," Ping said to Ethel.

"Did that guy call you John?"

"Yes," Ping said.

"Why?"

Ping shrugged. "John is good name, Bible name. It okay."

"Could be worse, eh, b'y?"

"You telling me," Ping said with a tired chuckle. White people sometimes called him John. As far as he could tell, this wasn't meant to be offensive, so he didn't care.

At last they reached her apartment door.

"Goodbye," Ping said.

"Excuse me," Ethel said. "Where do you think you're going?"

"Oh," Ping said, a blush rising in his cheeks. "Home. Go sleep. Wake early tomorrow."

"Did ya want to come in?" Ethel said as she opened her door. "I'll put a pot of Tetley on."

"No," Ping said. "Is okay. I go home."

"No," Ethel said. "Come in. Have a drink. I'll make you something stronger if tea's not to your liking."

"No, no," Ping said. "I go. I tired from travelling."

"Jesus, b'y," Ethel said. "Just get in the friggin' house before the neighbours sees ya."

Ethel had a small one-bedroom apartment inside the house. A casual clutter took up nearly every inch of the place. The bed was unmade, and the only thing in the entire space that looked tidy was the bar cart. Ping stood awkwardly inside the doorway.

"You wait here while I get changed," Ethel said, and she stepped behind a body-length folding screen, scarves, boas, and costume jewellery hanging off its corners.

"Heh, okay," Ping said, feeling heat radiating from his cheeks.

"Y'know," Ethel's slinky shadow called out from behind the screen, various garments falling to the floor, "my mother always told me to never let a man see me in my pyjamas."

"That good," Ping said, trying to not look at the screen, instead anxiously staring at a rather intricate cobweb forming in a corner near the ceiling. He knew he should be thinking of Hua Ling but it was hard to remember her in this instant.

"Yeah," Ethel said. "Luckily I'm not wearing any pyjamas right now."

"That good," Ping said again, nodding, beading the sweat off his brow with a hanky. "I always listen to Mom advice."

"As a matter of fact," Ethel said as she stepped out from behind the screen, "I'm not wearing anything at all."

1941

24

UNHAPPY ROAD

"I can't believe it's been ten years," Gao said as he stepped off the station platform.

"It hasn't been that long," Ping said. "Last time I saw you was only two or three years ago."

Gao stretched his arms. "I mean ten years since we first arrived here. Since we first met."

"Oh," Ping said. "Yeah. I'm not sure how much has changed since last time you were here. I have a car now."

"Yeah, you told me in your letters."

"Oh," Ping said. "Yeah." Enough time had passed that things had grown stiff between the two men. They were old friends, but now that they were together again, both of them found it difficult to know what to say to one another. Still, Ping was excited to have an old friend back in St. John's, and Gao was excited to leave New York City behind once and for all.

"I'm just glad to be away from the city life," he said.

"Really?" Ping said. "America, it seemed nice to me." His time in New York had grown in his estimation in the years since his visit.

"America, Newfoundland, it's all the same. It's the people there, their attitude, their . . . speed. I couldn't take to it."

"Well," Ping said, unsure what to say next. "I'll bring you to the place where I'll have you working."

They walked out of the station. Downtown St. John's was mostly the same, a few more paved roads, a few less farm animals. A lot fewer men. Most of the businesses that Gao could remember had since closed down. Hans' Shoe Shoppe looked as if it had been firebombed. But many things remained the same. There were still children running around and pointing and staring. Some of them came running now towards Ping and Gao, hands on their faces, pulling their own pallid skin back so their eyes slanted and yelling a bunch of nonsense words between giggles.

"Ching chang ding dong!" one child yelled.

"Clang clang!" another yelled.

"Chinese, Japanese, dirty knees, look at these!" the first child yelled.

Ping and Gao had stopped being bothered by this type of behaviour long ago. The comparison to the Japanese, well, they didn't care for that very much. They kept walking until they reached Ping's car.

A 1940 Chevrolet panel truck, all black and big round curves. The sides were emblazoned with painted words: SNOW WHITE LAUNDRY LTD.

"It's for work," Ping said. "Makes it easier delivering the laundry."

"Wow," Gao said, stopping outside the passenger door to size up the van. "I don't remember seeing rides like this when we first came here."

"There were a couple around," Ping said as he hopped in the driver's seat. "None like this, though."

Gao kicked a tire and extinguished his cigarette before getting in the van. "So business must be going well," he said.

"Yeah," Ping said. "Those laundry machines, they really changed things. We have dry cleaning now too."

"Who would've thought you could clean things dry?" Gao said as Ping took the car out of park and began the short drive to Harvey Road.

"I got a good deal on this," Ping explained. "A furniture company ordered a half-ton version of this Chevy and when it showed up, it was a one-ton. They didn't want it, so I was able to get a good price."

"This city," Gao said, staring out the window as Ping drove. "It's just as I remember it."

"Okay, this is the place." Ping parked outside a nondescript building a few doors down from the movie theatre.

Inside, the floor was laid with an extravagant patterned carpet, and tables and chairs were upholstered with the finest linens. The walls were covered with a red velvet fabric, and electric candles and lanterns hung from the ceiling. Along the back was a small stage with a mic and a stool and an organ built into the wall. Next to it was an elaborate bar slightly raised above the rest of the restaurant, fully stocked with liquors of every type. Three women, two of them on ladders and one on the floor directing the other two, were hanging up a large painting. The painting depicted three men with long beards, one in a green robe holding a baby, one in red carrying a curved green sceptre, and an older one in yellow holding on to a peach.

Gao nodded in appreciation.

Ping said. "We've got these too." He walked over to a wooden crate and pushed aside its cover. Inside were dozens of circular wood carvings of the symbols for double happiness, prosperity, longevity, and status. "We're going to arrange them into an archway," Ping explained. "Right here by the door."

"This must've cost quite a bit," Gao said. "The whole place, I mean."

"It's always the way," Ping said.

They looked at each other.

"I didn't mean . . ." Ping began.

"It's fine," Gao said.

"Oh," Ping said. "Do you remember Ethel? She used to teach me English?"

"Yeah," Gao said. "At the church."

"She and her sisters are going to work here too. That's them, helping me put the place together."

"William Seto Ping," Ethel called out. "C'mere, me love, and tell me if this looks level to you."

"Talk in English around her," Ping said to Gao as they approached her. "She gets suspicious when we don't."

Marge and Vile were on either side of the painting, pushing it back and forth little by little.

"Whaddya think?" Vile called out. "Can I get off this jesus thing yet?"

The painting looked as level as one could expect.

"It look good," Ping said with a chuckle. "Yeah, you come down. Get off there before you hurt you self."

"This must be the great Upton Gao," Ethel said. "It's a pleasure to meet you."

"You may have met before," Ping said. "He learn English at church too."

"Yes," Gao said. "I remember you."

Ethel paused, scrunching her face. "No, me son, I don't remember ever seeing the likes of you before. I remembers the other ones, the ones that died, but I don't remember you."

336

A silence fell between them as Marge and Vile came down the ladders.

"I like that," Marge said, gesturing towards the painting.

"Will bring good fortune," Ping said. "I glad to have you all here as team."

"No," Marge said. "Thank *you*, Mr. Ping."

"I'm only here because I'm getting paid," Vile said.

"Is still good team," Ping said. "This is Gao. He a great chef. He, uh, cook the food for us."

"I s'pose that'll be one thing we won't have to do around here," Vile muttered.

"Vile," Ethel warned.

"Hello," Gao said with a big smile.

"He was the one gave me cookbook," Ping said. "Remember?"

"Jesus, yes, I remembers that," Ethel said. "You were learning English from that friggin' book and everything you said sounded like a recipe. 'I was walking at fast speeds for thirty seconds to a minute.' 'Just a pinch of happy.'"

"I still have book," Ping said to Gao.

"Really?" Gao said.

"Yes," Ping said. "Is here in kitchen."

"Can I see?"

"Of course," Ping said and redirected his attention to his staff of Squibb sisters. "I show Gao the kitchen. You girls organize the wooden symbols."

"But we don't know what they mean," Ethel said.

"No matter," Ping said. "Just arrange by shape. No one have to know what they mean."

Once they were in the kitchen the two men resumed speaking in their dialect.

"Are you and her—?" Gao raised an eyebrow.

"No," Ping cut him off. "This is where you'll be working."

A nice kitchen, but small. A big fridge, a couple of gas ranges and a big hood. There was even a special compartment for a wok.

"What do you think?" Ping asked as he passed Charlie's old cookbook to Gao.

"It's great, it's great," Gao said. "You have a menu worked out yet?"

"No," Ping said. "You can do it. Just cook whatever you liked cooking in New York."

"I thought you'd want more authentic dishes," Gao said.

"I want whatever sells," Ping said. "You can cook fish too. Fish and chips. Stuff from that book."

Gao stood there, thumbing through the old, stained pages.

Ping raised one hand to his temple, massaging it. "Do you have ideas for a name?"

"You don't have one yet?"

"No. I was thinking something like Seven-A or Five-A. Something like that."

"Why?" Gao asked as he closed the book.

"Seems easy for white people. Not too Chinese, nothing hard to understand."

"Like the Globe?"

"Exactly."

"Call it the Globe Two."

"Heh, no." Ping shook his head. "Bad omen. Seven-A is more like good luck."

"I don't like it," Gao said. "It should be more mysterious, enticing."

"Globe Two is mysterious?"

"That was just a joke. What about something like . . ." Gao's eyes lit up. "Hollow Bamboo."

"Isn't that what your restaurant was called?" Ping asked. "We can't use that again."

"We just called it Jook Sing," Gao said. "We didn't translate. Here, you can call it Hollow Bamboo."

"That seems like in bad taste," Ping said. "It might give the wrong impression of me."

"No one will even know what it means."

"I don't know," Ping said. "I don't want my creation to be hollow bamboo."

"Look at where you are," Gao said. "That might be out of your control."

"I'll think about it."

"Who's cooking with me?" Gao asked, as he thumbed through Charlie's book again. "You?"

"No," Ping said, waving the notion away. "I know a guy. We'll have to drive out to him, though."

"We should've left earlier," Ping muttered.

"Why?" Gao asked from the passenger seat, looking at a crudely drawn map. "How long does it take?"

"About an hour," Ping said. "Maybe an hour and a half."

"Lots of time," Gao said, checking his watch. "It's almost three now. We'll be back by seven, just in time for supper."

"Yeah," Ping said.

The roads were only intermittently paved throughout the city and once they were beyond the city limits, the roads were nothing but dirt and trees.

"Reminds me of the trains," Gao said as he stared at the landscape blurring by.

"Yeah," Ping said. "I was just thinking that."

"So," Gao said. "We need to catch up."

"Yes," Ping said. "You first. Tell me all about New York."

"Eh, you don't want to hear about that," Gao said. "The people are loud and they move fast. Everyone's in a rush. You were there, you saw it. I want to know about you. I want to know how you afford all this. I especially want to know about you and Ethel."

"Ethel?" Ping said, squinting as he tried to distinguish which dirt road to turn down. "She's just a friend. She's an employee now."

"C'mon, man," Gao said. "You've been around this girl for ten years and nothing has happened?"

"She's a nice woman," Ping said. "But just a friend. I am married, you might remember that. I have a family."

"So what you're saying is, you don't care if I make a move on her?"

"I don't care what you do," Ping lied. "But, no," he added. "I can't have two employees involved romantically. It's a very bad idea."

Ping had long since determined that what happened between him and Ethel was a matter only for him and her to know about. He was married. He had a family. There were responsibilities he needed to consider, and optics. Granted, Ethel was something of a salve to his unending loneliness in the West. Nights spent entwined together with the blinds shut and the lights off, the taboo of it all only making everything feel that much better. And that much worse. There was always an emptiness to it, sneaking out through the back door to throw off the neighbours. Never being able to go on a date in public. Indeed, all of his success felt empty to him. He couldn't have the life he wanted; he couldn't allow himself. And he wasn't even sure which life of his he wanted anymore. He drove the car faster.

Gao narrowed his eyes and looked at him. "All right," he said. "But who says it would be romantic? Not everything has to be romantic."

"You have the map for one reason and one reason only. To guide me. I'm not being guided right now."

"Fine," Gao said, and scrutinized the map. "I think you just keep going straight."

"I thought I took a turn somewhere around here," Ping said.

"If you know the roads so well, why do you need me to look at the map?"

"Usually Little Joe shows me which roads to turn on," Ping said. "I think I'm supposed to turn here. I'm taking this turn."

"You and Little Joe, driving around this place. I never would've thought I'd see the day."

"He's a nice guy," Ping said. "It's not like it used to be. He just makes sandwiches for kids now."

"Old grey mare," Gao crooned in English. "She ain't what she used to be."

Ping waited, wondering whether Gao was done singing. "But, yeah," he said. "We drive around the island, Little Joe and me, make sure all the Chinese people are connected through the association. The more people that arrive in St. John's, the more that end up somewhere out here. It's important to keep the community together."

"Is it really a community if it's spread out across an island?"

"It's a community spread across the world," Ping said. "You know how lonely it gets here. Even when I'm surrounded by my own people, it's lonely. I can't imagine how some of the people out here feel, alone in places where nobody's ever seen anything like them before."

"All right," Gao said. "I get it. You're the big shot community leader now."

"It's not like that," Ping said. "The main reason we come out to all these people is to collect money for our War Relief Fund."

"Oh yeah," Gao said. "I remember you mentioning something about that."

"Three dollars a month from every Chinese person on the island," Ping said.

"So it's gotten easier to send money back home?"

"Oh, yeah," Ping said. "The banks have better technology now."

"Do you send much back to your wife?"

Ping winced. "I . . . I haven't been able to contact them since the war with the Japanese began," he said. "It was bad enough before. Maybe one, two letters a year. Now, nothing. For years."

"Mm," Gao said. "I haven't heard from my family in years either."

Neither of them really knew how to talk about the ways in which their isolation was intensified by the emotionally harrowing wars, but there was a solace in their solidarity.

"Sometimes not hearing anything is a good thing," Ping said. "Little Joe . . . he recently received word that his wife had been killed during a bombing."

Gao looked out the side window. "I'm sorry to hear that," he said.

"So anyway, we collect money and send it over. Just a little way to . . . do something. A bunch of troops that were here were just sent to Hong Kong."

"Newfoundlanders?" Gao asked.

"Some, I think. Mostly Canadians."

"Whole world is upside down," Gao said absently. "We're over here, they're over there."

A silence fell between them and they both listened to the car's radio, cycling back and forth between heavy bouts of static and far-away whispers of some Christian show, the gospel of Christ sandwiched between white noise.

"Do you ever see Bessie?" Gao asked.

"Who?"

"Bessie. My language buddy."

"Oh," Ping said. "I have no idea."

"Blond," Gao said. "Curly hair."

"Haven't seen her," Ping said. "Maybe a nurse for the war? A few of the women from the church did that."

A silence fell between the two men again. Ping relied mostly on painted wooden road signs in figuring out where he was going. He had been out here with Little Joe once, a few months ago at the beginning of summer. There was a guy out near Placentia, he had opened up a restaurant in a shed. Nothing more than a wood stove, a wok, a counter to take orders from, and a bed under the counter, out of sight. Just a shed on the side of the road. A nice view of the ocean and nothing around him.

"What about the reverend?" Gao said.

"He passed away a couple of years ago," Ping said, with a slight shake of his head. "Well, he's presumed dead. He was on a boat that sank. They never found his body."

"That's terrible," Gao said. "He was always nice to us."

"They never found the boat either," Ping said. "Maybe he's still out there somewhere."

"What about his family?"

"Not sure," Ping said. "Maybe we should see if his daughter would play organ at the restaurant."

Ping and Gao arrived at the shed about an hour after they'd left the city. They parked the truck underneath a hand-painted sign that read RENNY'S CONFECTIONERY. There was barely enough room inside the restaurant for Ping and Gao to stand together. A thin young Chinese man sat behind the counter smoking a cigarette and reading a book, with his glasses precariously balanced on the tip of his nose. He wore a long-sleeved sweater that was too big for him, with small ropes tied around the cuffs so that the baggy sleeves didn't impede him.

"Hey, Renny," Ping said.

"Oh!" Renny looked surprised, quickly putting down his book. "Hello, Mr. Ping. What brings you out here?"

"Did I mention to you last time that I was opening a restaurant? I want you to meet Upton Gao. He's going to be my chef."

"Very nice to meet you, Mr. Gao."

"Now I didn't drive out here just so you two could meet each other," Ping said. "Renny, I want you to work for me."

"Oh no, Mr. Ping," Renny said, shaking his head. "I can't. I have to run this place."

"I know life out here can't be easy," Ping said. "Come to town. We've got a really nice restaurant built on Harvey Road. I'll pay you good money. Probably more than what you make here."

The men stood around debating the logistics of such a move. Renny could sell the shed or hold on to the land, et cetera. Eventually, they agreed that Renny would make a decision within the next three days. Ping and Gao left the roadside shed and stared out at the ocean. Several ships were out on the water, big and small. Two huge naval cruisers, one British, one American, surrounded by a bunch of tiny warships. Big blue waves crashed into light brown rocks and the air tasted salty. The sun was beginning to set, so the men started the drive home.

It wasn't long before darkness began to set in and Ping found it harder to see the road signs, scattered as they were. Gao found it difficult to navigate the map, and Ping started to wonder if the man even knew how to read a map. He pulled over a couple of times, to get a better look at a sign on the road, and then he tried to line that up with the map. This worked to variable degrees. He thought that maybe if he kept driving straight, he would make it back to St. John's. And so he drove.

It was night now and he was driving through a dark forest. Sometimes he'd see a flash of light or he'd feel an urge to take a turn or even just stop but he kept going. They clung to a road by the coast, hoping that it would eventually lead them to the city. So dark, no lights other than his own headlights and an occasional beam of passing light from a lighthouse. Gao dozed off in the passenger seat. Ping judged him for this but found himself dozing off too. Struggling to keep his eyes open, he fixed his eyes on the beam of his headlights, nothing but dirt road and patches of grass and then something ran in front of him.

Several somethings.

Ping slammed on the brakes, stopping so hard that the truck's rear wheels left the ground and the truck toppled onto the driver's side with a loud dry thud.

"What the hell?" Gao said.

"I . . ." Ping started. "I thought I was about to hit something."

"Well, did you?"

"I'm not sure," Ping said, his eyes struggling to focus.

Just beyond the windshield, trapped in the beam of the headlights, were dozens of little birds. Their bodies were half black and half white, with big multicoloured beaks, orange with yellow lines and black spots. Their eyes were black and rimmed orange and it almost looked as though they were smiling. The longer Ping stared at them, the more of them seemed to arrive, until he could swear there were hundreds of them out there around the headlights. More and more little birds gathered in the light until, counted among their ranks, was a pair of green rubber boots.

"Jumpin' dyin' tanight," the rubber boots yelled. "Are you fellas okay in there?"

"Is he talking to us?" Gao said.

"Mudder!" the voice called out. "Mudder! Dem jesus birds did it again!"

Ping struggled to understand where the voice was coming from.

"Oh, it's you lot," the voice said quietly. "Jesus, should've known the way they drive. C'mon, fellas, get out of there, let's get you set back up."

It took a few minutes to establish what had happened. Once Ping and Gao were out of the truck and it was determined that they weren't injured, only dazed by the accident, the man in the rubber boots helped them push the one-ton truck back right side up. It wasn't an easy task, and a farm horse was enlisted to help right the fallen vehicle. The rubber boots belonged to Cory Cox, a teenager who lived with his mother just off the main road. These car accidents were semi-frequent, Cory explained.

"Dem birds, right, dey're called puffins," he said. "Dey live on dat island over dere. It's called Puffin Island."

Ping and Gao stared blankly at the boy while he told them this.

"Basically, da puffins, dey likes to eat during da night and dey lets da moonlight guide dem where ta go. But sometimes, cars and trucks and all dat drives by, right, and da birds gets confused and thinks dem lights on the front are da moon, right, and dey comes over. Gives da drivers an awful fright, all dese little birds coming out of nowhere, right."

346

"Yeah," Ping said, anxious to leave.

"Every morning, I collects all the birds over here and puts 'em in me boat and brings 'em back to dere little island. I s'pose I could leave 'em here, but there's nothing worse than waking up to a yard fulla dead birds."

"Right," Ping said.

"Although, I s'pose if it was turrs, that'd be all right." Cory grinned at the men.

"Heh," Ping said. "It's always the way."

"Yes, dat's the trut', ain't it? What are ye fellas doing out here at night anyways? Could've hit a moose or anything?"

"I recruit a cook for my restaurant in St. John."

"Oh yes now, a cook! Where to?"

"My restaurant," Ping said.

"Yeah," Cory said, "where to?"

"On Harvey Road," Ping said.

"Unhappy Road?" Cory said, frowning.

"No, no," Ping said with a smile. "Har. Vey. Road."

"Oh," the boy said. "Harvey Road. Never heard of it. Now George Street, I heard of dat before."

"Cory, b'y," a woman's voice called through the air, "come in out of it, you're liable to catch a chill out there."

"All right, Mudder," Cory yelled back. "Listen, fellas, you're more than welcome to spend the night here. Just park your truck up by da house. It'll be easier for you to figure out your way back to town tomorrow, in the daylight."

And so the men parked their laundry truck by Cory Cox's house, just off the main road by Puffin Island. They said they would sleep in the back of the truck, not quite comfortable enough to sleep in the young man's house. The boy brought out some of his nan's quilts for the men to sleep with.

"You're liable to freeze ta det out here," he said as he handed the men the quilts. "Is really no trouble for you to sleep in the house, we don't mind. Are you sure you don't want to come in?"

Ping and Gao slept in the truck.

And just under all of this, just over the edge of that there cliff, on a beach down below, two men walked on the rocky shore under the cover of darkness. They paced up and down the beach, discussing the future of the world. What a funny pair, these two men on the beach were, one short and stout, a cigar hanging out of his mouth, his bald head gleaming in the moonlight, attracting more than a few puffins. The other man was tall and thin, with glasses that reflected the gleaming light off the other's bald head. This man had a wheelchair with him but found it too hard to navigate on the uneven rocks. Instead, he stood and walked very slowly, swinging his hips back and forth in such a way that the iron braces on his legs could move just so, balancing his weight on a cane. And these two men talked and talked and came up with a document that would change the shape of things. And although the document would never truly exist, its contents never written down, its signatures never signed, it was something agreed upon and heard the world over. And the strangest thing of all is that even though this document had nothing at all to do with the Chinese, no mention of them at all, its creation meant that one day, several years down the road, the walls would come down and Chinese women and children would be allowed in to Newfoundland.

All because of two men walking on the beach.

1942

25

THE HUNTING TRIP

"Service!" Ping yelled. "Service!"

Marge arrived to grab another hot plate out of the kitchen.

"You can't let people wait like that," Ping said to her. "If food get cold, they hate us. We have reputation."

Marge silently took the plate and headed back out to the dining room.

It was a busy night, as always. Every table in the room was filled and there was a waitlist for others to get in. Ping checked himself in the mirror by the service hall, made sure his tie wasn't askew, made sure his hair was perfectly coiffed. Appearance was important. It always was, but especially here, especially now. The 7-A had been praised as the best restaurant in the city, and he had to make sure that he looked like he owned the best restaurant in the city. His clientele, most of them were the finest of St. John's, the bourgeois elite, politicians and men rich enough to be able to afford to miss the war. The rest of the clientele was made up of American servicemen and members of the Navy who wandered in from a hostel for soldiers just a few doors down the road. Some called them heroes; Ping called them customers.

A banjo was being played tremendously fast out in the main dining room. Ping took a deep breath, fiddled with his tie once more, and walked out. The 7-A was a glamorous place, all rich white people in their best dinner attire. Bow ties and top hats, elegant dresses, ornamental canes, the whole gamut. Ping loved to circulate through the dining room on nights like this, to see and be seen. It was a strange turn of events. It was no longer frowned upon to be at a Chinaman's establishment. Now it was exotic, a badge of honour, something these patrons could go home and brag to their friends about. "Ernest took me to the 7-A last night and it was amazing. The food was served in a pineapple, like the pineapple was a plate."

Ping surveyed the room. A local banjo act was strumming his four-string while simultaneously humming a tune into a harmonica, playing while Addie was on her break, probably out back having a smoke. There didn't seem to be any problems Ping needed to tend to. The room looked happy, sounded happy. As long as he heard laughter out here, he knew it couldn't be too bad.

Ethel was tending to a booth in the back, a rich guy waving some bills at her, her blushing and batting her eyelashes, knowing how to work the room. Marge was over in the service hall, staring at a plate. Vile was taking drink orders.

Ping peeked into the kitchen. Gao and Renny were cooking as fast as they could. Ping walked back out and took a seat at the bar. This had been his routine as of late. Work at the laundry all day, managing the orders, doing the paperwork, writing up receipts. Then after he was done his clerical duties, he'd pop down to the restaurant, just to check in, make sure everything was going smoothly, have a drink at the bar and be there to shake the hands of whosoever wanted to meet the owner. He had a good view of the stage from here, and tonight was a special night. When service slowed down later, Gao and his band were going to do a couple of songs. Ping hadn't seen them perform yet, and although he was trepidatious about letting Gao leave the kitchen, he was excited to see his friend do what he loved.

He lit a cigarette, ordered an old-fashioned, and waited. After the banjo player left the stage, Addie took her seat behind the organ again and started playing some dinner music. In the beginning, she had played nothing but hymns, and it drove business down. But over time, she learned some secular music and things were good.

A little after eleven service had slowed enough that Ping could reasonably declare that it was okay for Gao to take the stage. Gao went out back to change into his performance clothes. Ethel took the mic to introduce the band.

"All right, b'ys," she said, not quite loud enough to quiet the rowdy crowd. "There's a band taking the stage now, so let's give a warm welcome to the Chinese Singing Cowboy and the Barrelmen."

Gao walked onto the stage in an ivory suit with a shiny red tie and a big cowboy hat. His band formed behind him, the banjo player, a drummer, a guitar player. All white men.

"Hello," Gao said in stilted English into the mic. "For our first song, we will perform Dean Martin song from new movie."

The banjo player blew a tune into his harmonica, a soft, strange tune. The bass player hummed along to the harmonica, giving it an ethereal feel. Ping took a sip of his drink. He hadn't heard this tune before so it must be from a movie he hadn't seen yet. He was too busy for the picture shows nowadays, trying to keep two businesses afloat.

Gao sang something about cowboys dreaming in his deep baritone voice, with a wavering delivery. It sounded like an error but it was perfect. It gave the line some emotion. He sang with a nostalgic sadness, and Ping could remember all those days on all those boats and all those trains listening to Gao singing the same folk song over and over again. And Ping had always felt that Gao's voice didn't quite fit that song about San Francisco and gold and moms and whatever, but his voice felt right here. Ping shook his head as he stubbed out his cigarette.

He turned his attention back to Ethel, over at that rich guy's booth again. Ping could've sworn that he saw the rich guy pointing towards him, but now that he was looking at the table, the rich guy was shrugging and looking at Ethel. Ethel shook her head and then looked in Ping's direction. Ping gave her a nod, as if to say "It's fine."

The rich guy stood up and began to walk over towards Ping, but Ethel shushed him and pointed to the stage. The rich guy took his seat again. Ping finished his drink. He had stopped listening to the music after a line about a gun and a pony. Gao and his band were good, but this type of music wasn't for Ping. He felt a little stomach sick now. He got off the stool and went into the bathroom, its brilliant light bulbs a stark contrast to the dark velvet lighting of the dining room.

"Mr. Ping," the young bathroom attendant said. "You don't look so well."

"It nothing," Ping said, looking at an unusually pale reflection in the mirror. "I think I just drink too fast."

"Do you need anything?" the attendant said. "A cigar? A razor?"

"Is okay," Ping said. He splashed water on his face and grabbed a towel from the attendant.

By the time Ping took his seat on the stool again, Gao had retreated from the mic and the banjo player had stepped forward. The audience was roaring with laughter. It was the first time Ping had taken a good look at the banjo player. He was bald at an unusually young age and he had thick-rimmed glasses. He wasn't singing so much as he was just talking into the mic, doing some kind of comedy routine set to music. The bass player was playing a jaunty tune on an accordion, and the drummer kept a steady beat. And although the audience was laughing, the story the banjo player told seemed to be a darker one, a rhyme about someone being refused entry to heaven.

When the banjo man finished his rhyme, the laughter from the audience was deafening. Ping lit another cigarette and watched Gao take the mic again. He sang a song about a big iron on his hip, and while Ping knew this was probably a reference to a gun, he couldn't help but remember the irons they'd used at Fong-Lee and imagined having a big one strapped on his hip like a weapon. He sighed.

The band performed a couple more songs, nothing too extravagant, more country songs and more funny spoken pieces. When they were done, it was time for last call. Gao and the banjo player came over to the bar.

"Hey," Gao said in English. "My bandmate want to meet you. He say he know you."

"Oh?" Ping said, squinting at the banjo player.

"You have to excuse me," Gao said, turning away. "I go see Agnes." Ping hadn't noticed Gao's girlfriend in the audience. He had asked them to keep their relationship away from the customers' eyes, unsure of how the clientele would react to a white woman dating a Chinese man.

"Hi." The banjo player stuck out his hand. "We met years and years ago. Do you remember me?"

"I'm sorry," Ping said. "I not sure."

"I used to own a bar downtown and you came in one night with Fong Choy."

"Oh!" Ping said, the memories of that night coming back to him. "Yes, yes, I remember."

"Eh, it was only a chance meeting," the man said. "We may as well be strangers. I just remember your name, is all."

"Heh," Ping said. "Mr. Ping."

"Joey Smallwood."

"Nice to meet you," Ping said. "Again. You like 7-A?"

"It is truly one of the finest establishments in the city. And you've got a wonderful singer cooking for you here."

"Yeah, yeah," Ping said. "His voice very good at this type of music, very nice."

"Ain't that the truth," Joey said. "Well, I'll leave you to it. I only stay out late once a week 'cause I got a pig farm to be tending to."

"Okay," Ping said. "Have good night."

"Just let me talk to him, just—excuse me, excuse me—let me talk to him," a man's voice rang out. It was that rich guy, and even now, Ethel stood between him and Ping, trying to keep him from going over.

"Just take me word for it," she said.

"Mr. Ping!" the man yelled out. "Just a moment of your time, please. I am merely an admirer of your establishment, that is all."

"Yes, yes." Ping stood up and sauntered towards the man, gripped his hand in a shake. "Ethel, anyone want speak me, you let them speak me. Is fine."

"Fine," she said as she walked away.

"Oh, Mr. Ping, you are the gentleman of repute," the man said. "I simply wished to extend my thanks. My thanks for this abso-lutely wonderful establishment you have here, I mean, it's just mir-aculous. I feel like I've been transported to the Orient the moment I walk in through the doors."

"Thank you," Ping said with a nod. Ping could vaguely remem-ber meeting this man before, on a rainy night at the Woodrows' house. "Your name?"

"Richards DuMont."

All this fuss made sense to Ping now. Dicks. The man who had always loved Ethel. She hadn't spoken of him in years, but Ping remembered how she'd mention him time and time again during his language lessons. And at the Woodrows' garden party. Ping thought Richards looked a lot older now.

"I love everything about the 7-A," Richards continued, "just everything, from the drinks to the waitresses. I come here pretty often, I'm sure you've noticed me. Look, I just wanted to invite you to a hunting trip with me. Nothing too fancy. I have an estate just outside the city. It'd be an honour and a privilege to have you out there, just for a couple days, and we can talk. I am positively fascinated by your people's . . . perseverance. I'd love to discuss some business with you."

"That sound good," Ping said. "Fun, yes."

"So you'll do it?" Richards said.

"Yes," Ping said. He knew their past, but was this what Ethel was trying to stop him from doing? *She's crazy*, Ping thought. "I never been hunting but I want try."

"This weekend," Richards said. "I'll send a car for you."

Richards DuMont's estate was on a beautiful piece of land in a valley between two mountains. There must have been a farm somewhere nearby, as there was such an overwhelming scent of shit in the air that most visitors gagged for the first few minutes they breathed in the air. But then it wore off and they got used to it.

A fancy black car picked up Ping on Saturday morning and drove him out to this estate. A one-story building, significantly wider than it was tall, with sharp and dramatic angles, stood at the end of a long dirt road, although it seemed to Ping that most things outside the city were at the ends of long dirt roads. A row of nice cars was parked around a fountain outside the front door.

The butler directed Ping to a room where he was to change into a garish bright orange sweater to prepare himself for hunting with Richards.

"Moose," Richards explained. "There's a lot of 'em here now and we're gonna find one. You can bring back some of the meat to that wonderful chef of yours and see what he can do with it."

"Oh yes," Ping said. "Very good idea."

"Me and Gao go way back," Richards said with a big smile. "Or, well, I know him at least. He may not know me. My dad helped him ship some precious goods to New York, if you catch my drift."

Ping and Richards wandered through the woods behind the house for a couple of hours. Ping had never shot a gun before, but he liked the weight of the rifle in his hands and he could imitate the poses one should take with a rifle from all the movies he had seen over the years. Holding the rifle reminded him of his child-hood, playing with sticks, pretending to be the men in the diaolous. Ping didn't like to remember this. After all, it was still a weapon. The same type of weapon that saw his friends reach their untimely ends. Ping swallowed. He tried to think of something else.

Ping and Richards wandered for hours, never saying much. On occasion, Richards would stop to have a snack and offer Ping some carrots he had brought along. Then he would put his hands up to his mouth and make some sort of weird sound that was wet and loud and Ping thought it would probably scare off an animal before it would attract one. Ping remembered the noises that the moose had made on the *Caribou* and they sounded nothing like this. They didn't encounter any moose.

They wandered into a bog and saw a pair of long, spiny legs from a distance.

"Oh my," Richards said, raising the rifle to look down the sight. "Looky there."

Far down at the end of the bog stood a peculiar sight. Two pink flamingos, one pecking at its legs, the other just standing there looking around. Ping stared at the long, pink birds.

Bang!

One of the tall birds fell to the earth as easy as a rock through a window. The other flamingo flew off in a hurry, zooming through the woods until it was no longer visible.

"That type of bird," Richards said. "Why, I never in my day."

They dragged their boots through the moss until they got to the bird.

"I'm glad we got at least one," Richards said. "Otherwise no one would believe me."

They dragged the bird back to the house and gave up hunting for the day.

Richards had a modern home, with a glass fireplace and big luxurious leather chairs and small mirrored tables. After changing back into their normal clothes, the two men sat at either end of the fireplace and the butler brought out two snifters filled with some peaty Scotch. Ping found the first sip abrasive, like breathing in pure smoke, but the second sip was more palatable, and by the third he had grown to like it.

"You hold the glass like this," Richards explained, half of his face illuminated by the fire. "Around the little round bit. The heat of your hand warms up the Scotch ever so nicely."

"Yes," Ping said. "The heat, you can taste."

"The heat you can taste," Richards repeated with a shake of his head. "You people have a way of being so wise with your words. It's . . . remarkable. Just remarkable."

The only thing Ping could think to say in response was *it's always the way*, but he thought this might be the rare occasion where the phrase might actually hit the wrong notes.

"Do you like hunting?" Richards said. "Did you have fun?"

"Is nice," Ping said. "Being outside. Easy to work too much, stay inside too much. Outside nice."

"Yes," Richards said with a nod. "Now, look, as I'm sure you've already surmised, my motives in bringing you all the way out here were not limited to just the cultural experience of a Newfoundland hunting trip. No, I brought you here to discuss business."

"Okay," Ping said and took a sip of his Scotch.

"Or, rather, one particular aspect of your business. Now, you see, Mr. Ping, I love the 7-A. I love everything about it. It's tremendous, really, really tremendous. And the thing about it is, when it comes to you people, you come here with not a dime in your pockets, not a cent to your name, and you come all the way over here to do what? To live. And you have a hell of a time doing it. Why, I can't even imagine what it must be like."

Richards stopped as if he expected Ping to talk about what it's like, but Ping didn't say anything.

"And the 7-A," Richards continued. "You and the 7-A. Why, what a remarkable success story, for you to rise from nothing and now you own a place people want to go to. It's just fantastic. And I'm sure it is due in part to your diligence, your absolute cunning, as a businessman. But I think even you yourself have to admit, your success also rests upon your team. And what a wonderful team you have. You take Gao, for example. Multitalented. Multilingual. Why, no wonder half my folks want your people to leave. You're just too talented. You're like moss on a rock that grows into a mushroom. You people thrive on survival. It makes you stronger."

Richards raised his glass to toast, and Ping mirrored the action, though he was unsure that he really wanted to toast Richards's sentiment.

"Other members of your team too. Like Ethel. You talk about a ravishing young lady." Richards made a fist and bit it with an eager glee. "Never in my days, I swear to you, Mr. Ping, I swear to you. Which brings me to the matter of which I wish to speak to you. Now, you see, I'm a wealthy man, Mr. Ping. I deal in imports and exports and, much like yourself, I am not from around here. I too am an immigrant, even though my skin may be white. It's a funny situation we have ourselves in here, all these immigrants and descendants of immigrants and descendants of descendants of immigrants."

He stood up from his chair and walked to a window that framed the vast forest behind his estate. "The first person to live on Newfoundland, year-round that is, was breaking the law. Now, I'm not talking about those Indians. Their histories aren't written the same as ours. No, I'm talking about Europeans. You see, when England first colonized this little island in the middle of the frigid Atlantic, the King himself decreed that no one was to live here. That's right, the royalty didn't think the conditions here were livable. So they made it a rule, it was against the law to stay on this island. Then some knucklebrain got it in his head and thought, *Well, what are they gonna do about it?* and he stayed here and survived a winter somehow, and the monarchy didn't do anything. So then another man moved here and survived and another man. And soon enough you have on this very island a whole community of yahoos from throughout Europe, gathered here to fish and break laws, as it were. And the King did nothing. What are you going to do, sentence a hundred people to death? Easier to just leave 'em here and forget about 'em. So that's how it began. The original celestials were people whose skin looked like mine."

Only half of the man's body was illuminated by the light, and for some reason Ping thought of Shaowei.

"Now, you may be thinking to yourself, *Why am I hearing this?* Why, it is to establish something, a precedent, if you will, for the type of community you and I have found ourselves in, that we dragged ourselves to from our own disparate parts of the world to end up here together at this very moment. Now, listen to the sounds of my home, Mr. Ping."

Richards stopped talking. All Ping could hear was the crackle of the fire. Maybe the footsteps of the butler on carpet far off somewhere.

"Do you hear any screaming children, Mr. Ping? Do you hear any nagging wives? You hear nothing, correct?"

"Yes, is very quiet house," Ping said. "Peaceful."

"Well, Mr. Ping, the time has come for the peace to end. You see, I live comfortably here, and in fact I no longer require the inheritance to which I am entitled. But you see, Mr. Ping, and I'm sure you can relate to this sentiment, money begets more money, don't it? There's never enough of it, is there?"

Ping shrugged.

"You might be familiar with my father, Old Member Higgs, and if you are familiar with him, then I'm sorry to be the bearer of terrible, no good, bad news, but he's on his deathbed, I'm sorry to say."

"I sorry to hear," Ping said. He had never heard of Old Member Higgs.

"Well," Richards continued, "you'll be relieved to know that the old coot is remaining stubborn as always and now he's demanding that I marry before he dies. He said I got a beautiful nest made here, now all I have to do is trap my bird, and that once I trap my bird, I'll inherit a bigger nest. And I'm not talking about that flamingo, although I will most assuredly get it taxidermied. No, Mr. Ping, I am referring to a wife of course."

"Oh," Ping said. "Okay."

"Now you see, Mr. Ping, this is where my interests and yours collide. You see, I've run my fingers through my little address book time and time again, and I just can't settle on any girl. And these are wonderful girls, Mr. Ping, wonderful. Beautiful, smart, wealthy in some cases. But none of them intrigue me. None, that is, except for your darling waitress Ethel."

Ping slightly choked on a sip of Scotch, the flavour of peat rising through his sinuses.

"I've known darling Ethel for years, and she's always been the one that got away, as the platitude goes."

"Oh," Ping said, thinking about all the nights he and Ethel had spent together. "Yes, yes, she speak of you many times. When she teach me English, she talk about you all the time. I remember, I not even know English and she keep saying 'Richard, Richard, Richard.'"

"Ahem, the name is Richards. And yes. Yes, that does sound like her. Now, here's the funny thing about that. Young Miss Squibb, well, she is not interested in me in the slightest. Never has been. I hadn't the faintest idea why. I mean, usually the money is enough but I can be quite charming too, y'know. But then I start asking around. And I start hearing some things. And then I start looking for myself. And I start piecing things together. Piece. By. Piece."

Ping shook his head in confusion.

"It's to my understanding that you moved here, round ten years ago now? A decade, if you will. And in that time, most curiously, you and Miss Squibb have been frequently seen together. As you yourself just said, she taught you English, and I hear that she got you a nice job at the lieutenant-governor's house and then you got her a job. People say that the two of you go to movies together and you've been seen sitting next to each other on the train. Now, others might fear miscegenation, especially seeing as that sister of hers—Marge, is it?—well, that sister of hers has been seen cavorting around with one of those negro American soldiers, so it must run in the family, a taste for exotica. And again, Mr. Ping, I do not judge. I do not. I have been to Polynesia and let me tell you, the pull of the exotic is entirely understandable to me. No, Mr. Ping, I do not judge miscegenation in the slightest. What I would judge is an adulterer."

Richards leaned on his heels and let his last words hang in the air. "It's to my understanding you're married, Mr. Ping?"

"Yes," Ping said. "I have wife in China."

"And it's to my understanding that it's illegal for you to bring women and children of your kind here, is that so?"

"Yes," Ping said.

"And it's also to my understanding that all men, the world over no matter their race or creed, that all men have the same appetites and desires. I'm speaking carnally, of course, and I don't expect you to answer that one, Mr. Ping, as I do know the answer and no amount of protesting will cause me to think otherwise."

Ping said nothing.

"Old Member Higgs always says a stiff cock knows no conscience. Vulgar, I know, but you know Dad. He has a non-discriminatory way with his words. And correct too. Men—we are driven by one desire. To put a bird in our nest, to put it politely, and we might mask that desire behind other things, like accumulation of wealth or some other silly pursuit, but it's always true that there's really just one motivation. Now, Mr. Ping, it's to my understanding that you haven't seen your wife in ten years, a decade, as it were?"

"Right," Ping said.

"Right," Richards continued. "Then how curious it is, that a man such as yourself could spend ten years away from his wife and not find another outlet for his desires. I'm not looking for an admission of guilt, Mr. Ping. I am merely presenting the facts. A man away from his wife for ten years, spending ample time around another woman. It just makes sense, Mr. Ping. But a wife is a wife, and even if that coupling was arranged for you, I'm sure there exists in you a desire to bring your wife and child here, to this very town, laws be damned. Right?"

"Well," Ping stumbled on his words. "Yes."

"Then what a terrible situation you would have on your hands there, hypothetically of course, if you were to have a wife and a mistress in the same town, in the same room as each other. What a nightmare."

Ping nodded. "Yes, but—"

"Oh, Mr. Ping, just wait, let me speculate a little further. As you and I both know, there is no way of bringing your wife and child here. But if the option was presented to you, I'm sure you would accept. Especially seeing as there is a tiny bit of conflict known as war going on the world over right now, and war's filthy fangs have certainly sunk into your neck of the woods too. What I mean to say is, surely you wouldn't abandon your family in a war zone, even if you were in love with another woman."

Ping nodded again. He knew Richards was right, but he was afraid of where this was going.

"Well, then, let me get to my point. Ethel doesn't have the time of day for me and I am supposing that that is because she is in love with you. What a predicament. Being in love with a married man and the whole married aspect of said man is far, far away on a plot of land that may as well be in outer space. What I am proposing is this. I want you to fire Ethel, or, in other terms, break up with her.

Tell her you don't want her at the restaurant, you don't want her in your life. Bequeath her to me, in essential terms. There might seem to be no benefit in that to you, but let me suggest this to you, Mr. Ping. I am a wealthy and powerful man and I have friends in many high places, friends that I have met at your very establishment as a matter of fact. And I think we can spin a narrative around you, as being a noble man, who owns several businesses, and donates money, and stepped up to the community plate during this time of war. You are a leader, sir. And you know what a leader deserves? His family."

Ping leaned in, eyebrows scrunched.

"Now you may recall those first Newfoundlanders breaking the law and getting away with it. My point being is that laws are malleable. What I am proposing to you is that I can use my influence in conjunction with your image to strike a deal and get your wife and child admitted to this country. All you have to do is give up your other woman. How does that sound?"

Ping sat back in his chair, his hands shaking. He rested the Scotch on a round mirrored table.

"It's a reasonable deal, Mr. Ping. Let's have dinner and you can think about it."

They moved into Richards's elegant dining room with its long table, at least twelve feet in length. The butler had prepared the place settings, with Richards sat at one end of the table and Ping at the opposite side. A large gold candelabra stood in the centre of the table, one of its candle holes empty, the wax having fully burned off.

"I must apologize for the seating arrangements," Richards called out down the table. "I'm accustomed to hosting large crowds."

The meal passed by mostly in silence. The first course was a strange salad consisting of one big lettuce leaf, one slice of tomato, and one slice of mozzarella. Ping stared at the plate, wondering if it was served wrong. The main course was a moose heart, served with some puréed parsnips and roasted shallots. Some sort of sauce made out of the moose's blood was balanced delicately in an onion petal, looking like a small fragile bowl.

"This is a very special part of the moose," Richards called out. "I usually save it for New Year's but today is a special day after all."

Lemon meringue pie for dessert, the meringue whipped to wispy points, some of which had been crisped brown while others remained pure white.

Ping ate the meal dutifully. It would've been rude not to. But his body felt like every successive bite was poison, everything was too much, and he couldn't stomach any of it. With the last bite of his slice of pie, Ping was relieved to know there would be nothing else he'd have to eat after this.

"Why, Mr. Ping," Richards yelled out. "You finished that slice awfully quick. Have another."

"No," Ping said, unable to yell back, fearing that he might vomit. He felt unusually warm now too and wished for nothing more than being able to loosen his tie and have an opportunity to walk through fresh air.

Richards rang a little bell within arm's reach of him and the butler walked into the dining room carrying another slice of pie on a plate, which he went to put in front of Richards.

"No, not for me," Richards said. "For him, for him."

The butler brought the plate to Ping. He weakly picked up his fork and stabbed the tip of the slice, bringing it to his mouth, biting into it. The saccharine-sweet meringue, the bitter-tart lemon, the fatty crust. He struggled to swallow and knew he had made a mistake.

"Toilet?" he called out. He thought of Ethel when he said this, back when he first had language lessons in the gymnasium.

"Just behind you on your right," Richards yelled back.

Ping ran, swinging open the door, but he wasn't quite fast enough. He vomited all over Richards' expensive-looking green floral wallpaper. It came out of him so fast and so strong that it knocked over a flower vase balanced on top of the tank. It was empty anyway.

Richards, hearing the glass shatter, rushed down to see what the matter was. "Oh, Mr. Ping," he said. "Was it my boy's cooking?"

"I do it," Ping said, panting on the floor, yellow and red liquids dripping on either side of his mouth.

"Well, that much is apparent to me, Mr. Ping," Richards said. "I can see what exactly you have done."

"No, no," Ping said, mopping the corners of his mouth with his cufflinked wrist. "Ethel. I fire her. I do it."

"Oh goody," exclaimed Richards. "I'll get to work on our agreement immediately."

"I sorry," Ping said, gesturing to the oozing mess on the walls.

"Oh, don't worry your little heart about that," Richards said. "Wallpaper was due to be freshened up anyway."

And so on the following day of work, Ping fired Ethel in front of the entire staff at the 7-A. He found himself unable to eat that day.

"Is not enough business for three Squibb," Ping said before service was to begin. "So I think Ethel should leave."

"Yes now," she said with a laugh, as she wrapped utensils in fine cloth napkins. "Come off it, b'y."

"I serious," Ping said. "We no need you. We fine."

"I'm sure," she said, continuing to stack the wrapped utensils in an old milk crate.

"I not kidding. You go."

Ethel stopped wrapping the utensils, resting an unfinished one in the crate, the napkin folded to fit utensils inside but no utensils, just empty space. "Are you fuckin' serious?" she said.

"Yeah," Ping said, walking towards the bar, unable to make eye contact with her. "You no work here anymore."

"So, what? This is my two-week notice?"

Ping stepped behind the bar, grabbed a rocks glass and a sugar cube. "No notice. You go. You gone."

"Why the fuck are you doing this?" she said, stomping towards the bar.

The rest of the staff stood throughout the dining room quietly.

Ping grabbed a bottle of bitters, soaked the sugar cube with them, and then he used a brass muddler to mash the cube inside the rocks glass. "Is business," he said. "We no need you. I sorry. Is business."

"Business? You greedy fuck, you're letting me go because of what? Money?"

"Yes," Ping said, his voice wavering, his hands slightly shaking as he poured a couple of fingers of bourbon into the glass.

"You, you, you . . ." Ethel was shaking, tears welling in her eyes, each iteration of "you" sounding madder and madder. "You . . . you . . . you." She stomped over to the crate of utensils and pushed it over. "You think my sisters will keep working here after you fire me, you fuckin' Jew?"

Ping, puzzled by her remark, shrugged.

"Look at me!" she screamed. "Look at me!"

Ping stared at the lone ice cube he had dropped into his drink, watching it float around.

"Look me in the friggin' eyes!" she screamed. "What is it? Why?"

Ping merely shook his head, unable to look at her.

"Did it all mean nothing to you?"

Ping swallowed and continued to shake his head. For the last decade, she had meant everything to him.

"Nothing? You think it was easy for me to be seen with you? You know what people said about me? They thought I was a hooker just 'cause I was with you."

Ping knew that to be true, that the police marked any white woman seen with a Chinese man as a woman of the night. He wanted to tell her how much she meant to him but that this was a matter of honour.

"I hate you," Ethel said. She walked out the door and slammed it behind her.

Marge and Vile just stood there.

Ping looked up at them. "You two," he said. "Wrap utensil with napkin."

He sipped his drink as the two sisters gathered the mess Ethel had made on the floor.

"You're just pulling her leg, aren't ya, Mr. Ping?" Marge said.

"No. I sorry, no," he said, before turning his attention to Gao and Renny. "Go! Do prep. Don't stare at me. Stare at me won't make cooking easier. Go."

Service was a bit bumpy that night, as Marge and Vile had to fill an Ethel-sized hole in the team. And although Ping feared that the two sisters would leave, they found the tips better without Ethel there and only grew to like their jobs more. Sure, behind the scenes they would no doubt commiserate with their sister.

"What a prick," Vile would say.

"I couldn't believe," Marge would say, breathy. "I just couldn't believe it."

But they still showed up bright and early on payday. After all, this was just a lover's quarrel, and while Ping might have thought their affair was a grand secret, it was an arrangement that had been apparent to everyone who worked at the 7-A.

Richards held true to his word. He arranged passes and permits and documents allowing Ping's wife and child to come to Newfoundland. He was even able to arrange an array of communications through the British military to get the message to them faster. They responded back with confirmation that they would be coming. And so Ping waited. Although ten years had passed, it hadn't become any easier to get from one side of the world to the other. If anything, travelling such a long distance was more difficult now and infinitely more dangerous. So he waited. And he waited.

He waited through September, hearing nothing about any arrival. He waited through October, patiently reading the newspapers in the mornings, hoping to not see a headline about a passenger ship being sunk in the Pacific. One morning he awoke to a headline announcing the sinking of the *Caribou*, hit by a torpedo off the coast of Port aux Basques. His heart was racing. He read the article over and over again. Could they have been on it?

"The *Caribou* struck by a German torpedo. She sank after five minutes." Ping read those words repeatedly, adrenaline making the tips of his fingers feel electric. "Nearly all the ferry's life rafts were instantly destroyed or sank after being hit by the underwater missile. The ship sank too fast for the few remaining rafts to be used in time." Did Hua Ling and Wai know how to swim? Ping never knew how to swim. But anything could've happened in the last ten years. They could've learned.

It was all that was in the paper for days. A few days later, accounts from survivors began to be published. One man who balanced an oil drum on a wooden plank to escape described how "all the lights went out. Couldn't see. But I knew where I was to, I knew what way to go. When she got hit she listed over, took water aboard. Well, the people that were down in steerage, they never had a chance. They couldn't get up because she was all flooded with water. They were drowned like rats down there."

Ping felt dazed reading that, like he might pass out. Words stuck in his mind. The people who were down in steerage, drowned like rats.

"It was dark," the man said in the paper. "But you could hear people screeching. All over. And then the cattle drowning."

Survivors were taken to Sydney because Port aux Basques didn't have a good hospital. Maybe they were there. Maybe they got out. It was a rare time where Ping felt part of the larger St. John's community, as it seemed everyone knew someone who was on that boat, and everyone, yellow, white, or otherwise, was waiting, praying that their loved ones had made it off alive. War had reached the shores of the island and along with it a deep sense of anxiety and loss. Even if your loved one did make it, something had been irreparably lost.

In the days after that, a list of all the passengers' names was released, both alive and dead. The list didn't name Hua Ling and Wei. Although Gao and Renny said Ping should be happy that they weren't on the list, this absence only made Ping feel worse. It was months and they still hadn't showed up. So he waited some more.

The onset of winter was cold that year. The wind seemed harsher, louder. And although Ping never cared much for Christmas anyway, he had Marge and Vile decorate the restaurant with some metallic tinsel and fragile lights.

It was the night of December 12 when Ping noticed a strange black smoke billowing under the doors of the 7-A. It was a busy night, more seatings than usual, as would be expected before

Christmas. And it wasn't unusual to see smoke roll in under the door, but usually of the cigarette variety, not thick, black smoke like this. Ping put on his coat and hat to go outside and see what was the matter.

Just up the road, the Knights of Columbus hostel for the soldiers was ablaze. He ran back inside and evacuated the restaurant. In the coming days they would learn that nearly a hundred people were killed in the blaze and another hundred had been seriously injured. The press speculated that it was another attack by the Germans, although Ping could easily imagine a naval man drunk off too many cocktails at the 7-A stumbling back and dropping a cigarette on a stockpile of toilet paper. He wasn't sure how to feel about this notion, and although the restaurant had to be closed for the rest of the Christmas season due to severe smoke damage, Ping never dwelled on either of these issues too much. Instead, he was holed up in his laundry on Aldershot Street, waiting and waiting.

In February, he received a tattered, soggy postcard in the mail. The image on the front depicted Vancouver's harbour. On the back was a small paragraph, Hua Ling's calligraphy. "They wouldn't let us in," she had written. "They said that they didn't believe Wei was your son. So they sent him back. I'm going with him. Will send another letter when we are home."

1949

26

THE NIGHT THE ROADS CHANGED

Ping rested his soggy hat on a hook as he entered the apartment above his laundry. He sighed as he flicked on his desk lamp and slumped into a creaky revolving chair, the cold March rain pitter-pattering on a window. Clinging to his tongue was a memory of scallions from an afternoon scone. He looked at the clock. Seven. He was waiting for midnight. It was a nice lunch, he thought. Good to see her again.

He had run into her on Water Street the week before, saun-tering into a movie theatre on the arm of some handsome beau as Ping was leaving. They chatted for a moment. Ping had just seen *White Heat*, and Ethel was dragging this guy in to see *Jolson Sings Again*. It was the first time they had seen each other in years. Sure, sometimes he'd see her hanging out with Marge and Vile, back before the restaurant closed down. But that was years ago, when there had been nothing but tense silences and sullen glares. The world had changed since then. A lot of things had changed.

Later that same night, when Ping was back in his loft above the laundry, his phone rang.

"Hello?" he said, half expecting it to be some bozo looking for a rush on his laundry.

"Hey," Ethel's voice echoed through the tinny receiver. "Want to go get a lunch sometime?"

They made plans to meet the next day for a cozy bite at the lobby restaurant of a newly opened hotel. What had interested Ping most of all when they ran into each other at the theatre was that the man on Ethel's arm wasn't Richards DuMont. He still looked like a man of wealth, but it wasn't Richards, that's for sure. Ping had tried hard to not follow up on what had happened between those two. He forbade Marge and Vile from talking about it in front of him. It wasn't long after that the restaurant had closed. No Ethel DuMont. No Hua Ling. No Wei. It seemed to him that everything he had done years ago was for nothing.

The Newfoundland Hotel was nice, renovated in the hopes of a big influx of tourism, with confederation and all. Ethel was already seated there waiting for him. She still looked beautiful to him, radiant even, but despite this, Ping knew it was for the best if he kept his attraction to her repressed. She had on a puffy jacket, and though it was warm inside the hotel, she refused to take it off. The hotel was a classy place, big slabs of green rock and marble pillars, and a couple of glass sculptures behind the bar. The menu was fairly light. Devilled eggs, cheese and scallion scones, lemon squares. Two scones were ordered.

"I surprised you want talk to me," Ping said to her.

"Well, Jesus, b'y," she said as she lit a cigarette. "Why wouldn't I want to talk to you?"

Ping stopped, unsure how to even describe why. "Because when I fire you job," he said.

"Oh," Ethel said. "Is that all you did? Just fired me, nothing more to it than that?"

Ping frowned. Maybe he should've stayed home.

"I'll tell you why I wants to talk to you, I wants to talk to you because I always wanted to know why. What it was you and Richards were up to. Neither of ye are of any interest to me anymore. But Richards always denied that he made you . . . fire me."

Ping felt sick again. "You not with Richards?" he asked.

"Jesus, b'y, that's old news. Sure, do you know the war's over?"

"Heh," Ping laughed.

"So?" she said. "If you're not going to tell me either, then I'll leave."

"Okay," Ping said with a sigh. "I tell you. You remember when Richards take me hunting?"

"Yes, I remembers that. I remembers trying to stop it too."

"Yes," Ping said. "He send nice car for me, drive me to fancy house. We go hunting for a little bit, not find anything. Then we go back to his house. He say to me, 'You break up with Ethel, right away, and I get paper allow your family to come here.'"

"He did not," Ethel said.

"Yes," Ping said. "Richards say, 'Oh, it very easy. I rich guy, I change rule for you if I want. You a good businessman, easy.' But he want me to fire you, he want to marry you."

"Oh my goodness," Ethel said. "It all makes sense now."

"Yes, yes," Ping said. "He make me decide that night. I get so nervous, I get sick all over his bathroom. But I do it. I want my family safe."

"Safe?" she said. "Sure you people have never felt safe here, have you?"

Ping couldn't think of anything to say.

"I remembers Marge and Vile telling me about that," Ethel said. "'Bout your wife coming over. And I figured that was why you fired me. But then Marge said they never showed up."

"Is true," Ping said with a slow nod. "Never show up. I wait and wait. They never come."

"So whaddya think? Richards never gave them the right documents?"

"I not sure," Ping said. "I think maybe he give right document but my son— I am not the father. I not sure the word in English. I not the father and my wife not the mother?"

"Jesus, b'y, what is this, a riddle?"

"Heh. No, I just not sure the word. You never taught me. You a bad teacher."

Ethel laughed. "It takes one to know one, you know that, right?"

Ping paused. Both of them had been playful but something felt off to him. "Anyway," he said. "I not sure the word, but my wife, she not give birth to our son."

"That's called adoption, me duckie. You adopted him."

"Yeah," Ping said. "He adoption son, so someone say he not my son, they send him back."

"So they're still in China," Ethel said. "This makes so much sense. You must be looking forward to tomorrow."

"Tomorrow?" Ping said. "When roads change?"

"Well, that too," she said. "But aren't the laws around you people changing tomorrow too?"

"Oh," Ping said. The significance of the day had been almost lost on him and now, having been reminded of it, he remembered the days, weeks, he had spent waiting, wondering where they were. "No, I not excite."

"Sure you went through all that trouble to get them here," Ethel said. "Now he should be able to enter, right?"

"I . . . I not sure," Ping said with a wave. "What happen you and Richards?"

"Just wait now," Ethel said. "You aren't planning on bringing your family here now?"

"I not want to talk about it," he said.

"You're going back to China, aren't ya? You're leaving us here, aren't ya?"

"No," Ping said sternly. "I not go back to China. I have business here, I can't leave."

"Sure, can't you get someone else to run it?"

"No, no," he said. "Then I lose money. Richards and you, what happen?"

"So you're not bringing your family here and you're also not going back?"

Ping exhaled heavily. "They dead," he said. "They die in war. They not come here, I not go there. They dead."

"Your scones," the waiter said, placing one plate with two scones on the table.

After receiving that postcard back in February of 1943, Ping waited for another letter for months. Months and months, until a bitter and sour disposition took hold on him. He no longer felt sick, he felt ravenous. He became a voracious consumer of food and gained forty pounds in six months. And still he waited. Sometimes he would even go and sit at the train station and peer through the crowds of people disembarking from the cars and look for them. Maybe they had tried again, maybe they would show up.

Never did they show up.

News from the European war fronts was easy to obtain, covered in the papers and on the radio and in newsreels before the picture shows. And although all the Chinamen knew that a war was being waged back home, it wasn't too easy to get any information about that one. When Allied troops were in China, it would be reported in the papers. Ping repeatedly read about the exploits of a Newfoundland dog named Gander who had been promoted to sergeant in the Canadian Army. On several occasions the dog had halted enemy Japanese advances. This string of articles came to an end when Gander caught a Japanese hand grenade in his mouth and ran into a cluster of enemy troops, killing himself but saving the lives of countless Canadian soldiers. The soul of Gander joined those of a thousand other Canadian soldiers who died defending Hong Kong. Ping and the other Chinese men pored over and analyzed these articles for any mention of location, any piece of information that might indicate something more about what was going on back home. Indeed, it had been easier to learn about the exploits of a Newfoundland dog in China than it had been to learn about the plight of the Chinese.

As such, it came as quite a surprise to Ping when he was at the theatre once and the week's war newsreel was titled "Chino-Japanese War: Authentic Pictures of CHINESE TROOPS in Action."

"Hundreds of days of war in the Far East," the British-accented narrator reported, "hundreds of days of bucking shots and whining shells and on nearly every one of those days, hundreds killed and maimed." The footage showed grand naval ships in harbour, dozens of soldiers carrying supplies around. "As the opposing armies advance and retreat, dragging each other to and fro across the central plain like wrestlers locked in a death grip, they turn China's fertile countryside into a scarred and scorched wilderness." Footage of water cannons firing, of seaplanes taking off, of trenches and raised bayonet rifles.

"The Orient contains much that is beautiful and now, war! Must it go on?" Soldiers aimed guns at planes flying over. Shattered windows, pulverized buildings, troops dragging carts down dirt roads. Dramatic music played over footage of soldiers rushing onto a battlefield, accompanied by a chorus of loud brass instruments and incessantly rolling snares. "As China's tragic struggle drags into its sixth year, we present these dramatic pictures from the Chinese side of an actual battle far into the wild and mountainous interior. China's army is ill manned, ill trained, and ill equipped but still it struggles on." The scenery almost looked familiar to Ping, the rocky mountains, the overgrown greenery. Had he walked through there? Impossible to say for sure, but now it was war-torn, with cannons hidden inside bushes and explosions destroying the countryside.

"In filming these amazing pictures, the cameramen took almost as much risk as the soldiers, moving forward in twos and threes on the deadly job known in warfare as contact with the enemy." A feeling of certainty came over Ping as he sat in the theatre, illuminated by the black-and-white glow of the screen, showing men who looked just like him, fleeing their towns, running as fast as they could to escape bombs and cannon blasts and explosive shells. The idea had crept into his mind time and time again over the years, one that he had never been able to shake, and now he was certain. Wei and Hua Ling were dead. They had to be. There was no other way to account for their silence.

"Such is the indomitable spirit of the Chinese people," the narrator proclaimed before the newsreel cut out on footage of a diaolou exploding.

Ping had frozen in his seat. Maybe they weren't dead, maybe they were hiding. But then he thought about it some more, and he was again certain. He felt sick again and slumped lower in his seat in the theatre. How could he possibly have expected them to make it here? He tried to block the thought out of his mind, he tried to focus on the picture, some Cary Grant vehicle. He couldn't. He left the theatre and walked home and couldn't stop thinking: *they're dead*.

Of course, that was years ago now. That was before the war was even over. And when the war did end, Ping felt hopeful for a few weeks, as he thought maybe now he would hear from them, maybe now they would write and say, "Hi, we're alive." But no such letter came, and this idea in his mind grew bigger and stronger and all the more encompassing. They were dead.

He focused on the laundry. The restaurant was too social, too many couples, too many white people to smile at, too many government officials, too much disappointment. He avoided it altogether until one day Gao suggested they should probably close down.

"No business," he had said. Ping was happy to get rid of the place.

After the waiter placed the scones on the table, Ethel was quiet for a moment. Then, "I . . . I'm sorry, b'y, I never even thought. How rude of me."

"Is okay," Ping said. "I not want to talk about it anymore."

"Okay," Ethel said.

"You and Richards?"

"Oh," she said. "He was some friggin' weird, b'y, like he thought just 'cause he had money he could act right strange. I went out with him for a couple months but I just couldn't stand him, not even for a million dollars."

"I thought you marry him," Ping said.

"No, b'y, I would've never married that. Jesus, no."

"So you single now?"

"I've been seeing a new guy now, Frank, and it's going good. Sure you seen us at the movie theatre?"

"Oh," Ping said.

The two of them sat in the lobby restaurant for three hours that afternoon, nibbling on scones and kicking around old times. Learning how to say "toilet" in a church gymnasium. Christmas at the Woodrows' house, the fire roaring and a Cuban cigar in everyone's stocking. Seeing those marvellous Disney animations, the way those lines could dance. Late nights at the 7-A, back when Joey Smallwood was just a face in the crowd. That time Marge just stared at a plate and everyone thought maybe she'd had some sort of aneurysm. Good memories.

"You ready for tomorrow?" Ethel said, once all the tea was drunk and the scones were nothing but remnant crumbs on a fragile plate.

"Tomorrow," Ping said, "nothing change. One day, I am Chinese in Newfoundland. Next day, I am Chinese in Canada. Except I not go anywhere. Buildings not change. Car still drive. Nothing change." Family still dead, he thought.

"Hey now," she said, "that's not true. You gotta drive on the other side of the road starting at midnight."

Newfoundland would officially become a part of Canada then, and amidst all the changes that would come with that status, Ping was most tired of hearing about the changes with the roads. Everyone had always driven on the left side of the road. It just made sense—it wasn't logical to drive on the right side of the road like those on the mainland or those idiot Yankees. But this was part of the compromise of joining Canada: you had to drive on the right side of the road like a damn fool. This was a rare time where Ping agreed with the locals, that it was stupid to change this. But at the same time, he really didn't care. There had been protests in the streets by people who never knew the likes of the lives his people had lived.

"Yes," Ping said. "Right. But still, nothing change. You wake up tomorrow, nothing change."

"Don't be so dour," Ethel said. "At least one of your friends must be happy. Gao, or somebody, must be able to bring their family here now."

Of course, another curious thing was to result from confederation: the head tax would be revoked and Chinese women and children would be allowed to immigrate to Newfoundland. Once World War Two was over, the Canadian government decided that their anti-Chinese laws were a little hypocritical in the face of the defeat of Nazism. The Newfoundland government didn't feel it was hypocritical at all and left their laws in place: pay big money at the front door, and no women and children. But joining Canada would change that.

"I not sure," Ping said. "Lot of things change."

"See," she said as she put on her hat. "You said nothing changes, but now you just admitted it. Things change."

"Things change in world and society because war. Things change here because money."

They walked out the front door of the hotel and kept dry under the extended burgundy-and-gold awning.

"This was nice," Ethel said.

"Yeah," Ping said. "Is good to clear the air."

"Hey," she said. "I never taught you that one."

"I have many teachers," Ping said as he lit a cigarette.

"Let me bum a smoke off ya," she said.

Ping lit her cigarette, pushing down on the back of his Zippo until that small ball of flame flew up and ignited the dry tube.

"All right," she said. "Well, I'll be seeing you."

"You drive?" Ping said.

"No," Ethel said. "I'm gonna walk."

"In freezing rain?" Ping asked. "No way. I drive you home."

He had parked just around the corner, on the other side of Duckworth Street.

"Say," she said. "Whatever happened to Gao and that woman he was dating? Agnes, was it?"

"Her parents no want her with Chinese. They threat violence. So he had to let her go."

"Jesus, b'y, that's just terrible."

They walked towards Ping's truck, and as they crossed the street, Ping linked his arm in through hers to help her step over a puddle. A car slowed down on the other side of the road. The driver's window rolled down.

"Why don't you find one of your kind, you fucking chink!" the driver yelled and then sped off, tires screeching.

"You fucking prick!" Ethel yelled back, waving her handbag in the air.

Ping acted as though nothing had happened.

"Aren't you mad?" Ethel asked as they sat in the Snow White truck.

"Is just words," Ping said. "I get used to it. It's always the way."

After he dropped her off at her house, he drove back to Aldershot Street and it occurred to him that this was probably the last time he would drive on the left side of the road. Once he was inside, he sat back in his chair and sighed. Ethel was right; Gao would be able to bring his parents here now, and a woman they had arranged for him to marry. Lots of his friends were planning on bringing their families here.

He went into the bathroom. Maybe he'd have a shower. He thought about what he had said to Ethel that afternoon. *They dead.*

Should've said "they *might be* dead." He knew the difference. Why didn't he say something? Just didn't want to talk about it. No shame in a little misleading. They might really be dead. He looked at himself in the mirror. It had been almost twenty years since he'd seen Hua Ling. He had spent so much time as an immigrant, he'd forgotten that he was also a husband. Now tomorrow, he'd be an immigrant again in another nation. Strange world.

He planned on walking somewhere at midnight to watch the traffic. Maybe Rawlins Cross. The papers had been predicting huge car accidents starting at one stroke after midnight. The buses had their doors on the wrong side now, people would have to get in and out in the middle of the road. It was sure to be chaos. Maybe he'd call Gao and they could go together. He should've asked Ethel.

Why hadn't he thought of that? Maybe he could still ask her. He could call her right now. Yeah, that's what he'd do, he'd call right now and ask her out again. But then again, she said she was seeing Frank now. Stupid Frank. *They dead.* Maybe they aren't. Sure, it was something he had thought of often, a notion that was at first so displeasing that he spent hours, days, weeks crying over it, wishing he had been there, wishing he had never left. But as the years passed, the idea took on a perversely comforting notion: if they were dead, he didn't have to wait anymore. He didn't have to wonder. But of course, he still wondered.

They dead. Maybe he said it so that Ethel would think they were dead. He wouldn't have to tell her the difference. He didn't have to tell anybody anything. People would talk. They would anyway. They could . . . But no. He wouldn't put her through that. Sure, even this afternoon, boom, right off the bat. But wouldn't it be nice? Wonder whatever happened to Marge and that negro. Did Ethel say Marge had a kid? Should've asked. *They dead.*

Well, if they are dead, then he's free to move on. Free to not grieve. Hell, he'd spent his life grieving. Even before they were dead, even before he had left, he started grieving that moment in his mom's kitchen, when they were tying up those dumplings—twenty-five? No, do thirty—right then and there, he knew exactly how it would be, that a rooster could take his place if he left. He never should've left. If he had been born in the West, there's no way he would've listened to his mom. He would've argued with her, he would've talked back. But that wasn't his way.

They dead. Well, they might as well be, as terrible as it may sound. And who is this Frank anyway? Fuck Frank. That's how they say it, right? Fuck him. If they were alive, they would've contacted him by now. Maybe they didn't want to leave either. Plus, two months in steerage on those coffin ships, who could blame them? Why not just call her, just call her and see what she's doing? He hates the phone, so empty, so strange, so staticky. Why not just go back there? Hop in the truck right now and knock on her door and ask her to go watch the cars with you. As friends. Well, you don't need to say that part. Just ask her and see what happens, see where it goes. Hop in the truck. Hop behind bars. What time is it?

11:55. Where does the time go? *They dead.* She's not.

Ping threw on his hat and coat. He rushed out the door. He strapped his wristwatch to the steering wheel, just in case he needed to switch sides of the road while he was driving. He drove up Aldershot Street as fast as he could. Gower Street isn't that far. Just a couple turns away, really. Would she even be awake? Of course. Of course she'll be awake. Everyone should be awake to watch their country die.

Midnight. Ping swerved into the opposite lane of traffic, which had now become the correct lane of traffic, just as he pulled onto Gower Street. He brought the truck to a screeching halt outside Ethel's house.

"Whoa," somebody called out from a window above. "Hey, you crazy chink, you're driving on the wrong side of the road!"

"Is the right side now!" Ping yelled into the sky, unable to place which house the voice came from. "Is right side of the road now!"

Ping ran up the steps of Ethel's house, pounded on the door, took a step back and looked up at the windows. The lights were on.

"Hello?" Vile said, opening the door just a crack.

"Hello," Ping said, out of breath. "I come to see Ethel."

"She's in for the night."

"Is urgent," he said.

Vile squinted at him. "Hold on," she said and shut the door. Muffled behind the door, Ping could hear her yelling. "Ping is outside, Ethel. Ethel! I said Ping is outside!"

"What does he want?"

"I don't know. He says it's urgent. Next time you plan on having a frenzied Chinaman show up on my doorstep in the middle of the night, could you let me know ahead of time?"

"I *didn't* know," Ethel said as she opened the door. "Ping, b'y, what's the matter?"

Ping stared at her eyes, that chaotic unruly hair, those nicotine-stained fingers, that attitude, every blemish and foible that had allured him for years radiating off her glowing face.

"I," he stammered. "I going to . . . to ask if you . . ." Ping looked her in the eyes. "I love you," he said.

Ethel's jaw slightly dropped. "Didn't you notice?" she said, gesturing in the air.

He looked her up and down. She was wearing a light blue nightie and it looked almost too small because her stomach had swollen into the shape of a huge egg.

"I'm pregnant," she said.

1999

27

THE LETTER

A knock on the door jostled Ping from his afternoon nap in his favourite chair. He hobbled out of the seat, still dazed from his snooze, and opened the front door. It's that guy, the doctor who's a big deal in the association now. What's his name, Dr. Kris something? He was wearing a baggy windbreaker, with a tie-dye pattern on the shoulders and the Gucci logo on the chest.

"Hello, Mr. Ping," the middle-aged doctor said. "May I come in? An important letter come for you to the association."

"Okay." Ping let him in with a sigh.

"If it a bad time, Mr. Ping, I can go!"

"No, no," he said. "Just my back, get tired when I sit down for too long. Come in, please. You want tea?"

Ping led Dr. Kris to the back of the house, but the doctor got distracted by the numerous pictures on shelves in the hallway.

"You have beautiful family, Mr. Ping," he said.

"Yes," Ping said as he sat down at the dining table. "Some of them turn out all right."

"How many children?" Dr. Kris asked. "It seem like they multiply in every picture."

"Five of mine," Ping said. "Plus Steve and Silas."

"Mr. Ping, this a big house, but I can't imagine seven young-sters, seven teenagers, running around in here."

Ping coughed. "Well, it just me and Ethel now," he said. "Better that way! More peace, more quiet!"

The doctor tapped on one of the framed photos sitting next to Ping's abacus. "Is that a, uh, a monkey?"

"Yeah, yeah," Ping said. "You say you have a letter?"

"Here in Newfoundland?"

"Yeah, back in the seventies, kids want a pet. So we get monkey."

"A monkey lived in this house?"

"Dr. Kris, I am tired, I usually nap at this time," Ping said.

"Yes, well." Dr. Kris made his way to the table. "A letter come for you. I thought it was odd, mixed in with the association's mail. Must be from someone who doesn't have your address."

"Yes," Ping said. "Let me see."

"It from China." Dr. Kris procured a thin envelope from an inside pocket of his Gucci jacket.

Ping coughed.

The return address was messy and hard to read, the characters smeared together from months of travelling through post offices. Ping tore open the envelope. Inside was a small square of paper that had been folded several times to make it fit in the envelope. Ping unfolded the paper. The letter was written in Taishanese.

Dear Dad,

As I kneel before you. In a blink of an eye, time has passed. I hope this letter finds you, and finds you well. I am deeply sorry to tell you of this, but Mom is dying. I am uncertain if you have received our previous correspondences. We tried sending letters to the address of 7-A but have never heard a response, and sometimes have even had the letter returned to us many months later. We have caught wind of the Chinese Association of Newfoundland and are sending this letter to their address in the hopes that this reaches you before it is too late. Mom wishes to see her husband one last time before she dies. Please respond to this letter. I am once again sorry if we have ever offended you. Please forgive us.

Seto Wei

Ping's hands shook, and he thought it was probably because he was getting old.

"Everything okay?" Dr. Kris said.

"Yes," Ping said, his voice wavering. "I . . . I just, um, not expect this."

"Your hands are shaking very bad," Dr. Kris said. "I can give you a checkup anytime."

"This letter," Ping said. "This letter is from my son."

"Which one of the seven?"

"Another son."

"Oh," Dr. Kris said, and grinned. "You must've been very busy when you were young man."

Ping began to sigh and it turned into a cough.

Dr. Kris patted him on the back. "Mr. Ping, you really must come in for checkup."

"What are you doin', coughing up a frickin' lung again?" a voice yelled from upstairs. "Jesus, b'y, you're gonna rile up the dogs."

Dr. Kris chuckled. "Mrs. Ping would probably like you to get checkup too."

Ping rested his head in the palm of his hand as the letter shook out of his hand and onto the floor.

"It's just checkup, Mr. Ping," Dr. Kris said. "Nothing to be concerned about."

"I not concern about checkup," Ping said, batting away Dr. Kris's hand on his back.

"Did the letter upset you?" Dr. Kris said, squinting to try to read the letter out of his peripheral.

"I have to go," Ping said. "I have to."

"Mr. Ping, really, no trouble for me to bring my equipment here. I know you old laundrymen have trouble getting around. It's time of your life now where you can sit back and let younger generation take care of you. You earned it."

"I not want checkup!" Ping yelled. "I not care! I go back to China!"

"Jesus, Mary, and Joseph," Ethel said as she stomped down the stairs. "Dr. Kris, what are you doing here, b'y, angering me husband?"

"Mrs. Ping." Dr. Kris stood up as she walked into the dining room. "I did not intend to cause any stress—"

"Go back into the Health Sciences out of it, b'y, you ol' quack."

"I'm sorry, Mrs. Ping, I—"

"I'm just joking, b'y, that's all. Now, what seems to be the matter down here?"

"He give me letter, from China," Ping said, his shaking hands picking up the letter to show Ethel.

"All right, and?"

"Is my son," Ping said as he handed the letter to Ethel. "Look!"

Ethel looked at it for a second before tossing it down on the table. "I can't read those jesus things, b'y," she said.

The matter was settled quickly. Ping would return to China, but he was too old and feeble to go on his own. Someone needed to take care of him. Ethel, she was too old too, and Ping was sickened by the prospect of both his wives meeting each other. So it would have to be one of Ping's children who would travel with him. Most of the kids couldn't find time off work. Bruce was making dentures in some factory behind the mall. Michelle was managing the pet department at the new Walmart. Curt had moved to the mainland and was a Mountie somewhere out West. Jim was working in a plastic factory, making playground slides and containers for disinfectant wipes. Steve was in jail, and even if he wasn't, he wasn't Ping's son anyway. And Silas . . . well, no one really knew where Silas was, but that was his way. Silicon Valley, probably.

The only child who could travel with Ping was his firstborn with Ethel. Bill worked with the Coast Guard, two weeks on, two weeks off, so he had some time during his off weeks to take care of his dad. He wanted to see China anyway. He'd spent his whole life on the ships being called a Chinaman and a chink and meanwhile he had never even seen the country that defined him. So it was settled.

"Be wary of the kung flu," the travel agent warned. "It'll get ya!"

Within a month of receiving the letter, William Seto Ping and Bill Seto Ping found themselves flying over the Pacific Ocean. It was a strange relationship that the elder Ping had with all his children. He didn't like to talk about the past. He kept a stoic and humble attitude, and anytime someone asked him about the past, he would brush it off.

"Is long time ago, I don't remember."

"Is fine, is nothing."

"I was young. It not important."

"All I want is apology from government. I not need to think about what happened."

The most anyone had ever heard him talk about his younger years was when some student filmmaker from the university came into the house and did a documentary about the early Chinese immigrants in Newfoundland, during which time Ping talked at great length about his struggles. *The Last Chinese Laundry*, it was called, and Ping had been the focus of the film as he was indeed the owner of the last Chinese laundry in St. John's. Snow White had outlasted every other Chinese-owned laundry.

It was closed now, of course, the popularity of home laundry machines having been a death knell to his industry. Ping remembered when he first saw the personal washing machine, in a window display at Woolworth's on Water Street. As he peered through the window at the model of the ideal home laundry room, signs promising consumers that they would never have to go to a laundry again, Ping couldn't shake the memory of Shaowei from his mind. Shaowei had said something about cleaning salmon in San Francisco until someone invented some machine called the Iron Chink that could clean the fish and then Shaowei and everyone he ever knew was out of a job. Maytag Washing Machine, General Electric Iron Chink, all the same.

Even so, Snow White held on long enough for them to make a movie about it. It didn't go fully bankrupt until the early nineties, by which time Ping was retired. Still, he was quite proud of the fact that he had owned the last Chinese laundry and he would often play the VHS tape for visitors. "Look," he would say, only half-jokingly, "they made a picture about me. I am star."

Ping had packed the tape in his suitcase so he could show his family back in China. Easier to just show them the film than have to tell the story. Besides, he couldn't remember half of what happened anymore anyway. Then he took the tape out of his suitcase and put it in his carry-on. Just in case his luggage got lost. Then he took it out of his carry-on and put it in the breast pocket of his suit. Couldn't be too safe.

As he was zipping his suitcase closed, he thought of another item he wanted to bring with him. He hurried downstairs to the bookcase, pushed aside his favourite chair, and skimmed through his small collection of Chinese books. His fingers grazed over the spines of several aged, wizened titles before settling on a particularly withered copy of Pu Songling's *Strange Stories from a Chinese Studio*. He ran his finger over the Taishan address written inside the front cover. He remembered the man—boy, really—dragging a heavy briefcase behind him on the train, his unadulterated enthusiasm for the many delights of the West, his clothes stained red, tomato juice, blood.

Ping barely slept on the flights, simply amazed by how fast anyone could travel to China now. It wasn't his first time on a plane. He had taken Ethel and the kids on a couple of family trips back in the seventies, to Disney World and the Montreal Olympics. He hadn't flown since then, as the task of managing seven children was too strenuous to make a vacation worth the money. "Never again," he had said after the Olympics. "Never."

But this, this was different. On the overnight flight to Hong Kong, the stewardesses had handed out blankets and slippers and bowls of congee and even alcoholic beverages. The seatback screen was playing a James Bond marathon. Ping relaxed in his seat with glee, watching the old Sean Connery films and thinking of days even further in the past. Of weeks and months travelling the Pacific Ocean and indeed the entire continent of North America, one inch at a time. Now they travelled swaths of land and sea in mere seconds.

Ping dozed off during the opening credits of *You Only Live Twice*, Nancy Sinatra crooning to him over the exploding lava, swirling oriental colours, and the suggestive silhouettes of dancing Japanese women. He dreamt of the flowery years of his past. Of both his wives, of teaching his classes, of holding babies in his arms, of drinking baijiu and laughing with his friends, of sitting in tall grass and watching the sun go down. He remembers those vanished years, like looking through a window during a snowstorm, everything that *was* buried by everything that *is*, in perpetuity.

"Was that a long flight or what?" Bill said, stretching his arms, as they waited for their luggage on the carousel.

"Back in my day," Ping said, "it take two, three months to travel this far."

"And I bet you walked uphill to school both ways too, huh, Dad?"

"Matter of fact, yes, I did."

Ping's suitcase rumbled down the conveyor belt, followed by his second piece of luggage, an old and battered red-trimmed briefcase.

"Geez, Dad, why'd you bring an old thing like that? We're lucky it survived the flight."

"Always the way," Ping said. "You young people don't know value in old things."

Ping struggled to lift the briefcase, recalling the young Wong's similar struggle. When you're young, you're weak, then you grow old and become weak again. Ping thought better of his explanation to his son. "This old thing," he huffed, "belong to an old friend. He pass away long, long time ago. I gonna bring it to his family."

The two William Pings stayed in Hong Kong for the night. The harbour was still clogged with boats. Women still sat on street corners, slinging oranges out of wicker baskets. Raw meat still hung on hooks in store windows. Pots of clams still boiled over as a lineup formed down the block. But the people had changed. Gone were the traditional garbs of his day. Now people wore everything and anything, yellow Nike sweaters, purple suits, electric blue dresses, tattered windbreakers, and dirty sneakers. At night the streets were aglow with a dazzling array of fluorescent lights and neon signs, advertising everything from Taiwanese Beef Noodle to Tomokazu Japanese Restaurant to McDonald's. So too had the buildings grown taller, driven up, up, up by all that lay underneath. The horse track was still over there, a glow emanating from it into the night sky.

In the morning, on the ferry leaving the island, they sailed past Macau, and when they reached land, a Jeep was to drive them to Hoiping. Soon enough, they could see the dilapidated diaolous on the horizon, some slanted over like the Leaning Tower of Pisa, all riddled with bullet holes, windows shattered from shell blasts. Hoiping, too, had changed. They drove past hardware stores and coffee shops. They drove past an old graveyard being excavated by a tractor. They drove past power lines and zipping cars, boarded-up wells and collapsed bridges. They passed by Chinamen dressed in the newest Western fashions. It was a strange place. Some of the houses still looked like the old huts Ping remembered, plain little cottages built of necessity. Other houses were big and contemporary, looking like mansions in the West. Homes built of foreign money, of faraway currencies, of dreams come true.

The Jeep stopped in front of a cottage Ping could remember. The two Pings got out of the car. Ping stared at the old house. It was even smaller than he remembered, and its walls were still a washed-out pink, the concrete still cracked at several points. A man was sitting outside.

"Dad," the man called out in Taishanese. "Dad. It's been so long."

Ping shook his hand, sternly. Who was this man? What happened to that baby boy? A strange thought crept into his head: this man could be anybody. That child he left behind could have become anybody. Ping could've run into his son a thousand times and never known it. Then he hugged the man calling him Dad.

"Where is your washroom?" he asked. "It's been a long morning."

"Around back," the man said. "Where it's always been."

Ping found the old hole in the ground. He sighed as he undid his pants and struggled to squat down. His back felt like an old rusty iron and he groaned as he attempted to bend over. He gave up and pulled his pants back up.

"Dad," Bill called out from around the corner. "Do you need help?"

"What I need," Ping said with a huff, "is a toilet. We have to buy toilet for here, this no good."

Wei and Bill were standing next to each other and what a strange sight it was to see. Two sons, two firstborns, two lives. The kids looked a little similar, Ping thought, even though he recognized that to be impossible.

"Come in and see Mom," Wei said. "She's been waiting for sixty years."

Ping followed him into the house. It was just as he remembered it. Kitchen over there, bedroom in the back. Arguing with his mom over not wanting to leave. And hanging on the wall, a yellowed photograph of a young man sitting on a stool and beaming at the camera. Ping felt lightheaded.

"We have so much to catch up on," Wei said as he noticed Ping looking at the old picture. "But go, go see Mom. She's waiting for you. Go fulfill your duty. I'm sure you've been waiting a very long time for this."

Ping scrunched his eyebrows for a moment, then slid open the bedroom door. He had remembered a beautiful, vibrant young woman, with tiny, soft curves. What lay in the bed looked like a deflated balloon, nothing but skin and bones, jowls and sags.

"Go on," Wei said. "Do what you have to do."

"She . . . she an old woman," Ping said, in English. She lay there staring at the ceiling, a corpse that could still blink. She made noises like grunts. Ping was reminded of his grandmother and wanted to leave.

"I think they want you to have sex with her," Bill said.

Ping looked back at him, eyebrows raised. "I know what they want. But she an old woman. She very old. This not the woman I marry. I not have sex with her."

"Dad, you're an old person too," Bill said.

"What, you want me affair on your mother with this old woman? This sick, this disgusting."

Wei was smiling, looking from one to the other. He didn't know what they were saying.

"Didn't you kind of have an affair on this woman with Mom?"

"You don't know what you talk about," Ping snapped. "This very different. This . . . gross."

Wei said, "It is her dying wish to be able to be held in your arms once more."

Hua Ling made a small noise.

Ping sighed and shut the door.

"My back is killing me," Ping said over supper later that afternoon. "We need to go somewhere and buy a toilet."

"You couldn't find the hole?" Wei asked.

"I found it. But it's no good for me. I can't bend down like that anymore. We'll get you a good toilet, like what they have in the West. It's way better."

The following day, they drove to the shopping district and bought a ceramic toilet at the hardware store. They set it up over the hole in the backyard. Ping sat on it to demonstrate its use to Wei.

Wei didn't have a VHS player.

"It's a really good movie," Ping assured him. "And I'm not just saying that because it's about me. It's very educational. They show it in schools sometimes."

The days passed by so fast, it almost felt like a dream. They visited the farms Ping had frequented as a child, the old well he used to drag water out of, the old school he used to teach at. He visited his mother's grave several times. She lay resting out in the middle of a field. He knelt before her grave and asked for forgiveness. He did the same with his grandmother's grave and Lee's grave. All the while, Hua Ling lay catatonic in her bed. Wei had a wife and child of his own. They lived in a different part of the city and he felt ashamed to admit that he didn't spend as much time as he should taking care of his mom. He owned a hair salon and his family lived in the apartment above it.

And of course, they talked about what happened way back when. Ping found it upsetting to hear what Wei said about it, the attempts to immigrate to Newfoundland. It was with great shame that he listened to Wei speak of how Hua Ling worked long hours in the rice and vegetable fields to support the family, how she used to carry fifty-pound baskets of dried fish for over five kilometres, each new piece of information making more sense of the shell of a woman that had greeted Ping from her bed. And although he listened closely, some part of Ping just didn't want to hear about how they had to sneak out of the town under the cover of darkness, of the struggles of trying to cross the Pacific during war, of trying to evade the Japanese. He especially didn't want to hear about how they were turned away at the border, how they had to spend weeks at sea coming back, how Hoiping was seized by the Japanese, how seven martyrs used the diaolous to protect the city, how the martyrs fell and were beheaded in front of the town library. Ping didn't want to hear any of that. He couldn't—didn't want to—imagine how hopeless it must have felt, how absolutely miserable they must've felt, that day in Vancouver when they started the voyage back to China. It made him feel sick.

The address in Wong's book was located in Taishan, a nearby city. Wei arranged for a car. Bill and Wei attempted to go with him, but Ping politely declined, and took the old briefcase with him to the waiting car.

"An old friend," Ping explained to his sons. "No worries."

It took little over an hour to get to the address, a small cottage much like his family's house in Hoiping. Ping took a deep breath and knocked on the door.

A middle-aged Chinese woman opened it. She looked to be around the same age as his Western children and he was disappointed. "Hello?" she said.

"I'm sorry," Ping said. "I think maybe I have the wrong address." He wasn't sure what or who he had expected to find here.

"What address are you looking for?" the woman asked.

"Oh, uh." Ping took the old book from his jacket pocket. He showed her the address scrawled inside the cover.

"Yes," she said. "This is the place."

"Do you know a young boy named Wong?" Ping said before catching himself. "Er, well, not a young boy, I suppose. Did you ever know a man named Wong that lived at this address? Maybe when you were a child? Or before then, probably."

The woman looked at Ping and sized him up, the cut of his suit, the age of his case. "No," she said. "I haven't. Our name is Wah."

"My mistake," Ping said, stuffing the book back inside his jacket. "Sorry to have bothered you." He turned to head back to the car.

"Wait," she called out. "Let me get my mother."

The woman closed the door and Ping stood outside. He could hear the murmur of voices inside. A moment later, an older Chinese woman, roughly the same age as Ping, came to the door.

"My daughter says you are asking about a man named Wong?"

"Yes," Ping said.

"Come in."

Ping followed her as she hobbled towards a well-worn chair in the living room. He saw the daughter walk out the back door and slam it behind her.

"Have a seat."

"Thank you." Ping sat down and took the book out of his pocket. "I'm looking for the family of a friend of mine, Wong."

"That is not our name," the lady said. "Our name is Wah."

"Yes," Ping said. "Your daughter told me. I think I likely have the wrong house."

"No," she said. "You don't."

The woman stared at him while her daughter came in from the backyard, holding a live chicken by its feet. She slammed the bird on a chopping block and then just as quickly slammed a cleaver through the animal's neck. Ping was briefly shocked by this, then a smile crossed his face as he realized that the action was both an affront to his Western sensibilities and a pleasant reminder of a long-ago familial past.

Ping said, "How can that be?"

"The man you are looking for," she said, "he had fake immigration papers. We had no family in the West so we had to pay someone to fake it."

Of course, how could Ping have forgotten this. He remembered Shaowei saying it on the train. "We're made of paper."

"Oh, yes," Ping said, placing the briefcase on the table in front of him. "Of course. I've brought you some of his things."

"He's sending over some stuff to us, is he?"

Ping looked at her. What did she mean? "I'm sorry," he said. "What relation are you to the man we're talking about?"

The woman stared at Ping, sizing him up in the same way her daughter had. "I'm his mother," she said.

Ping knew this was a lie. It was simply impossible. The woman could not have had a child the age of Wong. If she had said "sister," he would've believed that.

"Oh?" he said, his grip tightening on the briefcase handle.

"Yes," she said in a cold manner. "I miss him very much."

Why would she lie? Maybe she hadn't. "I do too," Ping said.

A slight tic in one of her eyes. A large pot of water began to burble and boil over. The daughter lifted the lid and dipped the bird into the steaming liquid.

"We all miss him," the woman said. "Very much."

What did it matter if they really were Wong's family? In the grand scheme of things, Ping had ventured to the address in Wong's book. Maybe the book had never belonged to him. Perhaps it was part of the forgery. After all, he was a paper son. Maybe it was all fake, just words put on paper and nothing more than that. Wong had wanted to bring things home to his mother and sister. At the very least, this was *a* mother and sister.

"Yes," Ping said. "Well . . ." What to give? What to keep? "This book belonged to him." He passed it into the woman's hands.

"Oh," she said. "Thank you."

"I must be going," Ping said. He stood up to leave.

"Just the book?" she said.

Ping looked at her, at the sun-faded, crazing-cracked walls, at the chicken being plucked in the kitchen, at the old furniture, at the humble garments. What did it matter if this wasn't the right mother and sister? This was all the mothers and sisters left behind, this was everyone left behind.

"And this," he said, passing the case over to the woman. "This was his briefcase. As I'm sure you know."

"Ah yes," she said. "His beloved case."

"You'll find some of his belongings inside. I am certain he would've wanted you to have it."

"Thank you very much," the woman said.

Ping gave her a nod and turned to leave, but then looked back at her. "I owe a great deal to your son," he said. "He changed my life."

"Me too," she said.

That night, Ping took his families out to supper in a restaurant off the main street in Hoiping, which was still populated with stands. A row of motorcycles were parked outside the front door. Ping, Bill, Wei, his wife, and his boy were seated around a large round table in the back of the establishment. Although Ping would normally order for a table, he deferred this time to Wei, as his mind was still focused on the events of the afternoon. Wei ordered a whole roasted duck for the table, as well as congee with pork blood, pork buns, a rice wrap, noodles with beef, and a variety of dumplings—vegetable, taro root, sesame with peanut sauce, and more. The food was good, but still Ping's mind was elsewhere, divided, put into two disparate places at once. He felt somewhat sick and excused himself from the table.

As he walked to the washroom, a song came over the restaurant's speakers, a rendition of "Southern Nights" that sounded as though it had been filtered through a tube. This was something Ping had paid attention to during the meal, the restaurant's eclectic selection of Western music, ranging from a big band version of "It Ain't Easy Bein' Green" to a choral arrangement of "Heigh-Ho." And now this strangely ethereal version of "Southern Nights." The bouncy, upbeat country hit that Ping used to hear on the radio in Newfoundland was replaced by a distant interpretation.

The song made Ping feel nostalgic, which he supposed was the point of the song anyway, a feeling that this rendition especially highlighted. Something in the swirly, searching piano notes, the dreamy atmosphere of the vocals, and even the sparse, somewhat oriental, percussion. He looked around the crowded restaurant, searching through the faces, and it was as if he had walked into his dream from the plane, as though he could see everyone—everything—he ever knew sitting at these tables.

In the back by the counter, there was Ping as a young boy after another hard day at the well, his father cutting up an apple with an old knife, handing pieces down to him, clean, crisp, fresh. And then over there in the corner, there was Ping as a young man, Mr. Poy, with his friends, spilling baijiu over spent duck bones. And that long table in the front, there he was with Hua Ling on their wedding day, his mother not too far away, a resentful smile crossing her face— not resentful, no, for it wasn't always that way—a warm smile, a welcoming one. And Grandma too was smiling, chatting and eating with her friends. And in the middle of the room, there Ping was with Hua Ling again, this time trying to feed a spoonful of congee into baby Wei's mouth, drool-drenched porridge sputtering out of his mouth. At the table next to that, there he was again, now with Gao and Wong and Shaowei, at the Globe, tasting fish and chips and grimacing at first, then coming back for a second bite. "It's not so bad," they said.

Now Ping could see outside the restaurant's window, himself and Gao drinking Dewar's in the streets of New York, laughing at the threat of an alien invasion, knowing that the aliens invaded long ago and that if there's more here now, well, they're probably just looking for a better life. And at a stand outside, there he was with Ethel and Marge, out for a snack at Fong's on a late night in Carbonear. An order of chicken balls, which for Ping was, even then, just an echo of the deep-fried foods of the West.

Just as he reached the door to the washroom, Ping shook his head and took another look back at the tables. Still, he could see the past: a late night in Montreal, a delayed flight home, the whole family pushing their way into an all-night deli, Ping trying to feed his seven children and muttering, "Never again, never again." And now he found himself outside the washroom in Hoiping once more muttering, "Never again, never again," for indeed those days were gone, gone, gone. He was waiting now outside the stall for the one Western-style toilet, although the squat toilets were unoccupied. Once seated, Ping noticed how a McDonald's arches outside the small window made the white-tiled washroom glow yellow, neon light glinting off the edge of the ceramic bowl.

On the walk back to his table, he paused in the mouth of the dining room and looked around at the tables again. Now he saw the faces of lonely souls and wild ghosts, the room filled with dozens, hundreds, thousands of his fellow immigrants that never had the chance to do what he had done: go back, go home. But what did it mean? What did it mean to live out the dreams that you knew others could not fulfill?

And he could see a different life. He could see himself saying no to his mother, straining their relationship, but keeping things good with Hua Ling. Could it have been that simple? Could he have simply said, "No"? He could see himself raising Wei, he could see himself being there in the cold, lonesome evenings, holding his wife close, maybe trying for one of their own. He could see himself fighting for his country, shielding his family from war, being a martyr for the cause. He could see himself teaching and growing old, his waist expanding behind his desk in the same way the city did, getting bigger, growing West. He imagined his old friends from back then and he could see himself growing old with them, watching the years go by as the fellows around the table dwindle and disappear, some overseas, some into different towns, different jobs, different responsibilities, and some—inevitably all—buried or burned.

He could see it all so clearly in that moment. Shaowei and Wong would still be wandering the earth someplace, old men with hip and heart problems and lingering coughs and families of their own. Ethel married off at some beautillion, birthing a totally different caravan of children, being the matron of some other man's lineage. And what of Ping's children with her? What would have become of them? Nothing. Nothing at all. Their union was one of two worlds and had he not been there, there would be no Ping children, and what then? These are the choices sacrificed, the things lost down the diverging roads in that far-off yellow wood. Maybe he was wrong. Maybe Ethel would have married another Chinaman, birthed his hyphenated lineage. But what world was better off, the one where Poy became Ping or the one where Poy stayed put? There is no answer. In life, you always make the wrong choice, even if you make the right one. You always lose something.

He thought of the Wah women he met that afternoon. If they were everyone left behind in the East, then what he was seeing now was the opposite. The legion of faces haunting Ping's vision in the restaurant were the ghosts of everyone left behind in the West, of every man who didn't get to go home, of every soul buried alongside the railroad spikes, of every person tossed aside like discarded laundry equipment. Ping was living the dream but it felt like a nightmare.

"Hey," Bill said. "Are you okay?"

"Huh," Ping said. He looked around again. No ghosts, no legion of faces. Just a normal restaurant and normal people, eating, drinking, living.

"You've been wandering around the room for the last five minutes," Bill said. "You look unwell."

"Oh, I sorry. I just . . . remember the old days. So long ago."

"Yeah," Bill said. "I bet a lot has changed since you were here."

"It always the way," Ping said. "Everything change. Everything."

"Do you miss it?" Bill said.

Ping paused. "Miss what?"

"The way things were."

"You know," Ping said, "is a story in the Bible, about a lady who keep looking back. She turn into pillar of salt! Is not good to keep remembering. Is good to move on."

The sun was shining and the air was redolent with the scent of new crops. Hua Ling had never budged from her bed. As the driver was putting their bags in the back of the Jeep, Wei took Ping aside.

"I . . . I don't know how to ask this," he began. Ping already had a good idea of where this was going. "But Mom, I think she could die any day now. I don't know how I will pay for the funeral. We . . . I'll probably have to sell the salon."

"No worries," Ping said, patting Wei on the back. "You have my address now. You will receive what you always deserved."

Wei was speechless for a moment. "Really?"

"It's me that should be kneeling before you," Ping said. "Call me. Or write me. Let me know what happens."

"Mom always said a day would come where Seto Poy would return and save us."

Ping laughed as he got in the Jeep. "I haven't been Seto Poy in years," he said. He shut the door and laughed again. "Do you want hear joke?" he said to Bill.

"Sure," Bill said. There hadn't been much conversation he could understand on this trip. Not many people spoke English.

"Okay, so," Ping said. "There is a husband and wife, and the wife, she about to go on a long trip, go far, far away. The wife say to her husband, 'Oh, husband, I know you miss me so very much while I am gone,' then the husband say, 'Miss you? It worthwhile to send you away for fifty bucks!'"

Bill chuckled. Behind the Jeep, there was a loud smash, and the two Pings looked back to see big white pieces of ceramic clatter all over the ground.

"I guess they didn't like the toilet," Bill said.

Ping was happy to sit in his big chair once again and not dwell on the past. He liked to spend his afternoons watching the soaps and the game shows. He liked *Wheel of Fortune* the most because it made him think of when he first met Ethel and she was helping him to spell words. And there was something so enticing about watching that wheel spin, that anything could happen to the person spinning the wheel, that one minute you might spin and land on a million dollars and the next minute you might end up bankrupt. Anything could happen.

Sometimes he would babysit his grandchildren. Their parents would just drop them off and he'd watch TV with them, or fall asleep in his chair while the kids played in his lap or under his chair. Sometimes they'd watch the game shows together, although the kids always seemed more interested in those Flintstones gummy commercials where those cavemen used animals like appliances. He guessed there was supposed to be something funny about watching those guys use big birds to make cake batter or whatever but he didn't get it. He liked the part where the animals had a begrudging yet blasé acceptance of their labour-dedicated lives. Now that was comedy.

And for the weeks after he returned from China, this is how he spent his days, watching TV and entertaining his white grandchildren. Cooking beef and broccoli and telling the kids that the veggies were mini trees. Reading them storybooks and writing down translations alongside the English words. Someone, one of his children's wives, although he couldn't remember which one, had given him a storybook, *The Story about Ping*, to read to the grandkids when they were over. The wife had thought it was cute or ironic or something.

It told the story of a duck named Ping who lived in a boat that had two wise eyes on the Yangtze River. The duck never fit in with the other ducks and one day, the boat leaves him behind. And then some birds almost kill the duck and then a Chinese family captures the duck and tries to cook him and then the duck gets stuck in a barrel and so on. Eventually the duck ends up back on the boat with the two wise eyes. It was written by someone named Marjorie Flack and it bothered Ping how often the grandkids wanted to hear this story. But he read it to them all the same.

Dr. Kris returned and did a checkup on both Mr. and Mrs. Ping. Ethel was diagnosed with cancer. Ping's heart was broken. What would it mean to live in a world without Ethel? He didn't want to find out.

One night during a fretful dream, only a few weeks after he had returned from China, William Seto Ping died.

MARCH 2020

28

THE MONUMENT

I woke up.

Groggy, I struggled to remember who or where I was. Or when. I was lying on top of a bed in a small hotel room. I sat up and looked around. There was a TV on the wall playing a nature documentary about some strange little animal. "Known by locals as the mountain cow," intoned a British voice, "this fourteen-toed critter is the official animal of Belize! This animal and its ancestors have been around for thirty-five million years."

"Mo," I called out, addressing the screen. "Mo . . ."

There was no response. Perhaps it had all been in my mind. God, I hate endings like that.

"Mo," I cried out again, not wanting it to be over yet. "Eat my dreams. Eat my dreams. Eat my dreams."

The TV went silent.

"What do you want?" I heard the spirit's strange voice emerge from the television's tinny speakers. The voice close yet far, recognizable yet totally alien.

"Mo," I said. "Please, is it over?"

Mo slithered out of the TV, its lengthy body stretching out of the pixels on the screen. The spirit spiralled around the tiny room, the accommodation being too small to contain its elongated form. "It is never over," Mo said. "What is dead may never die."

"Yeah, I think I've heard that one before," I said. "But I have so many questions now. What . . . what was in the briefcase he gave those women?"

"It's open to interpretation," Mo said.

"Was it money? Like how he found the briefcase?"

"It's open to interpretation."

"But you said you were showing me things as they were or always are or something like that. You must know what he did."

"Well, whatever you decide he did with the money and whether or not he returned it," Mo said with a twinkle in its eye, "that says a lot about you and how you view the world."

"What? How?"

Mo sighed, its tongue lolling out of its mouth. "Fine," it said. "I made that part up."

"What?"

"I made that part up. Little white lie."

"But you said—"

"I know what I said," the spirit boomed. "Obviously the brief-case part is made up. Things don't happen like that. You work hard, you earn money, you get lucky and succeed or you don't. That's life."

I sat there on the bed, turning the spirit's words over in my mind.

"I mean, think about the whole 'dogbane nation' thing," Mo said. "They're not even speaking English. It doesn't make sense."

"Wh . . . w-was it all made up?"

"No, it wasn't all made up. There are falsehoods, but they are derived with sincerity and candour. It was a true story. A love story.

The overarching narrative was true. The important parts are true. But sometimes you need to let fiction fill in all the details of life, spruce it up with bits and pieces from here and there, fill in the latent cultural vacuum. There is more truth to this than you know."

"Are . . . are you Shaowei?"

"No," the spirit said with a sigh. "I am not Shaowei."

"But why—"

"Look," Mo said, slithering back towards the TV, "I'm done. I've taken what I wanted from you. It's over."

"What? What did you want?" My Patagonia sweater?

"I told you his story," Mo said as the screen reabsorbed its body. "Go forth in his world and determine the truth for yourself."

"Wait, Mo!" I called out, but the spirit was gone.

For a moment there was silence, and while I felt compelled to call out to the spirit again, I knew that I shouldn't. A robotic female voice came from the TV.

"Did you say 'Play "Mo Money, Mo Problems" featuring Mase and Puff Daddy by the Notorious B.I.G. from the album *Life After Death* (Deluxe Remastered Edition)'?"

I sighed and rubbed my eyes. "Yes," I said.

I rolled out of bed and got used to being on my feet again. How long was I out? A couple months it seems, but that can't be. My jeans didn't fit the same as they used to and I was pretty sure I was going bald. I mean, I still had hair, I just thought there was less of it. After a quick breather, I left the room. A quiet day in the hotel. No noisy children, no kitchen clangs. I made my way down to the lobby and found the door locked.

I unlocked it and let myself out, wandering onto Duckworth Street. The sun was high in the sky, but the city was quiet. I could still faintly hear the music playing from my room upstairs. Cars parked alongside the roads but no traffic. A pair of surgical masks tumbled down the road in the wind. Gross. Some dwindling snow-banks lingered on the sidewalks and a pothole on the road exposed an old rail line. Typical. I walked down the street thinking how strange it was, to stand in places he stood, to see what became of his old haunts all these years later. I walked towards a familiar route from the past: Tai Mei Club to Fong-Lee Laundry. All the restaurants were closed, the cafés empty. No one was around. I didn't see a person for my whole walk. How weird. There's money to be made on a day like this.

I passed by a pub, which despite being closed had left out their chalkboard. A strange cartoon drawn on it, an oriental-patterned bowl with a grinning bat suspended above it by a pair of chopsticks. It read "DON'T EAT BAT SOUP, EAT OUR HOUSE SPECIAL MOOSE STEW!" Odd.

I don't care for soups or stews. Never have.

I made a stop outside a furniture store to look through the window as Pop did before me. Inside were refrigerators and stoves, washers and dryers. No mannequins, no displays of happy housewives. The lights were off inside and all I could really see in the window was my solitary reflection surrounded by dust-covered appliances. I still don't look Asian. There was a sun-bleached notice in the window that read, "Times have changed and so have we . . . for now. As we prioritize our customers' wellness and being, we remain closed due to the ongoing health crisis. Common symptoms of the China Plague include fever, coughing, difficulty breathing, loss of smell/taste, conjunctivitis, and abnormal bruising in the toes. Stay home, stay safe."

What the fuck was going on?

Across the street was a centuries-old churchyard, leafless trees slumped onto shrivelled icy grass and cracked headstones, the ancient church pointing a jeering finger at the unpleasant sky as the wind wailed maniacally from over frozen and frigid seas. I remember being told that once during a great flood, all the old decaying corpses floated out of their tombs here and drifted through the water-filled streets. Look at this sight now from a certain angle and it would resemble an image from a tourism campaign, an elegantly elegiac church looking over a still winter harbour, calm waters, clear skies, the Narrows framing an endless expanse of ocean, little Cabot Tower looking down with a wistful eye. It was a peaceful Newfoundland scene, but knowing what it hid, I hated it. I hated the mocking sun, the hypocritical church, the festering streets, the sinister signs. Everything seemed tainted with an abhorrent contagion and inspired by a poisonous alliance with obscured supremacies.

I continued on down that familiar footpath, following their Sunday routine, but I felt as though I had eyes on me, like that scene in *Snow White*, as if being outside was illicit and dangerous. I arrived where Fong-Lee was, on the corner of Holdsworth and New Gower. But there were no more Chinese laundries. Indeed there was no business here at all. Instead there was a big rock, with a big glossy picture and some engraved words, sandwiched between a strip club (whose marquee read "WE'VE TESTED POSITIVE FOR CO-EDS-19!") and a sports bar. The picture memorialized on the big rock was the one taken outside the Nickel Theatre. I see my grandfather in the picture. I see a lot of faces I recognize. I almost feel like I can see myself and Mo in the background, standing inside the theatre and watching the photo get taken from a window.

I remember being here when they unveiled this a few years ago. It was a meagre reception, attended by some members of the Chinese Association and also one NDP leader who didn't end up getting elected anyways. I remember thinking, *All their struggles and all they get is this big rock?* But a rock is better than nothing.

The words on the rock told a simplified narrative of their history:

In 1906, the Government of the Dominion of Newfoundland imposed a $300.00 (three hundred dollars) head tax on each Chinese immigrant entering the country. This discriminatory legislation remained in effect until 1949. This monument is dedicated to the memory of those Chinese immigrants who travelled from their homeland seeking a better life.

Right next to these English words was a series of Chinese characters that presumably said the same thing, although I had no way of knowing that for sure. And I supposed some local must've thought that the monument was deficient as is, as they had taken it upon themselves to spruce it up, alter it from the way it's supposed to be, with a special new flourish. It surely didn't have this detail when they unveiled it. And although I wished I could remove this unofficial addition to the official monument, it somehow made the whole thing feel more truthful.

Scrawled in bright yellow spray paint on top of the engraved characters on the big rock: CHINK.

It's always the way.

AUTHOR'S NOTE

When I set out to write *Hollow Bamboo*, for the better part of a year I wrote nothing. I chalked it up to the fact I'm a distractable procrastinator. But I was also contemplating the question, Who am I to tell this story—this tale detailing race, unjust labour, hardships, violence, tragedies, and occasional triumphs for the early Chinese community of Newfoundland and Labrador? Although it was the story of my family, it was a story I felt uncertain about telling; though, if not me, who would tell the story of my immigrant grandfather? Two generations out and just one-quarter Chinese, I find these qualities of my mixed racialized experiences curious, untidy, and difficult to distill in any simple metric.

It came to me in the shower on an autumnal morning to frame the story with a severe and stylized first-person frame, a move to be as transparent as possible in instructing the reader just what privileges distinguish me and my experiences from those in our community who experience racialization more often and in different degrees than I do in my very comfortable life. I aimed to render my fictional self in unflattering and inarguable terms: a white-passing idiot.

I'm not as ignorant as the fictionalized version of myself, however useful he is in establishing my privilege in relaying a fantastic historical imagining of my grandfather's life. Hell, it felt good to kick that version of myself out of the book. In contrast to what faux Will says in the first chapter, I have in fact seen several anime shows, enjoyed most of them, and even know that they're from Japan, not China. (But worry not, dear reader, I'm sure I'm still a colossal asshole in other ways.) My writing practice continues to develop and deepen, and I strive to continue to engage meaningfully with my fellow Asian-Canadian artists across this sometimes antagonistic, sometimes nurturing country of unlikelihoods.

Telling this story honestly required uncomfortable, charged, and "problematic" language, whether that be the proliferation of hate speech directed towards the Chinese people who came to Newfoundland, or even sometimes the dialogue of Ping himself. Although the novel isn't afraid to dabble in the chewing gum, duct tape, and glue that is absolute fiction, I strived to do a faithful rendition of both the time period and my grandfather as he was. I based this portrayal of him on many sources: family anecdotes, his own writings, audio recordings of him talking, and his starring role in the NFB documentary *The Last Chinese Laundry*. It was through these sources, wedded to my own childhood memories of him, that I crafted Ping's voice and his pragmatic ways. The documentary in particular was a great resource, and I recommend watching it if you're interested in hearing about some of the events in this novel in his own words. Filmed nearly sixty years after his arrival in Newfoundland, the film was very helpful in understanding specifically the cadence and pace of his voice, to ensure an accurate rendition of his English delivery.

For the rest of the novel, much of the narrative was informed by deep research into contemporaneous newspapers, newsreels, and speeches from politicians, among other historical documents. Despite the light touch throughout, writing this novel was a difficult, emotionally heavy process. Having to read and imagine terrible acts of racially motivated violence daily, and to in turn craft language to reflect the worst of my grandfather's experiences, was a solemn task.

Much of the novel was written during the early days of the pandemic, and it became clearer than ever that these violent acts are still ongoing, with an increase in xenophobia against Asians in light of misplaced blame for the virus. It is easy to dismiss what happened to Ping and his contemporaries in this book as some tragic footnote from long ago, but it is not. The importance of the first-person frame is not only to signal to you, the reader, up front exactly who I am. It is to tell you that it is not just a story of my grandfather surviving precarious migration, racism, and violence in the yesteryear: it is a story of us all struggling with how precarious justice and equity are to this day.

ACKNOWLEDGEMENTS

Thank you to the first William Seto Ping, without whom none of this would've been possible. Thank you to my parents, Bill Ping and Violet Ryan-Ping, for being constant cheerleaders of their "strange kid." Thank you to the late Silas Kung, to whom I truly owe so much.

Thank you to Lisa Moore, my wonderful mentor who really allowed this project to flourish. Thank you for all your support and notes along the way. Thank you to Benjamin Dugdale, for being an amazing second reader, an absolute inspiration, and a great friend. And thanks to all the other people who read parts of this book along the way and helped shape it to what it is today: Ryan Clowe, Eva Crocker, N. Page, Miriam Richer, and Madeleine Thien.

Thank you to Martha Webb for believing in this project and for your wonderful suggestions on how to further improve this tome. Thanks to Jennifer Lambert, Shaun Oakey, Canaan Chu, and the whole team at HarperCollins Canada for the incredible, thoughtful edits.

Thank you to Remzi Cej, Jamie Chang, Gordon Jin, and Margaret Walsh for sharing so much incredible knowledge of the past with me. Thank you to the many other sources which informed the historical part of this fiction, including the *Evening Telegram* (St. John's), the *Daily News* (St. John's), contemporaneous news reels, *Newfoundland Quarterly*, *Cape Breton's Magazine*, Heritage Newfoundland and Labrador, and countless other sources at the Memorial University Archives. Thank you to the Chinese Association of Newfoundland for providing a way to connect with my heritage.

Thank you to Jennifer Lokash and the entire Faculty of English at MUN for letting me write this book. Thank you to the Landfall Trust for giving me time to edit this book in their wonderful Kent Cottage. Thank you to Angela Antle, Michelle Porter, and Santiago Guzmán for being early supporters of my work. Thank you to Christa Eastman for giving me my first storytelling gig. Thank you to the Connolly family, for (in chronological order) friendship, education, and employment. Thank you to Josh Ward, for everything. The world we have seen and known is embedded in these pages. Thank you to Ryan Rumbolt for saying, "You should write a novel about your family." Keep making that bread, dude. Thank you to Luke Kennedy, for pushing my mind to further and more absurd points in order to make each other laugh. Thank you to Sam Bishop for telling me what it was like to wander in Russia.

Thank you to Ian Cornelissen, John Green, Jessica Grant, Lewis "Skip" Fischer, and all the other educators throughout my life who taught me to work harder and see the value in myself. Thank you to Andreae Callanan for being the person who taught me the most in grad school. Thank you to Ken Pittman, whose culinary artistry at Seto Kitchen + Bar was a constant inspiration in my life. Thank you to Alicia Wong, for always being there for me.

And finally, thank you to the Canada Emergency Response Benefit, for the days of CERB and honey were surely the greatest of my life.